THE ENGINE
OF SURVIVAL

A Charlie Edmo Murder Mystery

R. J. SEILER

ISBN: 9798579100696 (paperback)

The Engine of Survival is dedicated to the memory of my mother-in-law Eleanor Mae Dixon, my biggest supporter, and to my dear mother Arlene.

Excerpts from my 2020 Kirkus Review

An SF mystery series starter in which FBI agent Charlie Edmo must solve a high-profile case involving one of the first genetically engineered human beings.

Seiler pens a futuristic murder mystery with a science-fiction bent—one that's heavy on the science. Genetic modification is the name of the game, and it's clear the author put a lot of effort into researching the topic to make the tale feel as realistic and lifelike as possible.

Fans of police-procedural novels will enjoy this work, as it follows the rigid guidelines of witness interviews and evidence gathering and takes very few liberties when it comes to proper investigation techniques.

An often engaging future murder case with a well-rounded protagonist.

ACT I

1

Monday, December 19th, 2050

There are a lot of ways to get from birth to death, and they all work.

The killer was composed as he prepared to murder the most famous genetically enhanced man on the planet. He knew his calm was the result of his own recently completed genetic modifications. But the man was still surprised. His heart would normally be pounding in these circumstances, yet he felt relaxed, and in complete control. If asked, he would be unable to fully explain how this felt. In his mind's eye, he could see his fear and other emotions on what could best be described as a series of dials. Dials he could turn up and down, or even off, with a simple thought.

Maybe I should dial up the fear?

The killer knew there was good reason to be fearful. His prey was young and strong, and possessed world-class genetic enhancements equal to, or better than, his own. Given his immense wealth, the victim likely possessed a state-of-the-art personal defense system. The killer would need to be on his toes. There was no room for error, and his orders were clear. Murder Quinn Conner, and destroy the body, as soon as possible. And leave absolutely no trace of viable DNA.

Crouched on top of a large boulder, the murderer placed his rifle against a nearby tree. There was thick cloud cover, and the forest was pitch black. Despite a complete absence of light, the killer's genetically enhanced visual cortex allowed him to clearly see the trail beneath him. The trail crossed a small meadow surrounded by forest before it disappeared to the left behind another large granite boulder. The boulder was the size of a small building and sat about seventy-five feet to the west of him. A small creek flooded parts of the meadow to his right.

There was nothing on the trail. The dark forest was deadly quiet.

He should be here by now.

A few minutes later his app-watch vibrated, and the man glanced at the device strapped to his wrist.

Quinn Conner had left his father's estate on his nightly hike.

He'll be here in fifteen minutes.

Earlier that evening, the killer had administered an injection into his thigh that armed his body's metabolism optimizer. His body had responded in several ways. First, the man's immune system went on full alert, flooding his blood stream with genetically enhanced white-blood cells. This increased his body's ability to recover quickly from trauma and help heal wounds rapidly. The amount of fuel available to his muscle cells increased, and his internal organs maximized their respective functions. Lastly, the injection temporarily boosted the flow of blood to his brain, providing him with an exceptionally clear mind, even when under immense stress.

The man could feel the changes to his body. He felt strong and indestructible. His ability to sense his environment was acute. The killer was completely focused on the task at hand. His body and mind were prepared for battle.

Reaching into his shirt pocket, the killer removed a small metal canister. Unscrewing its lid, he switched on the ten tiny drones stored in the canister. The man had built the drones himself. To the untrained eye, they appeared to be large mosquitoes. Only a microscope and trained eyes could detect the true nature of his deadly creation.

His enhanced hearing detected the footfall of a single person walking, still a long way off.

That would be Quinn Conner.

Tapping a series of commands into his app-watch, he watched as half the insect drones leapt upward from the canister and hovered in the space above his head. The drones were slightly louder than the real insect, and he could clearly hear the buzz of their tiny wings.

Now I wait.

The man planned to launch half the drones as soon as his victim came into view. If these drones failed to reach their target, the extra distance would allow time for a second wave of weapons to be launched.

Each mechanical insect carried a lethal dose of Aconite, a substance capable of killing Quinn Conner in seconds. His victim would die from either paralysis of the respiratory system or cardiac arrest. The Aconite would break down after entering his bloodstream, leaving only traces of aconitum alkaloids, chemicals that can only be detected by a gas chromatography or mass spectrometry, if they could be detected at all. The FBI could apply these tests, but they would never get the chance, as the killer planned to destroy the body.

Leave no trace of viable DNA.

The footsteps were closer now, and the murderer stood very still. After a few moments, he saw his victim come around the large boulder and enter the meadow. Quinn Conner walked toward him in silence, his head down to protect his face from the wind and the few snowflakes that had started to fall.

Standing quietly, the murderer held his finger poised over his app-watch.

Now.

The killer activated five drones and watched as they disappeared into the darkness.

His victim had exactly eight seconds to live.

The killer began to count the seconds, but to his dismay, Quinn Conner quickly stepped backward until his back rested against the boulder, obviously alerted to the danger. The man watched in amazement as a swam of tiny drones suddenly appeared out of nowhere and surrounded the man.

The murderer checked on the status of the insect drones on his app-watch. He was amazed to see that only one drone remained aloft. He watched as it too disappeared from the screen.

His drones killed my drones.

He calmly entered the command to launch the remaining drones. Responding immediately, the tiny drones launched straight into the dark night and headed toward Quinn Conner. Taking no chances, the man sent a second command to the drones. This command altered the drone's attack mode to be more aggressive.

Turning his attention back to the target, he could see Quinn Conner had his back to the large rock. The killer assumed he was still protected by a swarm of drones.

Looking back at his app-watch, the killer watched as his

five insect drones approached their target, and disappeared from the screen, one by one.

Shit.

The murderer dropped the empty canister into his jacket pocket and calmly moved to implement his backup plan. He reached to his right and picked up the dart rifle leaning against a nearby tree. He had prepared the rifle as backup in the case of a drone failure, never expecting all of his drones to be destroyed so easily. The weapon held five darts, each armed with the same poison as the drones.

The man looked toward his target, rifle in hand.

But Quinn Conner was already moving away from the killer. He had ducked to his left, behind the large boulder, and disappeared.

The killer leapt off the rock and accelerated quickly to a full sprint, chasing after his target. He crossed the meadow and rounded the boulder, immediately glancing up the trail. The path rose steeply in front of him, but it was empty.

He heard a faint sound to his left and turned just in time to see a tree branch crashing into his face.

The killer crumbled to the ground and lay still, his rifle falling in the mud.

Returning to consciousness within seconds, the killer saw Quinn Conner sprinting up the trail the way he had just come. His victim moved fast, working furiously to create distance between him and his pursuer.

But the steep trail prevented him from getting far.

Retrieving his weapon, the killer got to one knee and fired three darts in rapid secession. The first two darts were aimed several feet to the right and left of his target. As the killer expected, Quinn Conner's defensive shield of drones reacted to the errant darts by splitting in half.

The killer took advantage of the opening and shot the third dart into the back of Quinn Conner's neck.

He was dead before he hit the ground.

Ignoring his broken nose and the cuts on his face, the man sprinted up the trail until he reached the body. He removed the dart from the victim's neck, placing it in his pocket. The swam of drones disappeared as quickly as they had appeared. The killer quietly searched the area for the other two darts. He wasted fifteen valuable minutes looking for the errant darts, but with no luck.

Nobody will have a reason to look for the darts because the body will not be here.

The killer returned to where the victim lay and began lifting the body.

Just then, he heard the footfall of a single person. The killer estimated the sound was less than a half-mile away. Then he heard a dog's bark, and for the first time felt a moment of panic.

Somewhere up the trail someone with a dog was moving toward him.

The murderer's first instinct was to kill the intruder and his dog. But he only had two darts left in the rifle. Instead, he decided to hide and wait until he could get a better look at the interloper.

After moving the body into the underbrush, the man quietly entered the thick forest above the trail. Holding his rifle, he hid in a deep shadow, fifty or so feet from the trail. He could see portions of the trail in both directions.

Feeling a strong rush of adrenaline, the killer realized he had made a mistake. The intruder's dog was sure to discover the body. The animal may have already picked up its scent. And no way the animal would not, at some point, notice him as well.

I need to leave now.
But I was ordered to destroy the body.
He quickly made his decision. The murderer would wait to see if the dog discovered Quinn Conner's body. If the animal found the body, he would quickly make his getaway.

The murderer evaluated his surroundings looking for an escape route. He decided the safest route was uphill, directly away from the trail. Sitting quietly in the shadows, it wasn't long before the killer saw the intruder and his pet appear on the trail. The dog was a large German Shepherd, and the man looked very fit. In fact, the man looked ex-military.

The killer took a closer look at the intruder.

He looks so familiar.

The killer turned his attention to the dog. He watched as the animal caught wind of the nearby body and started yelping. The assassin watched as the dog, and then it's master, approached Quinn Conner's body.

It's time to go.

Moving silently through the forest, the killer found his way to a pre-arranged location near Westwood's outer wall. Using his app-watch, the assassin sent a signal to his contact inside Westwood. The murderer knew the security measures for this portion of the wall would be disarmed in seconds and would remain so for the next fifteen minutes.

Out of habit, he waited a full five minutes before passing through an unguarded gate. Once outside of the wall, the killer made his way back to his vehicle and drove away.

2

Monday, December 19th, 2050

I hate being a DNA molecule, so much to remember.
Geneticist's Joke

Charlie Edmo was just about to dismiss his Monday morning seminar on Genetics in Law Enforcement, when he noticed the faces of his fellow FBI agents signaling him through the glass of the classroom door. Several students chuckled. Charlie stopped his lecture, wished his students a happy holiday, and let the class go. As the students filed out, the two agents stepped inside the room, and with a brief nod had Charlie follow them both outside.

Something is up.

A couple of the departing students glanced at the two men curiously, but most of the class members knew their professor worked for the FBI. It was one of the reasons Charlie's class was so popular.

'Jack, Brad, why so gloomy?' Charlie asked, once the three men were outside and alone.

'We got a body,' Jack said, like he was talking about his lunch.

'Where?' Charlie asked.

'The *where is* important, but it's the *who* that's really important,' Jack said.

'Do tell,' Charlie glared at Jack.

'You have to guess. Think big.'

'Tell me now!'

Jack hesitated, 'Quinn Conner, Hawke Conner's son. Not officially confirmed, but it's him.'

Quinn Conner and his brother, Alex, were among the first, and without doubt, the most famous genetically engineered persons on the planet.

'Whoa!' Charlie said, staring at Jack, 'Where was the body found?' he asked.

'Westwood, near Hawke Conner's estate. According to the local police, the death looks suspicious,' Jack concluded.

Henry 'Hawke' Conner was founder and CEO of Genetic Services International (GSI) and was likely the richest man on the planet. As such, he was also America's leading spokesman for the human genetic engineering industry, and a regular guest on national news shows. GSI was headquartered on Washington's Kitsap Peninsula across the Puget Sound from Seattle. Hawke Conner lived with his wife, Abby, in the gated community of Westwood, on nearby Bainbridge Island.

'You didn't come all this way just to tell me Quinn Conner is dead?' Charlie said.

'No. We came all this way to see the look on your face when we tell you Hunter has assigned you to lead the investigation,' Brad smiled.

Charlie went into shocked silence.

Every internal alarm system in his body screamed loudly.

Once his initial shock wore off, Charlie spoke.

'That makes absolutely no sense. Hunter hates me,' he said.

'Unless he's giving you a chance at redemption?'

Charlie laughed.

'Pretty unlikely, and I don't need redemption,' he said. 'Still, I've haven't left my desk for months. He'll never forget what happened.'

'So why give you such a high-profile case. Unless . . . " Brad hesitated.

The three men had the same thought.

If things go badly, Hunter will throw me under the bus. He needs a fall guy, and I'm it.

'We're screwed,' Charlie concluded.

'Yeah. Merry Christmas. This is going to be fun,' Jack said.

'And to think I was headed home early,' Charlie said.

'You could find some reason to refuse the case,' Brad offered.

'That's a real possibility. He might be trying to force me to retire, and maybe I should,' Charlie replied.

'If you retire, he gets his way, and if the investigation goes badly, he's got you to blame. Win-win for him,' Brad explained.

'Right. But what if I'm successful?' Charlie asked.

'Ever the optimist. But I got a bad feeling about this one, Charlie, you need to pass,' Jack pleaded.

'I'll think about it. Let's head to Westwood. You can tell me what you know on the way,' Charlie said.

Jack punched a code into his app-phone, and they walked toward the edge of campus to meet their car. The colorful autumn leaves were like a second bloom of spring flowers, and frozen enough to make a crunching sound as they walked. The sky was overcast and Charlie could feel a few stray raindrops on his face as they approached the vehicle. The air held a winter's chill and carried enough moisture to make anything but a heavy coat worthless.

The FBI vehicle was waiting. The three men entered the car, and once the doors closed, a computer-generated voice queried Jack for his identification and password. After he complied, the same voice asked in a warm tone.

'Where to?'

'Take us to Westwood on Bainbridge Island, and turn up the heat,' Jack instructed.

'I am only authorized to take you to the gate at Westwood. I am not authorized to enter,' the voice stated, with seemingly less warmth.

The three men heard the heater fan come to life

'That will do,' Jack responded.

Accelerating quickly into traffic, the car headed for the Seattle ferry terminal. The vehicle would board a vessel for the twenty-minute ride to the city of Winslow, on Bainbridge Island. Traffic was light, and the car moved quickly through downtown Seattle. Most of the storefronts were empty and boarded up. A steady drizzle had started to fall, and the day seemed as dreary as the abandoned stores. Charlie remembered holidays when these streets were crowded with cars and the sidewalks thick with shoppers . . . the window displays illuminating the night. Those days were gone. As they passed Pioneer Square, Charlie could see dozens of homeless men huddled around fires, fighting off the damp air. Others filled nearly every unused doorway. Sadly, he shook his head at how much his city had changed in the past twenty years.

The advent of driverless cars made traffic congestion a thing of the past, and they made good time. It also allowed the three men to discuss the case without distractions.

'The call came in this morning at two-ten. According to the

report, Hawke Conner received an alert from his son, who was hiking nearby. Why he was hiking in the middle of the night is beyond me. Apparently, there was a holiday party at his estate last night. After receiving the alert, Mr. Conner took their dog and went searching. He was alone. I'm not sure what time that was, but I can find out,' Jack said and stopped, waiting for questions.

'Go on, Jack,' Charlie said.

'Hawke Conner found the body in what used to be called Gazzam Lake State Park. It's now part of Westwood. It's adjacent to the Conner's property, less than a mile from the house. He called the head of security for Westwood, who then called local police. Winslow police are currently on scene. According to the initial report, Mr. Conner has confirmed that his son, Quinn Conner, is deceased. The cause of death is unknown.'

'Who's in charge at the scene?'

'Ben Hayward. He'll meet us inside the gate,' Jack answered.

'Good man.'

'Hunter instructed us to call him once the initial walk-through and interviews with the family are completed. He's arranging a press conference for this afternoon, in time for the evening news, of course,' Brad added.

'Hunter will see this as his road to glory,' Jack added.

'No doubt. A high-profile case like this. Chance to get back East,' Brad said.

'No reason to celebrate until he's actually gone,' Jack chuckled.

'Too late, I already feel happiness in my heart.' Charlie quipped.

Brad and Jack smiled.

The three men discussed the upcoming holidays for the remainder of the trip. All three men knew what this investigation meant for their holiday plans. Charlie, as always, had half his tribe arriving for the holidays. He and his wife, Anna, entertained guests often, and Christmas was no exception. Charlie was looking forward to spending time with his aging grandparents, especially his grandfather, Frank.

As the three agents talked, Charlie remembered how pissed off his grandfather had been when he'd announced his intentions to work for the FBI.

'Didn't anyone tell you? The FBI shoots Indians. Why the hell would you work for them?' he had bellowed, then added in a softer voice, 'you always were a straight-arrow.'

But Charlie took the job. The FBI was looking for geneticists, and Charlie had just graduated from the University of Washington near the top of his class. It was what Charlie wanted, the chance to excel in a white man's world.

That was over twenty years ago, and Charlie still loved his job. But in recent months, he had started to think about a change of profession. It had started when his current boss, Special Agent in-Charge Ross Hunter was transferred from the New York office to Seattle. That was three years ago, and Charlie and his new boss had never figured out how to get along. Special Agent Hunter was an ambitious jerk entirely focused on his career. Charlie could never decide whether naked ambition was ugliest at the FBI, or at the University of Washington where he was also employed as adjunct faculty.

One reason Charlie didn't resign his position was because he was blessed with a great team. He had worked with Jack Lee for over a decade. Jack had been a homicide detective with the Seattle Police before joining Charlie's team. Charlie was close to Jack and knew he had plans to spend a quiet

Christmas at home with his wife, who was battling an untreatable form of cancer. Charlie worried that she would now be alone during much of the holidays.

Jack was staring out the car's window, so Charlie took the opportunity to take a good look at his long-time partner. The man had aged in recent months, and Charlie could see all the pain generated by his wife's sickness etched on his face. Like most of his best friends, Jack was nearly a foot shorter than Charlie. Charlie had always wanted a tall friend, but he always seemed to connect with men who were short, but strong enough to kick his ass. Jack was no exception. He was stout as a fence post and quick as a cat. Charlie once saw him leap onto a garbage can, climb over an eight-foot wall, and tackle a suspect. The man was in handcuffs before Charlie arrived to help.

Switching his gaze to Brad, Charlie took a moment to consider how things were going with his new partner.

Charlie knew Bradley Grant and his wife, Gayle, were scheduled to travel to California on Saturday. They were planning to visit their two grown children. Brad had joined his team the previous year, after the death of Charlie's long-time partner, Hank. Brad was an expert in gene-editing and was working for GSI when he was successfully recruited by the FBI. Brad provided Charlie with an intimate knowledge of the human gene-editing industry, along with an outstanding background in bioengineering.

They were all part of an FBI division charged with enforcing federal laws regulating the human genetics services industry. The need for a 'genetics' division within the FBI was created when Congress, in 2019, and in response to rapid advancements in the science and business of human gene editing, passed comprehensive legislation overseeing the emerging industry.

Overnight a new area of public policy was created, and the FBI scrambled to find ways to enforce these new and complex laws.

One of the strategies developed by the FBI was the formation of small, regional, investigative teams comprised of bioengineers, geneticists, and members of law enforcement. Charlie, Jack and Brad were one of three teams located in the Pacific Northwest. They were based in the FBI office building in downtown Seattle. Among their many responsibilities was investigating the deaths of all genetically modified Americans, the so-called designer babies.

Their car departed the ferry, driving directly toward the main gate at Westwood. They passed through the busy village of Winslow, where most residents either worked for the ferry system or inside Westwood. These jobs allowed Winslow to avoid the fifty percent unemployment rate common in most parts of the country. Charlie could see a few boarded-up businesses, but unlike Seattle, plenty of stores were decorated for the holidays. The drizzle had turned to rain, and most of the shoppers walked with open umbrellas.

As their car departed Winslow, Charlie's thoughts drifted to his boss, and for a moment, retirement sounded good.

It's what the Man wants.

But Charlie was not one to lightly abandon his life's pursuit. After all, he had passed through personal and professional hell to reach his goal of working for the bureau.

Charlie recalled the first day he had walked through the doors of the FBI academy. His reputation had preceded him. Word had leaked that Charlie had submitted a letter of recommendation from a former director of the FBI as part of his application package. This news had landed with a thud. To make matters worse, immediately after being hired, Charlie had sued his new employer and won the legal right to keep his long ponytail, a source of great pride to him.

As a result, from the moment he walked through those hallowed doors, Charlie was viewed as an outsider, as someone filled with the simmering anger common to the red man - an ambitious jerk with a huge ego who had made it into the FBI on the backs of his Native American heritage.

At the time, this was exactly the reputation Charlie wanted to project. He felt protected by his tough-guy exterior. He would be left alone and could use his status as an outsider to fuel his ambitions. But inside he felt a huge sense of accomplishment for having achieved the only goal that mattered to him – a secret and the very satisfying feeling of having overcome the rocky start to his life.

Rocky start? That is an understatement.

As they approached the entrance to Westwood, Charlie's daydream came to an end.

Charlie could see the arched gate and high wall that separated Westwood from the rest of the island. The wall stretched for some distance in both directions. The forest was clear for fifty feet outside the wall, and he knew a variety of unarmed security robots, motion sensors, razor wire, and an army of armed human guards awaited anyone foolish enough to approach the wall. Westwood, like the other large gated communities around the country, was designed to not only provide lavish surroundings, but also a completely secure environment. The locals called it *Freakwood,* referring to the high percentage of its residents who were genetically enhanced adults.

The three FBI agents passed through a variety of security measures. The fact they were federal agents didn't impress the guards, and it took several minutes before they were admitted. They were required to leave their firearms with the guards and wear security badges firmly attached to their suit coats that allowed their movements to be tracked anywhere inside Westwood.

Ben Hayward greeted them and immediately led them to a waiting car. Ben was Chief of Police for Bainbridge Island. Charlie had worked with him on a couple of cases in the past.

'Takes about ten minutes to get to the Conner Estate,' Ben said as their car drove them south. 'They're waiting for us. Their attorney will be with them. I left two of my officers in the park with the body. I also ordered five officers to canvass the neighbors. I've seen the body. It looked like someone moved it off the trail, and there was blood coming from his nose and ears. Clearly a suspicious death in my book.'

'It'll be a high-profile case, regardless of the cause of death. We do things by the book. Maximum documentation, understand. When we get there, Jack and Brad will go to the crime scene and do the initial walk-through. I'll interview the family. Any chance the area is accessible by vehicle?' Charlie asked.

'Nope. Quinn Conner was found near an old maintenance road. The road was used when it was a state park, but after it was added to Westwood, the road was blocked off and made into a trail,' Ben responded.

'Okay. Ben, I need you with me to witness the family interview. Then we'll go see the body.'

Driving southwest into the interior of Westwood, Charlie noticed the rain was soaking a thick blanket of overnight snowfall. Snow was rare on the island, and the branches of the plentiful conifers, not used to the heavy load, slumped steeply downward. Charlie knew the day's warm air would soon free the trees of their burden. Already, blocks of snow were falling to the ground with loud thuds.

Charlie had been to Bainbridge Island a couple of times in recent years, but still marveled at how it had changed. It had always been a home to the wealthy, along with a healthy mix of working-class Americans. The island was popular because it offered an environment of quiet beauty and was only a short ferry ride from the city. All this changed when GSI, Genlabs, and several related industries selected the Kitsap Peninsula as their business hub. Overnight, the Kitsap Peninsula and the surrounding area became the desired residence for hundreds of millionaires and thousands of other highly paid workers. These wealthy families began buying homes on Bainbridge Island in large numbers. Land developers, always on the lookout for this type of opportunity, employed every means imaginable, including applying pressure to local officials to use eminent domain laws, and in some cases getting targeted legislation passed, to take advantage of the boom. Quickly, this group of developers opened the largest gated community on the west coast, Westwood, encompassing nearly a quarter of the island.

Arriving at the Conner estate, the four men exited the car. The rain had stopped, and as often happens in the Puget Sound, patches of blue sky battled with the clouds for a place in the firmament. Charlie estimated the main house and adjacent buildings, including horse stables and a private helipad, covered several acres. The entire complex sat on the western slopes of the island above the waterfront. Outside the complex of buildings, the property was heavily timbered. Charlie could see the Olympic Mountains here and there through the cloud cover. The view would be stunning on a clear day.

The four men were greeted by the head of security at Westwood, Brent Barns. After introductions, Charlie asked Brent to accompany his two partners to examine the body.

'Sure, I hope you brought boots. It's a long walk and pretty muddy,' Brent said.

Jack and Brad looked at each other.

'I thought you guys were Boy Scouts. Isn't that a requirement for the FBI?' Charlie said, wondering to himself if they even owned boots.

Charlie and Ben headed for the main house to question the Conner family, while the other agents followed Brent to a nearby building to find suitable footwear.

Hawke Conner greeted Charlie and Ben at the door. Charlie saw a proud man carrying the heavy burden of losing a child. The mainstream and tabloid press had run countless stories about Hawke Conner. Most described him as superhuman, brilliant, strategic, tireless (he was rumored to never sleep), and possessing the uncanny ability to be a step ahead of those who dared to compete with him. Some claimed he was an actual mind reader. The rumors were endless.

Hawke Conner's road to wealth was a classic American success story. His journey had begun at MIT in 2018. While there, he had met Gordon Kelly, and together they had developed technologies that transformed society.

Most Americans knew their story. Hawke and Gordon were the first to develop the technologies needed to safely engineer designer-babies in large numbers. More importantly, their advancements offered parents new options for genetically enhancing their prodigy. The list of enhancements included improvements across the physical, intellectual, and emotional make-up of their sons and daughters.

This was just the beginning. Soon, Hawke designed the nanomachines capable of removing strands of genetic materials from the cells of living adults and replacing them with customized protein sequences. These cells would then utilize the new genetic blueprint every time they recombined and created new cells. Over time, this resulted in permanent changes to the person's genetic code, which manifested in numerous improvements to their physical and intellectual abilities.

Gordon Kelly discovered how to customize human genes so they could be used by Hawke's nanotechnology. Gordon's research focused on using the nanomachines to splice out undesirable genetic sequences in the DNA, and then replacing them with his own custom-designed genetic material.

The potential of these new scientific tools proved limitless and opened the door to an entirely new industry. No longer were scientists limited to just modifying the human genetic code during the embryonic stage. Within the limits of these emerging technologies, living adults could now be genetically enhanced.

Like all globally famous people, members of the public either hated or worshipped the two men. Their fiercest critics accused Hawke and Gordon of working to create a new subspecies of super humans. Others shouted the two men sought to destroy the human species, and still others claimed they were usurping the power of God. Some spoke openly about their plots to rule the world.

Other Americans had nothing but praise for the work accomplished by the two men. The application of genetic engineering in mass immunization programs had eliminated dozens of genetically driven diseases, saving countless lives. It had reduced violent behavior in thousands of individuals, and significantly decreased the incidences of certain cancers, alcoholism, depression, obesity, autism, and other less known maladies. Regardless of how the accomplishments of the two men were measured, they had transformed society, and maybe the human species as well.

After introductions, Hawke Conner led them to a room where his wife and attorney were seated.

'Agent Edmo and Chief Hayward, this is my wife, Abby, and my friend and personal attorney, Frank Kaminsky,' Hawke said, as they entered a small room.

Abby Conner looked like someone working hard to contain her grief. Her face was puffy and blotched red. Charlie couldn't imagine losing his own daughter.

'To be clear, my role here is to support Hawke and Abby as their friend. But I'm also their personal attorney. The Conner's have experienced a profound trauma. I insist this be kept as short as possible,' Frank said.

'I'll do my best to keep this brief. Are there other family members in the house?' Charlie asked.

'Yes. Quinn had a brother. Alex is still sleeping. We haven't told him,' Mr. Conner replied.

'Anyone else?' Charlie asked.

'No one else,' Hawke answered.

'At some point I will need to speak with Alex.'

'I'm not sure he'll be up for it today.'

'Tomorrow is soon enough. I'll also need a list of everyone who attended the party last night, as well as all employees working at the estate. Please include any temporary help hired for the holiday party.'

'No problem, I can generate a list when we finish,' Frank offered.

'Thank you. I have some questions for both of you. I would prefer to ask these questions now, while your memory is fresh,' Charlie said.

Hearing no objection, he continued.

'Mr. Conner. Can you tell us what happened, starting with when you last saw your son?' Charlie asked.

As he began to speak, Charlie struggled to separate the man talking from the one on the national news. His voice, usually so calm and confident, was edged with anger and insecurity. His infamous youthful appearance had turned against him, and he looked like an emotionally crushed child. He was about six feet tall, with a slight frame that looked bigger than it was, due to the generous cut of his casual business suit. A suit that now hung like a tent over his slumped form. His jet-black hair was cut short and tinged with grey. His face was clean shaven and unexpectedly tan, better suited for the Southwest.

Charlie focused on Mr. Conner's words.

'Last night was our annual holiday party and we entertained about a hundred family members and friends. Both boys were here, as was Quinn's wife, Ella. My partner Gordon Kelly and some other folks from Genlabs were here. The party was a huge success. Everyone left by eleven-thirty, except Ella and Gordon. Quinn decided to go for a walk; I remember it was a few minutes after midnight. Ella was tired and decided to go home. I poured drinks for Gordon and myself, and we sat and talked for a few minutes. Then Gordon headed home, so I went to my office to work. I noticed an alert from my security firm. Quinn's defense system had been activated,' Hawke stopped.

'What does that mean?" Ben asked.

'As you can image, security is a big deal for us. Among other precautions, each member of the family is monitored by a personal protection system when off the premises. Quinn was fully protected whenever he took a hike. I receive security alerts if something is wrong,' Hawke said.

'So, you received an alert?' Charlie asked.

'Yes. At the time, I was not that concerned. Quinn was drunk when he left for his hike. I wondered if it wasn't a false alarm. It's happened before. So, I quickly searched the rest of the house, but I couldn't find him. I took Tiller and went outside. I didn't intend to go far. I was just going to look around the yard. Quinn could have come home and passed out anywhere. Like I said, he was intoxicated.'

'Were you armed?' Ben asked.

'I don't own a gun, so no,' Hawke answered.

'Then what happened? You decided to go look for him?' Charlie asked.

'Yes, well no, not exactly. Tiller was itching for a walk, so I headed south toward the old state park on Quinn's regular route. I was searching for Quinn, but part of me was convinced he was still somewhere in the compound.'

'So, tell us about finding your son,' Ben said.

'I didn't find him, Tiller did. Quinn was lying in the brush just off the trail. I didn't see him, at least not at first. I noticed Tiller acting strangely, he was yelping a bit, like something was wrong. I went to investigate and saw my son's body,' Hawke answered flatly.

'Was he conscious at any point?' Charlie asked.

'No signs of life.'

'Did you see anybody on the trail, or any signs someone else was there.'

'No, no one, though it was clear his body was moved.'

'Thank you,' Charlie said and turned to face Abby Conner.

'When was the last time you saw your son?' Charlie asked. To this point the woman had not made eye contact with him.

'I saw him about eleven-thirty last night. He was with Alex,' Ms. Conner answered, 'Forgive me for asking, but when can I have my son's body?'

Her eyes bored into Charlie's.

Abby Conner would be considered beautiful in nearly any culture. Charlie wondered if her universal appeal was a result of surgery, augmented with genetic enhancements. If so, he marveled at how tastefully the doctors and genetic engineers had done their work. Many of her naturally occurring features, the things that combined to make her face and body beautiful, were slightly enhanced. She was tall. Charlie guessed she stood just under six foot. The curves of her body were slightly pronounced, reflecting the latest trends in body types. Several dozen strands of her hair glimmered with the smallest flecks of flashing red and green lights. Charlie assumed it was her hairdo for the Christmas party.

But her eyes were Abby Conner's most powerful weapon. Her genetically enhanced irises were a storm of slow-moving colors, changing constantly from blue to green to brown. It was hard to not be overwhelmed by her stare. Charlie noticed Ben was struggling to avert his gaze. She was both alluring and intimidating at the same time. Charlie could sense the power she had over him and he didn't like it. He averted his gaze, noticing Mr. Conner was staring at him.

'We're almost done, Ms. Conner. I'm on my way to the scene as soon as we finish here. Your son's body will be taken to the forensic lab at the Center for Disease Control in downtown Seattle. The law prescribes that an autopsy be performed,' Charlie answered, looking back at Ms. Conner. 'It may take some days or weeks before your son's body will be released.'

Abby Conner stared at Charlie, and he saw she was fighting a losing battle with tears. He decided to move on.

'After the party ended, what did you do?' Charlie asked.

'Hawke was talking with Gordon, so I said my goodnights and went to bed,' she said.

'So, you were in the house all night?'

'Yes. I slept for a bit, but then I heard a shout. I could see

Hawke out my window, running toward the house, and I knew something was wrong.'

Abby hesitated in order to gather her emotions.

'Do either of you know why he took a walk so late at night?' Ben asked.

'He had a habit of taking long walks late at night. His enhanced vision allowed him to see at night,' Mr. Conner answered with a hint of pride.

Ms. Conner nodded, 'Hawke's right; he liked hiking at night. It was the only time he could be alone.'

'So, he always went alone. Risky for someone so famous.'

'As I said, he was well-protected by my security systems,' Mr. Conner said.

Apparently not that well protected.

'Okay, thank you. That's all for now. We'll head to the scene. Please remain available in case I have more questions.'

Charlie left the room with Ben.

'What do you think?' Ben asked, once they were outside.

'Time will tell. I didn't catch any red flags,' Charlie answered.

'That's the closest I've been to somebody so famous, and so enhanced,' Ben said.

'Me too. Meeting Abby Conner was like being introduced to the elf queen in *Lord of the Rings*. More intimating then I expected,' Charlie added.

'I agree, it was weird. How could you ever tell if they're lying? It's like reading the face of another species,' Ben complained.

Triggered by Ben's comments, Charlie's thoughts drifted into a sea of bad memories. Walking in silence, Charlie relived his partner's recent death.

The events from last year were still fresh in his mind. It had been a tough case from the start. Charlie had been contacted by a disgruntled former employee from Genlabs. He made some outlandish claims against his former employer and then disappeared. It was his sudden disappearance that caught Charlie's attention.

Pulling his team together, Charlie had pushed hard to recruit another informant inside Genlabs. After weeks of work, Charlie thought he had found a potential informant. A meeting was arranged. But the whole thing was a trap; Charlie and his partner were shot and left for dead. His friend and partner, Hank Eckmeyer. died two days later. For reasons that were never shared with Charlie, the FBI suspected a genetically enhanced person was involved. But after months of investigation, the bureau still didn't know who had shot them and no motive for the shooting was ever uncovered.

As a result of the follow-up investigation, Charlie was severely reprimanded, and had never gained his boss's confidence again.

After his partner's death, and the first time since his youth, Charlie suffered a personal crisis of confidence, and the mandated sessions with the agency's psychologist had only made Charlie feel less secure. In some ways, he was glad Hunter had assigned him to a desk. Sitting at a desk for month on end had done Charlie some good. While he was unable to rid himself of all his demons, he was able to solidify one powerful goal.

No genetically enhanced person would ever get the best of him again.

Charlie's thoughts drifted to his boss's actions.

Its clear Hunter wants me gone.

So why hand me such a high-profile case?

Charlie didn't believe for a minute that Agent Hurter had suddenly become a generous man. Something was up. His boss needed a fall guy should the investigation go south. That much was clear. But Charlie wondered if there was something else behind Hunter's decision.

If I'm going to refuse this case, it needs to be today.

Charlie's focus returned to the present.

He followed Ben through the woods toward the place where Hawke had discovered Quinn Conner's body. The rain was heavy, and the trail was sloppy and difficult to navigate in places. Charlie had borrowed a raincoat and boots from the Conner's but was still struggling to stay dry. The path led to the old park boundary, where it met the former maintenance road, and the walking got easier. The steep dirt road hugged the hillside, but gradually dropped toward a large granite boulder and flat meadow. A rain-swollen creek divided the meadow, flooding into the low-lying ground on either side of the stream. Half-way down the hillside, Charlie could see Jack, Brent, and Brad searching the area where he presumed the body was located.

'What's the story?' Charlie asked when he arrived.

'Not sure. No signs of a struggle or blunt force. As Ben said, there's a bit of blood coming out of his nose and ears. It looks like the body was dragged from the trail and hidden in the undergrowth,' Brad said.

'Show me the body,' Charlie said.

The body was slumped on its side below the right side of the road. The side of Quinn Conner's face rested in the mud. His eyes were closed, and Charlie could see blood had flowed from his nose and pooled in the dirt under his nostrils. A small amount of blood was visible in his left ear. The body was covered with a fast-melting coating of snow. It looked like he'd been dead quite a while. He was dressed for wet weather. He wore thick pants and a well-worn raincoat that covered a wool sweater. Quinn's leather hiking boots were covered with mud, and he wore a white cap on his head. He looked like he was sleeping, and Charlie resisted the urge to shake him awake.

'Did you get pictures and video?' Charlie asked, 'I want to turn over the body."

'Yeah, we're done,' Jack answered.

Charlie pulled his latex gloves on and gently rotated the body until it was on its back. The men could see a few drops of blood escaping Quinn's other ear.

'It was cold last night, but he didn't die of exposure. He's dressed for the weather and is familiar with these woods. It's not like he was lost.'

'The blood from his nose and ears suggests poisoning,' Brad said.

'You mean alcohol poisoning?' Jack asked.

'No, I mean the old fashion kind of poisoning. Need a toxicology report to be sure,' Brad added.

'This is clearly a suspicious death. We need call it in,' Charlie said.

'Given the body was moved . . .' Brad pointed out.

'Should I call Hunter now?' asked Jack.

'Are we all in agreement?' Charlie asked.

Brad and Jack nodded.

'I'll call him when we get back to the house. I'm going to recommend he dispatch a full forensic team. I suspect the shit is about to hit the fan,' Charlie lamented.

Charlie and Ben hiked back to the Conner's house while Jack and Brad remained with Brent and continued their investigation at the scene of death. When they arrived, Charlie paused outside the Conner house to call his boss. Ben stood nearby listening to the phone conversation.

'Sir, I appreciated the opportunity. I was surprised to be assigned the case,' Charlie said.

'Right. Just don't screw it up. Work quietly and stay out of the news cycle. All public comments go through me. Got it? So, what's the verdict?' Hunter asked.

'Clearly a suspicious death. The body was moved into the underbrush. We need to open a full investigation. I don't have to tell you,' Charlie started to say.

'I hope this isn't more of your Indian bullshit. We've been through that once before.' Hunter said, sounding drunk.

His boss was speaking so loudly that Charlie was forced to hold the phone at arm's length. Charlie could see Ben grimacing. Hunter continued to provide clear evidence that political correctness was a thing of the distant past.

'Are you sure it wasn't hypothermia? Wasn't he drunk?' Hunter asked.

'His father said he'd been drinking. But the body was moved, and there is blood coming from his ears and nose. This is not consistent with hypothermia. Sir, you need to let me do my job.'

It wasn't the first time Charlie had made this request. It was like banging on the side of an old television set in a losing effort to improve reception.

'And it had to be during the fucking holidays, for Christ's sake,' Special Agent Hunter complained.

Charlie knew better than to respond.

'Fine, but this one goes strictly by the book. Shouldn't be a problem for a straight arrow like you. I'm going ahead with the press conference at four-thirty. I'll have another press conference in the morning; have your report on my desk by nine a.m. I've already ordered a full forensic team to your location. They'll arrive by copter in the next thirty minutes. Understand?' Hunter ended the call before Charlie could respond.

'Your boss sounds like a bigger asshole than mine,' Ben said.

'Yeah. Quite a leader. One of the few people I want to punch,' Charlie admitted.

'My boss is just lazy. Likes social events, free food and booze, preferably booze. He's definitely not interested in police work,' Ben said.

'Hunter's ambitious, and East-coast rude,' Charlie said.

Ben nodded in agreement.

'Shall we face the music?' Ben asked.

Charlie and Ben went back to the main house to update the Conner's. Hawke Conner waited at the door.

'Mr. Conner, may we speak with you and your wife again?' Charlie asked.

'She's with Alex,' Mr. Conner said, 'please follow me.'

Charlie noted a flicker of concern on his face when he mentioned his son.

Following Mr. Conner to a large sunroom, Charlie found Abby Conner sitting with a young man who he presumed was their remaining son. There were two untouched coffee cups sitting on the table nearby. Based on the look on their faces, she had already shared the bad news with Alex.

Hawke introduced Alex Conner to Charlie and Ben. He refused to make eye contact, and Charlie could see his face was filled with anger. He looked a great deal like Hawke, though he hadn't developed his father's talent for hiding his emotions.

'Alex, I will need to ask you a few questions. But the forensic team will arrive by copter shortly, so I don't have time right now. Please be available tomorrow morning,' Charlie said.

'I'm sure I'll be here, given what's happened,' Alex said.

'Thank you. We'll be touch.'

'I'll look forward to it,' Alex said smartly.

Unfazed, Charlie continued.

'I have a quick update.'

He turned to Mr. Conner.

'Do I need my lawyer?' Mr. Conner asked.

'That's up to you. But you should know, we're treating this as a suspicious death.'

'You think my son was murdered?' Ms. Conner asked.

'There's never been a murder in Westwood, and I doubt there is one now. Sounds like someone's got an overactive imagination,' Alex said looking at Charlie.

Charlie didn't speak for a moment.

'I hope you're right. We'll have to wait for the forensic team to determine the precise cause of death.'

'And how long will that take?' Alex asked.

'Days or weeks, depending on the evidence,' Charlie said.

'Weeks. Are you kidding? That's not acceptable,' Alex spoke harshly.

'This is a high-profile case. It's important we get it right,' Charlie said.

'Yeah, the FBI is famous for that,' Alex continued his attack.

'That's enough,' Mr. Conner stated firmly.

Charlie and Alex locked eyes.

Their stare down ended when they heard the helicopter approaching. Charlie and Brad said their goodbyes and rushed to leave the house.

DNA

September 17th, 2018
Journal Entry #1
Gordon Kelly, Doctoral Student, MIT

Today was my first day in the genetics lab at MIT. I was impatient as the image of the DNA molecule emerged on my computer screen. The molecule looked like a random piece of tangled yarn. But as the minutes went by, software churning, the details of the famous molecule materialized. The piece of yarn turned into two ladders that twisted and joined. Then the rungs and rails of the ladders became tiny neon rods of green, blue, red, and yellow as the software assigned colors to each of the four nitrogenous bases.

I heard the chime sound, indicating the image of the DNA molecule was fully compiled. I had waited to see this image since my twelfth birthday; the day I fell in love with the field of genetics. Here was the blueprint for all life; the once secret code governing the creation of all living cells; the true arbiter of life and death; the difference between health and disease, happiness and depression; and the place where all genetic inheritance was decided; this tiniest of things, with an incomprehensibly vast memory of our specie's past.

Some believe the existence of DNA proved there is a God, citing the elegance of its molecular structure. Only God could create such a beautiful thing. If I had any religious leanings, I might agree. But I don't think that way. I know the DNA molecule is not God, instead it's a living collection of forty-six chromosomes, twenty to twenty-five thousand genes, and about three billion DNA base pairs. The DNA molecule is the result of eons of human evolution, nothing more.

To me, proving the existence of God using the DNA molecule is misguided at best, and pure stupidity, at worst. The primary question facing humans is not whether DNA proves the existence of God; but rather, 'how human do we wish to remain?' The cat is out of the bag, and evolution is no longer in charge of the human genetic code. Permanent changes to the human embryo, the so-called germ line, can be done by lab technicians. Changes to the human germ line cascade forever *into our future. The world is fundamentally changed and too many people only care about justifying their ancient beliefs.*

Still, many in my field insist I continue to compare the DNA molecule to God, at least in casual conversation. Subconsciously, they argue, floating this meme will help people accept our controversial work. Doesn't the Bible tell us to help the disadvantaged . . . to go forth and prosper? God has given us this gift. Isn't it our responsibility to use the technology to improve the human species and eliminate diseases?

I don't know if comparing the DNA molecule to God will lead to an acceptance of our work, or anything else, but I am sure the human genetic code is now our responsibility. And today, for the first time, I saw its magnificent face.

It was Monday morning and Gordon Kelly sat in his office reading from his old college journal. His major professor at MIT had insisted her students keep handwritten journals. At the time, Gordon had considered it a waste of time. But now, decades later, he found inspiration in reading the entries. Gordon had developed a habit of reading a single entry each day before beginning work.

It was at MIT that Gordon had met Hawke Conner. Hawke Conner was three years older than Gordon, but the two men had hit it off immediately. Both were ambitious and brilliant students who shared a passion for the science of human genetics. During their years at MIT, they spent countless hours working together in the university's genetics lab, and Gordon considered Hawke to be his best friend to this day.

As doctoral students, their early research led to innovative and inexpensive ways of mass producing genetically engineered children, the so-called designer babies. These technologies would later form the foundation for their successful companies.

Next, the two scientists developed a panel of genetically enhanced viruses that could be used to immunize the general public against an array of genetically driven diseases. Government contracts soon followed, and the two researchers were on their way to wealth and international fame.

The two men were mentioned as future candidates for a Noble Prize.

But this was just the beginning. Hawke began developing nanotechnologies that could enter cells without triggering their defenses. Once inside the cell, the microscopic machines used the CRISPR Cas9 enzyme to splice engineered genetic materials into the cell's DNA. The tiny machines, released by the millions in a single injection, could be programmed to enter and modify any cell in the human body that contained DNA.

Gordon's research complemented Hawke's advancements in nanotechnology. He specialized in the creation of protein sequences or genetic materials that could be used by Hawke's tiny machines.

These advancements changed the world.

Prior to these developments, genetic engineers were limited to modifying the human DNA only during the embryonic stage. In other words, inserting the re-engineered genetic material into the mother's egg, and then placing the egg into her, or a surrogate's, womb.

However, little could be done to enhance the DNA of living adults. This new technology opened the door to a whole new industry. The sky was the limit, and scientists around the world began to take advantages of these new developments. Soon hospitals and medical clinics began offering a broad array of genetic enhancements for living adults.

Hawke finished his doctoral program first and founded Genetic Services International. GSI started by developing the first mass produced generation of designer-babies. The sales of designer-babies became the foundation of GSI success.

Gordon completed his dissertation two years later. He decided to start Genlabs as a subsidiary of GSI. It was a natural arrangement, and the two men grew wealthy beyond measure.

Gordon launched his new companies by announcing to the world the company would tackle the ongoing problem of human violence. The genetic markers associated with severe violence had been identified decades before, but without access to living DNA, nothing could be done to replace the harmful genetic materials. Hawke promised to develop nanotechnologies that could splice out these markers and replace them with benign bits of DNA.

After months of tireless work, Genlabs unveiled its new technology for reducing violent behavior in humans. The science was highly effective, eliminating violent behavior in nearly all persons who received the modifications to their DNA. And despite its huge cost, the procedure succeeded in reducing murder rates and decreasing episodes of domestic abuse.

These amazing developments were followed by advancements in significantly reducing obesity, mental illness, and the advent of dozens of other medical applications.

Hawke and Gordon were on a roll.

Gordon's daydreams fell away as his app-phone buzzed. It was a call from Special Agent Hunter. Gordon took a deep breath before answering.

'Gordon. I wanted you to know before it hits the news, Quinn Conner was found dead this morning,' Hunter paused.

'My god, are you sure?'

'Yes. The FBI will assume control of the case within the hour. From what I gather, it looks like a homicide,' he said.

'Tell me what you know,' Gordon said.

'He went for a walk after the Christmas party and didn't come back. His father got a security alert and went looking for him, early this morning. He found Quinn's body about a mile from the estate,' Hunter added.

'How did he die?' Gordon asked.

'Don't know yet,' Hunter said.

'Where will the body be taken?'

'The body will be taken to the CDC lab downtown. My guess it will be early tomorrow,' Hunter said.

'Got it. I'll be in touch. Let me know when your team is gone and I'll go to the estate,' Gordon said.

Gordon disconnected the call and sank back in his chair.

They have Quinn's body. Ramsey failed.

Thank God I own Hunter.

Immediately after Special Agent-in-Charge Ross Hunter had arrived in Seattle, Gordon worked to compromise the man. It didn't take much. Gordon learned from his contacts in New York why Agent Hunter was suddenly transferred from the New York office to Seattle; a huge demotion. The FBI agent had a weakness for kinky sex. Once Gordon understood this, the rest had been easy.

Gordon thought about his meeting with Quinn Conner on the previous Saturday morning. In response, his chest tightened as a huge dump of adrenaline entered his bloodstream. His heart began racing in response. Gordon sat motionless and took long, slow breaths, trying to slow his heart. It wasn't working. Panic filled his body. He started picking at the long scab on the top of his left hand. The wound sprouted small drops of blood.

Using a Kleenex, he dapped the blood off his hand. Opening a drawer in his desk, Gordon removed his medication. His hands shook and his mouth was dry. He gagged while swallowing the pills without water but managed to get them down. The bathroom was less than ten steps away, but it seemed like miles. Gordon took several deep breaths waiting for the meds to kick in. A few minutes passed. He felt his heart slow and breathing return to normal, the panic subsiding. His thoughts returned to the problem at hand.

The Ghost is showing his face.

What should I do?

He shuddered as he recalled Quinn reading the summary of his report and calmly reciting its devastating data. All he could hear was his ex-wife's voice.

So many are going to die.

His mind filled with images of bodies piled high, dirty and bloody.

What to do?

Gordon knew the answer.

Secrecy first. Then find the problem and solve it.

3

MONDAY, DECEMBER 19TH, 2050

Where you stumble and fall, there you will find gold.
Joseph Campbell

Charlie watched as the forensic team unloaded their gear. Once the equipment was on the ground, the helicopter lifted off and flew east toward Seattle. Charlie exchanged pleasantries with the team, and then, with Ben leading the way, the six men and women donned their packs and headed down the trail.

Watching the team file into the forest and finding himself alone and in no hurry to return to the Conner's home, Charlie called his wife, Anna. He wanted to tell her that he wouldn't be home for dinner. He also wanted to hear her voice.

'You gonna miss dinner?' Anna answered the phone without saying hello.

'Sorry. You aren't going to believe this. Hunter assign me to lead a huge investigation,' Charlie offered.

'That's doesn't sound right. It's not the Quinn Conner case, is it? It's on the news.'

'None other. They may never let me come home,' Charlie answered.

'Fine with me,' Anna chuckled, 'Listen, obviously we need to talk about this. But I'm cooking chili and drinking wine. Call me later, or better yet, get home,' she said and hung up.

Why doesn't anybody say goodbye anymore.

Returning to the main house, Charlie was greeted at the door by Frank, and led to the sunroom. Hawke Conner and his wife sat close together holding hands. There was no sign of Alex. The room was noticeably more tense then before. The south-facing room had filled with sunlight. The sun lit a wide array of potted plants and small trees. The warm temperatures and plentiful foliage made the room hot and damp. In a few minutes, Charlie's skin felt moist under his suit, and his long ponytail felt hot on his back. He wished he was back in the cold air of the forest with the forensic team.

'The forensic team is on their way to the scene. I expect they will work through the evening and maybe the night. Now, my apologies, but I need to ask some more questions. It won't take long.'

Hearing no objections, he continued.

'Can you tell me about your son, where he worked, his family, that sort of thing?' Charlie asked.

'Quinn is married, was, I guess.' Hawke slowly shook his head. 'His wife's name is Ella. Quinn works for our major subsidiary, Genlabs. I wouldn't allow both sons to work at GSI.' Hawke stopped.

'Alex works for GSI?' Charlie asked.

"Yes. He works in long-range planning,' Mr. Conner said.

'What does Genlabs do?'

'You may know the story. GSI got its start by selling designer babies, but really grew when, in 2026, it won government contracts to supply a panel of mass immunizations for an array of genetic disorders. GSI specializes in the nanotechnology used to deliver engineered genetic code into targeted cells. Genlabs was the original supplier of these engineered gene sequences and the specialized viruses that helped deliver them. When the government mandated additional immunizations for other undesirable features of the human genome, we worked closely with Genlabs in developing the new generation of engineered genes. Over time, Genlabs developed treatments for reducing several significant health problems. Last year, Quinn became director of their advanced research division,' Hawke added.

'So, he didn't work for GSI, but the distinction was artificial at best,' Charlie asked.

'No, the difference is important. He didn't work for me, and I didn't supervise him. I actually know little about what he does, or did,' Hawke shook his head slowly.

'Okay, so what do you know about his job?'

'He headed up Genlabs research division, as I mentioned. He signed a non-disclosure agreement, so he couldn't talk about any of his projects.'

'You run the parent company, but can't talk about work with your son?'

'We're not Genlabs' only client. There are legal issues involved. Given the huge black market for these technologies, the need for secrecy is paramount,' Hawke countered.

'Can you give me a simple explanation of his work,' Charlie pressed.

'Quinn supervised a number of research projects. You should talk to Gordon Kelly. He was his boss.'

'Tell me about Quinn's childhood,' Charlie asked.

'Quinn was a second-generation custom-designed child.

Most people don't realize the unpredictable nature of genetic programming. Our scientists excel at programming for intellectual and physical characteristics, but gene editing for emotional characteristics is less understood. It takes more finesse. We got lucky with Quinn. He had a magnetic personality, was kind and warm, and a wonderful addition to our business and family,' Mr. Conner stopped, from emotion, or something else, Charlie couldn't tell.

'He spoke his first words at two weeks and was walking at sixth months. As he grew, his exceptional abilities grew with him. He finished his doctorate program in genetics just before his fourteenth birthday. We were fortunate enough to have an exceptional nanny. She agreed to stay with the family beyond the usual timeframe. Quinn traveled with her and continued his studies in Europe for two more years, earning another advanced degree. About five years ago, he decided to settle down and went to work at Genlabs,' Ms. Conner filled in.

'Did Quinn have any enemies at work?' Charlie asked.

'I can't imagine. As I said, he was well-liked,' Mr. Conner answered.

'Can either of you tell me why someone might want to harm Quinn?'

'It doesn't make sense,' Ms. Conner said, shaking her head.

'Agent Edmo, please understand. No one living here would do this. Westwood has never had a serious crime. All the young people are genetically programmed to be non-violent, and the rest of us are too old. It must be an outsider. Westwood's security was breached, and someone is running loose inside Westwood,' Mr. Conner said.

'We checked that first. Brent says it's not possible. No one entered or left that isn't accounted for,' Charlie stated.

'Then they missed something,' Mr. Conner said.

'We'll keep looking. Any ideas how Westwood's security might have been compromised,' Charlie asked.

'That's not his area of expertise,' Frank observed.

"Okay, like I said, we'll keep looking,' Charlie restated.

'You mentioned a nanny. When did she leave your employment?' Charlie asked.

'When Quinn turned sixteen,' Ms. Conner explained.

'I need her contact information. I also want a complete list of the people who were at the party Sunday night. Please make sure the list is complete. We'll interview everyone, so please don't discuss the case with anyone. As I mentioned, Special Agent Hunter will hold a brief press conference later today and will arrive here to meet with you shortly after that. I don't have to tell you about what to expect when the press gets wind of this,' Charlie said.

'Mr. Edmo. We can handle the press, but mark my words, no one living inside Westwood is involved,' Mr. Conner insisted.

Leaving (the Conner estate), the FBI vehicle took Charlie back across the Puget Sound by ferry to downtown Seattle. Arriving at FBI headquarters in the late afternoon, Charlie was greeted by a message taped to his computer monitor instructing him to immediately come to Special Agent Hunter's office.

'The news conference is moved to six. I don't have much time, so tell me what you know,' Hunter said, once Charlie was seated in his office.

'The forensic team is on site and we'll know more by morning. I suggest getting an interagency team together for a morning briefing. I'll work on developing a written plan for guiding the investigation,' Charlie said.

'Fine. You questioned the family?' Hunter asked.

'Yes, well, the parents anyway. Alex was not available, and they asked me to wait until tomorrow to speak with him,' Charlie said.

'That was sweet of you. Why not interview him today? You're not intimidated by the Conner's, are you?' Special Agent Hunter asked.

Charlie was quiet for a few moments as he considered his response.

'Your vote of confidence is always appreciated,' Charlie said dryly.

'Toughen-up. There's a lot riding on this one. Given past events, I'm not sure I can count on you. This case must go well,' Hunter urged.

'If you're not sure, why the hell did you give me the case?' Charlie asked.

'You know why,' Hunter snapped.

'Yeah, I'm your fall guy,' Charlie said.

Hunter chuckled.

'I'm always on the lookout for ways to fuck with you.'

Charlie's chest filled with pain. Hunter never hesitated to use his partner's death as punishment.

'So, you're up to it?' Hunter interrupted Charlie's thoughts.

'Sir, I'm not intimidated by the Conner family, because I don't have enough respect for their lifestyle to be intimidated. I can handle this case. Unless you can show good cause, the case is mine,' Charlie said firmly.

'Fine. But I'm involved every step of the way. Keep nothing from me, you understand?'

'Yes sir,' Charlie answered, knowing that it was highly un-likely that he would comply.

'Arrange a meeting for the morning. Seven-thirty sharp. Get me your report for today in the next hour, and a draft of an investigation plan. Get the draft to me by morning. You're dismissed.'

My decision is made. I'm taking the case.

DNA

October 31st, 2018
Journal Entry #23
Gordon Kelly, Doctoral Student, MIT

Today in lab, my professor explained that during the semester, she would be discussing the so-called unspoken secrets of science from time to time. Those phenomena that border on the mystical, cannot be empirically proven, but whose existence is difficult to dispute. The first secret on her list; the Ghost in the Machine. Since the advent of computer software and artificial intelligence, machines have occasionally developed a mind of their own and done some very remarkable and unexpected things. A portion of these independent actions have never been fully explained by science. But as my professor pointed out, long before there was computer software, robots, and artificial intelligence, the Ghost in the Machine and its invisible hand has been at work. A mischievous energy working tirelessly to exploit the shortcomings of our engineering. For eons, men have used their increasingly formidable skills to check this unnatural force. But the Ghost is not reasonable, nor impressed with our skills. The Ghost bides its time, and when it finally acts, people usually die. We solve this riddle or perish.

Disconnecting from the call with Agent Hunter, Gordon leafed through the pages of his journal until he found the October 31,

2018 entry. He quickly read the words. Gordon loved the concept of unspoken secrets in science. He laughed to himself. His own words about the Ghost in the Machine had seemed so naïve but were now so relevant.

I'm at war with a ghost and this will not end well.

Turning his attention to the problem of Quinn's body, Gordon considered his options. Along with his devastating report, the DNA in Quinn's body contained enough evidence to destroy his business and life as he knew it. Quinn had tested his own DNA, and he was infected.

The body must be destroyed without raising suspicion?

And what to do about Quinn's report? It was over forty-eight hours since Gordon had received the written report from Quinn. He would need to act soon. He ran through the list in his head one more time. Quinn was the only person besides himself who knew about the report, and he was dead. There was still time to delete the report from Quinn's computer before others at Genlabs caught wind of it.

I'll need help finding and deleting Quinn's report.

Another big problem was what to do about Alex Conner. Gordon was pretty sure Quinn had told his brother about the report. Maybe even given him a copy. Alex looked right at him when Quinn was whispering in his ear at the party.

Am I just guilty?

Gordon didn't think so. He was involved with the Conner family enough to know Alex and Quinn were tight. Alex would need to be silenced somehow. It would give Gordon the time he needed to solve the problem and protect his interests.

The most time-sensitive issue is what to do about Quinn's body.

Opening a locked drawer in his desk, Gordon removed its false bottom. He took out a thin Clearcard, placed his thumb on front of the card, and waited for the screen to activate. An address appeared on the screen. Gordon memorized the address before removing his thumb. He watched as the message vanished. Gordon cut up the card, wrapped it in tissue, and stuck it in his day pack. He would bury the card later.

Leaving his office, Gordon walked to the nearest parking garage and climbed into a company car. He inserted a small datacube into the port on the dashboard. The software program on the datacube would remove any record from its on-board computer of where the car was going. Additionally, Genlabs' security division tracked the movements of all their vehicles. The software would make the car invisible to their tracking system. The car would look like it was still parked in the company garage. After the software was installed, Gordon instructed the car to chauffeur him through Winslow and to board the ferry to Seattle.

As he rode in the car, Gordon struggled to manage his panic. He had jumped on a path that offered few chances of turning back. He needed to move confidently, like he had done in the past.

But instead, Gordon was overwhelmed with uncertainty. He felt nothing but pressure and lacked deeper inspiration. He realized that was the different between the past and now. Before, he had found meaning in his work. After all, he had been working to save lives. But now, by any measure, this was dirty work, and he hated it. Gordon knew what he was doing was justified, but he was still filled with self-doubt. This made him feel weak and aimless.

I need to get a hold of myself.

Departing the ferry in Seattle, Gordon typed in the address that had been displayed on the Clearcard. The car confirmed the address and accelerated in the direction of Interstate 90.

After traveling east for an hour, Gordon found himself traveling down a gravel road in the foothills of the Cascade Mountains. The road lead to a gravel driveway protected by a steel gate. The gate was open, and Gordon took control of the car, driving until he reached a log cabin where a man stood waiting on the porch.

When GSI and Genlabs began to expand globally in 2030, their competitors multiplied accordingly. These enemies, both in the private sector and foreign governments, became increasingly aggressive in stealing their technology. Hawke and Gordon struggled to find ways of responding to these looming threats. They'd hired a series of private investigators and security firms, but after two years, and millions of dollars spent, none had done much good.

They finally landed on the idea of creating their own security firm and staffing it with individuals whom Gordon and Hawke would personally engineer. Their own security firm would allow them to do the necessary dirty work in complete secrecy. And using their own staff of custom-designed, and completely loyal, private investigators appealed to the sensibilities of both men. The idea was far from legal; federal law prohibited modifying the genetic code of individuals with the intent of having him or her commit crimes. But the men were beyond caring.

Gordon and Hawke worked quietly to develop the genetic blueprint for their private investigators and at the same time recruited a thirty-three-year old man to receive the experimental treatments. Once these steps were completed, Hawke and Gordon began the process of modifying his physical, intellectual and emotional makeup. It was the first time the two friends had worked together since college, and both men enjoyed the challenge. If they were successful, other men and women could be recruited, genetically enhanced, and used to staff their security firm.

The man was given a detailed false identity. His new name was Ramsey Lewis. Their future private investigator lived and trained near the Genlabs campus. He received daily injections of nanomachines that would imbed the genetic enhancements into his DNA. Ramsey did intense physical training and underwent a series of minor surgeries.

Over time, their investigator's new physical shape took form. His strength increased as his bones and muscles became hard as stone. His eyesight and hearing improved markedly. Other trainings imbued him with a high level of technical skills, taught him multiple forms of surveillance and counter-intelligence strategies, provided memory augmentation, weapons training and provided him with extensive expertise using explosives.

Ramsey was equipped with metabolism optimization. With a single injection, his metabolism would greatly expand its capacity to regulate his body for up to twelve hours. The injection worked in several important ways. His muscle cells could receive fuel at a much faster rate, which gave Ramsey great strength and stamina. Ramsey's immune system went on full alert, improving his ability to recover from injury.

But above all else, he was programmed to be loyal to Hawke and Gordon.

This was the man who stood on the porch of the cabin, waiting for Gordon to arrive.

'Mr. Kelly, I was glad to hear from you. Please come in. The water's hot,' Ramsey offered.

'Thanks, nice place here, quiet.'

'Yes, I like it that way.'

Gordon noticed his host's face was scratched in several places and Ramsey's nose appeared to be broken but said nothing.

The two men went inside, and Ramsey poured steaming water into the coffee press. He stirred the logs in the fireplace, and the men sat waiting for the coffee to finish steeping. A few minutes later Ramsey rose, filled two cups, and returned to his chair.

'Mr. Kelly. I know why you're here. I take responsibility for my failure to secure Quinn's body. Allow me to explain,' Ramsey started.

'Better be good,' Gordon said.

'I never anticipated someone would use the trail so late at night,' Ramsey explained.

'You fool. It was Hawke Conner who found the body. No doubt, alerted to your attack by his son,' Gordon said.

Ramsey sat quietly while he absorbed this information. Finally, he spoke.

'I screwed up. What can I do to make it right?' Ramsey asked.

'First, you still need to destroy the body. Our friend at the FBI has informed me the body will be moved to the CDC lab early tomorrow morning. The body will be moved by helicopter to the roof of the FBI building, and taken by ambulance to CDC's forensic lab. We should intercept the body before it gets there,' Gordon ordered.

Ramsey walked to his workstation and took a few moments to download a series of photographs of the CDC building.

'All ambulances enter the building through a heavily guarded door that leads into an underground garage,' Ramsey noted.

'Can we attach explosives to the ambulance before it gets inside? Then release a statement blaming some terrorists group?' Gordon asked.

'Might work. We need to know when the ambulance will

arrive. Once the ambulance enters the underground garage, it's too late,' Ramsey said.

'Hunter can tell us when the body leaves the Conner estate,' Gordon offered.

'That would give us a rough timeframe. Attaching the explosives isn't hard. It's being filmed on CCTV that's risky. If we know approximately when the ambulance will arrive, I can stand out of sight from the cameras and target the drones,' Ramsey said, pointing to a street map of the area.

'How do you know where to hide from the cameras?' Gordon asked.

'Watch this. I acquired a software program that displays every blind spot in the city. There are five hundred thousand cameras in Seattle. But even then, there are thousands of places to avoid being seen. See, look, three blind spots on our street,' Ramsey said confidently.

He pointed to the computer screen.

'Those are blind spots?' he asked, and added, 'Won't they search the vehicle?'

'My bombs will be very hard to detect,' Ramsey offered, 'want to see how it's done?'

Leading Gordon to a small outbuilding behind the cabin, Ramsey unlocked the door and the two men entered a windowless room. Ramsey turned on the lights, and Gordon recoiled at what he saw. On one wall were mounted several heavy weapons, ranging from assault rifles to grenade launchers. Boxes marked 'Explosives' were stacked in the corner. But it was the wide array of tiny drones scattered across a large worktable that caught Gordon's attention. The drones looked like a swam of insects.

'What the hell?' Gordon asked.

'You're looking at the latest in bomb-making technology,' Ramsey bragged.

'Impressive.'

'I can attach high explosives to dozens of the drones. The little critters are too small and fly too fast for the CCTV cameras to pick up.'

'Can they be ready by morning?' Gordon asked.

'Sure.'

'Will it be enough explosives? The body needs to be burned to the point where no DNA can be recovered,' Gordon said.

'The drones will fly under the ambulance and attached themselves to the top of gas tank. Virtually undetectable. Their gas tanks are always kept full. The explosion will be huge, and the fire will burn very hot,' Ramsey said.

'It will look like a terrorist attack?' Gordon asked.

'If that's what you want?' Ramsey asked.

'Yes. To the fullest extent possible.'

'Got it. Anything else?' Ramsey asked.

'There is something else. I need time to fix a problem at the company. There's a potentially damaging document. I need your help removing it from the company's servers, without leaving any trace. My computer skills aren't good enough. There can be absolutely no trace the document ever existed. You'll need to search the main servers as well as every employee's data storage, every g-message, and every backup system on and off campus,' Gordon advised.

'I understand, Mr. Kelly. How should I access the system?' Ramsey asked.

'Everything you need is here,' Gordon said, handing a data-cube to Ramsey.

'What else do you need?' Ramsey asked.

'There's another person who knows about the report,' Gordon said.

'Who's that?' Ramsey asked.

'Alex Conner.'

'Quinn's brother.'

'Yes.'

'You want him silenced?'

'Yes, but you can't hurt him, you know, just threaten him,' Gordon said.

'What should I say?'

'Tell him you work for cyber-security at Genlabs. Tell him you can't access some of Quinn's highly classified files. Tell him you can't find a recently completed project for the Department of Defense. Whatever. Ask him to help you figure out Quinn's passwords, anything. I just want to know if Quinn mentioned the report to his brother. That's all.'

'And if he did tell Alex about the report?'

'In that case, threaten him . . . scare the hell out of him. Otherwise say nothing,' Gordon finished.

Later, after finishing dinner, Gordon sat in a leather chair watching the flames flickering in the cabin's fireplace. Ramsey Lewis sat at a nearby desk looking at a computer monitor. He was preparing to search for copies of Quinn's report in Genlabs' massive information system. Gordon watched as Ramsey inserted the unlabeled datacube into the computer port and the software began to load. The software took advantage of a backdoor in Genlabs' data system. Once Ramsey passed through this door, he could conduct searches of every electronic device on campus, even those not physically connected to the system. If someone's app-phone or app-pad was anywhere on campus, it would be searched.

As far as Gordon knew, the only electronic copy of the report was stored on Quinn's data drive. Gordon had the only hard copy. Gordon had already confirmed that none of Genlabs' printers had been used to make another hard copy.

This didn't mean a copy hadn't been printed off-campus. But Gordon doubted that was the case. He was also worried about correspondences that might contain references to Quinn's report. Gordon wished he could search his employees' minds as easily as their data drives.

The software finished loading, and Ramsey typed in a series of search words provided by Gordon, including the tag for Quinn's report. He clicked the start button. Quinn's file containing the report appeared in the window within seconds. In a few minutes, the software finished its search. There were no other copies of the report on campus. There were no written references nor communications referring to the report.

Quinn kept his secret.

'It's ready. Do you want me to delete the file?' Ramsey asked.

'Yes, do it.'

Ramsey worked to delete the file and remove any trace of his work while Gordon went to pour two whiskeys. He returned to the computer with the drinks in time to see Ramsey click on the finish button. All traces of the report were gone. Gordon would be able to deny knowledge of its existence. Ramsey removed the datacube and returned it to Gordon.

'Next you need to clean up your mess; destroy Quinn's body. Then have a talk with Alex Conner,' Gordon said.

ДОД

Arriving home after ten p.m., Charlie found his wife, Anna, curled up in her recliner asleep. His body begin to relax as he watched the slow rise and fall of her breathing. He watched her closely as she slept, knowing she would soon wake. Anna's face was calm and radiant, and her hair was the same jet-black color as the day they met, though Charlie suspected her hair dresser had something to do with that. She was covered by an old Huston Bay wool blanket. He could see she was cloaked in her favorite bathrobe, and Charlie knew she was wearing lamb's wool slippers under the covering. Anna stirred, no doubt sensing she was being watched. Charlie knew he had just seconds before her eyes would open.

Anna George-Edmo was Eastern Shoshone and grew up south of Cody, Wyoming, near a small town called Meeteetse. Her ancestors were Plains Indians who hunted buffalo. Anna inherited her fantastic riding skills from them. She'd grown up on horseback and could easily out distance Charlie on a horse, a fact she never grew tired of pointing out. She worked at a local stable training horses for wealthy equestrians.

He quietly slipped into the kitchen to grab something to eat, a ploy that never worked. Sure enough, it wasn't long before Anna arrived and claimed her rightful place as the home's only cook. She sleepily reheated leftover chili, made with deer venison, her garden tomatoes, onions, and peppers. Anna took a frozen mug from the freezer, filled it from a jug of her home-brewed beer, and handed it to Charlie. She yawned as he ate.

'Hunter gave you the Conner case. I thought he hated you,' Anna said.

'He does. Hunter needs a fall guy, or he wants me to retire,' Charlie said between bites.

'If I thought we could survive on my paycheck, I'd tell you to quit. I know you're not happy,' Anna offered.

'Not always, but I need to work. Jobs are tough to find. If I quit, we might need to leave Seattle,' Charlie explained.

'Whatever happens we'll be fine. Tell me, is it really just Hunter, or is something else bothering you?' she asked.

'Maybe. Truth is, I'm sick of it all. If it wasn't for Jack and Brad . . . let me give you an example. Today I interviewed Quinn Conner's mother, Abby. She's in her mid-forties and looks like a teenage elf queen with big tits. Bred for pleasure, and to satisfy the cravings of her wealthy husband. She reminded me of a modern-day geisha girl. How am I supposed to care about these people?' he asked.

'They made it hard to like them. What gets me is how protective many feminists are of a mother's right to make these kinds of decisions for their unborn sons and daughters. I can remember when it wasn't like this. I wonder. Could you refuse to take the Conner case?' Anna asked.

'Too late for that. And no doubt I'm being set-up. But I plan to turn the tables on Hunter. Maybe this case will be my way out,' Charlie said.

'And how is that?'

'Not sure, but I will find a way,' Charlie said.

Soon after he finished eating, they went to bed, but not before Charlie removed his grandfather's necklace from around his neck and touched it to his lips.

As a result of his unstable family life, Charlie had lived with his grandparents on several occasions, sometimes for years at a time. It had all started on his tenth birthday. His thoughts drifted to his tenth birthday, and goosebumps skimmed across the surface of his skin. He was too young to understand it at the time, but looking back, Charlie knew his career in law enforcement had started on that day.

Remembering his tenth birthday filled Charlie with an intense anger and shame. Charlie had been forced to celebrate the birthday alone with his parents. At the time, his father was not speaking with any member of the family, and forbid school friends from visiting their home. Even though it was almost four decades ago, Charlie remembered that birthday like it was yesterday.

He recalled sitting quietly at the kitchen table, watching his mother as she attempted to light the candles perched randomly across the top of his birthday cake. It was an early evening in July, and the room was stifling hot. His father refused to open the small windows above the kitchen sink, arguing it would let in more hot air. The room was saturated with cigarette smoke, and the day's last rays of sunlight fought to penetrate the haze.

His mother's hand shook uncontrollably as she attempted to light the candles, and Charlie watched as his father grew increasingly impatient. She started to cry, and Charlie's father immediately lost his temper. Charlie could see the veins on the side of his father's neck pop out as his face turned a crimson red.

It was a sight Charlie had seen before. He wished his father's eyes would pop out of his head and roll across the floor, like in the Saturday morning cartoons, or his veins would explode, and his father's body would empty of blood.

Charlie remembered starting to cry as his father snatched the cake away from his poor mother, ripped the candles off the cake, and tossed them in the direction of the kitchen sink. He picked up a knife and angerly cut a large slice of cake for Charlie.

Then the most amazing thing happened.

Charlie's father slid the oversized piece of cake onto a small plate, and in one fluid, angry motion, spun the plate onto the smooth tabletop like it was a frisbee. Charlie was sure his father had wanted the cake to fly off the table and end up on the floor. Instead, the plate hit the surface with just the right amount of spin and skipped across the table in a perfect, sweeping arc, avoided falling off the far edge of the table by inches, before stopping precisely in front of Charlie.

'Eat up,' he said.

Charlie stopped crying and stared at his plate in amazement. Was this some sort of magic trick? Did his father do it on purpose? Neither of his parents seemed to have noticed what had happened.

He glanced at his father in time to see him cut a large slice for himself and begin eating.

'Aren't we goin' sing Happy Birthday?' his mother complained.

'And listen to your ugly voice. No thanks,' his father responded.

'Got to sing, and blow out the candles,' she said.

'Shut the hell up.'

Staring at her husband, Charlie's mother was quiet as she considered a response. After a time, she asked, 'Don't I get some cake?'

'Suit yourself,' he responded.

Charlie's father made a weak effort to slide the cake and knife a few inches toward his mother, and then continued stuffing cake into his mouth.

'I told you to get a store-bought cake. This cake's dry as hell,' he said.

Watching his mother stare at the knife, Charlie imagined she was going to pick it up and plunge it his father's heart. He could see the intense hatred on her face and Charlie remembered willing his mother to do it, to pick up the knife and rid their life of this mean little man.

Instead, his mother had grabbed a heavy glass saltshaker and hurled it at his father's face. The heavy shaker struck his forehead just above the left eye. Charlie watched in horror as blood started to pour down his face. His father refused move, and Charlie saw a trail of blood run down the left side of his face, drip off his chin, and splash onto the tabletop. His father remained motionless while a small puddle of blood formed on the table.

Knowing what was about to happen, Charlie ran out of the room. He sprinted into his bedroom, locked the door, and covered his ears. This didn't prevent him from hearing his father beginning to beat his mother. Charlie remembered standing in his room, hearing his mother beg for him to stop. He remembered having the sudden realization that his month was stuffed full of cake, and openly crying while he slowly chewed the sweet dessert.

Charlie knew his father might come for him next. So, he grabbed his baseball bat and crawled under his bed in preparation for another horror filled night.

But that night things had ended differently. A passing neighbor had heard his mother screaming and called the police. A giant man in a dark blue uniform had arrived and arrested his father, literally dragging him to a waiting police car as Charlie watched out his window.

Charlie's beloved mother was taken to the local hospital. He watched as the EMTs wheeled her to the waiting ambulance.

After his parents were gone, Charlie waited for several minutes before opening his bedroom door a crack. He saw a policeman sitting on their couch.

'Your mom said it was your birthday,' the policeman said when he saw Charlie.

Charlie slammed the door shut and turned the lock.

In Charlie's eyes, the man was truly a giant. His hands were locked behind his head and his legs seemed to stretch halfway across the room. He made the couch look like it was built for a child. His shiny black boot looked like tree stumps coming out of the floor. Charlie thought he saw a long, black ponytail, and a fearsome pistol hanging from his belt.

At least he is tribe.

Charlie considered escaping through the window.

Instead, he opened his door again.

'Sorry you had to see all that on your birthday. I'm Bill,' the man said.

'What'd you care?' Charlie asked as he opened the door wider.

'Just do.'

Charlie didn't respond.

'Believe me or not, your choice. Got any family nearby where you can spend the night?' Bill had asked.

'My grandparents are closest family, they live clear out by Grey's Lake,' Charlie had whispered.

'Okay, we'll give them a call in the morning. But tonight, you can stay with me. I already called my wife,' Bill offered.

'I can stay here,' Charlie suggested.

'No can do. Relax, we can bring the cake.'

That night had been the beginning of Charlie's journey to a different life.

The next day Bill drove Charlie to his grandparents' home. It was a two-hour drive, and Charlie had talked to Bill nonstop the entire way. Looking back, he now realized it was the first normal conversation Charlie had ever had with an adult. He now understood that on that day he had discovered that men could be something other than unkind.

Charlie would live with his grandparents for the remainder of the summer before being reunited with his parents at the beginning of the school year. In many ways, these were the best months of Charlie's short life. His grandfather was a highly skilled woodsman and rancher - and was eager to pass these traditions to his grandson.

His training had started immediately. Charlie's grandfather taught him to safely handle a variety of firearms. He could disassemble and clean every pistol and rifle his grandfather owned by the end of summer. Over time, Charlie learned how to track a variety of small and large game, including rabbit, grouse, deer and elk. His grandfather pushed Charlie to learn how to tie simple artificial flies and use a fly rod to catch trout. Spending countless hours in the woods with his grandfather provided Charlie with the skills and confidence needed to navigate in the backcountry.

Charlie soaked it all in happily.

During the first week living with his grandparents, Charlie had noticed a necklace around his grandfather's neck. The leather band carried a few simple glass beads tied on either side of a single fang. The fang was at least four inches long and yellow with age. The tooth had tiny black streaks etched along its length. He was fascinated by the fang and lay in bed that night wondering what kind of animal had such a fierce weapon. The longer Charlie laid there, the more frightening the animal became.

I bet it came from a saber tooth tiger.

In the morning, Charlie asked about the fang. His grandfather explained it had belonged to a grizzly bear. He told the story about a huge male bear that came through the ranch one day and killed a cow. His grandfather had shot the bear in the backyard. 'Right by the clothesline,' he said, while pointing out the kitchen window. 'Haven't seen a bear on the place since the day I made this necklace,' he concluded.

From that moment, Charlie coveted the necklace. Not because he found the necklace attractive, but rather he wanted protection from the bears he imagined were waiting outside.

On the day Charlie left his grandparents' home for the University of Washington, his grandfather draped the necklace around his neck. The amulet had remained with him ever since, and Charlie was comforted by its connection to his dear grandfather.

Climbing into bed, and as often happened during his decent into sleep, Charlie's saddest memories of his parents came to mind. Hardly a day passed when Charlie didn't recall the defining event of his youth - an event that made Charlie a minor celebrity in the national press, and later contributed to his acceptance into the FBI academy. Looking back, he realized that among the many factors that had led him to a career in law enforcement, his abandonment by his parents in the Idaho backcountry and his subsequent week-long fight for survival, was the most important.

Charlie's defining moment had begun when his parents, flush with a fresh supply of drugs, had decided to go camping. It was the summer of his fiftieth birthday. His parents loaded their old Ford truck with supplies, a small arsenal of firearms, and camping equipment. They plonked Charlie in the seat between them and drove east from Fort Hall toward the national forest. Charlie watched as his parents laughed and told endless stories about their high school years. Worst, he was trapped and unable to escape their relentless and unwanted affection. His father squeezed his left knee every time he shifted gears and his mother keep running her hands through his long, dark hair. Charlie was old enough to understand his parents were high, and resented their drug-induced attempts at being good parents.

Struggling to understand his parents, Charlie alternated between anger and pity. He felt alone and often thought of himself as the only adult in the family. He asked nothing of them, and that was exactly what he got. There was never food in the house, and if Charlie wanted clean clothes, he washed them himself. His parents had no idea about how he was doing in school and knew nothing about his personal affairs.

None the less, on some days Charlie pitied his parents. They had become victims and were without hope. His parents were convinced the white man had taken their lives from them. His mother and father had been born on the Fort Hall reservation, and out of pure stubbornness, would never leave, because leaving would deprive them of their right to be victims of the white man's oppression.

Resisting the urge to scream at his parents to stop touching him, Charlie instead stared out the truck window at the endless fields of potatoes, daydreaming about piles of French fries.

Charlie's father drove east for two hours before the foothills of the Caribou-Targhee National Forest came into view. They turned onto a wash-boarded gravel road, and the farmland soon gave way to a wetland occupying a huge basin. The basin was circled by minor mountain peaks that still held the remnants of the previous winter's snow.

Passing along the north shore of the huge wetland, Charlie could see areas of open water to the south. He could make out large islands of birds gathered on the water, while dozens of flocks flew overhead. In the pastures near the road sat countless black birds with oddly curved beaks and white spots on their breasts.

Charlie's father turned north onto a forest service work road that took them in the direction of Palisades Reservoir. As they slowly climbed, they entered the national forest and began looking for a suitable campsite. Charlie's father found a side road and followed it east for most of an hour. The road was steep and rocky in places, and the old truck struggled to make the climb. They finally came to a flat, high elevation valley divided by a small, well-braided creek. A circle of mountains surrounded the valley and Charlie sensed the road was the only way into the area. A perfect campsite was perched alongside the deep, flowing water. The valley was populated with a sea of Lodgepole Pine, and thick willow brush lined the banks of the stream. Charlie knew the stream would be filled with trout, and he was excited to do some fly fishing.

After setting up camp, Charlie's parents immediately retired to their tent. This began a three-day binge by his parents, alternating between sex in their tent and the preparation and consumption of meth. That night, Charlie was forced to cook his own dinner and eat alone. After eating, he climbed into his tent and tried to sleep over the sound of his parents frolicking in bed.

In order to leave before his parents woke up, Charlie climbed out of his sleeping bag before dawn and prepared for a day of hiking and fishing. The rays from an unseen sun blasted like a rocket across the sky above him and painted the highest clouds a brilliant pink. The morning's mist was beginning to rise from the creek and the grass meadows lining its banks, and Charlie suspected it would be a hot day.

After dressing, he fixed breakfast and tied a Pale Morning Dun to the end of his tippet. He packed a big lunch and filled his canteen with water from the creek.

Worried about bears, Charlie desperately wanted to take one of his father's guns for protection. He knew if his father caught him with one of the guns the consequences would be severe. But he was genuinely fearful of bears, so Charlie managed to convince himself to borrow a pistol.

My parents are too high to notice a missing gun.

I'll return the gun long before they notice it's gone.

Quietly approaching his parent's tent, he peeked inside to make sure they were both sound asleep. He could see them both in their sleeping bags and knew they wouldn't wake for hours. Walking silently in bare feet, Charlie went to the truck and slowly opened the passenger door. Several pistols and boxes of ammunition were stored in a cardboard box on the seat of the truck. Charlie quickly grabbed the biggest pistol, tossed the appropriate box of bullets into his coat pocket, and quietly close the truck's door.

Finishing breakfast, Charlie put on his boots, took his fly rod and headed for the creek. The loaded gun was safely stashed in his waist belt.

For the next two days, he spent his time fly fishing in the nearby creeks and going for long hikes - activities he could do all day, every day, for the rest of his life. The routine worked well for two days. Charlie would rise early and be gone before his parents woke. He would return to camp just before dark and hide in the trees near their campsite, spying on his parents. It never took long before they would return to their tent, after which, Charlie would quietly enter the camp, eat dinner, and climb into his tent.

But on the third morning, Charlie was forced to wait until his parents woke in order to discuss their plans for departing later that day. Around nine, his parents climbed out their tent and immediately began quarreling. It was clear to Charlie the drugs had begun to run out. Their quarrels soon turned to an all-out screaming match, and Charlie grabbed his pack and abandoned them to go for a hike.

When he returned a few hours later, their tents and the other camping equipment were loaded into the truck and his parents were impatiently waiting for his return.

'Where the fuck you been? I told you not to go far,' his father said.

'You didn't tell me we were leaving so soon,' Charlie stated, trying to hide his disgust.

'You callin me a liar boy?'

'Leave the boy alone, he means no harm,' his mother spoke.

'And where the fuck is my gun?'

'I saw a bear. I needed protection,' Charlie explained.

'You never touch my guns without asking, you little prick.'

'You were sleeping.'

His father took one step forward and back-handed Charlie across the face. His mother grabbed her husband by the arm, but he turned and punched her in the face. She fell to the ground whimpering. Blood began to pour from her nose.

'Don't touch her,' Charlie screamed.

His father came toward Charlie again, his fist clinched. His face was red with rage and the veins on his neck stood out like steel cables.

Charlie took several steps backward, turned, and started to run.

Then he remembered the gun was in his pack.

Charlie removed his daypack as he pivoted to face his father. He quickly unzipped his pack and retrieved the gun.

He pointed the pistol at his father, now only ten feet away.

His father stopped in his tracks.

'Get in the truck and leave or I will kill you,' Charlie spoke firmly.

'No, you won't, you're a fucking pussy.'

He slowly began to walk in Charlie's direction, his right hand pointed toward his son.

Charlie shot his father, glazing his left arm a few inches about his elbow. He heard his mother scream.

'You shot me, you little fuck,' his father shouted and holding his wound, moved quickly toward Charlie.

'The next shot is through your heart,' Charlie shouted and pointed the gun toward his father's chest. 'Get in the truck and leave,' Charlie repeated loudly. His voice trembled.

For the second time, Charlie's father stopped in his tracks.

'Easy boy. Okay I'll go, but she comes with me,' Charlie's father ordered.

'Not a chance,' Charlie said, the gun still aimed at his father's chest.

'Oh yeah boy. You better ask her,' his father shouted in the direction of his wife.

He slowly removed a small plastic bag filled with a white powder from his shirt pocket.

'Look what I have. Your slut mother is coming with me,' he said while waving the small bag in her direction.

Charlie looked at his mother's face and saw her eyes light up like it was Christmas morning.

'Where'd you get that?' his mother sneered, holding her bloodied nose with her right hand.

'Been saving it just for you. Now, get in the truck. We're leaving this worthless piece of shit.'

Charlie met his mother's gaze and saw a look on her face he would remember for years. Her expression when from the excitement at seeing the bag of meth to a sad realization she was about to betray her only child.

With a look of complete resignation, blood running down her face and staining the front of her blouse, Charlie's mother walked to the truck, climbed into the seat, and firmly shut the door.

She never once looked in Charlie's direction.

'You are officially disowned,' his father spat.

Charlie's blood boiled.

'You fucker, I've always been on my own,' Charlie screamed.

'Good, then it's settled.'

Charlie watched in horror as his father got into the truck and his parents drove away. He was fifteen years old and his parents had just abandoned him deep in the national forest. Charlie stood in the middle of their camp for a long time considering what had just happened. When it was clear his parents were really gone, he sank to the ground and cried, the gun cradled in his lap.

But it didn't take long for him to get over it. He realized he wasn't sad about his parents abandoning him. Not really. In fact, he was in complete agreement with their decision. Charlie was at ease with the notion that he didn't deserve a family and should be left alone to live or die. He was a lousy student, had no real friends, and was nothing but a burden to his family.

No wonder they left me here.

It never occurred to Charlie until years later that his parent had been crazy.

Charlie's first instinct was to follow his parents, and he walked a short distance down the road in that direction. Then it occurred to Charlie that his parents might be trying to teach him a lesson and would soon return.

I'll teach them a lesson.

With this thought in mind, Charlie donned his pack, stuck the gun is his waist belt, turned around and headed away from the road and deeper into the woods.

To clear his mind of these awful memories, Charlie focused on Anna's soft breathing. After he calmed down, Charlie shifted his thoughts to his first year at the bureau. Charlie had found it hard to fit into the FBI culture from the start. At the FBI Academy, there was a martial arts instructor who had it in for him from the first day of class. His name was Dale Louder, and he was from rural Utah. He came from a pioneer family who raised cattle on a large ranch south of Salt Lake City. He was the first in his family to earn a degree, but unfortunately, his college education had failed to erase some of his outdated notions about Native Americans. The man was never overtly racist, but made it clear he didn't believe Indians could be trusted to be FBI agents.

Charlie and the instructor were sparring one day while the other FBI recruits watched. In the middle of the match, Agent Louder grabbed Charlie's ponytail and yanked him to the mat and drove his forearm toward his throat. Charlie blocked the forearm, rolled away and sprang to his feet. He grabbed the man by the front of his shirt and lifted him off the ground with both hands. Louder tried to fight back, but Charlie held him firmly at arm's length. Charlie pinned him to the nearest wall, and said, 'Don't ever touch my hair again,' and then tossed him to the mat.

The instructor jumped to his feet enraged, and angrily charged Charlie. In a show of strength that was still talked about at the FBI Academy, Charlie blocked his advance, lifted Louder above his head and threw him across the mat into a pile of chairs.

The instructor never taunted Charlie again, but on no account would ever acknowledge his presence in class either.

Things weren't much different when he was assigned to the genetics division in the Seattle FBI office. He was the only Native American working in the building and often felt the stares of his fellow agents. Some agents couldn't stop themselves and joked about his long ponytail or quiet demeanor.

Charlie learned to smile and out-compete them all. It didn't hurt that Charlie was six foot two, weighted two hundred and thirty hard pounds, and was smarter than all of them. Over time his fellow agents came to respect Charlie's abilities.

〰️

Ramsey watched as the ambulance turned left and headed down the side street toward the entrance to the CDC's underground garage. Tall buildings lined both sides of the street, and Ramsey could just make out the earliest rays of the morning sun.

Working all night was exhausting, but exhilarating, and Ramsey was becoming increasingly excited about his plan.

I will be redeemed in Gordon's eyes, and that's all that matters.

The emergency vehicle was still several hundred feet away. There was no traffic, and parked cars lined both sides of the street. As Ramsey anticipated the driver slowed in response to the crowded lane. The vehicle was moving at walking speed by the time it reached Ramsey.

The emergency vehicle passed Ramsey as he sent a message from his app-phone to the ten drones assembled nearby. The tiny, insect-like drones had hidden themselves in the bushes and trees lining the street.

Receiving the command from Ramsey, the tiny drones sprang to life. The drones shot from their respective hiding places and swarmed just inches behind the ambulance's rear bumper. The drone's sensors located the target in a tenth of a second and the machines disappeared under the ambulance so fast Ramsey couldn't be sure it happened. The process took just seconds.

The ambulance continued its journey toward the entrance to the underground garage. Ramsey watched as the vehicle passed through security. He could see the guards using mirrors to check under the vehicle.

No problem.

He watched as the ambulance entered the garage and its door closed.

The drones would ignite in ten seconds. Moving further away from the CDC building, Ramsey made sure he was not visible to the nearest CCTV camera. He turned his head as the ambulance exploded. The sound was muted, but unmistakable.

4

TUESDAY, DECEMBER 20TH, 2050

Facts are stubborn, but statistics are more pliable.
Mark Twain

Marion Harper had worked many long, hard hours during her twenty-five-year career at the Center for Disease Control and Prevention. But on this Tuesday morning, she was feeling lazy. It was the holidays after all. She had a lab full of techs needing supervision, but Marion was hiding in her office, playing cards on her computer. She was thinking about her career and wondering if she could make it fifteen more years until retirement.

In her favor, the last twenty-five years had gone by in a flash. Her work had produced more excitement, joy, terror, wonder, and insights about life, than any job she could imagine. She hadn't been bored a single minute. But after decades of fighting infectious diseases around the world, Marion was tired down to her DNA.

Her thoughts slipped away as her app-phone rang.

'Marion. You heard about Quinn Conner?' her boss asked, when Marion answered the call.

'Of course.'

'His body arrives in ten minutes,' Dr. Peck said.

'You're kidding. So early. I knew we'd be involved, but. Well, I guess the FBI lab is not an option,' Marion said.

'You know the reason for that,' Dr. Peck said.

Dr. Peck was referring to the problems at the FBI lab recently reported in the press. Several important convictions had been overturned due to their negligence.

'We'll get the blame if something goes wrong,' Marion observed.

'It's great to be great. Stop by my office before you do your preliminary examination,' Dr. Peck said.

'I'll come now,' Marion answered.

Marion got up and left her office. She entered the lab and watched one of her technicians operate a gene-sequencing machine. He was processing a DNA sample that arrived from Asia overnight. The gene sequencing machines were new, as was much of the equipment in the lab. In the past five years, the federal government had funded a major upgrade of the CDC's Lab Response Network (LRN). Marion looked across the huge lab and felt more confident than she had in years. The CDC had never been better prepared to address a health emergency at home or abroad.

Before leaving for her boss's office, Marion called a colleague and asked him to come and supervise her lab while she was away. When the man arrived, Marion thanked him and exited the lab, walking to the nearest elevator.

Marion took the elevator to the top floor of the CDC building where Dr. Peck's office was located. She had just entered her boss's office, when suddenly the entire building shook violently.

The shaking was followed by the sound of a massive explosion.

𝕯𝕬𝕳𝕬

Charlie found a seat as his boss called the meeting to order. Special Agent Ross Hunter occupied the lectern in the front of the room. He seemed taller, and Charlie wondered if he was standing on a box. Hunter had taken the old-fashioned route to leadership in the FBI. He attended Yale University and entered the FBI Academy immediately after graduation. In a short ten years, Hunter rose through the ranks until he was assigned to a coveted position in the New York's FBI office. But Hunter had run into problems when he was arrested while having some very kinky sex at an establishment operated by organized crime. Charlie assumed it had been a set-up. (How else would the short, chubby, and balding man before him, standing on a box no less, seduce any woman?)

Special Agent Hunter was transferred to the Pacific Northwest as punishment. He hated the Northwest and blamed Charlie for every drop of rain that fell, making some strange connection between the constant showers and a forty-something Indian from Idaho. Hunter was entirely focused on one thing: returning to the center of the action on the east coast, and Charlie suspected he saw the Conner case as a promising way to get there.

Charlie sat alongside his two partners, the six members of the forensic team, and the other FBI agents assigned to the case. The large and windowless meeting room was buried deep in the inner sanctum of FBI headquarters in downtown Seattle. Besides the FBI agents, twenty law enforcement personnel representing nine other federal, state, and local agencies were present. This was a huge case, and everyone wanted a piece of the action. Charlie knew there would be much glory to share, if the case was solved quickly. And much blame to share, if not.

'Let's get started. You should all have packets. This is our preliminary plan for conducting the investigation into the death of Quinn Conner. As you all know, federal law requires the FBI to investigate the deaths of all designer-babies, so we have legal jurisdiction. The assignments for each of your agencies are listed on page three. Look this over but save your questions to the end. The FBI will maintain control of all stages of the investigation. Charlie Edmo will take the lead. Direct your questions to him. All evidence goes through us, understand. Chain of possession is critical,' Hunter paused.

'I don't have to tell you this is a very high-profile case. It may be the biggest case many of your people will ever work on. This one gets done strictly by the book every step of the way. Have your personnel document every minute they spend on this case. Our work will be closely scrutinized for years to come. Now, the forensic team worked through the night, and Amara will tell us what they discovered,' Hunter concluded.

'Thanks,' Agent Amara Dixon said, as she walked to the front of the room.

'Hawke Conner contacted authorities to report his son's death around one-ten yesterday morning. Winslow police were the first to arrive on scene. Charlie and his team were called and arrived on site at ten-thirty. Charlie's team did an initial walk through and determined the death to be suspicious. He requested our team be sent to the Conner estate. Hunter agreed to the request, and we arrived by copter at the Conner estate a few minutes before two p.m. Ben Hayward, detective from the Winslow Police Department, and Agent Edmo, met us at the Conner's helipad. Ben immediately took us to the scene,' she paused for questions. Seeing none she continued.

'Quinn Conner was a twenty-two-year old genetically-enhanced male. His parents are Henry and Abby Conner. As many of you know, the victim had a small amount of blood coming from his nose and ears. However, the amount of blood was not sufficient to cause death. The victim was in excellent health. Several possible causes of death will be explored, but it's far too early to speculate. The coroner estimates the time of death was between eleven-thirty Sunday night and one, a.m., Monday morning. The body has been taken to the CDC lab where an autopsy will begin in a few hours.' Dixon paused and removed an app-phone from her pocket.

Agent Dixon pointed her phone toward a nearby wall and beamed a series of photographs of the scene of the death as she spoke.

'Charlie and his team photographed the victim before and after examining the body. As you can see, Quinn Conner was found in thick underbrush laying on his side just below the trail. The victim was found less than a mile from his father's home,' she paused to display another photograph.

"Here is a series of close-ups of the victim's face. You can see the blood coming from his ears and nose. The area was very muddy. The team was unable to locate signs of a struggle, but the fact the body was moved indicates someone else was present. We'll have the results of the autopsy by the end of the day, but the toxicology report will take a few days. That's it,' she said.

Hunter pointed at Charlie, indicating it was his turn to speak.

'Thanks. Hopefully those reports will pinpoint the cause of

death. Turn to page two. Each of you is assigned to a team. The investigation will move along the usual lines. We'll take a close look at the family, Quinn Conner's place of employment, the employees working at the estate and do a records search of Mr. Conner. We'll question the one hundred or so individuals who attended the party the night of his death.'

'Do you know how you'll divide the workload?' Special Agent Hunter asked.

'As you can see on page two, my team will focus on Quinn's wife, extended family and his workplace. Agent Silas Seaman, our new techie, will conduct the records search. I've asked him to look at Mr. Conner's medical history, work history, finances, personal life and the rest. Ben will lead the team made up of SPD and the Winslow PD personnel. He will focus on the party goers and the employees at the Conner estate. Most of the party goers live in Westwood, so he will need to coordinate with Brent in order to gain access to these individuals. Last, we'll look at the possibility that an outsider penetrated the security at Westwood and committed the crime. Ben will liaison with the security team at Westwood to follow this line of inquiry,' Charlie finished and nodded toward his boss.

'A number of Westwood residents think an outsider is involved. There've been complaints about security,' Hunter interjected.

'Not likely. Brent assured me no one has entered or left Westwood who isn't accounted for,' Charlie said.

'You'd be stupid to ignore the possibility,' Hunter said.

'Don't worry, we'll look into it,' Charlie said, ignoring Hunter's choice of words.

He said nothing more, so Charlie continued.

'The rest of your assignments are listed in the packet. So, let's get to work. Twenty-four hours have passed so time is critical. It's the holidays, I know that; but I assume if you're here, you're giving it up for this case. I assigned your work accordingly. We'll meet back here tomorrow morning at 7:30.'

'Any questions?' Charlie asked. There were none.

At that instant, a dozen app-phones sounded, one after the other.

'There's been a bombing at the CDC,' Hunter shouted, after briefly speaking into his phone.

An hour later, Charlie, Jack and Brad sat with the other members of their team. They were all squeezed into the meeting room next to Charlie's office. Charlie had just gotten off the phone with a friend who was a first responder and was at the scene of the explosion. After he disconnected the call, Charlie spoke to the assembled agents.

'The ambulance carrying Quinn Conner's body exploded in the basement of the CDC building. Some group has claimed responsibility. Two EMTs were killed, and unfortunately the blast and fire completely incinerated Quinn Conner's body,' Charlie said.

'Could his body have been the target?' Jack asked.

'Can't rule it out. Though the CDC has been hit several times in recent years, so it could be a coincidence. Outside of us, only the Conner's and their lawyer knew where the body was going,' Charlie said.

'Regardless, we no longer have a body, which means we no longer have samples of Mr. Conner's DNA,' Jack said.

'We should be able to acquire a sample from another source,' Charlie said.

'I hope so. What's next?' Brad asked.

'The bureau has sent a team to the site of the explosion. We'll know more later in the day,' Charlie said.

'Okay. So, what's our plan of attack for today?' Jack asked.

'Jack, you set up the meeting with the wife and Nanny. Brad, work on Gordon Kelly at Genlabs. I want to meet with him this afternoon. The rest of you can focus on learning more about the parents and Quinn's brother,' Charlie said.

Alex wanted to grieve his brother's death, but all he could think about were the last words Quinn had spoken to him. He'd been arguing with his brother at their father's holiday party. It was one of their favorite past-times: a way to test the limits of their respective intellects in a way no one else could match. It didn't hurt that the debates upset Quinn's wife and their mother. Alex secretly relished their discomfort and was pretty sure his brother did too.

These spirited debates replaced the physical tests of will-power Alex and his brother had indulged in as teenagers. Not that Alex wouldn't still challenge Quinn to the occasional basketball game, during which one, or both, of them usually ended up bloodied. But to Alex and his brother, these games and debates were a way to stay bonded, and just as often, these contests ended in laughter.

That was why Alex was surprised when Quinn abruptly grabbed him by the shoulders, near the end of the party, and whispered in his ear, 'If something happens to me, find the report on my data drive.' Alex remembered how scared Quinn sounded, as he smiled uncertainly. Alex would never forget the look on his brother's face.

His perfect recall allowed him to remember every word uttered by his brother that night.

Alex wished he could erase these memories, but his enhancements wouldn't allow it.

'What report? What are you scared of?' Alex had asked, whispering.

'I think I'm being followed. Listen, if something happens to me, get the report. It will explain everything. Call Henry, he can help. Tell him it's on my data drive. The final report was saved as a PDF file yesterday, December 17th. The file has two layers of encryption. The password is SEAHAWKS2019 – typed forward and then in reverse order.' Quinn had said.

Sitting down on the couch, Alex tried to bring his full concentration to bear on his brother's death, but he failed. He was alone at his home in Westwood, not far from his parent's house. It'd been twenty-four hours since Quinn's body was found, and Alex's body pulsed with anger. There was a battle raging inside him, and he desperately craved an outlet for his pain.

For the first time in his life, Alex's genetic enhancements seemed worthless.

He tried to refocus.

Quinn was terrified about something, and now he is dead.

Alex's face flushed red as he applied his advanced analytics to the problem. In less than two seconds, he examined hundreds of pieces of information and replayed thousands of images from the past. Based on this internal exercise, Alex's reached a firm conclusion. He understood at least one truth behind his brother's deaths.

Our father is responsible.

Alex didn't know how or why, but his prick of a father was involved.

His mind made up Alex touched a button on his wrist phone.

'Hello Henry, Alex.'

'Alex, I'm so sorry about Quinn. I can't believe it. I fuckin' can't believe it. I'm not sure what to say. You know I loved him.'

'Thanks Henry. I know you did.'

'People here are real upset. They're having a meeting in an hour.'

'I bet. Listen, I need a favor.'

'Sure, anything, you know that.'

'Great, but I can't talk about it on the phone. Can we meet?'

Alex and Henry agreed on a time and place to meet and hung up.

Three hours later Alex and Henry met for lunch. Henry Chen was a senior scientist at Genlabs. Quinn had been his immediate supervisor for two years. Henry, Alex and Quinn had been friends since boyhood. They had attended the same private school for enhanced children and still got together for beers. Henry hugged Alex.

'So, what's up?' Henry asked, after they ordered lunch and had exchanged pleasantries.

'The FBI is treating Quinn's death as suspicious. If they're right, I'm worried it's related to his work. Can you tell me if he was working on anything that was 'hush-hush?' Alex asked.

'Not that I know of. Can you give me a better idea of what you're looking for?' Henry asked.

'It might involve some type of document, a top-secret report,' Charlie reported.

'Nothing comes to mind. Everything we do is secret. We work in silos, you know that. But I'll see what I can find out,' Henry offered.

'It's important. Check his data drive for a document dated Saturday, December 17th. The file's doubled encrypted. The password is SEAHAWKS2019, typed forward and then in reverse order,' Alex said.

5

TUESDAY, DECEMBER 20TH, 2050

I change, I stay the same.

One hour later, Charlie and Jack were driven by their FBI car to an apartment Quinn Conner and his wife maintained in downtown Seattle. The apartment was in a building not far from Charlie's office. Ms. Ella Conner, Quinn's wife of two years, had agreed to meet them there.

Charlie and Jack arrived at the penthouse apartment and were ushered into a small sitting room by the butler. The men sat in plush seats that Charlie suspected were once owned by French royalty. The walls of the room were a pink marble and matched the stone tops of the room's ornate furniture. A small sign posted on the nearby wall informed visitors the ceiling was painted using the *Di sotto in su* or 'seen from below' style.

After a few minutes, a small woman entered the room and sat in the remaining chair. During introductions, Charlie took a careful look at Ella Conner.

He immediately felt uncomfortable. She was twenty-six years old and possessed the body of a fully mature woman her age. But as Charlie's eyes came to rest on her face, he suppressed a gasp. Ella Conner looked like a very young girl, appearing far younger that Charlie's own seventeen-year old daughter. She possessed bright blue eyes, rosy cheeks, and perfectly painted red lips framing pearly white teeth. Ella Conner could have been Snow White's younger sister.

Charlie struggled to make eye contact with the woman.

Having done his homework, Charlie knew her appearance was the result of extensive genetic enhancements. When GSI first introduced designer-babies to the public, they offered three basic genetic profiles to parents. Beyond these basic plans, and for an additional fee, parents could choose advanced enhancements to the intellectual, physical, and psychological makeup of their prodigy.

But for many parents, even those with great wealth, the ten to fifteen million dollar price tag for a genetically enhanced baby was a deterrent. As a result, some parents choose to purchase more modestly priced genetic add-ons. But in Ella Conner's case, Charlie guessed her parents had an unlimited budget. In addition to focusing their resources on her youthful appearance and creating a face that never aged, Charlie knew she had genius level intelligence.

All Charlie could see was the child-like face, and it gave him the creeps.

'Ms. Conner, I am sorry for your loss, and I apologize for asking to meet with you so soon after your husband's death,' Charlie said.

'Thank you, Agent Edmo. Forgive me for interrupting, but I saw on my news feed there was an attack at the CDC building. Wasn't my husband's body taken there?' she asked.

'Yes, there was an attack. Emergency responders are still sorting things out,' Charlie offered.

'Did the bombing harm my husband's body?' she asked.

Charlie took a slow breath, thinking about what to say.

His hesitation betrayed him.

'I'll assume the worst until I hear otherwise. Please continue,' Ms. Conner said bitterly.

'Yes, well, as you know, we are treating your husband's death as suspicious. We want to move quickly, as this increases our chances of finding out what happened. Now, if you don't mind, when was the last time you saw Quinn?' Charlie asked.

'I saw Quinn, and his brother Alex, a little before midnight, at the Christmas party. They were having one of their arguments on the deck. They'd been drinking. I tried to get them to stop. But once they lock horns, there's no stopping them.'

'What were they arguing about?' Jack asked.

'They were arguing about Quinn's work. It was an ongoing debate. I finally gave up and went inside. That was the last time I saw my husband - drunk and fighting with his brother. Fitting, don't you think,' Ms. Conner said.

'Can you be more specific about what they were arguing about?' Charlie asked.

'I don't know. It was technical. I did hear something about Gordon, but he was always a source of disagreement.'

'You are referring to Gordon Kelly, Quinn's boss at Genlabs?' Charlie asked.

'Right, Quinn's relationship with his boss was complicated.'

'How so?' Charlie asked.

'My husband was in a tough position. He worked for his father's best friend. He was under tremendous pressure to produce. Research is the life blood of Genlabs, and by association GSI,' she added.

'Okay, back to their argument. Can you describe how intense it was?' Charlie asked.

'Nothing out of ordinary; certainly not violent,' she answered.

'You said they had these types of arguments before. Did any of those ever turn physical?' Jack asked.

'Maybe on the basketball court. Quinn ended up in the hospital once, I think. But they were never violent in my presence.'

Charlie stopped to write some notes.

'Can you think of any reason why someone would harm your husband?' Jack asked.

'No. He was well-liked, by everyone.'

'Was there anyone attending the holiday party that didn't get along with your husband?' Charlie asked.

'No, the party was for family and friends. Everybody loved Quinn,' she answered, her voice breaking for the first time.

'You said Quinn's work was an ongoing debate. Could there be a connection between some crisis at work and his death?' Charlie asked.

'Nothing comes to mind, but I don't know a lot about Quinn's work. It's all so top secret,' she answered.

'Okay. We'll be back in touch soon. Thank you. We'll do our best to keep you informed about our progress,' Charlie finished.

After saying their goodbyes to Ella Conner, Charlie and Jack headed back to the FBI building. As they traveled, Charlie thought about the interview with Ella Conner. Once again, he found it difficult to get a read on someone with genetic enhancements. Like a well-trained actor, her affect was so controlled it was impossible to interpret. Charlie was getting the faint, but unmistakable, feeling of obstacles arising in his path.

'Did you think Ella Conner is attractive? I'm struggling to

get my head around men's obsession with little girls,' Charlie offered.

'Hard to deny the sex appeal. But it'd be like having sex with a child,' Jack said.

'I think that's the point. Between you and me, I'm finding it difficult to remain nonjudgmental. My values are conflicting with my work. I might be old fashion, but I don't like where this is all headed. I'm finding it harder and harder to protect and serve folks who may or may not be entirely human,' Charlie said.

'You might be exaggerating, but I know what you mean. Feels like we created a monster and can no longer control it.'

'Except that's our job: to tame the beast,' Charlie concluded.

'Then we better get busy,' Jack added.

'That's what I'm trying to say. I'm not sure I can do it anymore,' Charlie finished.

After arriving back at FBI headquarters, Charlie asked Jack to contact the Conner's former nanny, Adele Peterson, and arrange to question her. Ten minutes later Jack called to inform him they would be meeting Ms. Peterson at 1:00 p.m., at her apartment.

Deciding he should be better prepared for the interview, Charlie left his office and joined Jack.

Charlie recalled how hard he had worked hard to recruit Jack to his team. Decades earlier, when Jack was still an SPD detective, they had worked together on a couple of cases. Jack was an exceptional detective, and Charlie knew he was interested in a career with the FBI. But Jack lacked the required college degree. On a couple of occasions, Charlie had encouraged him to return to school.

The next year, he was pleased to hear Jack had left the SPD

and was working on a degree in law enforcement. Later, after Jack earned his degree and had been accepted into the FBI Academy, Charlie worked behind the scenes to recruit him to his team. Jack was smart and tough, easy to get along with, and Charlie could rely on him under pressure.

Sitting next to Jack, Charlie watched as he did a quick background search on Adele Peterson. She lived in a converted steel shipping container near the old docks, south of downtown Seattle. Ms. Peterson was nearly fifty, unmarried, and had two sisters who both lived nearby. Adele and her sisters had grown up with their mother in Poulsbo. Washington, a small town on the Kitsap Peninsula.

Not surprisingly, Jack discovered Adele Peterson had not returned to work after leaving the Conner's employment. She fell victim to a national economy that had dramatically changed during her time as a nanny. In 2030, the global economy fell into a depression. As the global depression deepened and deflation in the U.S. settled in for the long haul, millions of Americans lost their jobs. Advancements in robotics and other forms of automation hastened this decline. Unemployment steadily increased until half the American workforce did not have jobs by 2035, and still didn't. Charlie knew that Adele Peterson, and others like her, had not stood a chance of finding work.

Ms. Peterson and millions of others were saved by the actions of the federal government. The high rate of unemployment created a fundamental problem for the wealthy and government policy makers. Without strong consumer spending, the rich would not stay wealthy for long. Consumer spending accounted for two-thirds of all economic activity.

Charlie still marveled about how Congress had solved the problem. Rather than focusing on job creation, policy makers created a new category of taxes on the very wealthy and their offshore corporate earnings. These revenues funded the so-called Universal Basic Income program. UBI was the term coined by the federal government for the stipends paid to millions of permanently unemployed Americans.

Adele Peterson survived on this government stipend. The stipend allowed her and millions of others to maintain a lifestyle just above the poverty line. Adele was lucky enough to own her apartment. According to a long trail of legal documents, Jack found out that Quinn Conner had purchased Ms. Peterson's apartment shortly after she left his father's employment. The deed to the apartment was in her name.

At twelve-thirty, Charlie and Jack climbed into an FBI car, which immediately headed for the woman's apartment. They talked about the case for a few minutes, and then sat quietly, staring out the car's windows. Along the way, Charlie saw the old Sears Building where older generations had shopped. Near the entrance to the graceful old brick building. Charlie could see dozens of party-goers and a row of ambulances with their lights flashing. The building was now a TwentyFour - one of a string of round-the-clock, low-life night clubs, popular across the country.

Once it became clear the jobs weren't coming back and the government stipends began to flow, millions of Americans faced a serious dilemma: what to do with their abundant time. (Charlie was among the lucky ones whose job was deemed essential.) Many unemployed Americans remained productive and got involved with civic projects or did volunteer work. Others became full-time rec-heads, gamers, or technogeeks. Others returned to school, joined clubs, and if they could afford it, traveled.

But some could not adapt to not working and started

partying, many until they died. There was a huge increase in the number of overdoses, accidental deaths, and suicides. Charlie knew this was why there were so many ambulances parked in front of the club.

As they approached the docks, Charlie could see Ms. Peterson's apartment complex. In the past decade, most of the docks and nearby industries had gone out of business. At the same time, the need for housing that was affordable to Americans only receiving a government stipend rapidly increased. Some clever developers bought dozens of the shipping containers that were rusting away along the docks. They converted them into apartment complexes, and Adele Peterson owned one of these units.

The car delivered them to Adele's apartment early. The apartment complex was a minor landmark. Each of the converted steel containers was forty feet long, eight feet wide and eight feet tall. They were welded into the shape of a pyramid. Each pyramid was made of twenty-one containers and was over fifty-feet tall. A spider web of welded stairs and walkways dominated the facades of the structures. They stretched, one pyramid after another, for the entire length of the decaying docks, separated only by the giant, old ship-to-shore cranes, their orange paint stained with rust.

The backs of the apartments all faced the dingy water of Elliot Bay, a poor man's waterfront property. The containers had originally been painted a series of primary colors, contributing to their reputation as a landmark. The former shipping containers were now covered with rust and black stain, and accessorized with piles of overstuffed, black garbage bags. Charlie could smell the mix of polluted saltwater and wet garbage.

They found Adele's apartment near the top of the second

pyramid. They were welcomed at the door by a tall, rangy, woman. She asked them to sit and offered water.

'Ms. Peterson, thank you for visiting with us on short notice. I'm sure you know why we're here,' Charlie began.

'It's because of Quinn,' her lower lip quivered.

'Yes, I'm sorry. I know you were close to him,' Charlie offered, 'I need to ask some questions and then we'll be on our way.'

'Okay.'

'First, tells us how you became a nanny for the Conner family?'

'I was selected after the usual search. I was surprised to be picked, honestly. It helped I was from the area and ranked at the top of my class. I was inseminated with Alex on January 1st, 2026, at GSI headquarters. Nine months later I gave birth to Alex and moved to the estate. I lived in the small house near the horse stables. It was like being in heaven. I had everything I needed and was well paid. I loved being a nanny and was pleased when they asked me to carry Quinn two years later,' Adele offered.

'How did the second pregnancy go?'

'Fine, everything went well.'

'Tell us about how Quinn and his brother were raised?'

Charlie watched as she paused to recall the boy's childhood twenty-plus years before.

'I was the primary caregiver, of course, but I had lots of help. The rest of the staff loved the boys. The Conner's loved their boys too but were dedicated professionals. They were remarkably disciplined about spending three hours every Sunday with the boys, and the occasional vacation, but that was about it,' she finished.

'They weren't a close family?' Jack asked.

'Not really. The boys were not bonded to their parents in the usual ways, even compared to today's standards. I don't know if it was their genetic programming, but when I compared them to my sister's kids, things didn't seem right,' Adele paused, and then added, 'I felt like it was a business arrangement.'

'How were Alex and Quinn growing up? Were they close?'

'They were as close as they could be,' she said.

'What does that mean?' Jack jumped in.

'Their father encouraged fierce competition between the brothers. He meant well, but Hawke was only capable of giving his approval to the winner, who was usually Quinn. He forced the boys to fight for his love, which he gave to them grudgingly. I hated Hawke for that,' Adele added.

'So, Quinn usually won?' Jack asked.

'Alex was nearly two years older. He won at first. But by the time Quinn was twelve or thirteen, he generally won. Quinn was gifted at everything,' she said smiling.

'If the genetic programming of both boys was identical, would they be that different?' Jack asked.

'They were similar in most ways. Both were brilliant and good looking. The girls loved them. But while Alex had his demons, Quinn had a warm personality. People were drawn to him, and Alex couldn't compete with that.' Adele paused. 'I remember when they were still boys. We were hiking near the estate and came across a stray dog. Alex walked toward the dog, talking to the poor thing. The dog kept growling and baring his teeth. I told Alex to stop, but he wouldn't listen. Alex was sure he could calm the dog down. He got too close and the dog bit him hard on the hand. I let it happen, to teach him a lesson, but then I felt bad because he was crying. Then, I'll never forget. Quinn walked up to the dog and literally stared him into submission. One second the dog was growling, and the next, he just laid down on his side. Quinn walked right up and rubbed his belly. He turned to Alex, and with the most compassionate expression, signaled for him to come and pet the dog.'

'Interesting, what about later, when they were teens?' Charlie asked.

'Raising genetically-enhanced kids is not the same as raising natural-born. Their childhood, if you can call it that, is short. Alex and Quinn were already on career paths by their early teens. It was all about their ongoing education and preparing lesson plans, field trips. I left when Quinn turned sixteen,' she answered.

'Did you stay in touch with Quinn?' Charlie asked.

'Not much. He bought this apartment for me, and I love him like a son. But I haven't spoken with him in months. Abby invited me to their holiday party, but I couldn't face it. Not my crowd,' she said flatly.

'Can you think of any reason someone would want to harm Quinn?' Charlie asked.

'The news said Quinn died of natural causes,' Adele said. She looked concerned.

'Quinn's death is officially listed as suspicious,' Jack pointed out.

Adele sat quietly for a time, her eyes slowly filling with tears.

'Why would anyone hurt Quinn?' she asked.

March 23rd, 2019
Journal Entry #57
Gordon Kelly, Doctoral Student, MIT

Today my professor discussed another unspoken secret in science. Our brain, the fundamental tool we use to conduct science, is relentlessly working to deceive us.

As you might imagine, this came as a shock. What, I don't really know myself? Or do I view my inner self through a fog of my own making? The scientific evidence suggests I do. My professor calls it autopoiesis; the notion humans don't perceive the world directly.

But why would my brain deceive me? The answer is found in how we evolved. The answer lies in the abyss between the ancient Paleolithic world where our ancestors were hard-wired by evolution, and the world of today. Everything we do; loving, hating, praying, begging, sweating, singing, dancing, fearing, killing, believing, and all the rest. All these emotions, all these things exist, because they somehow bestowed evolutionary advantage upon us.

However, my professor said, there was a price to pay for becoming such a clever species. Our brains were wired to make quick decisions, so I became a shallow thinker. Our brains instructed us to be safe rather than sorry, so I became fearful. Our brains were wired to resist change, so I began clinging to the status quo. Our brains were built to accept only information that agrees with what we've already deemed to be true, so I became easily manipulated. Our brains are constructed to survive, not to find truth. How could it be otherwise? We solve this riddle or perish.

Lifting his gaze from the old journal, Gordon focused his attention on the news flash scrolling across the bottom of the computer screen. There has been an explosion in the basement of the CDC building in downtown Seattle.

Gordon smiled.

One risk is eliminated.

Gordon felt no shame, but for a moment he wondered what had happened to the young man who wrote the journal entry decades ago - the bright-eyed grad student with a deeply inquisitive mind.

Gordon felt no regret about his journey from being that simple young man to the person he was today. He wasn't sorry for his descent into ruthlessness. It's how the world worked. Gordon knew he couldn't be both great and kind. Natural selection punished weakness and so did human society. Good things were not achievable without the occasional application of violence and an unshakeable commitment to the goal at hand. The world had never been changed by a passive person, no matter how nice, brilliant and well-argued he or she was.

These thoughts made Gordon feel like he was carrying the weight of world on his shoulders. Ensuring the long-term survival of our species was a heavy responsibility. In contrast, his spirits soared as he understood that he was a great man whose life had intersected with a precious moment in history.

All the elements Gordon needed to effect profound change were available to him.

Gordon possessed a profound scientific understanding of genetic engineering. It didn't hurt to have vast wealth, and one of the world's largest, most influential corporations in the world at his disposal.

Gordon didn't know why he had been chosen, and no longer cared. But he knew beyond a doubt that he had been born with the unique skills, and the force of will, to achieve his very lofty goals.

Gordon smiled.

They've summoned up a thunder cloud, and they're going to hear from me.

Gordon straightened a paper clip and used it to pick at the stiches on the back of his left hand. A row of black stitches repaired a long cut. Opening a box with a razor knife, Gordon's hand had slipped, and the blade had run across his knuckles. That was three weeks ago, and it wasn't a deep cut. But for some reason, he was unable to stop himself from playing with the wound. The cut should be healed by now. Instead, it was oozing small drops of red blood and yellow pus. The area around the cut was red and swollen, but he continued to play with the wound.

His thoughts were interrupted by the chime of his secure app-phone.

'All went well it appears?' Gordon asked, after answering the call.

'The fire burned hot for over an hour before they put it out. I'm sure no DNA survived,' Ramsey offered.

'Well done. You're forgiven. But no more fuckups, do you understand?'

'Understood. So now it's time to contact Alex Conner?'

'Yes. No time to waste,' Gordon said.

The three federal agents were scheduled to meet Gordon Kelly at four in the afternoon. Genlabs was located on the Kitsap Peninsula, and Charlie, Jack and Brad decided to save time and meet at the ferry terminal. They arrived in two cars, so Jack instructed one to drive itself back to FBI headquarters. The three men climbed into the remaining car and began comparing notes as the vehicle boarded the ferry.

'What did Ms. Peterson have to say?' Brad asked.

'Not much. As adults, Alex and Quinn were competitive, but close. They fought like cats and dogs as boys, and were not bonded to their parents, according to Ms. Peterson. Not a healthy family, in my opinion,' Charlie offered.

'Did she know anything about his work?' Brad asked.

'Nothing. She claimed his work was top secret, and he never discussed his research,' Charlie observed.

'Not surprising,' Brad said.

'What's the plan for Genlabs?' Charlie asked.

'We'll have an hour with Gordon Kelly and their corporate attorney. I arranged to question some of Quinn's closest colleagues, and I asked to search his office; permission was granted for both. One of their lawyers will be present at all times.'

'Did you ask about access to Quinn's data files?' Charlie asked.

'I did not. You're the boss, I left that for you,' Brad smiled.

Arriving at the Genlabs' campus, the three agents passed through security and were escorted to its main administrative building. The building sat in the middle of the campus. Charlie knew the campus covered sixty acres of forested land near the town of Indianola. He could see Miller Bay and the blue waters of the Puget Sound to the east. The tall buildings of downtown Seattle were visible far to the southeast.

After Brad was dispatched to search Quinn Conner's office, Charlie and Jack were taken to meet with Gordon Kelly. They found the famous man sitting in the middle of a large, wrap around desk, built of a single cross-section of a giant red cedar. The desk was polished to a high gloss finish, and all the items on the desk were perfectly ordered. Sitting next to him was a stocky woman, who Gordon Kelly introduced as the company's lead attorney, Kathleen Holden.

Charlie began by saying, 'Please accept my condolences. I'll begin by informing you the FBI is treating Quinn Conner's death as suspicious,' Charlie paused. 'This triggers a more rigorous set of procedures. In addition to today's interviews and the search of Quinn's office, we will need access to his data files. If the investigation expands, we will need full disclosure of everything related to Quinn's work,' Charlie said.

'He was murdered?' Gordon Kelly looked both confused and concerned.

'There was enough evidence to designate his death as suspicious,' Charlie said.

'I see,' Gordon paused, 'Okay.' He paused again. Charlie could tell he was carefully choosing his words.

'I'm sorry, but giving you access to Quinn's files will be a problem. Much of his work is highly classified, proprietary, or both. If the information became public, it could cost us hundreds of millions of dollars. I do not exaggerate. I loved Quinn like a son. I can understand how an outsider like you might assume his death is related to our research. But until you prove this, I will choose to believe otherwise. Kathleen will meet with our legal team in the morning and address your request. Meanwhile, I asked her to prepare for your questions,' he finished and looked away, dismissing them.

'I'll expect to hear from Ms. Holden once a decision is made. If not, I will file for the necessary search warrants. Now, can you tell me when Mr. Conner was last on campus?' Charlie asked Kathleen.

'Yes. Mr. Conner went through security on the day of his death, last Sunday. He arrived at 6:10 a.m. and left the campus at 2:30 p.m.'

'I assume working Sundays is not unusual?' he asked.

'No. Based on conversations with his co-workers, it was a normal workday. According to them, nothing was unusual, except he left early to help with his father's party,' Kathleen said.

'Can you tell me about his work? Is there anything that

stands-out about his job that might have got him killed?' Charlie asked, trying to reengage Gordon.

'Everything and nothing,' Gordon responded. 'All of Quinn's work was critically important to someone.'

'Is there anything else you can think of that might help us sort this out?' Jack asked. 'Forgive me, but maybe an office affair, or professional jealousy?'

'Someone else maybe, but not Quinn. He was solid and well-liked,' Gordon responded.

It was clear to Charlie the interview was going nowhere so he ended the meeting, thanked his host, and left to meet with Quinn's co-workers.

Charlie and Jack were led to a small meeting room where they were to conduct the interviews of Quinn Conner's colleagues. Spending the next two hours questioning Quinn Conner's co-workers was a monumental waste of time. Without access to Quinn's work files, Charlie and Jack were unsure what questions to ask. Additionally, the Genlabs scientists had all signed comprehensive non-disclosure agreements and were reluctant to share much information. Charlie and Jack were able to confirm Quinn was popular with his staff and considered to be an able administrator and a respected researcher. No one could think of a single reason why someone would harm Quinn.

ⅅⅆⅅ

'Is the building collapsing?' Dr. Peck yelled, holding on to the edges of her desk.

'That was some type of explosion,' Marion responded, as she got to her feet.

For a full minute, the two women were frozen in silence, waiting for the building to collapse beneath their feet.

The building stopped trembling, and the sounds of the explosion were replaced by sirens and alarms. They could hear the footfall of security personnel running down the hallway outside the office. One of the guards stopped and stuck her head in the doorway.

'Dr. Peck. Please close and lock the door. I'll be outside until we get the all-clear. Do you understand?' the woman asked.

Dr. Peck nodded yes to the guard, who closed the door and stepped back outside. Dr. Peck walked to the door and turned the lock. They could see the guard's silhouette through the bullet-proof glass.

'Another terrorist attack, and how many people just died? Just what we need during the holidays,' Lois said.

'I'm guessing someone made it into the basement,' Marion said.

Marion worried about the political fallout from this latest lapse in security. There had been other failures in safety and security at the CDC over the years, but three bombings in two years was unprecedented. Starting in 2033, the CDC came under serious scrutiny after three incidents exposed dozens of lab workers to anthrax, and one worker to Ebola. A sample of a deadly strain of bird flu was mistakenly sent to another lab. In 2036, another incident at the CDC headquarters in Atlanta costs the lives of three lab technicians who were exposed to a deadly genetically modified virus when there was a power outage and the airflow system failed.

The most serious incident took place in 2046. Terrorists purchased ten vials of anthrax from a disgruntled CDC employee. The vials were old and had fallen out of the CDC's inventory. Nobody noticed the vials were missing until they turned up in the Middle East, where they were used by a Sunni faction to murder several hundred Shiite men, women, and children.

The fallout in Congress and among the American people was severe. Most of the leadership team at the CDC were replaced, and an array of new safety measures were mandated by Congress. Tens of millions of dollars were appropriated for new equipment, security, and personnel.

Dr. Lois Peck survived this administrative purge and was asked to join the transition team charged with reforming the agency. She participated in a successful two-year effort to install new leadership at the top of the CDC. As a reward, the CDC granted Lois's wish to return to the Pacific Northwest where her aging parents and extended family lived. Dr. Peck moved to Seattle in 2048 and convinced Marion to join her there.

Marion couldn't image a better boss. The woman was an experienced administrator and gifted scientist. Dr. Peck was the perfect mentor for a budding young woman scientist like Marion. In her first decade at the CDC, Dr. Peck had assigned Marion to projects that protected Americans from health emergencies both in the U.S. and abroad. Marion spent four years in western Africa working to eradicate a new strain of Ebola, and another six years in Alabama supporting communities in fighting an outbreak of the zika virus. For the last sixteen years, she worked for the National Lab Response Network maintained by the CDC.

Marion's daydream was interrupted by an urgent knock on the door. Lois unlocked the door and the guard entered the office, urging them to leave immediately. The fire was still burning, and there were concerns about the structural integrity of the building. The women were instructed to wait to hear from security before returning to work. Marion and her boss exited the building via a freight elevator and headed home.

Returning to her townhouse by bus, Marion switched on her flatscreen and made coffee. News of the explosion was already flooding the airwaves. Watching the news made her worry about how soon she would be able to return to work. For a moment she wondered why. What part of her longed to hurry back to more death and dismay?

Am I heroic or just twisted?

Marion had had a very ordinary childhood. She had grown up on the coast of northern California near the small town of Point Arena. Her mom was a pediatrician and her father a psychologist. She was an only child. Marion's parents were low-key and loving caregivers, and Marion grew up in a happy household.

Given the happy childhood, Marion wondered what drove her so hard. She suspected it was her involvement in sports. In school Marion played basketball. She grew to five foot ten inches tall by sixth grade, and even though she had stopped growing, Marion still towered above many boys through her high school years. Some girls didn't enjoy being tall, but Marion loved exploiting her extra inches to intimidate the boys.

Thanks to her dad's coaching and hard work, Marion turned into a decorated athlete by her senior year. She had exceptional grades, and the combination provided her with multiple offers for athletic scholarships. She accepted an of-fer to play basketball at Harvard. She wanted to earn a bache-lor's degree and then attend their medical school. She played basketball for two years before a knee injury forced her to quit the team.

By then, Marion had met Dr. Lois Peck, and as a result, was seriously considering a career as an infectious disease specialist. Dr. Peck was a visiting professor and ended up being Marion's professional mentor and later her friend. Dr. Peck worked for the CDC and encouraged Marion's to keep her focus on infectious diseases. After completing her doctoral program, Marion went to work at the CDC. Dr. Peck had been her supervisor ever since.

Marion saw a message from Lois on her app-phone.

Just heard. Can't return to office until morning. Want to get a drink?

ᴎᴀᴎ

Charlie got home in time for a late dinner with his wife, Anna, and their seventeen-year- old daughter, Esther. Anna greeted him with a warm peck on the cheek, and Esther gave him a suspiciously long hug. Within moments, dinner appeared, and the family sat down to eat. Anna had prepared his favorite dinner: lamb stew, red potatoes, fresh corn, and salad. A tall beverage stood next to Charlie's plate.

Charlie was pleasantly surprised, as they never drank alcohol when Esther joined them for dinner. Charlie asked, and was told that mother and daughter had agreed it was the holidays, and just this once, he deserved a drink with dinner.

Charlie went on high alert.

Somebody wants something from me.

It'd been several days since Charlie and Anna had dined with their daughter, so there were lots to catch up on. The conversation revolved around the holidays and the upcoming visit from Charlie's grandparents.

Charlie's grandparents, Frank and Joyce Edmo, had spent their lives on a small ranch near Grey's Lake, Idaho, where they raised some cows, maintained a menagerie of other farm animals, but mostly had survived off the land. The ranch abutted the national forest, and the area provided great deer and elk hunting. The nearby rivers and streams were loaded with trout.

Recently, his grandparents had left the ranch and moved to a nearby city.

When Charlie went to live with his grandparents for the first time, it was like being dropped off in paradise. He was ten years old, the perfect age to developed a passion for the wilderness. Thanks to his grandfather, he learned to hunt, catch trout, ride a horse, and herd cows.

Charlie also learned what it meant to be a Shoshone-Bannock.

Charlie's grandfather was a quiet man from whom emanated an air of secrecy. He was so wrinkled his eyes often looked closed. Charlie only remembered seeing the whites of his eyes twice; both times were during an argument with his wife. His hands were gnarled from a lifetime of hard work, but his back was straight, and he hadn't lost a bit of his six-foot-four-inch frame. Frank Edmo was a legendary hiker. Young Charlie's legs had struggled to keep up with him on their long hikes looking for game.

Frank Edmo practiced many of the ancient ways of the Shoshone-Bannock tribe, and for years, Charlie was convinced he could perform magic. Even today Charlie wondered about some of the things he saw as a boy. One day, Charlie watched unseen as his grandfather left the house and spoke softly to a pair of ravens sitting in a pine outside the house. Charlie had never noticed the birds before. His grandfather tossed a few small pieces of meat on the ground, and both birds immediately glided to the food.

As the birds ate, his grandfather perfectly mimicked the sound of a hungry raven. Charlie watched in amazement as one of the ravens lifted off and landed on his left arm. He spoke to the raven in a whisper, and the bird received another piece of meat. The birds then flew away. Later, Charlie asked his grandfather about what he had seen.

'The ravens will never trust us, but they can be convinced to do our bidding. Next time watch them closely. They never stop looking at my eyes. They want to peck them out. To the raven, eyes are like chocolate candy. Like some of the people you might meet along the way, never let them get too close,' Frank Edmo had said.

Charlie realized his daughter was talking to him.

'. . . anyway, Amy got it done and she still looks Indian, mostly, and anyway, I can tone it down. So, what do you think?' Esther asked, her voice pleading as only a daughter can.

Charlie realized he was in deep trouble. He'd missed something important and he was firmly sitting in the no-win zone. He looked at his daughter. Like her mother, Esther was all Plains Indian. She was tall, beautiful and had a deep love for horses.

'I'm sorry. I was daydreaming and missed the beginning. What are we talking about?'

'Dad. Please. This is important. My future is at stake. Amy had it done and got a job right away.'

'What exactly did Amy get done?' Charlie pleaded, trying to catch up.

'GSI is having a holiday sale on all of their beauty packages. Amy's parents bought her one for Christmas. I have the money saved, almost all of it, anyway. Well, I would need a loan, or it could be my Christmas present,' Esther begged again.

'Aren't you beautiful enough?' Charlie asked.

'Dad, it's not that. You weren't listening. You're not going to like this. The process will make me look less like an Indian,' Esther blushed, and averted her eyes.

Charlie stopped dead. He fought back tears for a moment, and then felt a rush of hot blood torching his body.

'How do they do that?' Charlie was beginning to lose his internal battle to stay calm.

'It's a combination of genetic enhancements, cosmetic procedures and minor surgeries,' Anna added.

'So, you know about this?' Charlie asked his wife pointedly, blood pressure raising.

Anna nodded yes.

'Why would you do this?' Charlie asked his daughter, his voice growing louder.

'Nobody wants to hire an Indian,' she answered calmly.

'I got a job with the FBI,' Charlie pointed out.

'How's that going?' Esther asked smartly.

'What's that supposed to mean?' Charlie responded.

'Never mind. That's not the point,' Esther replied.

'And what's the point?'

'I don't want to look like an Indian,' Esther yelled.

''Being an Indian is an honor,' Charlie replied.

'Not to me.'

"I WON'T ALLOW IT!' Charlie lost it.

'I knew you'd never understand. I'm be eighteen in three months. I won't need your permission then,' Esther spoke calmly, but with firmness, and left the room.

Later, climbing into bed with a wife, Charlie sensed the air was thick between them and a fight was coming. Hoping to avoid this, he slipped into bed, turned off the lamp, turned his back to his wife, and pretended to sleep.

'Nice try. Before you go to sleep, please explain to me why you handled that so badly?'

'Esther should be proud to be an Indian. And there shouldn't be a way to change who you are, it's not right,' Charlie argued, as he turned to face Anna.

'It won't change who she is. It's a normal part of her world. Most of her Indian friends have done it, and the Asian kids are infatuated with changing the way they look too,' Anna said.

'That doesn't make it right. She's betraying her own blood. Her great-grandfather will die on the spot if he finds out,' Charlie argued.

'He doesn't need to know. In three months, she'll be eighteen, and after that, she might move out. We can't spend the next few months fighting over nothing,' Anna urged.

'It's not nothing. Her blood line is important, especially now. Besides, she doesn't have all the money, and you will not give her a dime,' Charlie said firmly.

'Charlie, you don't know the whole story. She interviewed today for a job she really wanted. Esther could tell the minute she walked into the interview they didn't like her. They didn't bother to call her back, and she heard from a friend another girl got the job. She's upset.'

'I don't care. There's got to be another way.'

'Great, you find a solution, but at least apologize to our daughter.'

'I will not. She needs to think about where she comes from.'

Anna grunted and turned over, pretending to sleep.

Why am I wrong even when I'm right?

Suddenly in a bad mood, Charlie tried in vain to sleep. His thoughts again descended into a pool of sad memories about his childhood. The day he was abandoned by his parents had become so imbedded in his personal history that Charlie had created a mental loop that frequently began to play itself during times of stress.

The loop always started with Charlie sitting in the dirt, crying as he watched his parents drive away.

The loop began to play again, and Charlie could see himself sitting in the dirt crying. Once he had run out of tears, Charlie remembered feeling freer than at any point in his fifteen years of life, not caring about being abandoned. Charlie had stopped crying and decided on a plan. He would walk to his grandparent's ranch. Charlie felt well prepared. He carried two sandwiches and three candy bars, a water bottle, his pocketknife, fly rod, a pistol with one box of ammo, and a small ax his father had left behind. He didn't know where their ranch was located nor how to get to his grandparent's house, but he knew their name, and this was a tight knit community.

Charlie would find his grandparent's ranch.

Charlie's first thought was to go after his parents. Instead, he abandoned the valley floor and hiked uphill, keeping the sun to his right. He calculated this would take him mostly to the south. He planned to adjust his bearings once he reached the saddle looming above him. He was pretty sure his grandparent's ranch lay far to the south and west.

The hillside was very steep and covered with short, dry grass. The summer sun baked the exposed terrain, and Charlie was soon dripping wet. To conserve energy, he used the many trails created by range cows and wildlife to crisscross the steep hill. But he was still consuming water at an alarming rate. As he climbed, Charlie came across a gulch holding a thick stand of timber. As he approached the stand of pines, Charlie could hear the soft trickle of water. He decided to rest and found a shaded area by the small spring. He refilled his water bottle, drank deeply, and filled it again.

Charlie stretched out on the grass, closed his eyes, and must have fallen asleep for a few minutes. He was roused by what he assumed was someone tickling his nose with a feather. But when he calmly opened his eyes, he was staring into the face of a large white tail deer. Charlie remained still as the four-point buck continued to sniff his face, his huge antlers looming over his body. The animal finally lost interest and wandered off.

That's a good omen.

Smiling, he got to his feet, donned his gear, and climbed up the hillside for several more hours. As dusk approached, Charlie realized he would not reach the saddle before dark, so he moved toward a nearby stand of trees. He was exhausted, and Charlie hoped the tall trees would provide shelter for the night. Charlie drank deeply before he began preparing a bed. Using his hand ax, he cut enough boughs to form a small bed and to cover his body. Charlie located the tallest tree in the stand and found a crevice among the exposed roots of the giant conifer. Laying half the boughs into the crevice, he crawled into his bed, covered himself with the remaining boughs, added a thick pile of dried leaves, and settled in for the night. After eating a few bites of his sandwich, he fell asleep.

After imagining huge bugs crawling over his body throughout the night, Charlie woke tired and a little scared. He made straight for the nearby creek, and after quenching his thirst, took one bite from one of his sandwiches. Charlie then went searching for edible fiddleheads, the fresh tips of the bracken ferns that are common in Idaho. Managing to pick a large handful, he slowly ate the fiddleheads. He took another bit of his sandwich in order to wash away the bitter taste of the fern. Using his hands, Charlie washed his face and drank from the creek again. He refilled his bottle before beginning the day's hike.

Leaving the stand of timber, Charlie finished the half-mile climb to the open saddle above him. Once there, he sat and surveyed the endless forest around him. The woodland stretched in all directions for as far as he could see. There were no signs of civilization.

Looking for clues to which direction he should go, Charlie surveyed the surrounding area for a long time. Finally, he thought he could see smoke raising in the distance. The column of smoke looked far away and was barely visible against the grey sky.

Based on his spotty memory of the area, the smoke was in the general direction he wanted to go. Even though it was hard to see, Charlie knew the fire would get more active as the day progressed. And where there is smoke there would be fire. Where there was fire, there would be fire fighters.

Getting back on his feet, Charlie picked his route off the mountain and started walking downhill in the direction of the fire.

As he hiked, Charlie kept his thoughts focused on his grandfather and the lessons he had imbedded in him. He faced two dangers. First, Charlie knew he couldn't wander the woods forever. He needed to find civilization, or he would starve. He was lost, but only a little. Charlie knew the knowledge that he was lost was the first step to getting unlost. He was confident he would eventually find a ranch or maybe a forest service work road.

Second, Charlie was worried his scent would soon attract a bear, or worst yet, a pack of wolves. His pistol offered little real protection against either threat.

Hiking for the entire morning gave the young man a chance to consider his new life. He understood that, once he returned to civilization, there was a chance he would be forced to reunite with his parents.

I can't let that happen.

He visualized telling the story to the cops about how his parents had abandoned him in the woods and left him to die. Charlie could see the looks of disbelief on the cops' faces. His parents could just say he ran away. No, his only hope was to find his grandparents and convince them to let him stay with them in secret.

As he hiked, Charlie, as he often did, fantasized about being a cop. He saw himself in the same dark blue uniform worn by Bill. Carrying a gun and telling people what to do. Arresting bad guys and driving a police car. Walking proudly down the street while being the center of attention. This line of thought occupied Charlie for hours and would sustain him in the days to come. More than anything Charlie wanted to be a cop.

Hiking at a brisk pace, Charlie found himself in a thickly wooded area. He started thinking about his grandmother's cooking and was lost in thought when he suddenly became aware of an odd noise above him.

Quickly scanning the trees around him, Charlie located the sound and immediately the hair on his neck stiffened. There was a young bear cub in the tree just feet above his head. The animal was alarmed and calling to his mother.

Immediately altered to the danger, Charlie reached into his waist belt and grabbed the pistol and disengaged the gun's safety. He turned to run up the trail he had just come down when he heard a loud crash behind him. Spinning around, Charlie saw the mother bear erupt into the small clearing, not fifty feet away. The sow stopped and lifted her nose in Charlie's direction. Knowing the bear could smell him better than she could see him, Charlie backed up until he rested against a tree while avoiding making eye contact with the animal.

I won't be threatening, and the bear will leave.

But not this bear. Charlie watched in terror as the sow charged him. The black bear was taking no changes and was soon approaching at full gallop.

Charlie firmly planted his feet in the soft ground and raised the pistol. He aimed at the bear's head and neck and opened fire. The first shot hit the ground just in front of the charging animal, but the following three shots found their mark. Charlie watched in horror as blood and bits of brain blew out the back of the bear's skull.

The huge animal, now crazed and wounded, faltered and almost fell. But Charlie watched in amazement as the bear raised his head, and, while staring directly at Charlie, keep coming at full gallop.

Firing the remaining four shots in the gun, Charlie prepared to be run over by the bear. He fell to the ground and curled up into a ball, waiting to die.

But nothing happened. He counted to thirty before he got the nerve to look in the direction of the attack. Charlie saw the sow lying not ten feet away. She appeared to be dead.

Taking no chances, Charlie reloaded the pistol and quickly moved a safe distance from the animal. He sat on a log for a long time watching for any signs the mother bear was still alive. He worked to slow his own breathing and beating heart. Watching his wristwatch, Charlie waited a full ten minutes before he decided the bear was dead.

Suddenly he remembered the now motherless cub.

He looked around but saw nothing. Charlie suddenly felt pain over what had happened. As a rule, hunters never killed an animal caring for, or about to give birth to, their offspring. Deer hunters killed bucks but seldom shot a doe. Charlie had made a huge mistake and was responsible for depriving the cub of his mother's care. Charlie had broken a fundamental rule: never move through the woods quietly in bear country. And now the cub was alone.

It occurred to Charlie he had a lot in common with the small bear. He wondered if the bear felt the same heartache as he did. Can the critter cry? He considered how long the sadness would last inside the cub's confused mind.

This bear is now my responsibility.

I need to do something.

Getting up slowly, Charlie searched the immediate area looking for the orphaned cub. It didn't take long. He found the terrified cub in the tree not far from the trail. The small bear was clinging silently to the trunk of a lodgepole pine ten feet above the forest floor, no doubt rattled by the gunfire.

Removing a small piece of a chocolate bar from his pocket, he climbed the tree and offered the candy to the cub. The cub growled at Charlie until he caught scent of the candy. Charlie calmly fed the candy to the cub, who devoured it immediately, somehow growling and chewing at the same time. Charlie dropped back to the ground and sat quietly munching on the corner of a chocolate bar.

It took most of an hour, but the bear finally backed down the tree's trunk until he found the forest floor, and immediately went looking for his mom. Following the cub, Charlie watched as the small bear found his dead mother. He watched as the cub lovingly nudged its mother and rooted around in her fur, looking to nurse on mother's milk.

This is my fault.

After deliberating for most of an hour, Charlie decided there was no chance the cub could survive without his mother. If the cub was older, there might be a chance he could save the bear. But Charlie couldn't see any way to feed the bear without starving himself. The bear needed his mother's milk and wasn't ready to survive on only solid food.

He removed his pistol and prepared to shoot the cub. He walked to the animal, now laying across its mother's body, and placed the barrel of the gun to his head. His grandfather had carefully instructed Charlie in the ways of the woods and that ethic included the avoidance of pain and suffering among all animals. Charlie would make sure the bear cub would be spared further suffering.

Without warning a powerful vision filled Charlie's young mind.

He suddenly understood that in his own small way, he was on a traditional vision quest. He hadn't realized the importance of what was happening to him. Charlie's mind flooded with fantasies about his quest. He was alone in the wilderness fighting for survival. The blood of a bear was on his hands.

This cub is my spirit animal, just like in the days of old.

For some reason, this thought pleased Charlie and he laughed out loud.

He put his gun away.

I'm going to raise this bear.

First, I need a leash.

Charlie removed all his clothes, and leaving his underpants and undershirt on the ground, redressed. He tore his undergarments into strips and used them to braid a strong leash several feet long. Charlie took off his belts and punched holes in the leather hoping it would form a collar of the correct size. He attached the end of the belt securely to the braided undergarments.

Taking another bar of chocolate from his pack, Charlie lured the cub to his side and securely attached the collar around the young bear's neck. Employing a combination of pulling on the leash and using the chocolate as a lure, Charlie moved the bear along. The cub growled the entire time, but clearly was discovering the wonders of chocolate and grudgingly followed Charlie.

Progress was slow, but Charlie beamed at this new development. This cub was his responsibility, and he immediately started thinking about how to keep his new friend alive.

But first, the bear needed a name. After much thought, he named his bear Ursula.

ACT II

6

WEDNESDAY, DECEMBER 21ST, 2050

His mind either jumps to conclusions or doesn't move at all.

'Grab your coffee and let's get started,' Special Agent Hunter announced.

He stood at the end of a table in the small conference room next to Charlie's office.

Charlie, Jack, Brad, Ben and Agent Seaman were seated around the table.

It had been forty-eight hours since the body of Quinn Conner was discovered. Everyone knew the so-called golden hours had passed; that precious time frame offering the best chance of finding the evidence needed to solve a crime. A sense of urgency was reflected in the faces of the team members, and even the aroma of fresh coffee and donuts was not enough to cheer them up.

'The press conference is scheduled for ten this morning. I'll need a written update from all of you by nine-thirty. So, Charlie, what have you got?' Hunter asked.

Charlie rose at his seat and remained standing.

'A message from a group claiming responsibility for the bombing at the CDC was posted online. Unfortunately, we can't confirm the authenticity of the claim. As we feared, Quinn Conner's body and all the blood samples we collected were destroyed in the fire,' he said.

'Then no autopsy?' Hunter asked.

'Right, and no blood samples for a toxicology analysis,' Charlie added.

'We need to locate a sample somewhere else,' Hunter said.

'I'll send an agent back to the murder scene to take another look. It's a long shot but we might get lucky,' Charlie said.

'Better chance checking his home. Send an agent there first,' Hunter insisted.

'We can do both. Won't hurt to have more than one sample,' Charlie argued.

'Fine. Was anything of value discovered in the last twenty-four hours?' Hunter asked.

'We questioned Mr. Conner's wife, and the Conner's former nanny, Adele Peterson, and spend several hours at his place of employment,' Charlie answered.

'Anything worthwhile?' Hunter asked.

'Nothing that amounts to much. Neither son was bonded to their parents. The nanny describes it as a business arrangement. The brothers were competitive but appeared to be close. We visited Genlabs and interviewed his boss and several colleagues. Not much of interest there. We're waiting to get access to his work files.'

'There must've been sometime there worth noting?' Hunter asked.

'I don't even know what questions to ask,' Charlie argued.

'Ask the usual questions,' he suggested.

'Which questions are those? His work is highly classified, and they aren't just going to let us waltz in and look around. Every employee at Genlabs signs a seventeen-page non-disclosure agreement. Just how do you suggest we gain access to classified information?' Charlie asked, irritated.

'So, what did you accomplish?' Hunter continued, seemingly unfazed.

'We discovered the brothers were drunk and arguing the night of Quinn's death,' Charlie said.

'Was it a serious argument?' Hunter asked.

'We're working to discover that.'

'That's interesting. What about access to Quinn Conner's work files? Isn't that a priority?' Hunter asked.

'I expect to hear from the attorney at Genlabs after we're done. If they don't comply with our request, I'll be asking you to file for the appropriate search warrants,' Charlie said.

'Just get it done,' Hunter said.

Charlie stared at his boss, waiting for more questions. There were none, so he continued.

'Ben and his team have finished interviewing the employees working at the Conner's Estate,' he said.

Charlie pointed at Ben and sat down.

'We interviewed the twelve men and women who work at the Conner's estate. All of them have worked for the Conner's at least three years and have passed extensive background checks. Unless one of them has some type of secret ax to grind, it's a dead end,' Detective Hayward said, still seated.

'What about the party goers?' Hunter asked.

'Interviewing the folks who attended the party may provide some leads. Minus the kids, about eighty people need to be interviewed. We should finish questioning all of the individuals by this afternoon,' Ben Hayward said.

'What about the outsider hypothesis?' Charlie asked, glancing at Hunter.

'Right, I almost forgot. We met with Brent Barns and he gave us access to all their security data. Their system is impressive. Five thousand cameras and countless sensors monitoring every inch of the wall, waterfront, and every residence in Westwood. That's over five hundred homes. We reviewed the data and watched footage starting four days before the victim's death and every day this week. There's nothing there. Unless someone hacked into their system, which seems unlikely, no one entered Westwood who isn't accounted for,' Ben finished.

'Don't give up on it. According to Hawke Conner, the Westwood security system isn't what it used to be,' Special Agent Hunter said as he stood.

'Will do.'

'Agent Seaman conducted a records search and an analysis of Quinn Conner's personal communication devices, as well as his bank, home and online computer files,' Special Agent Hunter said, and gestured to the rookie agent to begin.

'I'll keep this brief. Quinn Conner was the first genetically programmed baby allowed by federal law. He was born to much fanfare in 2028. There have been six generations of designer babies released by GSI since that time. A new generation of designer babies is released every three to five years, except for generations one and two. They were released just twenty-six months apart. Five million Americans have been born with genetic enhancements across those six generations. Mr. Conner was an exceptionally gifted person, with an amazing series of accomplishments for a man of twenty-two.'

'Stick to the case,' Special Agent Hunter interrupted.

'Right, sorry.' Agent Seaman hesitated. 'Our search of his

personal computer, app-pad, app-phone, and cloud files have turned up nothing to indicate anything suspicious. He was a busy researcher and family man. No porn, no girlfriends, no drugs or gambling - just work and family related correspondence. He's debt free, and by any index, wealthy. However, we did, by chance, find out something interesting about his brother, Alex Conner. Somehow Quinn Conner discovered his brother was receiving treatments at Genhancements, a famous black-market genetic services clinic. He joked about it to his wife in a routine correspondence. It may not be important,' Agent Seaman said.

'My team can follow up on that,' Charlie volunteered.

'Good. Another thing. I'm still haven't been provided with Quinn and Alex Conner's medical records. I'm getting stonewalled by GSI. The family doctor provided copies of their medical records right away, but those only cover their medical history starting on their fifth birthday,' Agent Seaman finished.

'I can ask about that Agent Seaman,' Charlie said.

The rookie agent nodded.

Charlie and the other agents never referred to rookies by their first names. It was an insider's joke, and a way to remind them of their proper place within the FBI hierarchy.

'So, what's missing,' Charlie asked.

No one responded.

'Don't be afraid to think outside the box. What we're doing may be too perfunctory. This case may rely on finding a black swan . . . ' Charlie didn't finish.

'Enough with the black swan crap. Just do good police work and the rest will take care of itself,' Hunter said. 'Now get to work.'

DNA

At eight a.m., Wednesday morning, Marion got the call informing her it was safe to return to work. She was told to be prepared for the worst. When she arrived at the CDC building, Marion met Lois and they were led to the site of the bombing. She was shocked to see her precious lab and all its equipment razed beyond recognition. Her own office was a pile of blackened chaos. Nothing was salvageable, and Marion's eyes filled as she realized what was lost. All her academic awards, including diplomas, and a countless number of gifts and memorabilia from coworkers and friends.

'You okay?' Lois asked.

'Not great. Looks like nothing survived. What the hell happened?' Marion asked.

'I assume it's the same group of terrorists that hit before.'

'What the hell do these people want? We're trying to help them. Pisses me off,' Marion urged.

'I'm with you, but we've got to carry on,' Lois said.

'There's a contingency plan, right? Other labs we can occupy?' Marion asked.

'Yeah. Already done. A temporary lab was setup overnight. Your office will be ready in a few hours,' Lois said.

'Well done Lois. Did you sleep at all?'

'No. I need to get home for some rest,' she answered.

As the two scientists spoke, the head of security approached. The two women could see him wiping soot from his hands with a rag, in preparation for shaking their hands.

'Some type of explosive device was detonated inside the underground garage right after the ambulance arrived. It's safe to assume the bomb entered the building via the ambulance. The subsequent fire burned up through parts of two floors before it was contained. An FBI forensic team is here investigating,' the man said.

'Any idea who might have done this?'

'A group has taken credit for the bombing; one we've heard of before. The FBI will get to the bottom of it.'

'Quinn Conner's body was in the ambulance. Was his body the target?'' Lois asked.

'We don't know. Maybe not. The bomb was detonated near two critical support columns. If the columns had failed, the whole building would have collapsed,' the man said.

'I'm glad that didn't happen,' Marion observed.

After completing their inspection of the bomb site, Marion walked with Lois up the stairs to her office. The main elevator was not expected to function for months. Once there, Lois used her phone to activate the flatscreen mounted on her wall, and the two scientists watched the news reports related to the explosion. There was still no mention of Quinn's Conner's body, just stock pictures of the CDC building and a brief mention of the recent bombings by terrorist's groups at other CDC labs.

As they watched the news, Lois scanned her computer screen for messages.

'I just got an alert from Karen at our lab in Spokane. Three men died in the past two days from unknown causes. The men were all genetically enhanced, so the Spokane FBI office has opened investigations into all the deaths,' Lois said.

'How'd they die?' Marion asked.

'Here, we can read it together,' Lois said as she turned the screen to face Marion.

Lois opened the first file and they began reading. After finishing their review of the file, they quickly scanned the remaining two reports. When they were finished, the two women compared notes.

'The fact they have so much in common worries me,' Lois said.

'Yeah, gender and age for one thing. Did you see all the men were second generation-designer babies sold by GSI?'

'How could I miss it? We need to call GSI and probably Genlabs. They can unravel this faster than we can,' Dr. Peck said.

'Could it be a flaw in their engineering,' Marion suggested.

'Do you know something I don't?' Lois asked.

'Not really, but when word gets out that we were looking into GSI there will be hell to pay. They'll sue the crap out of us. Their testing is very methodical. It's hard to imagine they'd have major problems and do nothing. I think it might be best to not mention them for a day or so,' Marion said.

'That's a big risk,' Lois offered.

'I know. But let my lab, have a peek first,' Marion pleaded.

'For now, I'll go along.'

'Thanks. You still need to convene the Health Advisory Network and asked them to issue an advisory. We can write the warning right now. We won't mention GSI. We'll see what comes up,' Marion said.

'If there are more deaths, the equation changes,' Lois said.

Two hours later the CDC issued an official Health Advisory Alert to public health officials, laboratories, hospitals, and clinicians nationwide. The alert didn't require any immediate action but did explain a health safety incident had occurred in the Pacific Northwest, and three men had died. The alert included details about the men's deaths and pictures of the damage to their DNA, but did not list their names. The alert didn't mention GSI or the fact that all three men were second generation designer-babies. It asked for members of the network to be on the alert for similar cases.

After the morning briefing, Charlie and Jack boarded

a car that was taking them to the Conner estate. As they rode, Charlie once again felt gratitude for living in the Great Northwest. There was an unspoken secret about the Pacific Northwest that can only be learned by living here. Americans living elsewhere saw only rain, wind, mountains and snow. If by chance one of these citizens visited the Northwest, they quickly become uneasy with its impenetrable forest, relentless moisture, steep terrain, and unpredictable waterways. These visitors usually head for home quickly.

But for those with the patience to endure (and those with lots of well-made outdoor gear), the Northwest offered bliss. This was the unspoken secret. Sun and warm weather were not uncommon in the Pacific Northwest. Far from it. During certain times of the year, the clouds grew tired of their assault on the land and retreated to sea. During these times, the Pacific Northwest became a lush, emerald-colored paradise.

Charlie's daydream ended when he received a call from Kathleen Holden, lead attorney for Genlabs.

'Mr. Edmo, I just concluded my meeting with our legal team. As Mr. Kelly indicated, the work done by Mr. Conner is highly sensitive. Our team needed to balance this fact with your request for full disclosure. Quinn was a valued employee and our friend, and I guarantee we want justice for him and his family. I am authorized to offer a compromise. Genlabs will provide a complete list and brief description of Quinn's projects. The funding source and a budget summary for each project will be included. This information can only be viewed by you, Mr. Edmo, and your boss, Mr. Hunter, and no one else. You will view these materials only in my presence. You may take notes, but no copies or any other form of reproduction will be allowed. Is this acceptable?' Kathleen asked.

'So, no access to his work terminal?'

'Not at this time.'

'That will work for now, but if we determine that any of Mr. Conner's projects are connected to this investigation, we will not hesitate to file for the appropriate search warrants,' Charlie said.

'That will not be necessary. If you can provide credible reasons to believe a specific project is germane to your investigation, we will respond appropriately. In the meantime, all his files will be on lock down and accessible to no one,' Kathleen answered.

'Fine. We'll accept these terms, for now. But I will need to consult with my boss.'

'I understand.'

'When can we view the information?'

'By end of today. Is that's acceptable?'

'Can you make it by sooner?'

'I can try. Someone will be in touch,' Kathleen said and hung up.

After passing through a crowd of reporters, Charlie and Jack arrived at the Westwood gate about ten a.m. They passed through security and were driven to the Conner estate, where they were ushered into the sunroom by Frank Kaminsky. Hawke and Abby Conner sat in the same chairs. Mr. Conner was dressed in a causal business suit, and his wife wore work clothes. Charlie noticed she had dirt on her pants, and a pair of gloves rested on the nearby table.

After pleasantries, Charlie began.

'I'm sorry to report the bombing at the CDC has destroyed your son's remains,' Charlie said.

Charlie's statement was met with several long moments of awkward silence.

'Was my son the target of this bombing?' he spoke angrily.

"We can't rule this out. It's also possible this was a random terrorists' act. This is the third bombing of a CDC facility in two years,' Charlie added.

His comments were again met with silence. Charlie decided to change the subject.

'I understand Alex will be available for questioning?' Charlie asked.

'Yes, he's on his way,' Frank said.

'Okay. Look, I'm sorry for the unfortunate circumstances. But I need to ask about the night of the party. You reported the last time you saw Quinn was at the party, and that he was with his brother, Alex. But you failed to mention they were drunk and arguing. This is important information. Why did you fail to report it?' Charlie asked.

'First, I did report Quinn was drunk. But arguing, are you kidding. They always argued. I didn't think much of it,' Hawke shrugged.

'How would you describe their argument? Was it intense?' Jack asked

'Very. They enjoyed the mental sparing. It's not like you or I could challenge their combined intellects,' Mr. Conner said. 'When they played sports as teenagers, someone always ended up in the hospital. I for one preferred their verbal arguments,' Mr. Conner offered.

'So, it used to be pretty physical?' Jack asked.

'No more than other brothers.'

'You said they often injured each other. Sounds serious to me,' Ben said.

'Asked and answered, please move on,' Frank said.

'Okay. Let's talk about Quinn's job at Genlabs. Did you remember anything happening at Genlabs that would give someone a reason to hurt your son?' Charlie asked.

'For the life of me, I can't think of a single reason. I agree, Agent Edmo, that Genlabs seems like the logical place to start. But the simple truth is, I don't know much about what Quinn did. I assume you spoke with Gordon Kelly. He would know much more about Quinn's job duties,' Mr. Conner said.

'We did. Anyone else we could talk to?' Charlie asked.

'There is someone else. Alex and Quinn have a boyhood friend who works at Genlabs. His name is Henry Chen. I can provide his contact information,' Ms. Conner offered.

'That would help,' Charlie said. 'One more thing. GSI won't release your son's medical files. I could get a search warrant, but I'd rather not. Can you request that the files get released?' Charlie asked.

'Not my call. It's up to legal,' Mr. Conner said.

'You have legal authority to release your own son's medical files. GSI won't win this in court. Your son's medical history is critical to the investigation, and we are required to fill in the gaps in the record.'

'I'll look into it,' Mr. Conner said.

'I'll expect Quinn's medical records to be delivered to me by the end of the day.'

Hawke Conner glared at Charlie, clearly a man unfamiliar with receiving commands.

After a few moments, Charlie continued.

'I want to get back to Alex and Quinn arguing at the party. Do you know what they were arguing about?' Charlie asked.

'Something to do with work,' Ms. Conner said.

'Did you remember anything they said?'

'Nothing,' Ms. Conner answered flatly.

'Mr. Conner?'

'Nothing that I remember. Maybe something about Gordon.'

'Okay. If anything comes to mind . . . 'Charlie said.

As they finished, Alex came into the room.

Hawke signaled for Alex to join them.

Abby Conner hugged her son briefly.

Charlie studied Alex Conner as he hugged his mother.

Similar to many genetically enhanced individuals, the young man exuded uncommon arrogance. He was taller than his father by six inches, tall enough to look Charlie in the eye. He had a stout frame and significantly more muscle mass than his father. Alex was strikingly handsome, and Charlie assumed his father's original DNA deserved some credit for that. Like his mother, Alex had amazing eyes. His irises spun slowly, like a kaleidoscope when the lens is turned. Charlie wondered if his irises would begin to spin faster, as Alex became more agitated.

'Alex, thank you for meeting with us. As you know, we're attempting the determine your brother's cause of death. Do you know anyone who wanted to harm your brother?' Charlie asked.

'No,' Alex said.

Charlie waited for him to volunteer more information, but Alex remained silent.

'What about your brother's job. I understand he worked on highly sensitive research. Can you tie anything at his work-place to a reason someone might have wanted to harm him?' Charlie asked.

'Not really. I work for a different company in a different field,' Alex said.

'Okay. Now I understand you were drunk and arguing with your brother the night he died. Can you tell us what the fight was about?' Charlie asked.

'It wasn't a fight,' Alex replied.

'What would you call it then?' Jack asked.

'A debate,' Alex said.

'What was the debate about?'

'We were debating whether genetic engineering was advanced enough to program the religious bullshit out of the Christian morons currently running our government,' Alex said.

'Was that an ongoing debate?' Jack asked. He was a practicing Christian.

'Not really,' Alex answered.

'So, nobody was angry?'

'No, what would we be angry about?'

'Just checking,' Charlie said.

'When was the last time you saw your brother?' he asked.

'I saw him in the house just after midnight. He was putting on his hiking boots and getting ready to leave,' Alex answered.

'You mean on his hike?' Jack asked.

'Yeah, he liked to walk at night. His night vision was excellent compared to mine,' Alex offered.

'Did you see him leave on his walk?' Jack asked.

'Yes, I saw him headed south. It was snowing lightly,' Alex said.

'What time was that?' Charlie asked.

'Like I said, a bit after midnight, maybe twelve fifteen at the latest,' he offered.

'Did you speak with Quinn? Were either of you angry?' Charlie inquired.

'You already asked me that. No, to both,' Alex said.

'You don't say much, why is that?' Jack asked.

'I'm answering all your questions to the best of my abilities.'

'Of course, you are. What did you do after he left?' Charlie asked.

'I had a couple of more drinks and went to bed,' Alex

paused. 'When I woke-up they told me Quinn was dead,' Alex said.

'You never left the house all night?' Charlie asked.

'I was at the party all evening. I went to bed and read until four-thirty. I slept in late Monday morning,' Alex answered.

'You were alone during those hours?' Charlie asked.

'Yes. Ella went back to the city. I was alone. Why?' Alex said.

'Just standard questions,' Jack answered.

'You're barking up the wrong tree. My father's right. Someone breached the infamous Westwood security system,' Alex argued.

'And how would someone accomplish that?' Jack asked.

'How would I know? I can barely get through the coded gate myself,' Alex complained.

▓▓▓

After FBI Agents Edmo and Lee left the estate, Alex and his father remained in the sunroom drinking coffee. It was the first time Alex and his father had been alone since Quinn's death. They sat without speaking, both men lost in thought.

While Hawke sat with his eyes closed, Alex took a hard look at his father's face. He realized Quinn's death was transforming his father. Hawke was holding his head at a weird angle, like someone was twisting his arm behind his back. Alex suspected if he were alone, Hawke would fall to the floor and curl up in a ball. Alex had never seen his father look so diminished and uncertain of himself.

But he could find little pity for Hawke. Alex's relationship with his father didn't allow it, and neither had Quinn's.

Alex recalled watching his brother stand up to their father when they were boys. Alex could never muster the courage to resist his father, but Quinn was fearless. There was one day when the divide between them blew wide open. Quinn was ten and had refused to clean his room for weeks.

'It's my room,' he had argued.

Adele, their live-in nanny, had asked Hawke to intervene. Hawke, who was rarely involved with the rearing of his children, immediately confronted Quinn, threatening loudly to take away his app-pad and ground him for two weeks.

Alex could still hear Quinn shouting his response.

'Why would I listen to you? You're not my father; some fucking bioengineer is.'

For just a moment, Hawke raised his right arm like he was going to backhand Quinn. Then he stopped himself and quickly left the room without a word. Alex was sure his father had heard them laughing as he walked away.

His daydream ended and he looked at his father's face again.

'What do you know about Quinn's death?' Alex blurted out.

Hawke opened his eyes and turned to look at his oldest son.

'Why would you assume I know something about Quinn's death?' Hawke asked, annoyed.

'Because you know fucking everything,' Alex responded strongly.

'Calm down son. I have no idea how Quinn died. It's possible he was murdered by someone trying to steal our secrets.'

'Why would someone, do that?'

'If I knew why, I would know who.'

'Are you going to find out?'

'I'm trying, I'm trying.' His father fell silent, searching for words. 'Alex, listen to me carefully. The FBI will soon gain access to your brother's medical records held by GSI. The FBI has also requested copies of your medical records. Once the FBI gets this information, we can assume the records will be leaked to the press. I need to tell you something before that happens.' Hawke Conner hesitated again. 'Alex, we lied to you, to the whole world. You're not genetically enhanced like Quinn was. Your Mom was too worried about the new technology. We used our influence to spread a false narrative about you to the press, and to get around federal law when Quinn was born,' Hawke looked away as he spoke.

Sitting speechless for a full minute, Alex could feel his scalp tingling as his heart rate skyrocketed. Bile rose in his throat, and he felt nauseous. Feeling such strong emotions was unfamiliar to Alex. His enhancements allowed him strong control over his mind and body. But for the second time that day, Alex felt his genetic enhancements were worthless.

Wait.

I forgot.

My father just informed me that I'm not enhanced.

I'm not fucking genetically enhanced.

By current societal standards, his parents were child abusers. As subsequent generations of designer-babies came along, the differences between them and natural-born children grew markedly. These differences manifested across the physical, intellectual and emotional characteristics of the children. Not only did newer generations have harder bones and stronger muscles, longer frames and better hair, teeth, eyes, etc., but the average difference in IQ between engineered children and natural-born children had grown to twenty-five points. Designer children were armed with metabolism optimization which allowed more high energy to be delivered to cells, giving them more endurance, and the capacity to heal from injury more quickly. Newer generations of designer-children were generally believed to have more char-ismatic personalities.

Alex felt his blood boil. Before he did something he would regret, Alex rose from his seat, and cast a nasty look in his father's direction.

'Fuck you, father.'

He left the house, climbed into his Porsche, and sped out of the driveway.

Heading north on the two-lane road, Alex over-rode the self-driving features of his Porsche and was driving danger-ously fast. Thankfully, the holiday season made for light traffic. It also freed him from any work responsibilities. Alex desper-ately needed time to sort this out.

As he drove, Alex could hear the voices of his father and brother echoing over and over in his head. Alex had never felt so confused and stupid at the same time. On top of Quinn's death, his father 's revelation was too much to comprehend. Alex thought about his childhood and fought back tears; his nose started running, and he could feel a serious headache coming on. The coffee he'd consumed with his father made him want to pull over and puke.

Alex was blindsided by his brother's death. But finding out he was born without genetic enhancements, knowing he was inferior to everyone around him, was more than he could with-stand. Believing he was enhanced gave Alex a sense of invin-cibility far beyond a normal young man's bravado. This sort of thing was not supposed to happen to him. He was indestruc-tible, and so was Quinn.

This was all undercut by his father's confession. His brother was radically different from him, constructed from a blueprint that was vastly superior to his own. He realized his whole life was a lie. His parents had acted in direct contradiction to federal law, risked going to prison and ruining their reputations, and worst, did something completely contrary to society's prevailing standards. Parents can have natural-born children, or genetically enhanced children, but they cannot have both. It's patently unfair to the siblings.

Alex was disgusted with them both.

Alex tried to imagine what motivated his parents to take the risk. Did his parents think they were doing what was best for the family - taking steps to ensure the longevity of GSI and the Conner legacy? Or was it just the need to have the latest technology - never being satisfied with last year's version?

Alex didn't know.

Wondering what clues he had missed, Alex remembered the first time Quinn had beat him in a game of basketball. Alex was fifteen and Quinn thirteen. They were playing in the driveway while their father, sitting at his desk, watched them though his office window. Alex played with passion. He wanted to grind his brother into the ground, as he always did. But his brother had grown bigger, stronger and was more intuitive. Alex lost, and not because he had an off game. They played three more games, and Alex lost them all.

He would never forget the look of disappointment his father had thrown his way as he came outside to hug Quinn. It felt like a changing of the guard, and Alex didn't play another basketball game with his brother for years.

Now Quinn is dead.

Alex decided to drive home. He needed a drink. When he arrived at the empty house, he noticed a message from Genlabs on his private app-phone. The voice message was from a man named Ray who worked in cyber-security at Genlabs. Alex didn't recognize the name. Apparently, the man couldn't open one of Quinn's classified reports, and wanted help identifying any passwords he might have used.

Feeling goosebumps slowly enveloping his entire body, Alex sat down hard on his couch.

I'm being contacted by someone looking for Quinn's report. He remembered his brother's words.

If something happens to me, find the report with Saturday's date.

Something was very wrong.

Rising from his couch, Alex walked to the wet bar and mixed a drink. He paced the room for a long time, drink in hand, thinking about what to do. Finally, Alex decided to call the man. He needed to confirm his suspicions.

'Hello, this is Ray,' a man's voice answered.

'Alex Conner returning your call,' Alex said.

'Thanks for calling back. Given the circumstances, I didn't expect to hear from you so soon. I'm sorry about Quinn. I worked with him a couple of years back,' Ray said.

'Thanks. How can I help?' Alex asked.

'I work at Genlabs in cyber-security. My boss has ordered that all materials related to his research be secured. I've been given the job of finding and securing these materials. I've found most of the passwords and the other encryption codes your brother used. But one has stumped my efforts. I wonder if I might pick your brain?' Ray asked.

'Sure, go ahead. But I'm not sure I can help,' Alex said.

'We've had success using this questionnaire before. It takes about ten minutes,' Ray said.

Ray spent the next fifteen minutes asking Alex a series of questions designed to identify potential passwords used by Quinn Conner. As the minutes went by, Alex become more unsettled and suspicious. He was sure the questionnaire was a pretense and wondered what was coming next. Alex was afraid. But he was determined to learn more.

Ray finished the questionnaire and said, 'Thanks for your help. I'll let you know if it works . . . I was wondering, did Quinn mention an important report he may have completed in the past couple of days. Genlabs' researchers work in such secrecy. I'm trying to confirm if a certain report even exists,' Ray said.

There it was!

Alex felt his heart pumping wildly.

'No, he never did. That's the document you're looking for? Sounds important,' Alex said.

'It is. Are your sure he didn't say something?' Ray asked.

'We both signed confidentiality agreements. We didn't talk shop,' Alex said, trying not to sound suspicious. 'Can you be more specific?'

'Not really. Listen, if you remember Quinn mentioning a report that was completed in the past week, please contact me immediately. And please, remember,' Ray's tone suddenly became harsh. 'For your safety, and for the safety of your family, never mention the report to anyone, now or ever. I'd hate to see someone else end up dead.'

Alex's heart froze as he hung up.

He started to feel panic over-taking him. Sweat erupted on his brow and his chest clinched so hard he nearly stopped breathing. The man had threatened him and his family. He knew about Quinn's report, and was probably responsible for his death.

The man killed my brother.

Trying to focus, Alex took several slow, deep breaths to slow his heart. He rubbed his face hard. Alex needed to think. He needed to talk to Henry Chen and find the report that led to his brother's death. Alex's thoughts swirled under the pressure.

I need to vanish.
I need time to think.

Minutes later he made up his mind. Alex used his app-pad to send an encrypted message to Henry. He filled a suitcase with warm clothes, grabbed a box of bottled water, topped a cooler with food, and loaded it all into the Porsche. Alex climbed into the car and drove to the marina in Winslow. Once there, he loaded the supplies aboard his father's yacht. Alex checked the fuel levels and started the motors.

Alex released the ship's moorings and cast off. He followed the Coast Guard buoys out of Winslow Harbor and into the choppy waters of the Puget Sound. He steered north toward the Straits of Juan de Fuca, and once in open waters, set the autopilot. He went below deck to warm up the ship-to-shore radio.

Alex had spent a lot of time on the yacht as a boy and loved being onboard. It was also the perfect hiding place and provided the privacy he needed to think. He also suspected his app-phone, app-pad and computers were all bugged, and he needed to speak with Henry Chen on an untraceable line. When he messaged Henry from his house, he'd given his friend instructions for contacting him on the ship-to-shore radio.

Alex expected Henry to hail him within the next hour.

Returning to the bridge to check the autopilot, Alex con-firmed the vessel was still on the proper heading. There was a brisk wind coming out of the west and three-foot waves broke across the vessel's beam from its port side. There was a heavy cloud layer, and the low visibility prevented Alex from seeing land. On the ship's radar, he could see the mainland to his starboard and the north tip of Bainbridge Island to his port side. His heading would take him through Admiralty Inlet and toward the Strait. Once clear of the Kitsap Peninsula, Alex would change course to the west toward Port Angeles. He planned to cruise until dark the next day, napping as he went along, and then drop anchor in its protected water. By then he would need fuel and to get some sleep.

Going back below deck, Alex went to the mess and heated water for coffee. He wanted to focus on his current predicament, but he'd hit the wall, and was suddenly exhausted. He closed his eyes and focused on his breathing, waiting for the water to boil. He remembered those rare times he sailed these same waters with his family. Many of his favorite memories happened on the vessel. His eyes filled as he thought about his parents in those days. Moments that transcended the normal coldness of their marriage and parenting. Alex had never seen his parents display affection in public, not so much as a peck on the cheek. He couldn't image things were different behind closed doors. But on these summer days, he watched as they held hands, and imagined his family as normal.

Alex recalled a day when he was standing on the deck of the yacht with his parents and brother. It was a hot summer day, and both the Cascade and Olympic mountain ranges stood painted against a blue sky. The lesser peaks of the San Juan Islands and Vancouver Island were visible to the north and completed a circle of glistening mountains around them. The yacht was cruising in the Juan de Fuca, heading west. Quinn was twelve, and Alex remembered his white blond hair and childish face. He was already five foot ten inches tall, deeply tan, and spouting confidence from every pore of his body.

Quinn had been in one of his expansive moods. He stood on the wooden deck above his parents. He refused to use the nearby handholds, balancing only with his arms and legs. The vessel was rolling hard, but this didn't stop Quinn from talking a mile a minute, his arms outstretched and knees bent, riding the vessel like it was a huge surfboard.

His words couldn't keep up with a quick mind racing through too many topics. In five minutes, Quinn wove together Greek mythology, biology, particle physics, chaos theory, cognitive psychology, and baseball - all while making a strong case why humans would ultimately succeed as a species. His parents were enraptured by the flow of consciousness being displayed by their youngest son. They both laughed and prodded Quinn to continue his tirade. His enthusiasm was infectious, and they all laughed freely.

The water boiled, and Alex poured the streaming liquid into the ship's French coffee press. He waited five minutes before filtering the grounds and filling a cup.

Sipping his coffee, Alex recalled a less pleasant memory. They were motoring through the San Juan Islands, headed for Friday Harbor. Quinn was eight, and they were wrestling on the ship's forward deck. Their father yelled at them to stop rough housing. Alex responded by looking at his father. Quinn took advantage and pushed him overboard. The vessel was moving at near full speed. If Alex's father had not immediately gone in after him, he might have been lost. In short order his father pulled him roughly aboard. The waters of the Puget Sound were freezing, and Alex was shaking violently. His father ordered him to bed without dinner. 'You let your little brother get the best of you. It's getting to be a habit with you, and I suggest you do something about it. I don't have time for losers,' he had said.

What a prick. Now I get it - why Quinn was always the favorite son.

Alex was sipping his coffee when his ship's radio came alive. It was Henry Chen.

'Hello, Alex, can you hear me?' Henry asked.

'Go ahead Henry.'

'Okay, I never used one of these before, pretty cool. Alex, where are you?'

'Out on the sound.'

'You okay?' Henry asked.

'Sure, just needed to get away. How's it going? Did you have any luck?' Alex asked.

'I did a search using the date you gave me. Nothing. So, I tried a bunch of other dates, still nothing. I decided to talk with Quinn's assistant, whom I trust. Bingo. She told me he was working on a top-secret project for Gordon. She assumed it was for the DOD but didn't know for sure. Does that help?'

'Maybe. Did she say anything else?' Alex asked.

'She mentioned a report was being compiled for Gordon, like I mentioned. The document should have shown up on Quinn's data drive. It's definitely weird it isn't there,' Henry added.

🧬

Returning from their visit to the Conner's estate just before lunch, Charlie and Jack found a message from Hunter instructing them to come to his office when they arrived.

'There you are,' Hunter said, as Charlie and Jack walked in.

Special Agent Hunter's office was on the top floor of the FBI building and offered a nice view of Elliot Bay. Immediately below them, the men could see a few vehicles moving up and down the old Alaska Highway. On the west side of the highway, the broad wooden walkway and the remaining waterfront tourist attractions separated the street from the tall concrete seawall. The seawall stood against the rising oceans. Charlie knew it had been expanded north to Everett in recent years. To the south, the same seawall swept around the far reaches of Elliot Bay until it met the steep cliffs of West Seattle. In the distance, Charlie could see the huge steel gates protecting the Duwamish Waterway.

'We just got back from the Conner house,' Charlie said.

'Anything interesting?' Hunter asked.

'Not much. Quinn and his brother argued often. Nobody seems to have paid it much mind,' Jack offered.

'But you did question Alex Conner?'

'We did,' Jack said.

'Did he admit to arguing with his brother at the party?' Chief Hunter asked.

'He said it was a debate,' Charlie answered.

'About what?' Hunter asked.

'Whether gene editing can make people stop believing in God, or something like that. I think he was being a smart ass. Both Abby and Ella Conner said they were fighting about Quinn's boss, Gordon Kelly,' Jack said.

'What else did he say?' Hunter asked.

'Nothing. Like I said, he kept his mouth shut. It's possible he was hiding something,' Charlie added.

'Okay, keep on him,' Agent Hunter said.

'One more thing. I got a call from Genlabs. They agreed to release information about Quinn Conner's research projects. It's not full disclosure but might be our best bet until we can justify requesting a warrant,' Charlie added.

'How much information are they giving us?'

'Not much. We can view a summary of his research projects and some budget details. No copies allowed, and we can only view the materials in the presence of their attorney.'

'When can we see it?' Hunter asked.

'I asked them to set up a meeting today after lunch. We could hear from them any minute,' Charlie explained.

'I'll cover the meeting at Genlabs. I got something else for you. SPD has located Genhancements. I want you to pay them a visit. According to our sources, the clinic is always on the move. It opens for a month or two, then moves to another location. Sometimes they rent space. Other times they just occupy an abandoned building. Here's the kicker. Clients pay fifty grand a year to join the clinic. They're issued a secure Clearcard. Best way to receive totally secure information. On the days the clinic is open, the address is distributed to those holding a card,' Hunter reported.

'Let me guess, it's open today?' Charlie asked.

'Right. We managed to get our hands on their Clearcard. The address for the clinic showed up at exactly eight this morning,' Special Agent Hunter said proudly as he handed the clear plastic card to Jack.

'Here's a warrant. I suggest taking backup,' Hunter said, handing him an envelope.

Charlie and Jack ate lunch as their car chauffeured them to the address displayed on the Clearcard. Charlie carried the federal warrant allowing him to search Genhancements. A SWAT team was already parked a block from the clinic awaiting their orders.

The car was headed toward a former industrial area along Federal Way, south of downtown Seattle. More than any other part of Seattle, this neighborhood underscored the decline in the city Charlie had witnessed since moving there over two decades before.

In many ways, the Seattle he loved remained the same. People got married, had babies, grew old and died. Fashion and hair styles came and went, and new music emerged. For those who could afford it, sports and travel remained popular. People went to movies, and politicians lied. Though much smaller than in the past, there was still an active local economy.

But since Charlie's youth, the huge gap between the very wealthy and everyone else had resulted in some radical changes in the U.S. economy. Prosperity only existed in small pockets across the country. The Kitsap Peninsula, Bainbridge Island, and areas east of Seattle were one of thirty or so prosperous regions in the country. Other wealthy areas in the western U.S centered around Portland, San Francisco, Los Angeles, Phoenix, and Salt Lake City.

These prosperous regions featured large-scale gated communities. Two types of gated communities had been built. Many of the five million genetically enhanced Americans lived in gated communities llke Westwood. The rest of the gated communities were occupied by naturally occurring, self-segregated groups of upper-class citizens, usually those who avoided genetic enhancements. Many of these were members of the religious right. Regardless, these communities had the world's best schools, security, and state-of-the-art infrastructure.

In many cases, these well-to-do areas were only a short distance from neighborhoods of great poverty. Crossing the line between these two versions of Seattle prompted Charlie to wonder why some people were driven to amass such large fortunes. He knew the very wealthy, once making up only one percent of the population, had grown to comprise five percent. In a country of four hundred and fifty million people, over twenty-two million were very wealthy. This segment of the population possessed nearly all the country's wealth.

Charlie knew from personal experience that this happened at the expense of the middle class, who now comprised only a quarter of the total U.S. population. This group was comprised of families who either had some inherited wealth or were among the lucky ones who still had good jobs. These individuals benefitted from choosing professions deemed to be essential, e.g. doctors, teachers, and fortunately for Charlie and his partners, law enforcement. These were jobs that could not be performed by robots or could not be eliminated by other forms of automation.

Half the population was supported by government stipends. The stipends kept these Americans living between ten and twenty percent above the poverty threshold. Many of these Americans supplemented their income by working for cash under the table - most in service-related jobs. Charlie knew the remaining twenty percent of the population were poor, and the areas of the country where they lived had collapsed into deteriorating, lawless neighborhoods.

Charlie and Jack were driving through such an area. Hundreds of manufacturing businesses used to thrive in the area, surrounded by middle-class neighborhoods. Many supported Boeing and the shipping industry. Nearly all of them were gone. Charlie saw endless rows of abandoned buildings and houses. Due to the constant rain, the structures were covered with vegetation. Parts of the buildings not covered with plants were coated with a layer of black moldy stain.

Every inch of open ground was overgrown with Scotch broom, Salat, bracken ferns, young maple trees, and blackberry vines. The vegetation spilled onto the streets in many places, and Charlie could see where cars created tracks through the greenery. It looked like a tropical jungle had rained from the sky and covered everything but two narrow tire strips through the pavement.

Without funds for road maintenance on anything but major highways, gullies and potholes formed on many side roads, including the one they were driving on. The software controlling Charlie and Jack's vehicle was struggling to navigate these obstacles. They were getting nowhere. The car kept hitting the holes and Jack finally assumed control of the car.

As Jack drove, Charlie could see some buildings were occupied by squatters. Charlie had watched a news story about one family that underscored an increasingly common trend among the permanently unemployed. As thousands of families lost their homes to foreclosures, entire extended families banded together and squatted in old businesses and manufacturing plants. Using materials from the nearby abandoned building, these families remodeled the interiors of the large buildings to provide warmth and comfort, and above all else security. Crime rates were high in these areas of the city. These clans were typically well-armed.

The family featured in the news report had moved into an old metal fabrication plant. Four generations of family members, totaling fifty-three men, women and children, lived under the same roof. The family cooked and heated the building using wood. Every tree in the surrounding areas had been cut down for firewood, and the abandoned nearby businesses were slowly being stripped of anything that would feed their hungry wood stoves. On some days, the smoke from their fires clouded the air surrounding Seattle in much the same way as the heavy car and truck traffic had done in the past.

Somewhere in this maze of ruined buildings and decaying neighborhoods was the most exclusive underground genetic services clinic in the Northwest. The emergence of the genetic engineering industry spawned a multi-billion-dollar underground trade for affordable genetic services. A vast majority of legal genetic services was only available to the wealthy. A complex and restrictive application process, combined with outrageously high costs, prevented all but the most well-connected patrons from accessing these services.

As a result, millions of Americans sought genetic enhancements through this underground network. These clinics, found in the back alleys of every town in America, provided a wide array of services, ranging from simple cosmetic enhancements to highly specialized gene modifications for those competing to become professional athletes.

Like underground businesses throughout history, some clinics provided genuine genetic enhancements to their clients, using technologies and genetic profiles pirated from GSI and Genlabs. These clinics offered treatments for genetic diseases and dozens of other medical problems. Other clinics were charlatans, providing genetic services that did little or nothing for their customers, or left them disfigured and sometimes dead.

The most popular underground clinics were those offering genetic services that appealed to the popular culture. Several clinics offered services that were holiday specific. Halloween clinics offered genetic programs that allow consumers to temporarily assume outrageous appearances. Charlie had seen his neighbors grow the hair of a werewolf overnight and others cultivate fangs like a vampire, only to watch these features disappear in days. Other clinics offered Christmas packages. Charlie thought of the red and green Christmas lights imbedded in Abby Conner's hair.

Hundreds of very popular underground clinics offered genetic services to customers who wanted to look more cross-cultural. Some customers paid huge sums to blend elements of different races, so they appeared to be less Caucasian, and more of a cross among Asian, Hispanic, Black or other races.

Other underground clinics fulfilled the requests for larger

breasts and penises, more sexually active wives, increased muscle mass, stronger bones, or pitch-perfect voices. Others wanted more hair, to be taller or shorter, improve their concentration, to be more beautiful, to have enhanced eyesight, and dozens of other demands.

Genhancements was not like these pop culture clinics. It stood above the rest as the only clinic in the Northwest to specialize in custom gene-editing designed to meet the exacting needs of the very rich. In many cases, these requests were clearly illegal. But regardless of the request, for enough money, their world class scientists would engineer any type of genetic modification within the limits of current technology.

Most customers walking through Genhancement's doors had wildly esoteric desires. Charlie had seen some weird examples on downtown streets and heard even crazier rumors. He had seen a young woman whose skin glowed green in the dark, thanks to an infusion of DNA molecules from jellyfish. Rumor had it one man asked that small angel wings be grown in the space between his shoulder blades. Genhancements had complied, for a reported fee of fifty million dollars. After a series of treatments, the man literally grew small wings that fit nicely under his clothes. Charlie's friend claimed the man only displayed the wings while making love.

Charlie's daydream ended as a voice in the dashboard warned the two men that they were approaching their destination. The two agents left the car and walked toward the building. It was located at the end of a dead-end street and abutted the old railroad tracks. An old sign on the building said, 'Fireside Stoves'. The front of the building was completely covered in vegetation, so the two FBI agents walked around to the side where they found a door.

The door was locked, so Charlie knocked loudly. A woman's face appeared on a screen built into the door.

'Can I help you?'

'I'm Agent Edmo and this is Agent Lee. We're with the FBI. We have a federal warrant to search these premises. Please open the door immediately. I must warn you there is an FBI SWAT team parked across the street. I would prefer to avoid asking them to join us, but unless this door opens immediately, I will make the call,' Charlie said.

'We just have a few questions,' Jack added.

Charlie and Jack held up their badges and the federal warrant to the camera.

The screen went dark. The two men could hear alarms sounding inside the building.

After a few minutes, a young man appeared on the screen.

'Agent Edmo. Please allow me one minute to disarm our security systems. Then I can unlock the door,' the man said.

'You have ten seconds to open the door or I call the SWAT team. I suggest you find your supervisor and open the door now,' Charlie spoke firmly.

After a few seconds a security robot opened the door and ushered them inside the building.

'Please follow me,' the robot said.

In contrast to the decaying exterior, the inside of the building looked like an upscale medical clinic. The reception room was filled with plush leather furniture and the walls were covered with walnut paneling. Jazz played softly in the background. The robot led them down a hallway and into a small office furnished with three leather chairs. The room had flatscreens covering all four walls and ceiling. The panels displayed various scenes and emitted scents from the local rain forest.

Within a few minutes, a nicely dressed woman entered

the room and greeted them warmly. She wore a bright blue, pin-striped, double-breasted business suit in the fashion of the day. The woman sported light orange hair featuring black streaks. Every finger was adorned with rings, and a string of earrings lined the rims of both her ear lobes.

'I'm Dr. Molly Wenger. Can I look at the warrant?' she asked.

Charlie handed the document to the doctor and watched as she scanned it.

'Pretty vague I'd say. But I'm happy to cooperate. What choice do I have? I understand you're looking for information. Since you didn't kick in our doors, I must assume this is about something that needs to stay quiet. Given recent events in the news, I can only assume you are here because of Quinn Conner's death. You have questions about his brother, who is a client. Am I correct?' Molly asked.

'And you can confirm Alex Conner is a client?' Jack asked.

'Yes, I'm his physician,' Molly said.

'Why did Alex Conner come here?' Charlie asked.

'Keep in mind I can evoke patient-doctor privilege,' Molly said.

'You work for an unlicensed and illegal clinic. I hardly think that applies,' Charlie pointed out. 'Let me ask again. Why did he visit your clinic?'

'Alex came for the same reasons most come here, to improve themselves. In his case, he wanted to be stronger without losing his athletic quickness. And he was always on the lookout for ways to sharpen his concentration,' Molly said.

'He already had the best genetic enhancements money could buy, why did he need your particular products?' Jack asked.

'I'm not sure he did. I've known Alex for three years. He would never admit it, but I believe he came here to improve his competitiveness with his brother. Alex had a real chip on his shoulder when it came to Quinn. He was a mellow guy, but mention Quinn, or worst yet his father, and watch out,' Molly said.

'Did he talk to you about this, or are you just speculating? Jack asked.

'I filled in a couple of gaps, but I got it right. He talked about Quinn and his father a lot,' she said.

'What else did he say about Quinn?'

'Be more specific,' Molly asked.

'Did he talk about anything at work that might be related to Quinn's death?' Charlie asked.

'That's the one thing he wouldn't discuss,' she said.

'Did he seem angry with Quinn?' Jack asked.

'Hard to say. They still talked.'

'So, it was mostly just a normal competition between brothers?' Charlie asked.

'It was more than that,' Molly said.

'How so.'

'Alex was obsessed.'

'But not angry?' Charlie asked.

'You should ask him.'

'We have,' Jack added.

'Tell us what he said about his father,' Charlie said.

'I don't know much. Lately, Alex was very uncomfortable talking about him,' Molly offered.

'Any idea why?' Jack asked

'No. But it was something personal between father and son.'

'So not work related?' Jack asked.

'No. I don't think so,' Molly answered.

'What makes you think it was personal?' Charlie asked.

'Something Alex said.'

'What was that?' Charlie asked.

'He was quoting someone. *It's not fleshes and blood, but heart which makes us fathers and sons*,' Molly said.

7

WEDNESDAY, DECEMBER 21ST, 2050

The heart has its reasons whereof reason knows nothing.

Blaise Pascal

April 10th, 2019
Journal Entry #78
Gordon Kelly, Doctoral Student, MIT

There is another unspoken secret in science, my professor said today. She'd just carried a chair into the middle of the room and asked the students to gather around her in a circle. I sat close by as she shared the insight.

Over one hundred and fifty years ago, she said, when physicists first started to conduct meaningful experiments with light, they noticed a very strange thing. When they observed light directly, it behaved like a particle, but when they stop observing the light, it acted like a wave. Somehow, the act of observing the light completely changed its physical state. Try as they may, no experimenter could account for this observation.

After decades of experimentation, scientists reached an astounding conclusion. Whereas physicists had traditionally focused on the forces governing mass and energy as they moved through time and space, they had overlooked another fundamental force in the universe, consciousness. Human consciousness (and perhaps that of other life-forms) is imbedded in the fabric of the universe in some unknowable way, like dark matter and dark energy. 'Never forget this,' my professor said, 'we are imbedded in nature, and our presence impacts the world around us, and our ability to measure and understand it.' We solve this riddle or perish.

The words from his old journal reminded Gordon of why he deeply loved science and had chosen genetics as his field of study. He knew mankind faced major challenges. Humans were saddled with a huge number of biological limitations in their physical, emotional, and intellectual makeup. These limitations were hiding in plain sight, yet most don't realize they existed. As a result, humans were struggling with a multitude of unsolvable problems.

Gordon was sure genetics, and only genetics, could eliminate the fundamental problems facing human society.

He sincerely wanted to improve his species and relieve suffering.

In many ways Gordon had succeeded. He was proud of his work, and this provided a sense of relief, at least for a few moments. The words from his journal reminded Gordon there was a bigger picture to keep in mind.

My work is what counts.

Then he remembered the CDC alert.

His heart sank and then it began to race.

Turning his attention back to the image, Gordon was filled with panic as he looked at the image on his computer monitor.

It was an image distributed in an alert issued by the CDC's Advanced Molecular Detection lab just minutes before.

It was the second time Gordon had seen the digital image. The first time was in Quinn's report.

This is happening too fast.

I'm losing control of the situation.

Gordon's secure app-phone rang.

'We got a problem,'' Ramsey said, when Gordon answered.

You got problems?

'What?' Gordon asked.

I followed Alex to his home. He was there for about an hour. He sent just one message, to an encrypted number at Genlabs. He then drove straight to the Winslow marina. He loaded supplies on his father's yacht, and before I could do anything he motored out of the harbor and headed north up the sound. I've lost him,' Ramsey reported.

'He has the report and has gone into hiding. Was he by himself?' Gordon asked.

'Yes, I didn't see another person on board.'

'Where he's planning to go?' Gordon was speaking to himself. 'Check to see if the Conner's own property in the San Juan's or Canada.'

'Got it. But he could just stay on the water and anchor at night. He could hold-up in a thousand places.'

'I know. But he'll need to come home eventually.'

𝕯𝕹𝕬

It was early evening when Charlie left his office and headed home in an FBI car. Charlie was thinking about something the doctor at Genhancements had said. Alex was not getting along with his father. Was Quinn's murder motivated by something as simple as a power struggle? Charlie tried to understand the immense pressure people like Hawke and Quinn lived with every day. He wondered if people with significant genetic enhancements were motivated by the same things as the rest of us. Do their brains work differently than mine? How are we different?

Luckily he was starving, and as the car approached his home, Charlie's hunger helped chased the murder case out of his mind. Instead, Charlie focused on sitting down for dinner with his grandparents, Frank and Joyce Edmo, who were waiting at the house.

The FBI vehicle arrived, and Charlie could see the house was stuffed with people. He exited the car and rushed up the stairs to his home. Opening the door, Charlie saw his grandparents sitting in his living room, surrounded by family. His grandparents rose to meet Charlie, and they hugged in the middle of the room. A couple of family members clapped.

Charlie was amazed at how little his grandparents had aged. His grandfather was an old-fashion cowboy and dressed accordingly. In the cowboy country of Idaho, Wyoming and Montana, the local garb was as standardized as a military uniform. Standard issue included cowboy hat and boots, faded Levi jeans, a belt buckle that was large (but not too large, this wasn't Texas after all), and a cowboy shirt. The outfit was accessorized with a sun-wrinkled face, uncombed hair, bowed legs, and a red bandana. Mud mixed with cow and horse manure frequently graced the footwear.

Charlie peeked at his grandmother, Joyce. Her eyes still sparkled when she smiled. Her entire demeanor exuded comfort. His grandmother was just over five feet tall and had grown nearly as wide.

Too much fry bread.

He remembered the hours spent sitting on her generous

lap as she recited the ancient stories of her people. His favorite story was about a people called the Nimerigar. The Nimerigar were aggressive little people who shot poisoned arrows from tiny bows. They killed and ate people and were especially fond of children. They lived in the nearby Wind River and the Pedro Mountain ranges north of Casper, Wyoming.

His grandmother always started the story by describing the discovery of a fourteen-inch-tall mummy in a cave near Casper in 1932. She said the mummy was proof the Nimerigar were real, and she had a picture taken from an old newspaper to prove it.

One Sunday in the late summer, when Charlie was ten years old, his grandmother placed him in the front seat of her old pickup and drove east. No matter how many times he asked, his grandmother refused to tell him the purpose of the trip.

'It's a big surprise,' she had said.

They arrived at the small town of Meeteetse, Wyoming in the early afternoon. The air was hot as his grandmother pulled into the parking area of a small drug store. She ushered him into the old wooden building and made Charlie cover his eyes.

His grandmother led him to the back of the store and told him to open his eyes.

Before him was a glass case containing the scariest and strangest thing Charlie had ever seen. He wanted to cover his face and raised his arms to do so. But he couldn't take his eyes off the creature in the case. He knew immediately it was the Nimerigar mummy.

The tiny mummy was covered with oddly folded, dried skin that stretched tightly around its tiny skeleton. The fourteen-inch high figure sat upright on its own tightly crossed legs. Both arms sat comfortably on the mummy's lap. The two limbs faced upward and were crossed left arm over right.

But it was the mummy's face that caught Charlie's attention. The face looked like it belonged to an insect. The creature's jaw protruded at a weird angle, and the mummy's chin narrowed to a slightly rounded point. The oddly shaped face featured an ugly sneering mouth. But it was the creature's huge eyes that were a source of Charlie's nightmares for years to come. Charlie could still see them protruding wildly, topped by high arching eyebrows.

Charlie let the memory slip away.

He backed away from hugging his grandparents. Charlie greeted his wife and daughter with a nod. No warm peck on the cheek or suspiciously long hugs from his wife and daughter tonight. Charlie was pretty sure he'd have to find his own drink.

The huge dining room table was covered with holiday foods. Glazed ham on the bone, wild duck, mashed garlic potatoes, a string bean casserole, garden salad and fresh baked cornbread. Several pies occupied a side table.

Dinner would start soon, and Charlie could hardly wait. But for now, the room was loud with conversation. Charlie loved the first hours after the family was reunited. He hadn't seen his grandparents for almost a year, and he knew their vigor would fade. But for these precious few hours, his family was deeply engaged with one another, and Charlie was pleased.

Anna announced it was time to eat. Charlie found a seat next to his grandfather, and Anna sat with his grandmother, Joyce. Once the rest of their guests were seated, Charlie rose to toast the cook and his grandparents. Glasses clinked, sips were taken, and the diners got down to eating.

'Grandfather, you haven't aged a day,' Charlie said between bites.

'That's because I'm already old as dirt,' Frank Edmo joked.

'Maybe older. At least dirt is useful,' Joyce teased.

'So, tell me about home,' Charlie said.

'Livin' in town is for the birds. Nothing to do but eat and get fat. I hunted this fall, but didn't shoot nothing, ' Frank answered.

'Yeah, you look fat. Where'd you hunt?' Charlie asked.

'Above the Palisade, near McCoy Creek. You know the place. Spent a week, saw lots of sign, but never had a shot,' Frank offered.

'No elk?' Charlie asked.

Yeah. Saw a bunch, but I didn't shoot one. I needed your help,' Frank said.

'Big animal, lotta work. You must be getting old,' Charlie taunted.

The truth was Charlie's grandfather was in amazing shape for a man well over eighty. Always an avid hunter and fisherman, Frank Edmo stayed in shape and connected to the old ways of his tribe by continuing to do both nearly every day of the year. Charlie knew the old man could still out hike many younger men.

A couple of hours after dinner, the two men retired to Charlie's front porch. They sat alone drinking small glasses of a fifty-year old single malt scotch. The porch provided a clear view to the south toward the city. Over the years, Charlie had watched as the lights of Seattle that once formed a solid skyline, became broken by intermittent patches of darkness. The men sat watching it rain and enjoyed the remaining city lights glistened through the dampness. They didn't speak for many minutes.

'Sometimes I almost like the city,' Frank Edmo finally said.

'You get used to it, but it's never home,' Charlie said.

'You need to come home, and not just for a few days. You

look like shit. You missed the powwow two years, maybe you're the one gettin old. You too soft to race?' Frank returned the taunt.

'Maybe, remember what happened last time, I ended up in the hospital,' Charlie admitted.

'You are too soft. Are you telling me that?' Frank couldn't resist.

'Maybe I'll come next August. Show the young bucks how to ride,' Charlie promised.

'I'll save all my money and bet on the other guys,' Frank snorted. 'Charlie, you need to meet my new city friends. I tell them you work for the FBI, but no one believes me. They all think it's illegal for Indians to work for the FBI,' he added.

Both men laughed; it was an old joke between them.

'Yeah, sometimes I can't believe it either, been over twenty years,' Charlie acknowledged.

'I'm thinking about quitting the FBI,' Charlie added quietly.

Frank sat silently for a time.

'When did this start up?' he asked.

'Been a while. Mostly since Hunter arrived,' Charlie said.

'You've had lousy bosses before,' Frank said.

'You're right about that. Maybe it's not just Hunter. I joined the FBI to make a difference, and I use to make a difference. But now I'm not so sure. Anna feels the same way. In Seattle, only the very wealthy can afford to own horses. It bothers her,' he finished.

'Always been this way. Money buys influence, and the rest of us get screwed. No reason for it to change. Are you really goin' quit?'

'Don't know yet,' Charlie answered.

'What would you do for a living? No jobs anywhere,' Frank said.

'I know. Like I said, I'm still thinking about it. One thing I know for sure, between you and me: we are not winning the battle to control our own DNA. Unless something changes soon, humanity will split in two,' Charlie finished.

Considering Charlie's words, Frank was quiet for a few minutes.

'What will the world look like then?' Frank wondered.

'We'll become two different species, with membership determined by how rich you are,' Charlie lamented.

'I'll be dead by then, thank god. Let's talk about something else. You still work with that Chinese fellow?' Frank asked.

'Jack Lee, yeah still my partner,' Charlie said.

'His wife still sick?' Frank asked.

'Yes. Doctors gave her six months. That was two years ago, but she won't make it much longer,' Charlie said.

'She needs to come to Idaho and have a sweat,' Frank suggested.

'Too late for that I suspect,' Charlie said.

'How's the new guy? What's his name?'

'Brad. He's fine. But I miss Hank. I still feel guilty,' Charlie admitted.

'Bad deal. Tough job you got. No wonder you want to quit. Maybe you're the one who needs a sweat.'

'What I need is justice, Kenu,' Charlie said, using the Shoshone term for grandfather.

'Life is long, my nagaha-dua. You may still find what you seek.'

'So, you always tell me.'

Both men sat quietly for a few minutes, lost in thought.

'Anna tells me you got a big case,' Frank said.

'Quinn Conner. He was the first designer-baby. No family can have that much money and be normal,' Charlie said.

'The same everywhere,' Frank said.

'Tell me about it. Esther wants to get fixed to look less like an Indian,' Charlie confessed.

'She told me. Is it really such a big deal?' Frank asked.

'Wow! You're the last person I expected to take her side,' Charlie said loudly.

'I'm not taking her side. Just trying to help her make good decisions,' Frank replied.

Then it dawned on Charlie.

His grandparents and wife were employing simple reverse psychology on his daughter.

That just might work.

He reached for the talisman his grandfather had given him when he left Idaho. He took the amulet from around his neck and handed it to his grandfather.

'This reminds us of who we are,' Charlie said.

'I change, I stay the same,' his grandfather replied, holding the bear tooth necklace for a few moments before handing it back to his grandson.

Charlie had great respect for his grandfather. He was a famous spiritual healer among the Shoshone-Bannock people. Tribal members of all ages, and from the far reaches of their ancestral lands, came to see Frank Edmo. Often his grandfather would lead these visitors to the sweat lodge near the farmhouse. He would build a fire for heating the rocks, and Frank would perform the ancient ceremonies. Many of these people were sick or dying. An old buffalo-skin drum would appear, and his grandfather would create one of the ancient rhythms and sing the holy songs, sometime late into the night.

Charlie replaced the necklace around his neck.

'You need to talk to Esther. No time like the present,' his grandfather said.

'You're right. I'll be right back,' Charlie said.

Charlie went into the house to find Esther. He found her with the other women in the kitchen. Charlie signaled for Esther to follow him into the empty living room.

'I didn't mean to shout last night. I'm sorry,' Charlie admitted.

'Fine. I'm sorry too. But you were out of line. It's your job. You have too much evil shit in your head,' Esther argued.

'You've always been embarrassed I work for the bureau. Why is that? You should be proud. Don't you know how hard it was for me to make it in the FBI?' Charlie asked.

'So, it's my fault? You're such an asshole' Esther said forcefully and returned to the kitchen.

I sense anger.

Charlie shook his head, went to the dining room cabinet, removed a fresh bottle of scotch, and returned to the comfortable chair next to his grandfather.

Later that night, Charlie quietly climbed into bed with Anna. The gentle sounds she made while sleeping were usually enough to send Charlie into a quick slumber, but tonight he was unable to slow his mind. Since he couldn't sleep, Charlie focused on the Conner case. Charlie realized the evidence didn't amount to much. A famous young man was dead. He was well-liked at work and happily married. According to his recent medical history, he'd been in perfect health.

Why would someone go to all the trouble of destroying Quinn's body? And without a body and a toxicology report, there was almost no physical evidence.

No one from outside of Westwood appeared to have infiltrated the heavily guarded community, and it was unlikely an employee at the Conner Estate was involved. None of the individuals who attended the holiday party appeared to have a motive. That left Charlie with either a co-worker at Genlabs, or an immediate family member.

He felt like he was missing something. A loud voice, no doubt from one of his crazy ancestors, was crying out from beyond the veil.

There is still much to uncover.

On the one hand, Charlie knew murder was usually committed by someone who knew the victim, often a family member. It was seldom premeditated. Usually something dark inside a person finds its way up through the cracks, and someone ends up dead, to the surprise of all.

But if this was poisoning, it had to be, by definition, a premeditated murder.

If it was poisoning.

His thoughts turned to Alex Conner. Alex had argued with his brother the night Quinn died. His family failed to mention this until asked. The whole Conner family painted their constant arguing and rough physical play as normal. But both young men had ended up in the hospital at one time or another. The brothers were viciously competitive, and Charlie could easily imagine things getting out of hand.

And then there was Hawke Conner. Alex worked for his father, but Quinn didn't. How did that fit in? There was no doubt that, by the time they were teenagers, neither Alex nor Quinn were emotionally bonded to their parents. That much was confirmed by the nanny. But what really struck Charlie was something the nanny had said. When the brothers were young, Hawke Conner had used his love to manipulate his sons. Charlie wondered if this created a deep jealousy in Alex toward his brother. A jealousy that grew and became twisted enough to motivate Alex to commit murder. One thing was for sure, something wasn't right with the Conner family.

The information provided by the doctor at Genhancements was also intriguing. Alex was paying huge sums for genetic enhancements so he could better compete with his brother. Why was this important to Alex? The doctor had said that Alex was no longer comfortable around his father. The reason for this was not clear, but it sounded like a typical 'family' falling out. Maybe Quinn and his father were feuding with Alex. But why?

Whatever was going on, it didn't sound to Charlie like the three Conner men had a normal, happy relationship.

In Charlie's opinion, Alex should be the first one added to the list of potential suspects.

But Charlie knew there were still huge holes in the case. For one thing, he knew next to nothing about what Quinn did at his work. There was a strong possibility Quinn's death was related to his classified research. Charlie vowed to find out. He would begin by focusing on Genlabs, starting the next morning.

Still unable to fall asleep, Charlie's thoughts drifted to the day his parents had left him alone in the back country of Idaho.

Smiling, Charlie recalled his decision to adopt the bear cub. He laughed about how hard it had been to hike with a young bear. It hadn't been long before he regretted his decision to care for the cub. A black bear cub is not a dog, and the critter hated Charlie's improvised leash. The cub dug under a rotten log, and Charlie was forced to dig him out. He climbed a small tree and, using the leash, tried to hang himself. And finally, the cub got tangled so often that Charlie was forced to carry the animal - an entirely different type of adventure.

It took several hours of tugging and physically carrying the bear for Charlie to make it two miles. This was unacceptable, and Charlie finally gave up and sat on the ground to think. Watching the cub hunt for food nearby, he thought about what little he knew about bears.

A sow and her cub are deeply bonded.
The mother sow doesn't need a leash.
The strength of the bond is about the sow's ability to feed her cub.
If my bond with the cub was stronger, I wouldn't need a leash.

Charlie removed a small piece of chocolate from his pocket and fed it to the cub. The cub was starving all the time and gulped the candy down. The sweet treat drove him crazy. He snuggled against Charlie's leg, looked him in the eye, and growled loudly.

This would work if I had a couple of hundred candy bars.

Knowing he would soon run out of food, Charlie wondered how he would feed himself and a growing cub. He had observed bears turning over rocks, sometimes huge boulders, in their constant search for food. Charlie decided to try his luck at being a mom to Ursula. Leading the cub to a nearby rock pile, Charlie began turning over rocks. Every rock had countless insects living in the soil beneath it.

It didn't take long for Ursula to catch on, and the young bear was soon licking at the insect colonies exposed by the overturned rocks. Using his ax, Charlie found some wet ground and turned over clumps of the swampy soil. Again, the cub pulled against his leash to get at the worms and insects residing in the wet ground. After thirty minutes of using this feeding strategy, Charlie not only formed a bond with the tiny black bear, but Ursula's enormous appetite seemed momentarily satisfied. The bear still growled the entire time, but at least he was being fed.

Charlie decided to remove the collar from the cub's neck and walk away. He caught the young animal and removed the leash, recovered his belt and threaded it onto his pants.

Moving down the trail, Charlie flipped over a few rocks as he walked. He was pleased to see the tiny cub following him, feeding as he walked.

This just might work.

Charlie and the bear cub continued in this way on their southward trek until, on the sixth day in the woods, they finally ran across a forest service road. By then, Charlie had run out of food, and, along with his furry companion, was surviving on insects, the few trout he had been able to catch, and a single grouse he had shot.

Walking in a hunger-inducted daze, Charlie didn't realize he was on a road until he stumbled and fell on the first flat ground he had encountered in days. The gravel and dirt road led south and brought Charlie to a small valley filled with cows. Charlie was pleased with himself. He was going to survive.

As he walked around a bend in the road, Charlie spotted a rancher working on his fence. An old Ford truck was parked nearby. He picked up Ursula and shouted to the man in the distance and smiled when he responded with a wave of his arm.

As Charlie approached, he could see the rancher take a camera from his truck and snap a picture. The picture of a shirtless, young man walking down a country road - backpack hanging loosely on his back, fly rod sticking in the air, pistol stuck in his belt, and a small bear cub in his arms - would later make Charlie a minor celebrity.

'Young man, name's Evan. You're not a sight I see every day. Are you lost?' Evan asked when Charlie stood before him.

'Not anymore. But I am hungry, and so is my bear.'

After hearing his story, Evan had driven Charlie and Ursula to his family's ranch. As they approached Evan's house, they were met by four cattle dogs who immediately went crazy when they caught scent of the bear cub, barking and assaulting the pickup in order to confront the animal.

Hugging the bear tightly, Charlie watched as Evan jumped out of the truck and corralled the dogs inside the house. Returning to the truck, Evan gathered the terrified bear from Charlie and let him loose in the dog run.

'You stay in the truck and keep an eye on Ursula,' Evan said to Charlie.

He ran in the house and returned after a few minutes with a huge bowl filled with dog food. He signaled for Charlie to get out of the truck.

'You feed the beast, he's your responsibility,' Evan had said.

Charlie placed the bowl just inside the enclosure and watched as Ursula began happily devouring the food. For once, the bear cub stopped growling.

Satisfied the cub was safe, Charlie entered the house where Evan's wife and the dogs were waiting for him. After introductions, she led him to the kitchen where Charlie enjoyed his first real meal in a week. After eating enough for two people, Charlie was taken to a bedroom where he was soon asleep. He woke the next morning to the news that Evan had been able to locate and speak with Charlie's grandparents. They had no idea Charlie had been missing. Evan had agreed to drive Charlie to his grandparents' home the next day. Evan had not mentioned the black bear cub.

ⅅⅅⅅ

For the first time since being hired, Ramsey wondered about the wisdom of following Gordon's orders. He knew the genes influencing his emotions were altered. Ramsey suspected the gratitude he often felt toward Gordon and Hawke were programmed into his DNA.

But now something else was stirring. He was conflicted, and the reason was simple.

Ramsey had observed his boss slowly deteriorating for months.

Gordon is becoming unhinged.

Ramsey needed to objectively judge his boss, but feared it was impossible. He decided it might be helpful to remember what he was like before undergoing the procedures that transformed him - to call upon his old self in order to see his way out of this mess. Ramsey wanted to set aside any forces within him that would impair his judgment.

But he struggled to remember his old self. Ramsey recalled the changes his body had undergone. His muscles growing larger and bones gaining density. Suddenly having night vision and the hearing of a bat. Ramsey watched as he added two inches to his frame. He recollected how his ability to remember information grew in leaps and bounds until he possessed perfect recall. He reminded himself of how great it all felt, especially noticing how other men and women looked at him.

But his memory of what it felt like to be his former self was much less clear.

Was I happier before?

Ramsey worried he had grown too serious, unable to recall the last time he had laughed out loud. And he was never content with anything, couldn't sit still long enough to watch a movie, and always felt paranoid. He was filled with a low frequency, but omnipresent, anger. At times, he would be ordered to hurt people and would look forward to it. Hurting people provided him relief from this mental state. But it never lasted long, and the anger always returned.

Ramsey had had a couple of girlfriends before the treatments. But since his transformation, his interest in the opposite sex was non-existent.

Was that Gordon's doing?

Ramsey called to mind the day before he had shot two FBI agents. Gordon had ranted for an hour about why the agents must die. Ramsey berated himself for not recognizing Gordon's insanity at the time, especially once he had ordered him to kill the agents.

But he'd fallen for Gordon's logic.

Ramsey had been played for the fool.

The next day, Ramsey had ambushed the two agents, and walked away without a care in the world.

What has Gordon done to me?

So, when Gordon had come to him with orders to kill Quinn Conner, Ramsey felt deeply conflicted. Ramsey wondered if he was being set-up to be the fall guy.

And now he wanted him to silence Alex Conner.

This is nuts.

I need to protect myself.

So, Ramsey had sent a copy of Quinn Conner's report to his personal app-pad, when Gordon had gone to pour whiskeys. He'd routed the document through Genlab's server. He was surprised how easy it had been to betray his boss.

What possessed him to take this step, to betray his loyalty to Gordon and Hawke, was beyond him. But he suspected it was a deeper instinct that had taken over. His own survival was at stake, and Gordon could no longer be trusted.

This was confirmed once Ramsey read Quinn Conner's report. He was glad he had taken it. He was in possession of information that was very valuable, and he now had the protection he needed. He could control Gordon and had something to trade with the FBI, should things go badly.

The world is about to get a big shock.

ACT III

8

TUESDAY, JULY 5TH, 2050

If you don't know where you're going, any road will get you there.

Old Rabbi

*T*he woman thought about how to get what she wanted. *A strict word here, and a stern look there. The smallest nudge to the weak minded. Rare praise with frequent admonishments. The ability to see many steps ahead. A deep capacity to understand human emotions and motivations. Knowing your opponent like you know yourself. A willingness to act when the time was right. These are the ways she would get away with her felonies. These are the methods she would use to ensure others are blamed for her crimes. This is how the woman would manipulate those she needed.*

The woman stopped daydreaming as the plane from Seattle touched down in Spokane, Washington. She hated all cities, and Spokane was no different. The woman longed to return to her rural home. To sit by the green river, watch the elk come down for their evening drink, or make the short hike to the hot springs near her ranch.

Just three more days.

But right now, it was time to do what needs to be done.

Checking into a hotel near the city center, the woman showered and changed into fresh clothing. While dressing, the woman considered what she was about to do. There was no hesitation or second thoughts. Her determination to implement the plan was unwavering. Her need for justice just as unfulfilled now as it had been decades before.

No, her thoughts were more centered around leaving her beloved home in the backcountry and eliminating any chance of ever seeing her daughter again. For her plan to work, the woman needed a clean break from her past, and this hurt deeply.

Who could have foretold, that the heart would grow old from loving others?

She checked her purse to ensure the invitation was there.

You are cordially invited to celebrate the
Twenty-Year Reunion of the Spokane County Chapter
of Second-Generation Designer Babies
sponsored by GSI
Claremont Hotel Ball Room
Downtown Spokane
7:30 to 10:00 p.m.

The woman went to her suitcase and removed a small metal box. Using a key hung around her neck, she unlocked the box and removed a single small glove. She slipped the clear, skin-tight glove onto her right hand and stretched it tight around her fingers, pulling its long sleeve up past her wrists. The woman pulled the cuffs of her blouse to cover the edge of the gloves and held her hand up to her face.

As she watched, the glove melted into her skin and disappeared.

She checked her appearance in the mirror.

I'm just an ordinary old woman attending an everyday event.

The woman left her hotel and walked the few blocks to the location listed on the invitation. Snow had started to fall, and the woman noted that most of the downtown buildings were permanently closed - their unused doorways occupied by the homeless. The few businesses that remained open were decorated for the holiday, though the woman saw few shoppers. She arrived at the reunion early and enjoyed an excellent glass of wine. The woman watched as the guests arrived. It wasn't long before the room was filled and the speeches began. She stood by the snack table for the entire presentation, clapping politely as needed.

She made a point of meeting and shaking hands with as many of the other guests as possible. She knew these guests would mingle with other guests. They would shake hands with dozens of other second-generation visitors.

Who knows how many will become infected?

Later that night she boarded a short flight to Yakima. She had another twenty-year reunion to attend the following evening where there would be many more hands to shake.

Then I can go to my sweet home.

9

THURSDAY, DECEMBER 22ND, 2050

I yam what I yam.

Popeye

Minutes before the Thursday morning briefing, Charlie's app-phone rang. He was alone in his office nursing a third cup of coffee. His head hurt, and the coffee was just making him thirstier. He was sitting at his desk with his eyes closed, wishing someone would bring him a glass of water.

Attempting to focus on his notes, Charlie opened his eyes, but he was soon distracted with thoughts about Hawke Conner. For such a famous and powerful man, he sure has become invisible in the context of the investigation.

I need to press him harder.

Just then Charlie's app-phone rang.

'Agent Edmo. Hawke Conner. I'm calling to report that Alex is missing. He was expected for dinner last night and didn't show. He's not responding to our attempts to contact him this morning. He and I quarreled yesterday after you left. He stormed out and I haven't heard from him since,' he said.

'When did you last see him?'

'Yesterday around one, not long after you left.'

'Did you go to his house?'

'Yes, I sent someone over early this morning, but it was locked, and he wasn't there. His car was gone.'

'It's only seven-thirty. Maybe he's sleeping it off somewhere,' Charlie suggested

'He would answer our calls,' Hawke said.

'Maybe. Did you contact local police?'

'Not yet.'

'I suggest you call them.'

'I will. It's my fault we quarreled,' Hawke Conner admitted.

'I'm sure Alex didn't go far. Can you tell me why you quarreled?'

'It's personal. But had nothing to do with Quinn's death.'

'It would help to know.'

'I'm sorry. I can't tell you,' Hawke Conner said.

'You understand this doesn't look good for Alex.'

'I know. I know, but this has nothing to do with Quinn's death, I swear.'

'That's difficult to buy,' Charlie said.

'It's the truth.'

'Fine. I suggest calling Ben Hayward. Get the local police involved.'

'I will. Can the FBI help find Alex?'

'Not yet. Please, just call Ben,' Charlie said.

Special Agent Hunter called the morning briefing to order without Charlie being present. It was Thursday and had been seventy-two hours since Quinn Conner's body had been discovered. The team had worked both day and night since Monday morning, but had yet to find a cause of death, much less who was responsible.

The team continued to aggressively pursue leads. They had eliminated as suspects over one hundred men and women who knew or were somehow associated with the Conners. Sophisticated forensic analysis and rigorous investigations along several lines of inquiry had turned up nothing. They seemed no closer to solving the mystery. The promise of solving the case quickly, and basking in the glory of catching a killer, was slipping away. So was the prospect of spending the holidays with their families. As he started the meeting, Agent Hunter could sense the team's frustration at how the case was unfolding.

'I assume Charlie will be here shortly. I'm going to get started. The cause of death is still listed as unknown,' Hunter started to say.

At that moment, Charlie rushed in the door.

'Is there a reason you're late?' Hunter asked.

'I just got off the phone with Hawke Conner. Alex Conner has disappeared. Given what we discovered yesterday, I was going to recommend we bring him in for more questioning. He may be on the run.'

'Based on what evidence?' Hunter asked.

'We know that Alex quarreled with Quinn the night of the murder. The brothers were viciously competitive and have injured each other in the past. Hawke Conner was ruthless in exploiting their competition. Alex Conner frequently visited Genhancements in order to improve competitiveness with his brother. The doctor at Genhancements stated that Alex had recently feuded with his father. This is not the picture of a happy family,' Charlie said.

'Hardly enough evidence to justify an arrest,' Hunter said.

'Not an arrest, we just need to question him again,' Charlie said.

'I told you before to be more aggressive with him,' Hunter said.

'Actually, you told me to focus on the outsider theory,' Charlie said.

'I said do both.'

'That's not true.'

Charlie stopped for a moment, locked in a stare down with Hunter.

Hunter finally gave in and looked away.

'Okay, bring Alex Conner in for questioning, and if it's not too much to ask, find out what's behind this mess,' he said.

Charlie turned to face the members of his team.

'So, finding Alex Conner is our highest priority, but we still need to fill in some other gaps. I want a team at Genlabs this morning, and don't come back until we know more about Quinn Conner's work. Agent Hunter was briefed yesterday by Genlabs, so coordinate with him.'

Charlie ended the meeting.

Wednesday afternoon stretched into evening as Marion moved into her new office, emptied boxes and set up replacement equipment in the new lab. The space was located on the top floor of the CDC building, but unfortunately on the opposite side of the building from the freight elevator. Every box had to be carefully moved on carts from the elevator to the new lab.

As a result, Marion didn't return to her townhouse until just after ten. She was too tired to eat, so immediately took a long shower and climbed into bed.

Marion's thoughts returned to the hectic and tragedy-filled day. She knew she wouldn't sleep. There was a ritual that must be followed, even on those nights when she was exhausted. She would not sleep until every part of her day was examined thoroughly - usually more than once.

She wished her brain had an off switch.

Marion finally nodded off for a short time before waking up in a cold sweat. She was dreaming about some type of war zone. Marion could see dead bodies piled in a city square. Soldiers were lining up more victims against a wall to be shot. Not a single person seemed to care about human life. It held absolutely no value. In the dream, Marion ran from person to person, grabbing them by the shoulders while screaming, 'Life is golden, life is golden,' in their faces.

Shaken, it took another hour for Marion to fall asleep. She tossed and turned all night.

As a result, Marion was in a lousy mood when she arrived at her new office the next morning. There was a note taped to her door. The Health Alert Network team was meeting down the hall. Her presence was requested.

I need to perk up.

Dr. Lois Peck and the other eight members of the HAN team had already started when Marion walked into the room.

'Marion, good morning. Sorry to begin your day like this, but another five young men died overnight in Spokane. Several dozen other men are sick,' Lois said.

'Same profile as the other men?' Marion asked.

'Right. Early twenties. We're checking to see if they are all second gen,' Lois answered.

'Bleeding from the nose and ears?' Marion asked.

'Correct.'

'So, eight deaths and dozens are sick, and no idea of the cause. We need to mobilize a team,' Marion said.

'We're prepping two teams. They should be on their way to Spokane and Yakima within the hour. Right now, we're discussing language for a Health Emergency Alert. We'll also need a written statement for the press,' Dr. Peck said.

'Will it mention the victim's connection to GSI and Genlabs?' Marion asked.

'No choice. Our credibility is at stake. The alert will list everything we know, regardless of the political consequences. All the connections to GSI, second gen babies, and the role Genlabs played in engineering the genetic profiles of the victims. I suggest we stop short of calling this an epidemic. We'll use the term 'outbreak' for now. This is going to be a full-blown media circus as it is,' Dr. Peck said.

For the next three hours, the group finalized a draft of the Health Alert and composed a three-page written statement for the media. At one-fifty, the team submitted its final draft of the Health Alert to the agency's communications department. At preciously three o'clock EST, the CDC released to the world its last official Health Alert of 2050. At the same time an official written statement was released to the press.

After the release of the Health Alert, Marion returned to her office. It was one-thirty in the afternoon, and she was exhausted. She found a chair, sat down, and closed her eyes. She took ten deep breaths and massaged her face for a full minute.

Marion had been involved with seven major Health Alerts in her career, but they were nothing like this. The emergence of a dangerous new health risk, combined with the potential for huge political blowback, was overwhelming. A Health

Emergency Alert was the CDC's highest level of warning, and the fact it mentioned GSI and Genlabs directly would reverberate globally.

🧬

Arriving at the FBI building at one p.m., Charlie walked into his office and found a file sitting on his chair. There was a note from Special Agent Hunter. The file contained Quinn and Alex's medical histories. It had just been delivered by a GSI courier. *Hawke Conner came through.*

Charlie opened and read Quinn's file first.

The file covered his entire medical and legal history starting the day Adele Peterson was inseminated until Quinn's fifth birthday. After that, responsibility for Quinn's medical care passed from the GSI's doctors to the family doctor.

Charlie read for an hour, taking notes related to Quinn's birth and subsequent physical and psychological development. The report was fascinating and provided Charlie with a better understanding of how families deeply involved with genetic editing operate.

Suddenly there it was, at the bottom of the file.

The clue he'd been missing.

Charlie would never have suspected it. He scanned the legal document again. There was no mistake.

Charlie immediately sent messages to Jack and Hunter, asking them to join him.

Looking back at the document, Charlie wondered how the Conner's had pulled it off. To his recollection, no court had ever allowed a family to have a designer-baby and a natural-born child in the same family. It was a scandal, not to mention a Class 1 felony. It was fundamentally unfair to both siblings and was one of the few policy areas where Congress had held its ground against the industries' lobbyists.

But here was a signed court order allowing the Conner's to bring a genetically enhanced child into a family already possessing a natural-born infant.

I guess if you have enough money.

Curious about the history of designer babies, Charlie spent a few minutes researching GSI and Genlabs. He knew the companies were the first to offer designer-babies to the public. What he didn't realize was GSI released updated versions of their designer babies every three to five years. The only exception was the first and second generations of babies, which were released just twenty-six months apart.

Both Quinn and Alex were the pubic face for the first and second generations of designer babies and were iconic figures worldwide.

But Charlie now knew it was all a sham.

Charlie returned to his online research. He was reminded that the development of the CRISPR Cas9 technology by Dr. Jennifer Doudna, and her collaborator, Emmanuelle Charpentier, in 2014, was the big game changer. This sudden advancement made gene-editing technologies more available and much less expensive.

Industry immediately responded. By 2016, in addition to allowing parents to select the gender of their child, companies began offering cosmetically enhanced babies. At first, parents could only select eye color, hair color and skin complexion, and only if the changes matched one of the parents. This soon changed.

Hawke and Gordon's discoveries greatly expanded the science behind this emerging industry. This led to the rapid development of technologies for mass producing designer-babies.

By 2026, just months after Congress liberalized laws governing the practice, the world's first designer baby was born: Alex Conner.

Or so we all thought.

In the twenty-two years since his birth, wealthy parents had purchased approximately five million of these children across the U.S., and another three million globally. Based on public records, GSI/Genlabs held ninety-three percent of the world market.

Parents anticipated a release of the next generation of GSI designer-babies like a new app-phone or car. Parents who could afford these babies did their family planning in accordance with these releases. However, parents who already had a natural-born child were prohibited from purchasing a genetically engineered child, and once a family locked into having a genetically engineered child, there was no going back. It was against federal law to give birth to a natural-born child if the family had already purchased a designer-baby. If parents wanted a second child, they would have to purchase one from among the newest generation of designer-babies as they became available.

The Conners had somehow circumvented federal law and gone against all social convention. Charlie wondered why any parent would do such a thing - give one sibling a genetic advantage over the other. The research on this topic was overwhelming; this was an unhealthy practice and harmful to the less genetically sophisticated sibling.

Charlie considered other possible motives for the Conner's crime. Was it about ego and the need to establish a family legacy? He could imagine Hawke and Abby having concerns about the ability of their sons to run one of the largest companies in the world. After all, tens of billions were at stake.

Charlie looked up as Hunter entered his office closely followed by Jack.

'We have our smoking gun. Alex was not a genetically engineered child. The Conner's have been lying. Quinn got the royal treatment, but Alex was natural born. Somehow they managed to buy their way through the courts.'

Charlie handed the twenty-two-year old court order to Hunter.

'Wow, things just got a lot more interesting. No wonder Alex was going to Genhancements,' Jack said.

'Right. Let's assume Alex recently learned he wasn't genetically enhanced. Is that a motive for murder? This isn't covered in the textbooks,' Charlie said.

'Motive enough for murder? Maybe. I'm not sure the old rules about brothers apply here either,' Jack offered.

'Maybe not,' Charlie said.

'Alex must have known. Why else go to Genhancements?' Jack asked.

'Maybe. He may have sensed he was inferior and decided to do something about it. Denial is a strong force. I'm just not sure that's enough motive for murdering your brother. We need to bring Alex Conner in for questioning,' Hunter mused while looking over the court order.

'We need to arrest him. It's more than enough motive, People have killed for far less,' Charlie said.

'I still don't buy it,' Hunter said.

'What about the Conners. They need to be prosecuted. This judge was bought and paid for. If it was up to me, I'd throw the book at them and the judge who issued this court order,' Jack offered.

'That's a decision for someone above my pay grade. I'll prepare a memo for the director,' Hunter said

'But right now, we need to find Alex Conner. Will you issue an APB?' Charlie asked.

'I'll order the APB, for no other reason than to see if your theory holds water,' Hunter finished.

An hour later Detective Ben Hayward called Charlie to inform him that Alex Conner's Porsche had been found parked near the Winslow marina, and his father's yacht was gone.

Charlie called Hunter immediately and urged him to issue a federal arrest warrant for Alex Conner. A judge approved his request in less than an hour. A copy of the warrant and a description of his vessel was forwarded to local law enforcement agencies, the U.S. Border Patrol, and the U.S. Coast Guard.

Motoring his father's yacht around the Strait of Juan De Fuca provided Alex with the time he needed to reflect on his predicament, but unfortunately the fresh air also brought on an abundance of clear thinking. Alex soon realized his actions would look bad in the eyes of the FBI. Agent Edmo had specifically asked him to remain available for questioning. Alex realized he may face some type of legal trouble when he returned.

Also, being at sea prevented Alex from accessing the internet or communicating with the outside world. So, by the time sunset finally arrived, Alex was impatient to get home. But first, he needed sleep and to get fuel for the ship. He decided it was time to set course for Port Angeles. Arriving at the port around eight in the evening, Alex was pleased to see the harbor was void of boat traffic. Alex carefully navigated the entrance to the harbor and found a quiet corner of the bay. He dropped anchor and shut down the vessel's motors.

Once the vessel was secure, Alex went below and radioed the harbor master. He paid the harbor fees using a false name. He'd worry about getting fuel in the morning. Alex prepared a quick meal, drank a glass of wine, and fell asleep on the bed in his parent's stateroom.

Hours later, Alex was abruptly awakened when the stateroom filled with a blinding light. A ship's horn blared so loudly that it rattled the porthole above his head. He covered his ears and curled up in the bed. Suddenly a voice so loud it had to be God addressed him.

'This is Captain Lane of the United States Coast Guard. Please show yourself on deck with your hands raised above your head. This is Captain Lane of the United State Coast Guard.'

Already dressed, Alex climbed to the deck of the ship and raised his hands. The spotlight on the Coast Guard ship immediately found Alex, and he covered his eyes to avoid the blinding glare. Several armed Coast Guard sailors were already climbing onto the deck of the ship.

10

Thursday, December 22nd, 2050

They sicken of the calm, who know the storm.
Dorothy Parker

June 3rd, 2019
Journal Entry # 98
Gordon Kelly, Doctoral Student, MIT

*T*he Ghost in the Machine has an accomplice. My professor spoke of it today, describing it as one of the least understood and deadly phenomena in nature. It's the so-called Black Swan event. For three centuries, ornithologists believed there were only white swans. Then black swans were discovered in Australia.

Since then, the term Black Swan, has come to represent the knowledge that we do not yet possess. The Black Swan informs us that science is limited in its capacity to understand the world around us and to predict the future. Like the dark energy that binds our universe together, the Black Swan is a force that hides just outside the realm of regular experiences. It is always an outlier. Nothing points to its possibility. It is, by *definition, deeply unpredictable. The Black Swan event always comes out of nowhere, my professor said.*

But the most insidious, low-down, and underhanded thing about a Black Swan event, is that it convinces us to concoct puny explanations based on our hindsight, which is often incorrect. This ensures that future Black Swan events will continue to occur, easily exceeding our capacity to predict and prevent them. We solve this riddle or perish.

Suddenly wanting to vomit, Gordon stopped reading his journal. His heart was beating erratically, and he was dizzy. Gordon stood leaning against the desk to steady himself. After a few moments he recovered his balance and returned to his chair.

Gordon thought about the night he'd written the entry. It was the second semester of his first year in graduate school. He had just read *The Black Swan* by Nassim Nicholas Taleb. His mind was reeling from the author's ideas, and Gordon had felt compelled to record his impressions.

The next day Gordon left campus and went for a long walk. He wanted to be alone to think. A rainstorm forced Gordon to rush back to campus and seek shelter in a building near the edge of campus. Standing in the lobby of the building, Gordon could hear a woman's voice coming from the nearby lecture hall and peeked in the door. By chance, the topic of the lecture was Transhumanism. He found a seat and watched as a woman delivered a lecture about the moral imperative for using genetic engineering technologies to improve the human species.

It was like the proverbial light going off. On top of reading *The Black Swan*, hearing the notions espoused in this lecture moved Gordon to tears. He waited until the lecture was over for a chance to meet the speaker. The two hit it off immediately, and Gordon asked if she wanted to grab some coffee.

Within a year, they were married.

Ending the daydream, and glancing back at the journal entry, Gordon realized how prophetic his own words were - a clear warning from the past. His heart skipped a handful of beats and he closed his eyes. After a moment, he again looked back at the words he had written about *The Black Swan*.

These words predict my inevitable defeat.

How could I have been so unbelievably arrogant?

Gordon considered the eons of time invested by the forces of evolution in the human DNA. The billions upon billions of individual choices accumulating in billions and billions of tiny memories, each one reflected in the structure and function of DNA. The molecule was a mosaic of lessons in survival which inhabit every cell of our body.

The DNA is our engine of survival.

How dare I challenge this wisdom?

Feeling his heart beginning to pound, Gordon walked to his private bathroom to wash his face. Gordon looked in the mirror, placing his hands on either side of the sink. He could see sweat forming on his brow. His heart started to ache like a sore muscle. Gordon splashed cold water on his face.

The Ghost in the Machine, and its accomplice, the Black Swan, have come to collect their dues.

Abruptly, complete panic filled his chest and Gordon stopped breathing. He closed his eyes and waited for the rush to pass. But it didn't pass. It was happening again - an uncontrollable panic attack.

Gordon managed to take a shallow breath.

For six months Gordon had had periods of pure panic, during which he was incapable of doing anything but curling up in a ball on the floor, praying for his heart to slow.

Gordon began sobbing, which made it harder to breath.

He stumbled to his desk and sat down. He pulled up the Alert on his monitor and read it for a second time. Gordon had received the Health Advisory warning from the CDC's Health Alert Network earlier that morning.

My world is unraveling.

He opened his left drawer and found his meds. He opened the bottle and downed four pills.

Thanks to me, young men have died.

I can't wait any longer.

Gordon closed his eyes and waited for his meds to kick-in.

Thirty-minutes later his heart slowed, and he felt a small measure of calmness. He picked up his app-phone and called Ramsey.

'Good to hear from you Mr. Kelly.'

'Anything new?' Gordon asked.

'Yes. According to Hunter, Alex Conner was just taken into custody by the FBI,' Ramsey said.

'The cover up is unraveling. We're out of time. They'll soon have Quinn's report. It will lead them to Idaho. The FBI will be desperate to find Jane. We need to stop this now. You need to get to Idaho before the feds,' Gordon said.

'Do you have an address for her?' Ramsey asked.

'Not really an address. She owns the Daisy Tappan ranch on the Middle Fork of the Salmon River, in the Idaho Wilderness. Stanley is the nearest town. I've already arranged a flight from Stanley to the Flying B Ranch. You fly at four, mountain time, tomorrow. The Tappan ranch is a ten-mile hike from the air-strip. It's winter, so be prepared. Don't forget, the FBI is on your heels. You need to get there first. You know what to do,' Gordon said.

'I'll take care of it,' Ramsey said.

Gordon ended the call.

He sat staring into space.

What have I done?

He felt himself going over the edge again. His heart started racing and he felt faint. Gordon closed his eyes and rested his head on the desk. The room was spinning.

There's no turning back now.

I've set some bad things in motion.

Gordon remembered his meeting with Quinn on the previous Saturday. Quinn had predicted thousands of men would die.

The thought cycled again and again in his head.

He could visualize the bodies of young men piled high.

All because of my arrogance.

He was overwhelmed with guilt and was spiraling uncontrollably downward.

Gordon began to sob loudly. His hands trembled, and he was filled with confusion and doubt.

There was a knock on his office door.

'Not now,' he yelled in response.

The knocking stopped.

What have I done?

It suddenly became clear what he had set in motion. The cover-up had spun out of control. Gordon had just ordered someone to murder his ex-wife. Two ambulance drivers were already dead. Young genetically perfect men were dying. His debts had come due.

I don't have the strength to face this.

Gordon's remorse overwhelmed him. He slid from his chair and laid on the floor. He curled into a ball and cried.

After a time, Gordon crawled back into his chair. He was filled with sadness and regret. He felt empty and dead.

He unlocked the drawer on his right and removed the pistol

hidden under its false bottom. He used his thumb print to activate the weapon. Gordon placed the barrel of the gun in his mouth and pulled the trigger.

🧬

The woman watched as the page downloaded onto her apppad. It was a Health Advisory Alert from the CDC. She smiled and nodded to herself. The epidemic had begun. The woman's long-anticipated plans were working.

For two decades, the woman had methodically sought her revenge. For the first three years she had thought of nothing else. What is the surest path to justice? How can I get satisfaction? How can I destroy those who have hurt me? How can I not get caught?

Then she committed her thoughts to paper in excruciating detail. One step after the other, weaving the threads together into a human drama of her making. The woman worked to anticipate every possible reaction and countermove made against her and developed plans within plans in order to prepare for when the unexpected happened. Every possible flaw was considered.

Then another fifteen years engineering and testing the technology. The many setbacks and disappointments. The burnout and heartbreaks. The huge amount of funds spent. But now, success. Her first victims were dying.

I have something the world will soon want very much.

🧬

In less than an hour, Alex Conner was transported by coast guard helicopter from Port Angeles to Seattle, booked into FBI custody, and left under surveillance in an interrogation room. It was one a.m. Friday morning. Alex requested his family's attorney, Frank Kaminsky, be present for questioning. While they waited for Mr. Kaminsky to arrive, Charlie watched Alex Conner via the video camera. He looked relaxed and sat quietly staring into space. Alex was wearing blue jeans and an Irish sweater and was humming to himself. Charlie could hear his soft singing through the microphone.

Charlie was impatient. He wanted a crack at the man who was likely responsible for Quinn Conner's death.

'I'm going to tell him his attorney is on the way.' Charlie said.

'Charlie, you better wait for Hunter,' Jack said.

'I'll just make conversation.' Charlie said.

Jack shook his head from side to side.

'Don't do it.'

Charlie ignored him and left the observation room and went to speak with Alex Conner.

'Agent Edmo. I should have known it was you,' Alex said, when Charlie entered the room.

'What does that mean?' Charlie asked.

'I could tell from the beginning you don't like my type.'

'I'm just following the evidence, and it leads to you.'

'Believing something doesn't make it true,' Alex said.

'I not talking about beliefs or opinions. I'm talking about facts,' Charlie countered.

'What facts?'

'You had both motive and opportunity. For starters, you argued with Quinn the night he died and hid it from me. You have no alibi for the hours between the end of the party and six that morning. You were extremely competitive with your brother and put him in the hospital more than once. You're a client of

Genhancements and your physician disclosed you were getting genetic augmentation to help you keep up with your brother. But the clincher, and the motive for murdering your brother, was finding out the truth about Quinn. He's enhanced and you're not. That had to be tough,' Charlie paused for effect.

Charlie didn't want to push too hard, but he knew there were only moments before Alex's attorney, or his boss arrived.

'Quite a case Agent Edmo. Except none of it is true.'

'None of it?'

'Actually, all of it is true. It's your conclusion that's wrong.'

'Then tell me what happened?' Charlie asked.

'Why would I do that without my lawyer?'

'Because if I believe you, I'll be your advocate,' Charlie said.

Just then Frank Kaminsky bustled into the room

'Hold on there. What are we discussing?' he demanded.

'Nothing, just some background questions,' Charlie said.

'Don't let me find you alone with my client again. Do you understand?' Frank asked.

'Fair enough. Now that you're here, can we get started?'

'I need some time with my client,' Frank said.

'Take as long as you need. Wave to the camera when you're ready,' Charlie said.

Returning to the observation room, Charlie watched as Frank Kaminsky and Alex Conner discussed the case. Hunter arrived just as Frank Kaminsky signaled to the camera. Charlie and Jack returned to the interrogation room while Hunter remained to watch the questioning from the observation room.

'Alex Conner. You are being held as a person of interest in the death of Quinn Conner. You are not charged with a crime at this time. That could change pending the results of this interview and other evidence. You've been informed of your rights?' Charlie asked.

'Yes.'

'For the record, this is not a court of law, but if you perjure yourself, the FBI will prosecute. Do you understand?' Charlie asked.

'Yes.'

'My first questions are directed at establishing a timeline of the hours and days leading up to the death of Quinn Conner.'

'Stop. I had nothing to do with my brother's death. You need to listen to me. I know who killed Quinn and why,' Alex announced loudly.

Everyone stopped what they were doing and looked at Alex.

'This better be good,' Charlie said.

'Okay. Yes, at the party, I was arguing with Quinn. But that's not what's important. Quinn was afraid of something,' Alex admitted.

'What was he afraid of?' Charlie asked.

'I'm not sure, he said. *If something happens to me, find the report dated December 17th, last Saturday.*'

Charlie thought about this.

'He feared for his life?' Charlie asked.

'Yes, he was seriously frightened.'

'Why didn't you tell us this before? Seems pretty convenient,' Jack said.

'I was scared.'

'So, you lied?' Charlie asked.

'I wanted time to find the report.'

'Did you find it?' Jack asked.

'I'm working on it.'

'How?' Jack asked.

'We have an old friend working in Genlabs, I contacted him.'

'Henry Chen?' Charlie asked.

'Right.'

'What did he tell you?' Charlie asked.

'He said my brother was working on a secret project for Gordon Kelly and a report was generated, but its disappeared and is no longer on Genlabs' servers,' Alex said.

'So, you don't know what's in the report?' Charlie asked.

'No idea.'

'Yet you're saying this report is why your brother was murdered?' Charlie asked.

'I wasn't sure. But then I was contacted by a man who threatened to kill me and my parents. He knew about the report. I think this man killed Quinn.'

'Whoa, slow down. Who contacted you?' Jack asked.

'Last Tuesday, I got a call from a man who called himself Ray. He claimed to work for Genlabs. I found out later that was a lie. He claimed to want my help figuring out some of Quinn's passwords. The man was very convincing. He claimed to know Quinn. Then he threatened me if I ever mentioned the report.'

'What exactly did he say?' Charlie asked.

'He asked me if Quinn mentioned a report. I was already suspicious and denied knowing anything about it, but I don't think he bought it. He said, *If I happened to remember the report, for my own safety, and the safety of my family, I should never mention it, now or ever. I'd hate for someone else to die,*' Alex said.

'Word for word, that's what he said?' Jack asked.

'Yes. I don't forget things,' Alex said.

'Any idea who the man is?' Charlie asked.

'No. I'm guessing he's an industrial spy, trying to steal Quinn's research,' Alex said.

Leaving Alex Conner in the interrogation room with his lawyer, Charlie and Jack walked to Hunter's office. Charlie was shaken. His heart rate was elevated, and he wanted to lay down. He wanted to think about what Alex Conner had said. Was he telling the truth? If so, the case had taken a radical turn. New evidence had emerged. Another motive existed. Was Alex blowing smoke? And who was this other man? It all sounded like a bunch of lies. Charlie struggled to adjust.

They arrived at Hunter's office.

'I just got a call from Kathleen Holden. Gordon Kelly tried to kill himself,' Hunter announced.

'He's alive?' Charlie asked.

'Yes. You saw him earlier this week. What did you think?' Hunter asked.

'Compared to our first meeting, he seemed like a different man. I told Jack he looked like he'd seen a ghost. He had these stitches on his hand and he couldn't stop playing with them.'

'Could this be related to Quinn Conner's death?' Hunter asked.

'I don't see how. The press has run a couple of stories about his depression,' Charlie said.

'It's still a weird coincidence.'

'Could be,' Charlie said.

What'd you think of Alex Conner?' Hunter changed the subject.

'We need to find out if he is telling the truth as soon as possible,' Charlie said.

'Get the team together within the hour. We need a new plan,' Hunter said.

Forty-five minutes later the FBI team was assembled.

'We have some news, so let's get started,' Hunter ordered.

Everyone grabbed their coffee cups and hurried to a seat. It was the fourth morning briefing since the discovery of Quinn

Conner's body. The team of men and women had worked relentlessly to solve the case, and until now, had felt a sense of collective failure. But the team was feeding off a noticeable change in the demeanors of both Special Agent Hunter and Agent Edmo.

Something was up.

Rumors were Alex Conner had been found. The team could sense progress. There was a chance the case would come to a successful conclusion before the holiday, and this lifted their spirits.

Once everybody was seated, Hunter got started.

'There've been some new developments. Alex Conner was taken into custody by the Coast Guard around midnight. He was found on his father's boat in Port Angeles. He was flown to Seattle and arrived at one this morning. He was then interrogated by Charlie and his team. Based on the information he provided, which has for the most part, been verified, the investigation will be taking a new direction. Alex Conner is no longer a suspect in the death of Quinn Conner. He may face charges for obstructing an investigation, but for now, he will be released from our custody. Charlie will bring you up to date on his interrogation.'

Charlie walked to the front of the room.

'Alex Conner withheld some critical information during our initial interview. The night he died, Quinn Conner told his brother that his life was in danger. He told his brother that if something happened to him, he should find a report he had just finished. It's possible something contained in that document led to his death.'

'Does Alex Conner have a copy of the report?' Hunter asked.

'Apparently not,' Charlie answered and then continued.

'There's more. Two days after Quinn's death, last Tuesday,

Alex Conner was contacted by a man saying he worked for Genlabs. The man was looking for a special report. When Alex denied knowing about it, the man threatened to kill Mr. Conner and his family. Alex panicked and went into hiding, during which time he contacted Henry Chen, a friend of his at Genlabs. Mr. Chen confirmed the report existed, but nobody there has been able to locate it. Mr. Gordon Kelly, the one person who might know where the report is, attempted suicide two hours ago and is unconscious in a hospital. Everybody with me?'

Charlie stopped for questions.

'What do we know about the man who threatened Alex?' Jack asked.

'Nothing.'

'Is he suspected of murdering Quinn Conner?' Ben Hayward asked.

'Yes. Starting now, we're focused on finding Mr. X. He's our number one suspect. Our best guess is that the suspect is involved in some sort of industrial espionage against Genlabs,' Charlie said.

'Any idea what's in the report?' another agent asked.

'No. Agent Seaman conducted a search of Quinn Conner's data files but found nothing. We're seeking a warrant to search all the data servers on the Genlabs campus. I personally spoke with Henry Chen, and he provided the name of the co-worker who knew of the report. I spoke with this person and she confirmed Quinn had recently completed an important project. Because of the high level of secrecy surrounding the project, she assumed it was a Department of Defense initiative. This was an educated guess on her part,' Charlie said.

Charlie nodded toward Hunter, who stood and addressed the group.

'So, we have a new plan. Let's get this done,' Hunter said.

11

FRIDAY, DECEMBER 23RD, 2050

The ox is slow, but the earth is patient.

Working in a haze of bone deep exhaustion, Marion jumped when her phone rang. Starting Thursday afternoon, she and her colleagues had worked twenty hours straight, analyzing dozens of samples and reviewing countless pages of medical data collected from victims, only to be greeted by the news that another twelve young men had died overnight. This news nearly made her manic. A total of twenty men had now died in Washington State. She expected other states would soon begin reporting cases.

She answered the call.

'Marion. This is Agent Charlie Edmo with the FBI. We've met before, a couple of years ago. The Olivia case,' Charlie said.

'Sure, I remember. How are you?'

'Fine thanks. Listen, I'm running the investigation into the death of Quinn Conner. I just received the CDC's Health Alert and I've got a couple of questions,' Charlie said.

'This isn't a great time.'

'I know you're busy. But this may be related to the out-break,' Charlie answered.

'You think there's a connection?' Marion asked.

'It's possible.'

'Tell me what you know.'

'I believe the symptoms are the same,' Charlie offered.

'Blood coming from nose and ears?' Marion asked.

'Correct.'

'That's consistent with what we're seeing,' Marion stopped for a moment. 'But I'd need a DNA sample to be sure. As I remember his remains were destroyed,' she said.

'We got hair samples from his home. One of my agents will arrive with this sample in the next few minutes. I know you're busy with the outbreak, but if you could analyze the sample ASAP, it would help a lot,' Charlie said.

I'll try to get it done by the end of today. That's the best I can do under the circumstances,' Marion said.

'I can live with that. Call when you're done.'

At four-fifteen that afternoon, Marion stopped with she was doing and prepared Quinn Conner's hair samples for analysis. She placed the sample in the 3D projector and pressed the start button. In a few minutes, a digital, three-dimensional representation of his DNA was generated by the projector. The 3D image, about the size of a loaf of bread, hovered in the air above the projector. The machine allowed Marion complete access to the molecule. Using both hands, Marion rotated the image of the DNA until it was correctly positioned. She touched the image with her index finger and watched as the projector zoomed inside Quinn's DNA.

Adjusting the digital lens until she could see individual segments of protein, Marion used her molecular scissors to splice out a random section of the DNA molecule. She watched as the CAS9 molecule unlocked the DNA's double helix. Marion could see the CRISPR protein leading the molecular wrench to the correct location, and then watched as it spliced the segment of a gene sequence into the DNA.

Suddenly, there was a reaction from the DNA she had never seen before. But it happened so quickly she wasn't sure. Marion repeated the process several more times, each instance with the same result. Marion zoomed back out and rotated the DNA. She zoomed back in and took a few minutes examining other sections of the double helix. She repeated the process again and again, roaming through various sections of the molecule.

There was no doubt. The damage to Mr. Conner's DNA was very similar to what was happening to the DNA of the young men dying from the outbreak.

It would need to be confirmed, but Marion suspected there was only one reasonable conclusion to be drawn from the evidence.

This is something I've never seen before.

Marion realized a new type of disorder might be ramping up, and Quinn Conner may have been its first victim. A powerful threat had emerged, and it was unlike anything she had seen before. Past epidemics featured some type of new bug - a pathogen that mutated and managed to make the jump from an animal species to humans. But it was always a living organism with DNA molecules - DNA that could be sequenced. Treatments could be developed and tested in computer simulations. Once the treatment was approved it could be distributed to sick patients. Sometimes in a matter of weeks or months.

But this outbreak was totally different. No known virus or pathogen triggered the reaction. The DNA was attacking itself, reacting aggressively to the engineered genes that had been spliced into the victim's genetic material before they were born. Twenty-plus years after the birth of these young men, their original genes were reacting to the introduced genes like they were an invading virus.

Worldwide, GSI had sold about three hundred thousand second generation designer-baby boys. These babies were now young men between the ages of twenty-one and twenty-three. A vast majority lived in the U.S., but about thirty thousand lived abroad.

How many of these men will die?

Marion considered whether she had the energy to wage another battle - pitting her experience and scientific instruments against nature's onslaught, like they were some type of magic wand. In truth, Marion knew she was fighting a losing battle. The tools at her disposal were no match for these invisible and recklessly determined viruses, pathogens, or whatever the hell this latest foe would turn out to be. Marion shivered as she pulled her sweater on.

I'm trying to kill a charging elephant with a BB gun.

She meditated on the deeper significance of her work. Why do diseases exist in the first place? Where does the will and energy for these destructive viruses and pathogens originate? Like anti-matter, is there some type of 'anti-life' force hidden in the universe? If hell is on earth, was it manifested in these ongoing epidemics?

Marion didn't know the answers. She did know the only thing keeping the viruses and pathogens at bay was a constant reshuffling of our genetic code. And this could only be done via the natural human reproductive process. In other words, making babies the old-fashioned way. For some strange reason, realizing this energized Marion, and she started pacing her office.

Thinking about what to do next, Marion knew Lois was right. Despite a hostile climate, they needed to reach out to GSI and Genlabs. Their help was essential. But how to accomplish this? Marion expected GSI to file a dozen or more lawsuits against the government in the coming days. She also knew GSI would call upon its many friends in the national media to wage an attack campaign against the agency. Marion would need to work behind the scenes.

But first she needed to contact Charlie Edmo.

𝕯𝕹𝕬

'Agent Charlie Edmo, can I help you?'

'Hello. This is Marion Harper at the CDC,' Marion said.

'Thanks for getting back to me. Were you able to run Quinn Conner's DNA?'

'Yes, and it may confirm your suspicions,' Marion said.

'What did you find?' Charlie asked.

'The damage to his DNA is the same as the damage we're seeing in the young men dying from the outbreak. Quinn Conner may have been an early victim of this new disorder,' she said.

'He wasn't murdered?' Charlie asked.

'No, Agent Edmo. He may not have been murdered. But without a body, we can't be sure,' Marion said.

'The symptoms are the same?' Charlie asked.

'Yes. The men all bleed from the nose and ears. The bleeding is a result of rapid cardiac arrest.'

'Can you confirm Quinn's DNA was engineered by Genlabs?' Charlie asked.

'Sure, no doubt about that,' Marion exclaimed.

'We just learned Alex was natural-born,' Charlie said.

'That doesn't seem possible. He's the poster boy for designer babies worldwide,' Marion said.

'The Conner's had enough influence and money to circumvent federal and state laws, and to keep it a secret,' Charlie said.

'I can't image a motive for doing that to your kids,' Marion said.

'The whole industry is out of control, and I intend to do something about it.'

'I'm glad to help. Honestly, my boss and I suspected something weird is going on at Genlabs, GSI, or both,' Marion offered.

'I need to hear more. Let me ask, how sure are you that Quinn died of the same disorder as the other men?' Charlie asked.

'Very sure. Let me ask you a question. What was the time of death for Mr. Conner?'

'Between midnight last Sunday night and one Monday morning,' Charlie recited.

'That's a full day before the other men died,' Marion offered.

'Lucky for him,' Charlie said.

'You don't understand. Mr. Conner may be Patient Zero,' Marion offered.

'I'm not familiar with the term,' Charlie said.

'It refers to the first person to contract an infectious disease, usually after contact with an animal hosting the virus. But I'm not sure it applies here. Technically this isn't the same thing,' Marion said.

'We need to meet and compare notes. Can we come to your office now?' Charlie asked.

'Sorry, my office was destroyed. I'll call my boss and we'll be right over,' Marion promised.

Anxious to meet with the two scientists from the CDC, Charlie was pacing around the small meeting room like a bear in a cage. Jack and Brad sat and watched Charlie walk in circles around the small space - his huge frame towering over the seated men. Combined with his non-stop patter, Charlie's energy seemed to fill every inch of the room.

Charlie knew this mood all too well. His impatience had overpowered him, and he wanted closure desperately. He needed to physically grab hold of everything that stood in his way and toss it aside. Charlie was frustrated that life was not so simple. He resented the need for subtlety and nuanced approaches. Charlie wanted to use his massive strength to simple smash something to pieces. His body pulsed with energy.

Increasing his pace of movement around the room, Charlie began spouting off about how stupid he'd been during the investigation. As a result, he didn't notice Dr. Harper and Dr. Peck abruptly entering the room. The two visitors watched his tirade until Charlie noticed the new arrivals and stopped mid-sentence. The two women smiled and introduced themselves.

Charlie nodded at the two women. They were a study in contrast. Marion Harper was about Charlie's age. She was a couple of inches short of six feet, lean and fit. Marion was dressed in standard government garb, plain pants, comfortable shoes, and a drab white blouse with a couple of small stains from her morning coffee. The only exception to the otherwise dull wardrobe were her eyeglasses, which were large, purple and pointed. Marion had a pleasant face designed by evolution to make everyone around her comfortable. Charlie remembered why he had immediately liked her when they had worked together previously.

Dr. Lois Peck, on the other hand, needed her shoes to clear five feet and was built like a pear. She looked more like an accountant than a scientist. Charlie guessed she was in her mid-seventies. Her clothes made rubbing noises when she walked, and Charlie got a small electric shock when they shook hands.

'Sorry about that. Been a week,' Charlie said after introductions were completed.

'Can you share what you've learned?' he asked.

Marion provided a summary of her conclusions related to the death of Quinn Conner. She discussed the similarities between his death and the deaths attributed to the emerging outbreak. Marion shared her observations related to Quinn Conner's DNA, and outlined her opinion that a new type of syndrome was behind the death of Quinn Conner and the other young men.

The foursome sat quietly for a few moments.

'Do you know what's causing the outbreak?' Charlie asked.

'Not yet,' Marion answered.

'This throws a whole new light on our investigation,' Jack added.

'Right. That's why I've already spoken with Hunter. The FBI will redirect its investigation and start coordinating with the CDC. This is no longer a murder investigation. And given the disease appears to impact genetically modified individuals, our involvement is mandated by federal law,' Charlie offered.

'That's good news. Helps to share resources and intel. Along those lines, can you tell us what you know?' Marion asked.

'Hold everything,' Jack interjected. 'We've been conducting a murder investigation. We know Mr. Conner compiled a classified report the day before his death. Something in the report caused him to fear for his life. We also learned from Alex Conner that an unidentified man threatens to kill him and his family if they discussed the existence of the report. This same man indicated he was responsible for Quinn's death. So, forgive me, but I'm confused. You're telling us Mr. Conner wasn't murdered. Doesn't add up.'

'Without a body it's hard to confirm any theory about how Quinn Conner died. Maybe that's not what's important. Someone thinks the report is very important. Maybe the real question is why,' Marion stated.

'We're assuming Alex Conner is telling the truth,' Charlie added.

'Right. So, let's talk about what we do know? We know Quinn Conner worked for Genlabs, and the report was presumably generated as part of his job. This means others at Genlabs may have known about the document,' Marion offered.

'For instance, his boss Gordon Kelly,' Charlie added.

'Here's a thought. What if the report is related to the outbreak? Connect the dots. All the men who have died were designer-babies,' Marion said.

'Right. Maybe GSI and Genlabs were already aware of a problem,' Dr. Peck said.

'If they failed to report what they knew, this would point to possible criminal actions that has already killed dozens of men. This is the responsibility of the AG's office,' Marion said.

'I can pass that recommendation along to my superior. For now, our job is to stop the outbreak,' Dr. Peck said.

'Understood. But what if the report contains something helpful in terms of stopping the outbreak?' Charlie asked.

'What else do we know about the report?' Marion asked.

'All we know for sure is Quinn Conner complied it and told Alex to find the report if anything happened to him. This clearly connects his death to the report,' Charlie said.

'Okay. It's confusing but I'm convinced. We need to find

this report. If Marion doesn't mind, she can stay here and work with your team. I need to get back to my office,' Dr. Peck said.

ᗪᑎᑑ

A soft chime called him toward the light - a sound so faint it was easy to ignore. Then there was silence, and he returned to the darkness. Nothing to indicate where the sound had come from. Time passed. And there it was again, the same sound, drawing him toward the glow. More time passed, and finally, the light came within reach. He fought to get closer and shapes began to take form.

Waking from a deep unconsciousness, Gordon Kelly heard soft chimes from the nearby medical devices. He had no idea where he was and struggled to focus on his surroundings. His head hurt in places Gordon didn't know existed. He fought to ignite his visual cortex, willing his eyes to function. But the pain associated with opening his eyes was too steep a price to pay. Gordon fell back into darkness.

Later, Gordon woke again, and the noises around him finally made sense. He was in a hospital. The sounds came from the array of monitors and medical equipment attached to his body. He tried to move his head, but it exploded in pain. Using both hands, he very slowly moved his head from side to side. Gordon could feel bandages on the left side of his face. After several rotations, his neck muscles began to work, and he was able to look around the room with less pain.

There was a young woman he didn't recognize sleeping in a chair next to his bed.

Abruptly, Gordon remembered why he was in the hospital.

He was flooded with embarrassment. He had attempted suicide and somehow failed.

Gordon closed his eyes and rested. If he kept his head still, the pain slowly subsided. He became aware of a more concentrated source of pain in his left jaw and cheek. He tried to speak but was unable to move his jaws.

Gordon realized he must have held the gun at too great an angle and the bullet passed out his left jaw. Laying his head back on the pillow, Gordon sobbed quietly.

After a time, he regained control of his emotions and took a closer look the young woman seated beside him. It was his daughter. Gordon didn't know why had hadn't recognized her before.

He thought about the day she was born. Megan was a first-generation designer-baby. Gordon recalled standing with his wife, waiting for the signal that it was time to enter the delivery room. After what seemed like an age, a nurse came and led them to see their daughter. Entering the room, Jane rushed to the baby. The little girl was being held by their nanny, who had just delivered the little girl. His wife hugged and kissed them both. Jane thanked the nanny repeatedly for bringing Megan into the world.

Their nanny handed the baby to Jane. Tears flowed down his wife's cheeks as she turned and brought the baby to Gordon. Unlike natural born infants, Megan was more bright-eyed than seemed possible. They could tell she was already focusing both eyes on their faces. Within an hour, the little baby girl began cooing and smiled at her parents.

Now she is a beautiful young woman.

Gordon felt overwhelming shame for what he had done. But he also a deep sense of calm, which surprised him. The suicide attempt had cleared his mind. The panic was gone. He could be strong and protect his family. He had a plan and would stick to it. Gordon felt renewed.

His stirrings woke Megan.

'Thank God, you're awake,' Megan said, sleepily. 'I was so worried.'

Gordon nodded.

Moving closer to her father, she spoke quietly in his ear.

'Dad, you need to go slow. The doctors say you're going to be fine. They repaired your jawbone using a small plastic part made on a 3-D printer. The injury isn't too severe, but your jaw is wired shut until tomorrow. It will take a while for it to recalcify. But you'll be out of here in a day or two.'

Gordon nodded his head indicating that he understood. Gordon was grateful she was there.

'Once the wires are removed, you'll be able to start speaking. The jaw will be sore for another week, maybe longer. I've arranged for a portable communication system to be delivered, as soon as you're up to it.'

Gordon nodded in appreciation.

He used his hands to indicate he wanted paper and pencil. Megan left the room to find the two items and when she returned he wrote:

I'm so sorry. Didn't mean to make your life miserable. My handwriting sucks so bring the communication system anytime. I love you.'

'I'm just glad you're all right.' Megan hesitated, 'Dad, we're going to have a conversation about what happened. Okay?"

'I promise, but not now.'

'Fine. But I expect the whole story. Got it?'

'I understand.'

'One more thing. Mom called,' Megan whispered.

Gordon said nothing and stared into space for a time.

'Why?' Gordon wrote.

'She was worried,' she said.

'Not a word in fifteen years. Now she calls,' he wrote.

'I know. She saw you on the news,' Megan said.

'Did you talk to her?' Gordon wrote.

'Not for long. You know how she is on the phone,' she answered.

'Not much better in person, as I remember,' Gordon was still using pencil and paper to communicate.

'I know you hate her. But I miss mom,' Megan said.

'Did she want anything?' Gordon wrote.

'Not that she mentioned,' Megan said.

'Still hiding in Idaho?' Gordon scribbled.

'Guess so. She mentioned heavy snow,' she said.

'I'm glad you talked to her,' Gordon wrote.

'Been way too long,' she said.

Megan left to fetch the communication device. When Megan returned with the machine, Gordon was sound asleep. While he slept, Megan worked to master the device. Just before lunch, when her father woke up, she was a competent communicator using the device.

As his strength allowed, Gordon worked with his daughter to learn how to use the communication technology and was soon interacting with his nurses and Megan. The talking machine used a strong word prediction function, and Gordon was communicating at a high level in short order.

But after an hour working with the device, he was exhausted. Gordon needed to rest.

Reminding her father, she would return the next morning, Megan left for the day.

Before sleeping again, Gordon asked for an app-pad, ostensibly for reading himself to sleep. But as soon as Gordon was alone, he used it to send a message to Hawke. Gordon was pleased to see an immediate response. Hawke would arrive at the hospital as soon as he could get away.

He wanted to do more, but Gordon needed to rest and was soon asleep.

Gordon slept for several more hours and woke to find Hawke Conner standing next to his hospital bed.

'You look terrible,' Hawke offered.

'Thanks. You too,' Gordon countered, using the communication device.

'That's a nice piece of technology,' Hawke observed.

'Yeah, but the thing won't let me swear,' Gordon said.

Hawke smiled.

'Gordon. I'm sorry. I feel responsible,' Hawke said. 'With Quinn's death . . .'

'That's not it,' Gordon said.

'I let you down,' Hawke offered.

'It wasn't anything like that. Hawke. I was fine, but then I got some bad news, and I spiraled downward out of control. You know how I get,' Gordon said as his eyes filled.

'I do know. You should have called,' Hawke said.

'I was too far gone. You got your own problems, with Quinn's death. Listen, Hawke, there's something you need to know. You better sit down,' Gordon advised.

Hawke made no move to sit down.

'What are you talking about?' he asked.

'You heard about the CDC alert?' Gordon asked.

Hawke was quiet as he processed Gordon's words.

'A couple of months ago Quinn ran some simulations that indicated problems with the engineering for the second gens. I asked him to quietly conduct a comprehensive risk assessment. We suspected some type of degradation of the code. He shared his report with me last Saturday. Hawke, the results are devastating. I'm sorry. It's going to kill a lot of men,' Gordon pleaded.

Hawke stood next to the bed staring into space.

'The CDC alert didn't mention us?' he said.

'You know the truth,' Gordon repeated.

'That's not possible,' he said.

'The selfish gene is fighting back,' Gordon replied

'But the original simulations were fine.'

'You know what's wrong,' Gordon said abruptly.

Hawke stared into space, then he asked.

'Was the bitch right after all?'

Gordon didn't respond.

Both men remained silent for several long moments.

'This will be the end of us. Mark my words. We will not survive this. How did Quinn get a hold of her research? We went to a great deal of trouble to wipe her work from the record,' Hawke broke the silence.

'It must have come from her directly. His report completely relies on her findings. She was an ass, but ahead of her time,' Gordon said.

'You would know. You married her,' Hawke said.

'Not my best moment. Listen, we got another problem. Quinn gave a copy of his report to Alex. The feds have detained him, and I assume they have acquired a copy. You know what's going to happen next. They're going to be desperate to find Jane, and have no doubt, she will do her best to ruin us,' Gordon said.

'If Jane can prove we knew about the problem years ago, we'll never recover,' Hawke said.

'That's not going to happen,' Gordon said.

'Are you crazy? We can't contain this. It's time to come clean. I'm calling the FBI,' Hawke said.

'You will do no such thing. Ramsey is taking care of it,' Gordon said, using the communication device.

'What have you done?' Hawke asked.

'Ramsey is on his way to Idaho,' Gordon answered.

'To do what?'

'It's best you don't ask,' Gordon answered.

'Call him back now,' Hawke insisted.

'No.'

'Call him back or I will,' Hawke insisted.

'Hawke, it's too late for that,' Gordon said using the communication device.

DNA

'I'm going to personally make sure you both go to prison,' Alex shouted.

The three remaining members of the Conner family were arguing on the front lawn of the estate's main house. It was late afternoon and Alex had been released by the FBI and immediately taken by FBI vehicle to his parent's house. The FBI had warned Alex not to leave Westwood, and that he would be facing a variety of charges, including obstruction of justice.

'The FBI told me what happened to Quinn. Why am I not surprised? This family was never normal. It's a fucking marketing tool. I despise you both,' Alex yelled again.

'You don't mean that.'

'I do. I'm done with both of you,' Alex cried.

'Alex, I'm sorry; we're sorry. We're not perfect,' Abby Conner pleaded.

'No risk of that,' Alex barked.

'We screwed up, big time. We didn't know what we were doing. None of the parents did. Raising genetic-enhanced children was uncharted territory,' Abby admitted.

'How is that the point? You broke the law. You're responsible for Quinn's death. Hundreds more are going to die. You said nothing! You and Gordon. You said nothing! What were you thinking?' Alex bellowed, piling it on.

His parents stood speechless, looking at their son.

'We didn't know. The data was inconclusive,' Hawke finally offered.

'You're lying. You all knew. Twenty years ago. I read the news reports. Dr. Jane Neil, she told the world. You buried her. You call yourself a fucking scientist.'

'It wasn't like that. You weren't there. She lied about her data and we couldn't be sure. Her results couldn't be duplicated,' Hawke implored.

'Really. More lies. The truth is you're both greedy bastards,' Alex yelled.

'The truth is, we wanted to do some good, and that takes a lot of money. Your father has saved countless lives,' Abby said.

'Congratulations. I hope that's enough. Quinn died trying to fix your fuck-up. You started an epidemic. You're fucking monsters,' Alex spit out the last words.

'Quinn was going to die no matter what,' Hawke said.

'Thanks. Now I feel better. Well done, father. Who's next to die?' Alex asked.

'I don't know,' Hawke admitted.

'You don't know. Fine. I'll see you in hell, or at least in fucking prison,' Alex shouted.

Alex left the yard and walked to his car, and for the second time, drove away in anger. But this time, he had no intention of ever returning.

12

SATURDAY, DECEMBER 24TH, 2050

If a fool throws a stone in the sea, a hundred wise men cannot pull it back.

Returning to his office, Charlie sat at his desk and rested his arms on the flat surface. He lowered his head onto on his arms as his usual positive attitude was replaced with deepening discouragement. Gone was the initial excitement of the day. He could no longer wrap his head around the situation. Charlie felt lost and overwhelmed. His confidence was ebbing like a spring tide. He could smell failure - a scent he got use to during his last big case. Charlie struggled to trust his once reliable instincts.

Realizing he'd briefly nodded off Charlie quickly woke when he heard someone walking down the hall toward his office. He was surprised to see Hawke Conner come in the door. Hawke's demeanor hadn't improved, and if anything, Charlie thought he looked more stressed. Charlie peered closely at the man and realized it wasn't stress; instead, he was witnessing a high level of agitation. Hawke's hands were shaking, his back was slumped, and he looked pale.

'Mr. Conner. Please come in and sit down. Are you okay?'

'Fine. Can we talk?'

'Must be important for you to come all this way,' Charlie noted.

Hawke told a deep breath before speaking.

'Yes, thank you Agent Edmo. If you don't mind, I'll stand. How's the investigation going? Agent Lee informs me Quinn's death may be related to the outbreak in the news,' Hawke struggled to get the words out.

'A possibility. Dr. Marion Harper from the CDC has joined our team and believes your son may be among the first victims of the outbreak,' Charlie said.

'I see. We appreciate Agent Lee's efforts to keep us informed. In a strange way, this information is a great relief to Abby and me.'

Sensing the man was struggling to summon the nerve to speak, Charlie remained silent. Many moments passed before Hawke finally spoke.

'Mr. Edmo, I met with Gordon Kelly yesterday morning. As you can image, he is not well. I'm here to share some important information he provided. Gordon suggested the FBI may have acquired a certain report written by my son. By now, you understand the potential magnitude of the outbreak,' Hawke said.

'Let me stop you there. Alex told us a report does exists. We have confirmed this through several other sources, and now, by you. But our search for the report is ongoing. I can assure you we don't have the report. If you or Mr. Kelly know the location of the document, failure to share that information with the FBI is likely a federal crime,' Charlie said.

'Gordon went to great lengths to destroy the report. There are no copies,' Hawke said.

'That may also be a crime. Did you or Gordon Kelly read the report?' Charlie asked.

'I have not viewed the document. But I assume Gordon did,' Hawke answered.

'Why do you think that?' Charlie asked.

'He was very agitated when he discussed Quinn's report.'

'Unfortunately, I cannot question him until the doctors grant permission,' Charlie complained.

'Did he tell you what's in the report?' he added.

'No. Only that it involved an epidemic,' Hawke said.

'Does the report contain additional information related to the outbreak?' Charlie pressed.

'I assume that it does, but I don't know,' Hawke said.

'Are you sure there are no copies of the report?' Charlie asked.

'According to Gordon, there are no copies,' Hawke said.

'Can you convince Gordon Kelly to meet with us . . . preferably today?' Charlie asked.

'That's up to him. He's still very weak and can't speak. Please understand, Gordon doesn't know I'm here. He did not advise me to share this information with the FBI, and I doubt he would approve. I'm here because my son is dead, and I've discovered that I may have had a role in his death. I'm here in a feeble attempt to make amends,' Hawke said as his eyes filled.

'I get that. I have a daughter.' Charlie paused, 'I'm sorry, but I need to ask you some more questions.'

'Go ahead,' Hawke said, and took a deep breath.

'A man using a false name contacted your son Alex. He knew about the report and threatened to kill your son. Do you know who this man is?' Charlie asked.

Hawke was quiet for more than a few moments.

'I'm not sure, but he might be Ramsey Lewis. He's an investigator who works for Genlabs,' Hawke said, looking down.

Charlie sat quiet for a few moments.

'Do you know where to find Mr. Lewis?' Charlie asked.

Hawke took out a pen and wrote down an address.

'Gordon told me that Ramsey Lewis will be at this address until tomorrow morning. After that he will be gone,' Hawke said.

'To where?'

'I don't know,' Hawke lied again. 'Agent Edmo, there's something you need to know. This man is well-armed and possesses a number of genetic enhancements that make him extremely dangerous.'

'How do you know that?'

'Again, the information came from Gordon.'

Charlie quickly typed the address into his computer. After looking at the screen for a few seconds, he called Hunter and quickly brought him up to speed. He requested a SWAT team be assembled immediately. Charlie told his boss to have the team prepared for mountain conditions. He also requested a drone be deployed to the airspace above Ramsey Lewis's location and a helicopter be prepared for takeoff. He sent notes to Jack and Brad.

'Thank you, Mr. Conner. I know this was difficult for you. I'm sorry, but I've got to go,' Charlie said, and left the man standing in his office.

The FBI's Drone Control Center's pilot already had a bird in the air by the time Charlie walked into the room. He could see the drone's video feed on the main screen, which covered the entire south wall of the control center. The drone was headed east toward Ramsey Lewis's location. Charlie knew it wouldn't take long for the bird to reach the cabin which was located in western slopes of the Cascade Mountains, about sixty miles east of Seattle. The drone was flying just below the cloud ceiling, cruising at twenty-thousand feet. At that altitude, it's tiny, twenty-seven-foot length, was invisible to anyone on the ground.

The room was dark and almost entirely lit by the main screen and two rows of computer terminals. The drone's pilot sat in the middle seat of the first row. She operated the flight control stick and on-screen controls. The remaining workstations were occupied by various FBI specialists working to support the mission.

Charlie stood behind the pilot. He urged her to get into position, explaining he needed as much time as possible to recon the area. After a few moments, the drone pilot indicated she was on target. The computer automatically zoomed the aircraft's powerful lenses onto the site. A two-story, log cabin came into view. There were several small outbuildings near the cabin. It was a heavily forested, remote area. Charlie could sense the location was chosen because of its remoteness. It was a location that could be easily defended, while offering plentiful escape routes.

The property and cabin were adjacent to the Mt. Baker-Snoqualmie National Forest boundary. The cabin sat at an elevation of two thousand feet, and a heavy blanket of snow covered the area. The driveway and the cabin's large parking area looked recently plowed. Charlie noted the parking lot was empty, but there were lights visible in the windows of the cabin.

Is his vehicle parked in one of the outbuildings?

The parking area adjoined a long driveway which led west to a closed gate. The gate separated the driveway from the solitary road into the area.

To the north and east of the cabin, the drone's camera displayed impassible rock cliffs. These granite faces climbed toward the higher peaks of the Cascade mountains. To the south and west, the forest sloped toward lower elevations. There were large areas of open ground between the stands of trees. These meadows were covered in snow and offered an easy escape for anyone on a snowmobile. Worse yet, the thick forest offered countless places for a man on skis or snowshoes to hide.

This is not going to be easy.

Jack and Brad arrived with the SWAT commander, Joey Manning.

Charlie quickly shared his observations with the three agents. They all moved to another computer screen displaying an aerial photograph of the area.

'We'll need six snowmobiles. We can place them here, here, and here in groups of two. They can find cover in the forest,' Joey pointed to three areas on the screen.

'That will cut off the most likely escape routes,' Charlie said.

'Right. We should assume he has a snowmobile,' Joey said.

'I agree. How should we approach the cabin?' Charlie asked.

'Fast and hard. You said the suspect is genetically-enhanced, right?' Joey asked.

'Yes.'

'Credible source?' Joey asked.

'Yes, very reliable.'

'Then we need to exercise extreme caution. None of my

men are enhanced. Director won't allow it for SWAT members. I suggest we send the armored personnel carrier through the gate and storm the house. Surprise and overwhelming numbers are our best options,' Joey said.

'What about dropping your team by copter?' Charlie asked.

'Too much snow. We'd have to hover over the parking lot right by the cabin. No, we cut off his escape routes using the drone and snowmobiles, and then storm the house. The copter can hover out of sight. When the assault begins, Hunter can bring in the copter and reinforcements if they're needed,' Joey said.

'It's important he be captured alive,' Charlie said.

'We'll do our best, but the safety of my men comes first.'

'Got it. But keep in mind, a lot of lives might be saved if we can talk to this guy.

'Understood. We'll do our best.'

'Okay then, sounds like a plan,' Charlie said.

The convoy of trucks and SUV's transporting the FBI team and their equipment left the downtown Seattle building at four p.m. It was a wintery day, with heavy clouds and a swirling wind. It was already getting dark, except for a faint glow in the west from an unseen sun. Charlie knew it would be completely dark by the time they reached their destination. The weather forecast called for snow and strong winds at the higher elevations.

Seven vehicles left downtown Seattle. Three trucks pulled trailers, each loaded with two snowmobiles. A fourth truck carried their protective and cold weather gear, as well as the heavy weapons. The remaining vehicles carried Charlie and his team, as well as the other members of the SWAT. Trailing the convoy was a military-style armored personnel carrier sitting atop a tractor-trailer.

The convoy drove until they reached the small hamlet of Carnation. The town was located near an agriculture area near the foothills of the Cascade Mountains. Charlie knew the Tolt and Snoqualmie Rivers met near the city center, and numerous small lakes were hidden in the forest. In past decades, the charming town had been a favorite destination for day trippers from Seattle.

In the parking lot of city hall, the convoy stopped, and Charlie exited his vehicle to meet with local law enforcement officials. The county sheriff's office had agreed to secure all the roads leading into the area once the assault began. After discussing tactics and double checking that their communication systems were in order, Charlie thanked the local sheriff, and the FBI team left Carnation driving east. If there was a moon that night, it had yet to show its face. A strong wind filled the air with drifting snow, and it was becoming much harder to find open pavement as the convoy gained elevation.

The local Sheriff had identified a large roadside pullout where they could unload the snowmobiles and personnel carrier. When the convoy arrived at the pull-out, they parked and quickly offloaded their equipment. Charlie watched as the snowmobilers put on their cold weather gear, protective vests and strapped on their weapons. Dawning their helmets last, the men drove their snowmobiles off into the snowy darkness.

After donning their combat gear and going through their pre-assault checklist, the remaining ten members of the team loaded into the personnel carrier. Charlie, Jack, and Brad put on their protective gear, checked their weapons, and loaded into one of the SUVs. They planned to follow a short distance behind the armored vehicle. They left the remaining vehicles at the pullout.

Jack drove the SUV while Charlie sat in the passenger seat

and maintained communications with headquarters and the SWAT team. Brad sat in the back seat. After driving north for several miles, the two vehicles turned right onto the dead-end road leading to the suspect's driveway. They were headed east toward the Cascade Mountains. The road narrowed, and as predicted, a much heavier snow with flakes as big as silver dollars began to fall. Their headlights were unable to penetrate the whiteout, and the two vehicles slowed to a crawl.

The silence was suddenly broken by a crackling sound from Charlie's headphone. The drone and helicopter had been recalled to Seattle due to heavy snow.

'Boss, do we continue? No eyes and no backup. Maybe we should turn around?' Brad suggested.

'This is our one chance to get this guy. We have overwhelming superiority. It's still a go,' Charlie answered. He pushed the send button on the comm device.

'Listen up, due to weather the drone and copter were forced to bail. But the mission is still a go. Repeat, we are still a go. Are the snowmobiles ready?'

Charlie counted the responses until he accounted for all the teams.

He spoke to the driver of the armored personnel carrier.

'Slow down and be ready. The gate should be closed,' Charlie spoke.

Feeling his adrenaline starting to pump, Charlie noticed Jack was struggling to maintain his distance from the armored vehicle.

'Hard to keep your foot off the pedal when the adrenaline's pumping,' Charlie mentioned.

'Heart's pounding. This was easier when we were young,' Jack responded.

'Nah. Were smarter now.'

'No. Only less stupid. There's a big difference.'

'That was always true,' Charlie suggested.

'Somehow it's very different now. Loving someone is great and all, but a huge burden too. I'm sure you've noticed,' Jack finished.

'Worried about your wife?' Charlie asked.

'Can't stop thinking about it, and it's getting to me,' Jack confessed.

'That's why we need to catch this bastard, tonight. We can end this now, and you can go home,' Charlie offered.

'Fine, but not much Christmas joy this year,' Jack whispered.

The tall snowbanks on either side of the road made Charlie feel like they were traveling through a tunnel. After following a curved to the right, Charlie caught sight of the gate. It was still a hundred feet away. The driver of the personnel carrier saw it too and quickly sped up.

As the carrier's headlights found the gate, Charlie's heart stopped. The gate was built of heavy steel, reinforced by two stout concrete posts. There was a removable steel post in the middle of the gate. He shouted into the microphone, urging the driver of the armored vehicle to go faster.

In response, the carrier jumped forward and headed straight for the closed gate.

Driving about four car lengths behind the personnel carrier, Charlie watched in horror from his SUV as the carrier slammed into the gate.

The twenty-seven-thousand-pound armored vehicle stopped dead in its tracks.

The driver slammed into reverse, and the personnel carriers bolted backward, heading straight for their SUV. Jack slammed on his brakes and started to slide on the ice. But the other driver reversed direction and again plunged forward toward another encounter with the gate. Jack eased up on the brake and the SUV moved forward.

This time the gate gave way and the armored carrier shot onto the driveway, crushing the steel gate as it went. Jack rushed to follow, bouncing hard over the fallen gate. He caught up with the huge vehicle as the driveway narrowed. Charlie watched as the personnel carrier whipped branches and occasionally smashed into the tall snowbanks overhanging either side of the road.

Snow was flying everywhere as the personnel carrier burst into the parking area in front of the cabin. The parking area was a large enough for a dozen cars. It was a sheet of ice covered with a thin layer of snow. There was no sign the cabin was occupied. The building was dark and there were still no parked vehicles.

The driver of the personnel carrier slammed on his brakes. It slid briefly on the ice, and came to an abrupt stop. Jack halted the SUV just behind it, engine running and headlights on. A panel of lights mounted on the top of the carrier came on, and the area was flooded with light.

The large rear hatch of the armored carrier dropped to the ground and Charlie saw the SWAT team pile out of the opening.

At the same moment, Charlie saw the upstairs window of the cabin shatter, and two canisters, bellowing smoke, flew toward the men. A few seconds later, two more canisters flew from the window, then two more.

Within seconds, the entire area was filled with a thick smoke. The air was cold and heavy with moister, and the smoke settled close to the ground. The bright flood lights striking the smoke brought visibility to near zero.

Struggling the see anything through the smoke, Charlie

buckled on his helmet, and before Jack or Brad could stop him, bolted out the door of the SUV.

Charlie raced across the parking area toward the cabin.

Hearing the high-pitched whine of a snowmobile, Charlie looked to his left and saw a single beam of light piercing the smoke. A snow machine emerged from behind the cabin, turned to the left and headed directly toward him.

The driver was wearing a helmet and looking to his left toward the SWAT team and failed to notice Charlie's rapid approach from the right.

Charlie shouted a warning to the SWAT team as he moved to intercept the snowmobile.

The driver heard Charlie's cry and swerved sharply to his left, moving toward the nearby snowbank.

But it was too late.

At full sprint, Charlie leaped onto the rider's back, just before the sled plowed into the snowbank separating the plowed area from the deeper snow.

The snowmobile's engine roared as the machine plowed through and over the wall of snow. The snow machine had more than enough speed to rise out of the deep snow, and still carrying the two men, accelerated toward the dark forest.

Charlie's left knee slammed onto the rear seat of the snowmobile. He managed to get his left arm around the man's neck as his right arm flailed wildly searching for a handhold. His other leg was dragging behind him, leaving a trail in the snow.

His right hand found the handhold just as the driver turned to avoid a tree. Charlie was far from being balanced and came close to flying off the machine.

The driver sensed his chance and tried to force Charlie off the sled by elbowing him in the ribs. Charlie responded by letting go of the man's neck while straddling the rear seat of the fast-moving snow machine.

The driver reached around and drove his right elbow toward Charlie's face.

Charlie blocked the blow and gripped the snow machine tightly with his long legs. He grabbed the man's helmet with both hands and yanked hard back and forth until the rider lost his grip.

Both men flew off the machine and landed in the deep snow.

The snowmobile kept racing for another twenty feet before stopping in the deep powder, its engine stalled. The helmeted man landed at the edge of a deep tree-well, and unable to stop his slide, disappeared down the deep hole under the tree. Charlie landed on his side nearby. He struggled to regain his footing in waist-deep powder. The rider scrambled out of the tree well and thrashed toward the sled. Charlie leaped over the snow toward the man and weakly grabbed his arm.

The man turned and punched Charlie in the face. It was a hard blow, and Charlie fell back in the snow, nearly unconscious. It took a few seconds for Charlie to clear his head. By the time he was able to refocus on his surroundings, Charlie could only sit and watch helplessly as the rider waded through the snow to the snowmobile, re-started the machine, and raced away.

Charlie called for help, but the snowmobile had taken him far from the parking lot. He could see several members of the SWAT teams struggling in the deep powder, desperately trying to reach him. But they were minutes away.

Then without warning, the cabin exploded in a huge fireball. Charlie threw his hands to his ears, but the sounds were deafening. He felt the compression from the explosion pass over him. Through the trees, Charlie could see the flames climb a hundred feet into the air. The surrounding forest was flooded with an orange light.

Pieces of the burning debris started crashing down through the branches of the surrounding trees. Charlie heard several pieces land near him, and finally, a large piece of burning wood landed at Charlie's feet. He was too dazed to move.

In the distance, Charlie could still hear the high-pitched sound of the snowmobile over the sound of the burning cabin.

I hope our guys grab the bastard.

After a few minutes, the fireball dissipated and was replaced by a burning mass of wood and stone. The fire continued to light the surrounding area. Sitting in the snow stunned, Charlie struggled to recover. His hearing was hampered by a loud ringing, and his nose was bleeding from being punched.

While he waited for help, Charlie held his frozen hands to the piece of burning debris at his feet. After a few minutes, several members of the SWAT team arrived. After receiving a quick triage, Charlie followed their trail through the deep snow until he reached the parking lot. He glanced toward the cabin. The explosion had cleared the area of smoke, and he could see several members of the SWAT team being treated for injuries. Others were searching the area surrounding the burning pile of logs.

An hour later, over fifty law enforcement and medical personnel were at the site of the explosion. Charlie's hearing had improved, and he'd been cleared by an EMT. He was glad to learn that all the members of the SWAT team had escaped serious injury, thanks to their protective gear, and the fact that most of the men were moving away from the cabin at the time of the explosion.

Ramsey Lewis escaped without a trace. The suspect had

taken a path through the forest that bypassed the waiting FBI agents. The tracks of his snowmobile were followed for eight miles. They ended on a county road outside the perimeter established by the county sheriff. No snowmobile was found at the work road, and it was assumed he had a vehicle waiting. Ramsey had simply loaded his snowmobile onto his pickup and driven away.

Charlie, Jack and Brad sat in their SUV waiting for Hunter to arrive. The motor was running to keep them warm, and the three agents sat without speaking. Charlie watched as a member of the forensic team walked toward their SUV. Charlie noticed the woman was carrying a small plastic evidence bag. She was wiping it dry with a cloth rag.

The three men got out of the SUV and greeted the woman.

'Agent Edmo. I'm Susan House. One of the men found this in a tree well, near where you fought with the suspect,' Susan said, and handed Charlie the clear plastic envelope to him.

It contained a small data cube.

Two hours later Charlie and the team were back at his office watching Agent Seaman work to recover the files on what was presumed to be Ramsey Lewis's data cube. The process made Charlie nervous, mostly because he was clueless about what the IT specialist was doing, and he could only imagine disaster.

He watched as Agent Seaman carefully cleaned and dried the data cube and placed it in a data reader. Charlie was pleased as a long list of files started to appear on the monitor.

Christmas morning arrived as the files finished compiling.

Agent Seaman stood from his chair and stretched his arms upward.

'There was minor damage to the case, but the cube is fine. I've finished loading every file, but there are more than two thousand. Unless you want to look at every file, I need some search parameters,' he said.

'We'll need to look at every file, but for now, just start with files tagged by Quinn Conner and Gordon Kelly. See if you get a hit,' Jack suggested.

Agent Seaman finished stretching and sat down.

'Okay, here it goes,' the young agent said.

Charlie watched as Agent Seaman typed in the two names and click start. The search took seconds.

'Nothing.'

'Search by date. Try December 17th, 2050,' Charlie suggested.

Agent Seaman did as Charlie suggested.

'Charlie again watched as he entered the word into the search engine. The search took two seconds.

'Here we go,' Agent Seaman said.

Charlie watched in disbelief as the title page of a document flashed onto the screen. The Genlabs' logo was clearly visible, and the word, *CLASSIFIED*, was watermarked in big red letters.

The report's title was centered on the page.

Risk Factors Associated with the Genetic Engineering
of Second-Generation Designer Baby Boys
Quinn Conner, December 17th, 2050

Santa Claus was bringing happiness and joy to children around the world when Charlie finished reading Quinn's report. He glanced up to see Marion grimacing. She was just finishing her reading of the report. He could see she was fighting back tears. The epidemic described in the report was frightening. Charlie's heart filled with pain for the victims who had died, and for the fatalities to come. He realized Marion dealt with the real possibility of mass death every day. He marveled at her courage and was glad she had joined his team.

Both Charlie and Marion were lost in thought for several minutes as they assimilated the information contained in the report. They were seated in Charlie's office.

Finally, he broke the silence.

'I'm at a loss.'

'Me too. This is unprecedented,' Marion said.

'Who's Jane Neil?' Charlie asked, referring to a scientist mentioned in the report.

'She's the geneticist who got famous predicting the DNA molecule would ultimately figure out a way to reject engineered genes - the so-called Selfish Gene theory. She predicted exactly what we're seeing. Her research crossed my mind before. But she ended up being discredited for falsifying data. She was married to Gordon Kelly, by the way. This was over twenty years ago,' Marion said.

'Really. What happened to her?' Charlie asked.

'She was convicted of falsifying data. She claimed it was a setup, but ended up in prison for several years. Gordon divorced her while she was incarcerated, in what turned out to be a huge public spectacle. After being released, she disappeared,' Marion said.

'So, she predicted this epidemic decades ago.'

'Right, but her theories were discredited. They were unable to duplicate her results across several studies.'

'Was she setup?' Charlie asked.

'It was never proven. Billions were at stake, so it's not hard to imagine something dirty was going on,' Marion said.

'Quinn seemed to think Dr. Neil was onto something,' Charlie said.

'I picked that up. He relies on her methodologies to a large extent.'

'Was Dr. Neil, right?'

'Maybe. As I remember, she predicted there would be an epidemic among one or more generations of designer-babies, and that it would manifest in early adulthood. She believed human DNA possesses an almost mystical power to survive. She thought DNA would adapt and learn how to reject the engineered genetic material. She suggested that returning the DNA molecule to its original state, replacing every single engineered gene, was the only fix. She called it a Reset Button. This made her very popular in the national press, before her downfall. After that, she was treated shamefully,' Marion said.

'Is she still alive?' Charlie asked.

'I don't know.'

'We better find out,' he said.

'I agree. There were rumors she moved to Idaho.'

'We'll start there.'

'Right. So, what else?' Marion asked.

'Let's get some folks together. We need a new plan,' Charlie suggested.

Thirty minutes later Charlie sat in the FBI's small video conference room with Marion and Special Agent Hunter. Lois Peck was on the flatscreen, along with the director of the CDC in Atlanta. It was early Christmas morning, and the two women were both at home and dressed in their night robes.

After introductions, Dr. Peck opened the meeting.

'Are we sure this document is the one prepared by Quinn Conner?' she asked.

'Yes, as sure as we can be,' Hunter said.

'Can you tell us how the report was recovered?' Dr. Peck asked.

'While attempting his escape, the man who we assume is Ramsey Lewis was knocked off his snowmobile and dropped the datacube containing the report,' Hunter said.

'Pretty convenient. Are you sure of the man's identity? I was told you never saw his face?' the CDC director asked.

'He was wearing a helmet, so we weren't able to positively identify him. But based on the information provided by Hawke Conner, and the files found on the datacube, we're nearly certain it belonged to Ramsey Lewis. There are hundreds of files. Quinn's report was attached to a message sent to Mr. Lewis's personal app-pad account,' Charlie added.

'Do you know where it was sent from?' Dr. Peck asked.

'It originated from an IP address inside Genlabs,' Charlie said.

'You're sure of this?' Dr. Peck asked.

'We're working to confirm. We've obtained a warrant, and our technicians are in route to Genlabs,' Charlie added.

'But it sounds like the document in front of us is Mr. Conner's report,' the CDC director said.

'As I said, we're as certain as we can be. We just aren't sure how Ramsey Lewis acquired it,' Charlie said.

'That isn't important. It's the content of the report that's critical to our efforts,' Dr. Peck added.

'Before we get to that, there's one more thing. Based on evidence found near Mr. Lewis's cabin, it's a good bet he was responsible for the recent bombing of the CDC building,' Charlie said.

'How do you know this?' Marion asked.

'Explosive traces found near the cabin matched those recovered in the CDC bombing. Quinn Conner's body was likely the target of the attack,' Hunter added.

'That's important information and adds weight to your

conclusions about the datacube. So, I suggest we move on. Marion, can you summarize the report for us?' Dr. Peck asked.

Marion took a quick breath, ran her fingers through her long hair and began speaking.

'Mr. Conner's report confirms much of what we already know about the outbreak. First, the outbreak is confined to second gen designer babies and impacts only males, at least for now. At the molecular level, the actual driver of the disease is not understood, though it appears the original DNA in each cell type is attacking the engineered genetic material like it is an invading virus.' Marion stopped for questions.

'The selfish gene hypothesis,' Dr. Peck observed.

'Right. But Mr. Conner offers two new conclusions. First, he indicates that not all genetically engineered men will get sick, and only a portion of those who do contract the condition will die. Mr. Conner predicts between five and ten percent of designer-babies, individuals who are now young men, will die. There are about three hundred thousand of these individuals living worldwide. Based on this figure, between fifteen and thirty thousand young men may die.' Marion paused.

'My god, thirty thousand deaths,' the CDC director lamented.

'And this figure assumes the outbreak will not migrate to other generations of designer babies,' Marion whispered.

There was silence for a few moments as everyone shifting nervously in their seats and exchanged glances.

'Does he provide any kind of timeframe for the outbreak?' Dr. Peck asked.

'He does not. Nor does he give any indication of what segment of the population will be most impacted,' Marion said.

There were no more questions, so Marion continued.

'Second, Mr. Conner agreed with Dr. Neil's previously

reported contention that the only way to stop the DNA from destroying itself, is to restore the molecule to its original state - literally, to remove all the engineered genes from the DNA, and replace them with exact copies of the cell's original genetic code. It may be possible to substitute benign material in some parts of the DNA, which could potentially speed up the process.'

'Is that possible?' Hunter asked hopefully.

'Not really. The original DNA sequences for every genetically modified individual are maintained by Genlabs. But honestly, there hasn't been a lot of interest in the research community for developing a way to reset the genetic code to its original state,' Marion answered.

'So, these men are going to die, and we're helpless to stop it?' Charlie asked.

'We're not out of options yet. Quinn Conner mentioned Dr. Neil had developed some innovative approaches for treating the disease. Unfortunately, he was unable to locate most of Dr. Neil's original research. When she was convicted of falsifying data, her work was purged from the research base. But Quinn Conner was convinced she knows how to treat the disease,' Marion said.

'When did Genlabs first know there might be an epidemic?' Dr. Peck asked.

'Dr. Neil's research was widely known over two decades ago. But her work was discredited. GSI and Genlabs were in the middle of the whole scandal. After all, Dr. Neil was married to, and worked closely with, Gordon Kelly. If Mr. Kelly acted to discredit her when he knew her research was valid, he has blood on his hands,' Marion said.

'Is there probable cause to support opening an investigation into GSI and Genlabs?' Hunter asked.

'Yes, in my opinion, but your attorneys will need to read the report,' Marion stated.

'Understood. My legal team will review the materials and decide what action is appropriate,' Hunter announced.

'That will be interesting. Does anyone know if Dr. Neil is still alive?' Dr. Peck asked.

'My agents are looking for her now,' Hunter added. 'We've located a post office box in her name in Stanley, Idaho. We've got a call in to the postmaster, but it's the holidays, so no luck reaching her. There is no death certificate in her name on record, so that's an indication she's still alive. Though she could have died while living abroad.'

'Hold on. We need to go back. I need more assurances we're on the right track. Can you describe Mr. Conner's methodology? How did he reach these conclusions?' Dr. Peck asked.

'Mr. Conner replicated Dr. Neil's research design to a large extent, but he died before finishing the work. The report describes his preliminary conclusions. But his research is meticulous, and he used newer technology and had ten times the resources at his disposal than Dr. Neil,' Marion said.

'You are confident these results will hold up?' Dr. Peck asked.

'Confident as I can be without replicating Mr. Conner's research myself,' Marion responded.

'Okay. Anything else?' Dr. Peck asked.

'One more big revelation. Quinn Conner sequenced his own DNA and discovered that he had the condition. He knew he was going to die and was frantically searching for an effective treatment. I believe the man is a hero,' Marion added.

'Why was he able to duplicate Dr. Neil's work when nobody else could?' the CDC director asked.

'The previous studies were poorly designed . . . perhaps intentionally,' Marion said.

'Okay. I'm convinced. So, what's our next step?' Dr. Peck asked.

'Our job is to find a way to repair the engineering flaws, to find a reset button,' Marion said.

'We need a plan,' Dr. Peck said.

'First, we need to find Dr. Jane Neil. With Quinn dead, she just became a very important person,' the CDC director said.

'The FBI will find her if she's still alive, but she's a long shot,' Hunter said.

'I agree. That's why we need a comprehensive plan. But I'm too exhausted to think,' Dr. Peck repeated.

'You all need to get some rest. Here's a plan. Go home and get some sleep. If you can, spend a few hours Christmas morning with your families. I'll get preparations underway,' Hunter said.

'Preparations for what?' Charlie asked.

'We can't wait for this Dr. Neil to just show up. You need to get to Idaho with your team and find her. I'll arrange flights to Idaho for late tomorrow morning,' Hunter said.

'I should go, assuming it's okay,' Marion said looking at Lois.

'That's fine. I think it's a good idea. Didn't you meet Dr. Neil once?' Lois asked.

'When I was a grad student she lectured at Harvard, and I met her after the presentation,' Marion said.

'In that case, it will be good to have you along,' Charlie said.

'That's settled. The four of you can fly to Idaho. Find Dr. Neil and question her. If necessary, bring her back to Seattle. You can coordinate with our Boise office. They can provide logistics support,' Hunter said.

'Meanwhile, the CDC will mobilize the national network. We can set up an emergency response team and begin analyzing Quinn Conner's research for clues to stopping the epidemic. We need to hit this outbreak with everything we have. We can assume other parts of the country will be impacted soon,' the CDC director said.

Special Agent Hunter thanked her and asked for questions. Hearing none, he said,

'We can speak in the morning. For now, enjoy what's left of Christmas.'

He smiled, no doubt visualizing spending the next holiday season in New York.

Five minutes later, when he was alone in his office, FBI Agent Ross Hunter contacted Gordon Kelly.

Sitting in his hospital bed, Gordon was surprised to see Hunter's name on his secure app-phone.

'Special Agent Hunter. I wasn't expecting to hear from you,' Gordon said, using his communication device.

'It's important. Your man lost a datacube. It contained Quinn's report,' Hunter said.

Gordon was quiet as he considered this new development.

'I'd assumed you already got the report from Alex Conner,' Gordon typed.

'No. He never had a copy. The datacube was recovered when we raided Ramsey's home,' Hunter said.

How did Ramsey get the report?

'Okay, so the report will soon be made public. Any suggestions?' Gordon typed.

'I was hoping you had some ideas,' Hunter said.

'Tell you what, just stop worrying about the report,' Gordon typed.

'Fine. But what about this Dr. Jane Neil. She was mentioned in the report several times. Who is she, and why is she important?' Hunter asked.

'She's my ex-wife and she's not important. Crazy as a loon. Contacting her will be a waste of your time. Trust me,' Gordon typed.

'I've already ordered a team to Idaho in the morning to look for her,' Hunter confessed.

'Stop them. Now. Under no circumstance should you contact that woman,' Gordon typed urgently into the communication device.

13

SATURDAY, DECEMBER 24TH, 2050

We're always the last one to know anything about ourselves.

author

It wasn't until Ramsey reached his truck and finished loading the snowmobile, that he noticed the data cube was gone. By then it was too late. The data cube contained his only copy of Quinn Conner's report.

I've lost my leverage.

But then he remembered the FBI had likely already acquired a copy of the report from Alex Conner. Ramsey realized he now had little leverage with the FBI in any case.

I just can't get caught.

Gordon was another story. Ramsey wished the FBI had never acquired the report, robbing him of the protection it provided against his boss. The man was no longer stable and wasn't making rational decisions. But without the leverage provided by Quinn's report, Ramsey would have no choice but to follow Gordon's orders.

As he merged onto Interstate Highway 90 and began driving east, Ramsey grappled with what just happened. How did the FBI find him? Who was the man that knocked him off the snowmobile? Ramsey assumed he was an FBI agent. He was big, fast, and strong. Ramsey felt lucky to have escaped and hoped to never encounter him again.

Having come so close, this man will now hunt me with a renewed vigor.

I need to be very careful.

After driving through the night, Ramsey reached Boise. He immediately went to the nearest sporting goods store and purchased as assortment of outdoor winter gear. Next, he visited a camera store and purchased several cameras and related accessories.

After loading all his gear, Ramsey drove thru the morning and early afternoon until he reached the small mountain community of Stanley, Idaho. After eating a late lunch, he went straight to the tiny airstrip overlooking the village where a small plane and pilot waited for him. Less than thirty minutes later Ramsey touched down on the Bernard landing strip near the Flying B Ranch. The Flying B Ranch was located on the Middle Fork of the Salmon River, in the center of the largest roadless wilderness area in the lower forty-eight states.

No one was there to meet him when they landed. The pilot unloaded his luggage and the photographic equipment he had purchased in Boise. Ramsey was posing as a professional wildlife photographer.

'He's on his way. Pat's always moving, but he's never on time. I'll wait to hear from you about the return flight. After tomorrow night, the weather will shut us down for a day or so,' the pilot said.

'I'll give you a holler the day before I want to leave. I don't have a set time frame. Listen, do me a favor, don't mention this flight to anyone. My competitors might be watching,' Ramsey said.

'Mum's the word. Just keep an eye on the weather report. I need a good weather window to fly.'

Ramsey watched as the small Cessna took off and quickly disappeared in the narrow canyon. He could hear the roar of its engine echoing off the canyon walls long after the plane was lost from view. The light was fading fast, and the perfectly still air carried a strong warning of the cold night to come. Once the sound of the plane dissipated, there was total silence - an experience that always made Ramsey extremely uncomfortable. The snow on the ground seem to swallow every sound. It was the type of quiet that only happens in winter, when the birds have migrated south and all the animals, both big and small, were either hibernating or have moved to lower elevations.

Finally, a man appeared at the far end on the runway. As he neared, Ramsey saw an aging cowboy wearing a heavy oilskin duster and ratty cowboy hat. The outfit made him look bigger than he really was, and Ramsey guessed he weight less that one hundred seventy-five pounds. Ramsey could see a couple of dogs nosing around the ground in front of him.

Ramsey reminded himself he had registered under a false name.

'You must be Ray. I'm Pat Harren. Welcome to the Flying B Ranch. Let's get to the bunkhouse, daylight's nearly gone,' Pat said, when he arrived.

The short hike took the two men downstream to the north. The trail crossed the remaining flat ground by the airstrip before turning into a narrow path that traversed a steep rocky face. As they climbed higher above the river, Ramsey could see snow a few hundred feet above him, and ice covered the trail in places.

Leaving the steep terrain, the trail dropped quickly until the two men met the river again. A small lodge and several cabins came into view. Pat led Ramsey to his cabin and helped him get comfortable before leaving to feed the horses and prepare dinner.

An hour later Ramsey walked to the main lodge to eat.

'How 'bout a beer,' Pat asked, after Ramsey entered the building.

'Sure. Thanks. Beautiful place here. Amazing. I can hardly wait for daylight,' Ramsey said.

'You're a photographer?' Pat asked.

'Yeah. I'm an independent. Sierra Club is contracting with me to film the river and wildlife in winter,' Ramsey answered.

'Nice. You might see a few critters around,' Pat said.

'What can you tell me about the place?' Ramsey asked.

'The Flying B is mostly a hunting and fishing lodge,' Pat said.

'Any interesting history?'

'Sure. The Sheepeater Indians lived here, some say until well into the last century. There are pit houses and pictographs all over the place. And there's the famous 2000 fire. The perfect storm of forest fires,' Pat said proudly.

'Tell me about that,' Ramsey said.

'Sure. On August 18th, 2000 in the middle of the afternoon, the sky got dark and the wind came up like a hurricane. Over one hundred miles an hour. That pack bridge we hiked by; it was lifted six feet off its foundation. Three fires came bearing down on the ranch from different directions at the same time. The windstorm ahead of the fire lasted about 30 minutes. One fire moved six miles in the hour before it hit the ranch.'

'What happened when the fires hit?'

'We cut the fences so the livestock could run, and the Forest Service saved almost all the buildings. But a lot of wild animals died,' Pat said.

'Anybody hurt?' Ramsey asked.

'Some burns, but we all got in the river.'

'Cool story. So, this building was okay,' Ramsey said pointing to the lodge.

'It was a close call,' Pat said.

'Does it get busy here in the summer?'

'Sure. Rafters, fly fisherman, and hikers in the summer. We're full every night. People from all over the world. We get lots of hunters in the fall,' Pat explained.

'But winters are quiet. I'd like that,' Ramsey said.

'Usually. Two flights in one week is weird in winter,'

'Two?' Ramsey asked.

'Yeah. That's why I was late to meet you. I got a call on my radio. Another group is coming tomorrow. They're cops. I'm their guide. I'll be taking them upstream to the Tappan ranch. Ten-mile hike so I'll need to spend the night. You'll need to feed yourself tomorrow. I'll leave dinner in the cold box. I wondered if you could feed the animals while I'm gone,' Pat asked.

'Glad to help. Sounds like fun. Tell me about the hike to the Tappan Ranch. I might want to go there later in the week,' Ramsey smiled.

It was one-thirty Christmas morning when the meeting with the CDC ended. Charlie decided to sleep on the couch in the break room rather than go home at such a late hour. Marion borrowed a couple of blankets and headed to Charlie's office.

Jack rushed home to be with his wife, and Brad headed to his daughter's home.

Hunter went to his office to begin preparations for getting Charlie's team to Idaho the next day.

Waking at about six-thirty a.m., Charlie made coffee and went to his office to wake Marion. He found her reading a file and drinking tea.

She looked up and smiled when he entered the room, closing the file with both hands.

'Merry Christmas. I'm headed home. You're coming along. My wife's making an early meal after we exchange gifts,' Charlie said.

'No, Christmas is for family. I'm not comfortable barging it. Besides I have no gifts,' Marion said.

'Me either. No worries. You're coming,' Charlie insisted.

Marion agreed to go with Charlie, and after a ten-minute drive, the FBI car pulled into Charlie's driveway. The moment they opened the car doors they heard drumming and singing coming from inside the house. Charlie smiled. He knew some members of the family had been up all night.

Quickly leaving the car, Charlie and Marion slipped in the front door.

The entire family was gathered around Charlie's grandfather and two of his cousins. The men were pounding wildly on three small powwow drums using wooden beaters. They were chanting loudly. Charlie recognized the song. It was a vocable played after sunrise. His grandfather knew it was among Charlie's favorites.

Everyone in the room was focused on the music. Besides the drummers, Charlie's grandmother, wife and daughter, two sets of aunts and uncles, and a half-dozen children filled the living room. A bunch of dogs were scattered around the floor.

Anna waved at Marion and gestured for her to sit next to her on the couch. Marion went to sit with Anna while Charlie found a chair next to his daughter. Esther smiled at him as he turned to watch the singers.

It took another twenty minutes for the drumming and singing to end. Frank laid his drum and beater aside and wiped his sweaty hand on his pants before offering it to Marion. After introductions, coffee and fry bread appeared and their collective spirits rose. For the next two hours, Marion, her face plastered with a big smile, sat with Charlie's family as Christmas gifts were exchanged.

About nine a.m., a Christmas breakfast was served, and everyone found a seat at the large table. Normally the family ate Christmas dinner at 3:00 p.m. But knowing he'd have to leave soon Charlie had asked Anna to prepare a morning meal. He sat next to his grandfather, and Marion was seated between Joyce and Anna Edmo. The rest of the family was scattered around the table. Charlie used his coffee cup to toast the cooks, and to thank his family for changing their Christmas morning routine for him. Everyone lifted their glasses and cups and took a sip. The family began to eat.

After the initial eating frenzy slowed to a crawl, the conversation began again; increasing in volume until it reached its previous dull roar. The conversation soon turned to the news of the epidemic. Charlie didn't enjoy discussing work within the walls of his home. But his family was concerned about the outbreak, and he agreed to share what he could.

'Marion works at the Center for Disease Control. She's helping with our investigation and can talk about the epidemic. I've been involved with the investigation into the death of Quinn Conner. You've seen the news that he was not murdered. He was one of the first to die due to the epidemic. So now we're working to stop the outbreak,' Charlie stopped.

He waited for the murmuring to stop.

'I can't provide any more details. We are headed to Idaho later this morning to find a scientist who might be able to help,' Charlie said.

'Can the disease kill natural born?' Esther asked.

'No. As far as we know, it effects only people with engineered genes,' Marion explained.

'My daughter wants to buy the GSI beauty package. Will she get sick?' Anna asked.

'No, I don't believe so,' Marion answered.

'But you can't be sure. I tell you, stay away from this stuff,' Charlie said, looking at Esther.

'I plan to get the procedure,' Esther said calmly.

'But it may not be safe,' Charlie implored.

'Nobody knows that,' Anna added.

'I support Esther. She knows what's best for her,' Joyce said.

'Me too. Times have changed,' Anna added.

Esther nodded to them both. All eyes turned to Charlie's grandfather as he prepared to speak.

'Esther, you live in a world I know nothing about. But I see you as someone I can trust to make a good decision. You have always been wise from the time you were very young. I support your wishes, whatever they may be,' Frank Edmo said.

Charlie threw up his hands and tossed them all a dirty look.

Marion looked uncomfortable but was wise enough to remain silent.

She was, after all, suddenly in the middle of a family squabble.

Feeling his blood pressure rising, Charlie's first instinct was to tell them all to go to hell. He wanted to share stories of what he had seen. The disfigurement and death. The fallout from an industry that was out of control. Charlie wanted to shout the story of Quinn Conner and his sick, twisted family.

Then he heard his daughter's wise words above the ugly thoughts in his head. He understood her, if only for a moment. These awful things had found a way to get a hold of his heart. Years of proximity to tragedy had hardened his soul. The lens through which he saw the world was dirty and stained. His daughter was right.

Charlie could feel everyone's eyes on him.

His grandfather was right, she would make the right decision if left free to do so.

'I hear your voices. I've changed my mind. I support my daughter's decision. And, I will help pay for the procedure. Merry Christmas,' Charlie announced.

Esther hugged her father and cried.

At that moment Charlie's app-phone rang. It was his boss. He found a quiet corner and answered the call.

'The trip to Idaho is off. I contactcd the Boise office and their agents are in route to find Dr. Neil and bring her back to Seattle,' Hunter said.

'I still think my team should go. The local agents don't know the circumstances surrounding the case. There's not even a genetics team in Idaho,' Charlie pleaded.

'Not necessary. I briefed the agent in charge. Stand down and we'll meet later today,' Hunter responded.

'Understood. Can I at least provide a briefing to the agents in Idaho?' Charlie asked.

'Not needed. Focus on the black swan,' Hunter laughed, and ended the call.

Charlie sat in thought.

Something isn't right.

Hunter had been fully supportive of the plan to travel to Idaho. It was his idea. What changed his mind? Did he get orders from above? Or was there another reason? Charlie didn't know, but he did know what motivated Hunter.

Considering his options, Charlie went with his instincts and decided to call the FBI office in Boise. Hunter had ordered him to stay in Seattle, but he would never know about a call from home.

Spending the next thirty minutes speaking with several agents in the Boise FBI office, Charlie wasn't surprised to learn that Hunter had not contacted anyone there.

Hunter lied to me.

After returning to the party, he made a beeline to Marion. He signaled for Jack and Brad to join them.

'Hunter ordered us to stand down. No trip to Idaho. But listen to this, he claimed to have contacted the office in Boise. He said agents in Idaho would find Dr. Neil and bring her to Seattle. But I checked, and guess what? He never made the call. Hunter lied. Nobody in Boise was contacted by our office,' Charlie explained.

Why would he lie about that?' Marion asked.

'Hard to say. There's something he's not telling us. I need to get to Idaho and find out what it is,' Charlie lamented.

'Won't you get fired?' Marion asked.

'I hardly care. Hunter would love to fire me,' Charlie admitted.

'In that case, I'm with you,' Marion said.

'Me too. I can use sick days. Idaho in the winter. What could possibly go wrong?' Jack chuckled.

'What about you Brad? No pressure,' Jack asked.

'No pressure. Right. I'll go on the condition that if I get fired, I get to move in with Charlie and eat Anna's cooking every day,' Brad stated.

'Nobody's going to get fired,' Charlie said.

'You don't know that,' Jack replied.

'No, I don't. But based on Hunter's actions, I'm suddenly convinced that Dr. Neil might be more important than we think,' Charlie confessed.

'Fine. But without Hunter, how can we get to Idaho?' Jack asked.

'I'm going to call in a favor with a friend at the Air National Guard. They've got a daily flight to Boise that we can hopefully catch,' Charlie finished.

🧬

A cold, sunny afternoon greeted Charlie and his team as they deplaned onto the tarmac at Gowen Field in Boise. They were greeted by Captain Alaina McConner, the National Guard officer in charge. The nearby ground held a few inches of snow and the temperature was in the low twenties. To the north, just a few miles away, Charlie could see the high-rise buildings of downtown Boise snuggled against sage-covered foothills. The slopes of the foothills climbed upward until they reached steeper terrain, where the sage and open grassland gave way to forest. Several dozen homes dotted the lower slopes of the foothills and Charlie could see wood smoke pouring from their chimneys. High barometric pressure forced the smoke to linger above the homes and spread east across the valley.

Charlie took a moment and tried, without luck, to locate the Boise Zoo.

Thinking back, Charlie remembered the bear cub he had

cared for during the summer of his fifteenth birthday. Charlie and Ursula had gained brief international fame after they had survived a week in the wildness. The moment of their rescue had been captured in a single picture that had appeared in newspapers around the world. Charlie had loved Ursula and desperately wanted to keep the bear. But he was convinced by his grandfather that the best thing for Ursula was to find him a suitable home. Luckily, once word went out, their fame generated a fierce competition among zoos and big game parks to house the now famous bear. In the end, Charlie and Frank had selected the Boise Zoo. Ursula had lived at the Boise Zoo for twelve years before dying of natural causes.

Searching the horizon, he took a deep breath. Charlie smiled when he saw the Snake River Plain stretching effortlessly as far as his eyes could see. The ancient lava shield, lost elevation as it sloped westward toward Oregon and the mighty Snake River.

But to the east, the land tilted upward toward southeast Idaho, and his childhood home. The Snake River Plains were rimmed to the north by the Rocky Mountains. Far to the south, across a huge expanse of rolling sage land, Charlie could see the outline of the Owyhee Mountains. The surroundings made him feel at home.

After exchanging small talk for a few minutes, Captain McConner got to business.

'After our conversation, I assigned staff to find the local postmaster in Stanley. We located her and she was able to provide a physical address for Dr. Neil. Turns out she lives in the middle of nowhere, literally. Dr. Neil purchased the old Daisy Tappan Ranch on the Middle Fork of the Salmon River. It's in the wilderness area. The Tappan ranch is ten miles from the nearest airstrip,' Captain McConner said.

'Have you tried to contact her?' Charlie asked.

'Yes, using all means possible. So far, no response,' Captain McConner said.

'Did the postmaster know anything about Dr. Neil?' Charlie asked.

'Postmaster said she's never seen her. Someone picks up her mail, but she didn't notice anyone in particular,' the officer said.

'How do we get to this ranch?' Jack asked.

'You have to fly there in a small plane. I've arranged a flight from Stanley to Bernard air strip near the Flying B Ranch. It's the closest airstrip to the Tappan ranch. You could fly from here, but the weatherman is calling for fog tonight and tomorrow. Stanley is predicted to be clear of fog by late morning. The caretaker at the Flying B will meet you and act as your guide. His name is Pat Harren,' Captain McConner said.

'Can we fly and do the hike in one day?' Marion asked.

'Yes, assuming an early start. But days are short,' she said.

'What's it like out there?' Brad asked.

'The wilderness is steep and rugged. No communications. If you stay on the river, you'll be fine. Watch for big game animals. They winter near the river, and so do the predators that eat them, except for the bear of course. It's been an early winter, so you might hit snow and ice on the portions of the trail that are shaded. If you climb in elevation, the snow will get deep real fast,' Captain McConner offered.

'What's the forecast?' Brad asked.

'Another storm by tomorrow night. You have a small weather window. You need to get to the ranch by then. Once the weather shuts down, nobody goes anywhere for at least twelve hours,' she said.

'Assuming fifteen minutes per mile, we need at least two

and half hours of daylight for the hike. If we hit snow or ice, a bit longer. How long to fly to the Flying B Ranch?' Charlie asked.

'Twenty minutes, it's a short flight. It gets dark by four-thirty, earlier in the canyon,' she observed.

'We need to be in the air by noon or so,' Jack said.

'I hope the fog burns off by then. We're cutting it pretty close,' Charlie said.

'Best we could do. You've got headlamps and batteries if you end up hiking after dark,' she said.

'Hopefully not,' Jack said.

'Everything else you need is loaded in the back of the SUV. Take some time to look over the equipment. Should be snow-shoes, ice crampons, backpacks, food, water, sleeping bags and the rest, for all four of you. Here are roadmaps and top-ographical maps of the wilderness area,' Captain McConner said, and handed Charlie a long metal tube.

After organizing the equipment, the foursome loaded their carry bags and found seats in the SUV. Self-driving cars were illegal in the State of Idaho, and Jack was forced to drive. Nobody else had a driver's license. Charlie navigated from the passenger seat and Marion and Brad sat in the backseat.

After a slow four-hour drive, they arrived in Stanley. Their headlights pierced the night to reveal a small city limits sign. The sign indicated that forty-three hardy souls lived in the town. Charlie suspected far fewer residents braved the long winters.

Charlie had visited the Stanley Basin only once in winter. During holiday break his senior year, he and two friends had driven to Stanley with plans to snowshoe to a hot spring. After spending the night in a local hotel, they woke to a crisp, clear morning. Arriving at the trailhead, Charlie and his two friends decided to brave the twenty-degree below zero weather and make the two-mile hike to the hot springs. They finished the hike half-frozen. They plunged their cold bodies into the hot waters and cried tears of pain as their feet and hands thawed out. Charlie laughed at the memory.

A foggy morning greeted Marion and the three FBI agents. They burned time by drinking coffee and eating breakfast at the local Sawtooth Bakery. Just before eleven, Charlie was informed the fog had lifted and they were cleared to take off. The foursome drove to the airstrip located on a flat mesa just above the small town.

A thin layer of snow and ice covered the airstrip and the white powder twinkled like diamonds as the first rays of sunlight penetrated the fog and found the ground. As the small plane lifted off and banked to the northwest, Charlie saw the east faces of the Sawtooth Mountains gathering the rays of the late morning sun, reflecting the light in patches of bright orange and blood red.

14

SUNDAY, DECEMBER 26TH, 2050

We lack imagination and suppress it in others.

NassiamTalab

As the white man pushed from the east, and the Blackfoot, Crow and other tribes were forced westward, small bands of the Northern Shoshone tribe were driven into permanent exile in the rugged mountains of what is now the Central Idaho wilderness. These people learned to hunt the big horn sheep living on the steep canyon walls and were known as the *Tukudeka* or Mountain Sheepeaters. They roamed the canyons and mountains surrounding the Middle Fork of the Salmon River. These small bands of Native Americans lived along the rivers in pit houses; a type of shelter used successfully for thousands of years.

While disease and the U.S. government systematically destroyed other Indian nations, the Sheepeater bands were mostly left alone. That was, until gold was discovered in central Idaho. Miners soon began to infringe on tribal lands. In 1879, the murder of a group of Chinese miners was unjustly blamed on the Sheepeaters. The military was sent in, and one of the most embarrassing campaigns ever conducted by the U.S. Army took place: the so-called Sheepeater War.

General O. O. Howard, already looking for an excuse to subdue one of the last remaining tribes in the west, was sent to investigate the miner's deaths. In the first battle of this so-called war, the army destroyed a small Indian camp which had just been abandoned. Then, ignoring his scouts, General Howard ordered his troops to follow a trail down Big Creek into a steep canyon. A handful of Sheepeater warriors were waiting, and the army unit was ambushed. Two soldiers were wounded, and the company was forced to retreat to a nearby hilltop.

The following morning, the Indians set fire to the base of the hill, and the winds carried the flames uphill toward the army encampment. The soldiers escaped the flames, and when darkness set in, many were able to sneak past the Indians. The army lost twenty-one pack animals and all their supplies.

Provoked, several army companies spent the next four months chasing these bands of Indians, which included a handful of warriors carrying only eight firearms. In the end, the army failed to defeat the band. Many members of the small band ultimately surrendered to Umatilla and Cayuse scouts. From that time forward, the proud remnants of the Sheepeater band were forced to live on the Fort Hall Indian reservation near Idaho Falls.

Charlie Edmo was descended from these people.

As their plane gained altitude and left the relative safety of the Stanley Basin, Charlie looked with pride at the ancestral home of the Sheepeaters. As the plane cleared a snow-clad mountaintop, the Middle Fork of the Salmon River came into view. Its green water flowed through a magnificent canyon of steep granite faces that climbed hundreds of feet above the river. The snowline hovered far above the water, and the flat ground near the river's edge boasted sandy beaches and scattered trees. The combination of beaches, forest, granite faces, and open grasslands backed by snow-covered peaks, created a magnificent wintery scene.

Charlie relished watching his colleagues' first wide-eyed looks at the Idaho wilderness. He knew his partners seldom left the city. Their faces reflected wonder, along with a healthy dose of discomfort. Few were prepared for the vastness of the wilderness. Endless mountain ranges, roughly parallel, stretched out-of-sight to the north as far as their eyes could see. Steep and rugged failed to descript the terrain. To the northwest, Charlie could see the peaks of the Big Horn Crags peering above the valley fog. Everything was covered with snow, and the trees growing on the highest peaks were encrusted in pure white ice and snow, slumping over like old men. Charlie smiled. The landscape was unchanged and as breath-taking as he remembered it.

The pilot signaled he was beginning his descent and they would soon be on the ground. Charlie's heart raced as the plane descended between the canyon walls, and the river rose to meet them. As the plane lost altitude, the sides of canyon walls drew inward. The eyes of his co-workers grew wide as the plane banked hard to the right and its wings came close to the rock faces. Everyone relaxed as the aircraft cleared the cliff and lined-up with an airstrip in the distance.

As the plane touched down, Charlie sensed relief among his fellow travelers. It was just before lunch and Charlie was pleased to be on the ground ahead of schedule.

Charlie could see a man waiting near the airstrip.

'You must be our guide?' Charlie asked, after he deplaned. The pilot unloaded their packs as the men spoke.

'Pat Harren. Welcome to the Flying B Ranch,' Pat said, as he offered a handshake.

Charlie shook hands with the man and introduced the other members of his team.

'How'd such a young man end up in the backcountry?' Charlie asked.

'I was raised on the river,' Pat answered.

'That makes you a lucky guy.'

'Thanks. I never wanted to live anywhere else. I feel sorry for most city folk. Listen, if we're going to make it before dark, we better get moving,' Pat suggested.

'You got it.'

'I expected to see the Flying B Ranch,' Jack said.

'The ranch is about a half-mile in that direction, around the bend in the river,' Pat said, and pointed downstream. 'But we're going south,' he finished, and pointed upstream.

Maintaining a brisk pace, Pat led Charlie, Jack, Brad and Marion upriver toward the Daisy Tappan ranch. The cold air stung their faces, and the hikers all wore several layers of warm clothes. The cloud layer thickened as they walked, and a few snowflakes fell from time to time. After a three-hour walk, the five hikers left the trail and came to a large river bar. The river flowed around the bar on three sides. On its fourth side, the flat terrain was flanked by a steep granite cliff. The sand and rock bar had been built by the river eons ago and formed several acres of flat terrain. It was covered with wild grasses, sagebrush, and some ancient fruit trees. An old farmhouse and several cabins could be seen in the distance.

Arriving at the door of the farmhouse, Pat knocked loudly. The others stood waiting nearby, their packs still on their backs. When there was no response, he opened the door and called loudly into the building. His cry was answered with silence.

'There's a note in the door,' Charlie said, and pointed to a piece of paper stuffed in the door jam.

'Welcome to the ranch. Follow my tracks in the snow. JN,' Pat read aloud, after removing the note from the door.

'Jane Neil,' Marion said, 'She knew we were coming. Pat, did you speak with Ms. Neil?'

'Never spoken with her, she keeps to herself.'

'Well let's go ask her. There's fresh tracks in the snow,' Charlie said, as he pointed to the line of shoe prints leading toward a nearby side canyon.

'I guess we should follow them,' Pat suggested.

The five hikers stashed their backpacks in the house, and with Pat in the lead, followed the foot tracks in the snow toward a small frozen creek spilling from a side canyon. The creek bed was a quarter mile upstream from the farmhouse, and as they entered the side canyon, the tracks in the thin snow gave way to a muddy trail. The trail followed the small creek and took the hikers upward. Ice covered the creek, but a small trickle of water could be heard flowing under the frozen sheet.

The trail wove through Ponderosa pines and granite boulders for about a half-mile until it abruptly ended at a pool of hot water. A thick cloud of steam hovered above the pool, and a brief appearance from the afternoon sun caused the water vapors to glow fiercely in the still, cold air.

In the middle of the pool was a woman. She was naked and floating comfortably in the steaming water. Charlie could see her robe, a pile of towels, and snow boots sitting on a nearby rock. The only parts of her body not submerged were her toes, breasts and face. Her eyes were closed.

The hot pool was built in the middle of the creek bed on some flat ground. It was constructed of a simple rock wall about two feet tall and lined with a black plastic pond liner.

The oval pool was about fifteen feet long and eight feet wide. A black plastic pipe came down from the rock face above them and delivered a constant flow of steaming hot liquid. Another pipe supplied cold water from the creek. The pool had a drain at its bottom. There was a small wooden sign mounted on a nearby tree instructing them to remove the wooden plug after using the pool. The water looked clean, clear, and hot.

'Hello,' Charlie said loudly, as they drew closer.

The woman slowly opened her eyes, and showing no signs of modesty, smiled and sat up. She spoke in an unexpectedly strong and clear voice for someone who sat naked in front of a group of strangers.

'Welcome to the Daisy Tappan Ranch. I'm Jane Neil. I saw your message this morning. I've been expecting you. I would appreciate it if you would join me. It's a tradition. Guests are required to have a soak when they arrive. I have towels for each of you. Clothing is optional,' Dr. Neil chuckled.

'Thank you, but I'll pass. I'm FBI Agent Charlie Edmo, and these are agents Jack Lee, Brad Grant and this is Marion Harper from the Center for Disease Control. I assume you know Pat Harren from the Flying B,' Charlie said.

'I've heard the name, but we've never met,' Jane said.

'I've heard your name too. Nice to meet you,' Pat said.

'Marion, you look familiar. Have we met?'

'Yes, actually. Amazing you remember. I was an undergrad at Harvard. It's a pleasure to see you again,' Marion said, and added. 'If you don't mind, I'll join you. I'm cold.'

Dr. Neil nodded.

'Climb in. You were one of Lois's stars,' she said.

'Yes. That was a long time ago,' Marion said.

'I always enjoyed Lois's company. I assume she still works for the CDC?' Dr. Neil asked.

'Dedicated as ever. She passes along her greetings,' Marion said.

Marion undressed to her undergarments and slipped into the hot water.

The four men watched Marion awkwardly.

Charlie sat down on a nearby rock, and the other men did the same.

'Dr. Neil. This is an amazing place. How long have you lived here?' Charlie asked.

'I came here two weeks after I was released from prison. I've only returned to so-called 'civilization' twice since that day. I like it here, and the locals are genuine people,' Dr. Neil said.

'Good for you. It looks like paradise,' Marion offered.

'Dr. Neil, do you know why we're here?' Charlie asked.

'I have a notion, but I insist we wait until after dinner to talk business. This hot-springs is a holy place for me, and I suspect for your ancestors as well, Agent Edmo,' Dr. Neil said.

Charlie could tell by the way she emphasized his last name, that Dr. Neil knew he was a local boy. She knew he was from the rez, and Charlie felt a familiar jolt of belittlement.

He turned to meet her eyes, looking to challenge her, but she hurriedly looked away.

Charlie decided to say nothing, but he did take a closer look at Dr. Neil. She had the body of a young woman, small and thin, with surprisingly smooth skin. He noticed there wasn't an extra pound on her tiny frame. Dr. Neil was so small Charlie was sure he could lift her up with one arm. But there was a disconnect between her young body and a troubled face. Deep wrinkles creased her cheeks, and small dark bags underlined a pair of sad eyes. Wrinkles in her skin formed a braided tangle as they curved downward from the corners of her mouth. Her chin was highlighted by a deeply creased dimple. Partially frozen grey hair that hung stiffly to her shoulders framed a troubled face.

'No problem. We can wait. Not like we're going anywhere,' Charlie said.

'Thank you. I've got a true backcountry dinner waiting for us,' she answered.

After enjoying their soak in the hot water, Dr. Neil put on her robe while Marion took advantage of some nearby bushes and changed into dry clothes.

Charlie and the others followed the muddy trail back to the main house. Dr. Neil went inside to prepare dinner while Charlie and the others settled into their cabins. When they were done, the four hikers and their guide returned to the farmhouse. The late afternoon had turned to evening and the four men and Marion wore headlamps to light their way. Cold air from the nearby mountains had settled into the valley floor, and the frozen ground crunched loudly as they walked. Like sound waves over water, the dim light visible through the farmhouse windows threw a soft glow across a huge swath of the snow-covered meadow.

'I'm worried Dr. Neil is a bit unhinged,' Charlie spoke quietly as they walked.

'If you had gone through what she has,' Marion said.

'I didn't pick up anything. She seems matter of fact, but that's all,' Jack said.

'Must be my ancestors talking to me again, and they're mostly crazy. But I plan to keep an eye on her,' Charlie finished.

'I'm just curious what she has to say. I hope we didn't come all this way for nothing,' Marion said.

'Pat, what'd you think?' Brad asked.

'Couldn't say. Locals think she's crazy and mostly keep their distance,' he offered.

When they entered the building, Dr. Neil asked her guests to be seated. Within moment of removing their coats and finding seats, she laid out a solid backcountry dinner of elk roast simmering in a thick brown sauce, garden potatoes, salad and corn. A blackberry pie waited on a side table. Once dinner was on the table, Dr. Neil joined the five guests.

'It's nice to not eat alone. My staff has been gone for over a week,' Jane said.

'You have a staff?' Jack asked.

'Yes, I have a couple who tend to the livestock and clean the cabins. They're gone for the holiday,' Dr. Neil explained.

'The food looks delicious, and I'm starved. Thank you,' Brad said.

'My pleasure. I'm not use to cooking for so many,' Jane said.

'We appreciate the meal. When we arrived today, I realized I've been here before,' Charlie said.

'When was that?' Jane asked.

'A long time ago. I'm a little embarrassed. While I was in high school, I spent a couple of summers guiding raft trips on the Middle Fork. On one trip with paying guests, I flipped my boat, just over there,' Charlie said, and pointed toward the river.

'Obviously you survived,' Marion said.

'Barely. These are called the Tappan Rapids and are a modest Class III. But I learned that day that it's all about timing. I made a mistake, and my raft flipped so fast I didn't have time to react. I remember the boat hit a huge rock and turned sideways, just before we plowed into a wall of water. The raft fell over the heads of my four clients, including two kids. I was tossed downriver,' Charlie said, and laughed.

'Anyone hurt?' Marion asked.

'No, but once in the water, I discovered a few things about the river. It looks like gravity pulls the river in a straight line down the canyon, but really, the water defies gravity, and flows upstream in powerful reverse eddies. It turns sharply and plunges deep until encountering huge and hidden obstacles - rising in violent swells and whirlpools,' Charlie said.

'You learned a valuable lesson,' Jane said.

'I did. I learned that nature, in this case the river, has many lessons to teach us,' Charlie said.

'Bravo. Bravo. Agent Edmo. Well spoken. You're not a dullard after all. Living here has taught me the same lesson,' Dr. Neil said.

After eating and exchanging small talk for most of an hour, Dr. Neil turned to the reason for their visit.

'I appreciate your coming all this way. I apologize again for not attending to my radio and computer messages. I hardly ever look at anything connected to the outside world. I just saw the news about the outbreak that is killing these young men. I hope that's not why you're here,' Dr. Neil said.

'That's exactly why we're here. We have an outbreak on our hands that looks a lot like the one you predicted twenty years ago. We're here to find out if you have any information that could be helpful,' Marion said.

Dr. Neil sat silently for an uncomfortably long time. She finally removed her glasses and held them in her left hand. Using her right hand, the woman rubbed the bridge of her nose. She closed her eyes and didn't open them again until she had spoken for several seconds.

'Please understand. I'm still angry. I think about it every day. I warned everyone about an epidemic years ago. And now you come to my home asking for help. Takes fucking nerve. I was in prison for three years. I was disgraced. I lost my family.

I haven't spoken to my daughter in fifteen years,' Dr. Neil said bitterly, suddenly sounding like a different person.

The group sat in uncomfortable silence.

Charlie and Marion exchanged glances. Finally, Marion spoke.

'I read your case notes. I know you were set-up. I'd like to help make things right,' she offered.

'You can't make things right, so don't bullshit me.'

She paused, 'I knew someone from the CDC would come begging.'

'So, you can't help us?' Charlie asked.

'I didn't say that. And make no mistake about what's at stake. Thousands of men are going to die. I can help, but you will do what I ask. Because, in fact, I don't care about Gordon and Hawke's precious designer-babies,' Dr. Neil said harshly.

'Any failure to assist us is not only highly unethical, it's reason enough for me to detain you and take you to Seattle,' Charlie said.

'Are you threatening to arrest me? For what, having an opinion? Do what you must, Agent Edmo. But then you will learn nothing.' Jane exaggerated his last name for the second time.

'Hold on, Charlie. I want to hear what she has to say. What exactly do you want?' Marion asked, looking at Dr. Neil.

'I have some simple demands,' Dr. Neil said.

'The government is happy to listen to your concerns,' Marion spoke firmly. 'But this is not a negotiation. If you know something . . . Charlie is right, you need to share it immediately. I won't consider your demands until you tell me what you can do to save these men's lives.'

Charlie considered using the threat of arrest again but assumed the presence of three FBI agents spoke for itself. He noticed their guide, Pat, looked stunned by the sudden turn in the conversation.

'Rather than tell you, I'm going to show you. How about we all take a little tour of my facilities,' Dr. Neil said, as she abruptly rose from her chair.

The five surprised guests donned their boots and winter coats and followed Dr. Neil out the back door. She led them toward the granite cliff a couple of hundred yards behind the farmhouse. There was no light and they all used headlamps to see in the dark. When they approached the base of the cliff, Charlie saw the entrance to an old mine shaft he hadn't notice before. The small opening in the cliff was guarded by a dilapidated wood frame enclosing an old, rusted, steel door.

Dr. Neil unlocked and removed the padlock from the chain holding the door closed. She opened the old door to revel a shiny, stainless-steel entrance. The door featured a small computer screen with a blinking red light. She punched in a code and the group watched in amazement as the light turned green and the door opened with a loud hiss, reveling a brightly lit airlock. The airlock led to some type of scientific lab visible through the glass of a second inner door.

'Looks like my lab,' Marion said, as they passed through the airlock and into the lab.

'In part, we modeled it after the design of CDC labs, but with several innovations.'

Entering the main lab, Charlie surveyed the room in awe. It was built into the hillside in what appeared to be a huge mine shaft. The room was at least a hundred feet long and half as wide. Its high ceiling was solid rock that had been sprayed with some type of photosensitive plaster which filled the room with a bright light. The walls of the room were stainless steel, and the rows of tables that populated the space were covered with science equipment and computer monitors. A row of offices lined the left wall. The lab was empty of people but appeared to be in regular use. Computers were turned on and paper covered much of the available desk space.

'Where is everyone?' Charlie asked.

'My staff are home for the holidays,' Dr. Neil said.

'I guess your staff is more than just maids and ranch hands?' Charlie asked.

'Quite right,' Dr. Neil smiled.

'The lab is amazing. How did you get this done, and way out here?' Marion asked.

'There are dozens of unemployed miners around here, so digging the tunnel was the easy part. I told them it was a bomb shelter. People round here are mostly survivalist at heart, so nobody raised an eyebrow. Recruiting top researchers in secret was another story. That took time and loads of cash,' Dr. Neil admitted.

'Forgive me, but why?' Charlie asked.

'To find a cure for the epidemic,' Marion spoke quickly.

Dr. Neil shot her a glance.

'Yes, and we've succeeded,' she said.

A long moment of silence followed.

'Quite a claim. If that's true, why are you keeping it to yourself?' Charlie asked.

'I'm not. We just perfected the nanotechnology and finished testing and debugging the software. I'd appreciate if you would recognize what we've accomplished. I've spent years and tens of millions of dollars of my own money. I expect some gratitude . . . and I expect to get paid back,' Dr. Neil said firmly.

'Understood. Please accept my apology. It's just . . . why the secrecy?'

'Given my previous experiences, what would you expect?

I knew I was right, and I had a multi-billion-dollar settlement from my divorce. I didn't need the scientific community. Fuck them. I created my own, small though it is. And we've been successful,' Dr. Neil said proudly.

'What exactly have you accomplished?' Marion asked.

'Simply put, we built the genetic reset button. We can fix the DNA code for the second gens. We engineered a nanomachine that can recognize and splice-out engineered strands of DNA. The device then replaces the engineered strands with the original gene sequences or other benign genetic material. The machines work for every cell type in the body and are ready to be produced on a mass scale. There's just one problem,' Dr. Neil said, and hesitated.

'You have nothing to deliver to the cells,' Marion said.

'Right. I can splice out the bad stuff, but don't have access to the good stuff; the original genetic sequences for this particular group of men,' Dr. Neil said.

'Neither does anyone else. Genlabs keeps close tabs on its proprietary property. They won't give up the genetic profiles, unless a judge tells them to,' Marion pointed out.

'Even to save lives? Given the catastrophic PR disaster they're facing. I bet they can be pressured into giving up the data,' Dr. Neil said firmly.

'Can someone please explain what's going on?' Pat broke in.

Marion explained that she worked at the Center for Disease Control and was working with Charlie and the FBI. She outlined how the deaths currently in the news was connected to the alleged murder of Quinn Conner. She described how this was their reason for coming to Idaho to find Dr. Neil.

Pat shook his head in wonder.

'Now it makes sense why you're here in the middle of winter,' Pat said.

'Dr. Neil. You mentioned demands,' Charlie said.

'Yes. I've lost a lot that can't be replaced. But my work deserves recognition. My name needs to be cleared. I want my reputation back. That's my demand. I want my reputation fully restored.'

'Any suggestions how?' Marion asked.

'As a matter of fact, I do. First, arrange a major press conference, immediately. The CDC will formally present my discoveries to the world. I will be there to accept my due, and of course, answer questions. Second, in less than ninety days, the CDC will convene an international scientific conference to address the epidemic. I will provide the keynote address at the event and present my findings to the scientific community. Lastly, Congressional leaders will make a public promise to convene hearings with the goal of investigating the genetics services industry. I expect to be a key witness at these hearings,' Dr. Neil said.

'The first two are doable . . . they're somewhat under CDC's control. But getting Congress to act is another story. You know that,' Marion said.

'I'm not asking for that much. When this all goes public, Congress is likely to hold hearings anyway. These are my demands. I got screwed before, but not this time.'

'I can get in touch with my boss once we get to back to Boise. She can arrange the press conference in the next couple of days. Is that soon enough?'

'That will work.'

'You'll return to Seattle with us? Marion asked.

'If I must.'

'Then it's settled. We can radio for a plane to Boise and catch a flight to Seattle. My boss will arrange the press conference. We can meet with her once we return to Seattle to discuss your other demands.'

'None of you are going anywhere,' their guide said harshly. Charlie turned in time to see Pat Harren pointing a gun in his face.

'Your weapons on the table and then raise your hands,' he ordered.

Unstrapping his holster, Charlie placed his weapon on the nearby table and raised his hands above his head. Ramsey Lewis kept his weapon trained on him but maintained a safe distance. Charlie's eyes bored into the man as he gave up his weapon. Jack and Brad unstrapped and dropped their holsters on the table. Using the barrel of his gun as a pointer, the man herded the three FBI agents and the two scientists into a small office. Once they were inside, Ramsey closed the door behind them without speaking. He removed several small wooden wedges from his pocket and using the palm of his hand, drove them between the door and door jam. The door was firmly locked from the outside.

Exiting the lab through the airlock, Ramsey blocked the outer door open with a rock. He quickly ran to his cabin. Once there, he found his pack and unwrapped the two bricks of plastic explosives and the detonator he carried.

Returning to the entrance of the lab, he worked to assemble the simple bomb. No longer needing to pretend he was unable to see in the dark, Ramsey switched off his headlamp. His enhanced night vision kicked in and night became day. Ramsey unwrapped the bricks slowly and inserted the wire ends of the detonator into the plastic explosives. He taped the detonator and the two brick-size explosives together, double checking to see that the timer was securely held in place.

Holding the bomb tightly to his chest, Ramsey carefully climbed to the area just above the entrance to the lab. He cleared some rocks and slide the bomb under a large boulder. He armed its detonator, setting the timer for thirty minutes. Ramsey estimated there was enough explosives to destroy the door, and hopefully cover the small entrance with debris.

Returning to the main farmhouse, Ramsey finished eating the pie he'd left on the table. It tasted fantastic. After his genetic enhancements were completed, Ramsey had noticed several unexpected changes in his body. He had anticipated having more physical strength and stamina and had not been disappointed. Gaining night vision and radically improved hearing was also exhilarating. His metabolism was incredibly efficient. But it was the significant increase in his sense of taste and smell that was the most unexpected and pleasant side effect of the genetic-enhancement process.

Ramsey ate the last bit of pie and finished his glass of milk. He walked back to the cabin, packed his belongings, and glancing at his watch, noted he had five minutes before the bomb would explode. Ramsey left the cabin and stood outside facing the lab's entrance. As he stood waiting, the bomb exploded. He didn't flinch, instead, he took full advantage of his enhanced night vision to enjoy the fireworks. He waited ten minutes before hiking close enough to ensure the debris had completely covered the door to the lab. Satisfied, he turned away and headed toward the Flying B Ranch.

Without warning, a huge shock wave, accompanied by an ear shattering explosion, rocked Charlie and his colleagues. Several pieces of furniture toppled over, and several books flew off the shelves. Dr. Neil screamed and everyone covered their ears. They could see dust pouring into the room under the locked door. Jack removed his sweater and stuffed it into the gap to stop the flow of dust.

At that moment the lights when out and the room was dark.

'What the hell happened?' Marion asked.

They all put on their headlamps and switched them on.

'He blew up the airlock. He left us for dead,' Charlie said.

'Anyone live close enough to hear the explosion?' Jack asked.

Dr. Neil laughed.

'There's nobody for miles. Why is this happening?' she asked.

'Good question. I'm starting to think that man is not Pat Harren,' Charlie said.

'How about a wild guess. He's Ramsey Lewis,' Brad broke in.

They all remained silent for a few moments, lost in thought.

'That seems pretty far-fetched. How could he possibly know we would be here?' Jack asked.

'If he read Quinn Conner's report, he would know about Dr. Neil,' Brad answered.

'And we know he had the report,' Jack said, 'and it's likely he read it.'

'Then how did he get here before us?' Marion asked.

'Gordon would have known where Dr. Neil lives. When Mr. Lewis gave us the slip, I bet he went directly to Idaho. He could have caught a flight to the Flying B Ranch from Boise or Stanley. He knew we would have to fly to the Flying B,' Brad said.

'Another explanation is he's a local anti-government wacko. This is Idaho. Though I admit it seems farfetched,' Jack said.

'Too random. The man must be Ramsey Lewis,' Charlie said.

'Looks that way. We keep underestimating him. I bet Gordon Kelly is behind this,' Brad said.

'As we suspected all along. The good news is Gordon Kelly

will be in custody by now, and we now know what Mr. Lewis looks like. But what happened to the real Pat Harren?' Jack asked.

'You think that man works for my ex-husband?' Dr. Neil broke in.

'Yes. It's the only explanation. Ramsey Lewis is connected to Gordon Kelly, but we don't know exactly how or why.'

'Dr. Neil, what can you tell us about Gordon Kelly?' Charlie asked.

Dr. Neil stared at Charlie. She appeared to be lost in thought, but Charlie was pretty sure she was deciding if he could be trusted. Finally, she spoke.

'Gordon is a brilliant man. But he went over the deep end years ago. He's an example of how the DNA expresses itself in the real world. On one hand, Gordon was always the smartest guy in the room, and the only man truly capable of saving us from ourselves. If anyone could do it, he was Gordon. For a while, he fell for all that Transhumanism garbage and was too immature to understand how he was being used. Gordon is like a small boy who is easily manipulated. He's a lost soul,' Dr. Neil said.

'So, he's a fanatic. Is that why he's doing all this,' Jack asked.

'No. Genlabs comes first. I think he's trying to cover up Genlabs role in creating the epidemic,' Dr. Neil stated.

'I suspected as much,' Charlie interjected. 'A couple of years ago a former employee of Genlabs came to us claiming the company was engaged in some questionable activities. We found no evidence to support the claim. But now I wonder if those claims weren't true.'

'All I know is that Gordon is convinced we are all doomed without his help. He sees himself as a savior. But he's become evil, and capable of great violence,' Dr. Neil said.

'Witness our current predicament,' Brad pointed out.

They all nodded.

Charlie was suddenly distracted by a loud voice crying out inside him.

These people killed my partner and friend, Hank.

Charlie stared into space as the insight pierced his brain. His heart started pumping faster and he felt light-headed. He sat down and covered his face.

We were too close to the truth about Genlabs.

So, they killed Hank.

'What's up boss?' Brad asked.

'Nothing, just thinking. We need to get out of here, now! Dr. Neil, if we can get out of this office, is there another way out of the lab. I suspect the main entrance is out of commission,' Charlie asked.

'There is a back door . . . a tunnel really. The miner who supervised the project insisted on an emergency exit. But how are we going to get out of here?' Dr. Neil asked.

'Maybe the door was damaged by the explosion,' Charlie said, and walking to the door, pushed it hard with his shoulder. It didn't budge.

'I can pick the lock,' Marion said.

'And where exactly did you learn that skill?' Charlie asked curiously.

'Just something I picked up as a kid,' she answered with a shrug. 'But I need the right tool. A stiff piece of wire would work,' Marion said.

Using their headlamps, they all searched for a piece of wire, but without success. Finally, Jack dismantled a table lamp and recovered a piece of wire meeting Marion's specifications.

Marion walked to the door and got down on her knees.

Using the small length of wire, she worked on the door's lock intently for several minutes.

'Sorry. I've never seen a lock like this,' Marion said, as she got to her feet.

'Worth a try. There's got to be another way out of here. What about the ductwork for the heat system?' Charlie asked, as he walked around the room examining the ceiling with his headlamp.

Charlie located the ductwork carrying heat to the office. It hung from the ceiling and ran across the back wall of the office. A small vent in the side of the ductwork distributed heated air into the room. Using a chair to stand on, he removed the cover of the vent. The opening was far too small for a person to pass through.

'The ductwork might be big enough, but we need to widen the hole,' Jack offered.

Searching the dark office until he found a small metal toolbox, Charlie dug out a pair of wire cutters. For the next thirty minutes, he struggled to enlarge the vent hole. He finally managed to crave a hole large enough for a small person to fit through.

'Dr. Neil. You're the only one small enough. Can you fit?' Charlie asked.

'I can try. Lift me up,' Dr. Neil said.

Charlie and Jack lifted Dr. Neil up toward the opening. She wiggled, arms first, into the ductwork.

'I'm good. This is tight. Thank God I'm not claustrophobic. I'll be right back, if I can find a way out. I should take some tools,' Dr. Neil said.

Charlie looked around the room until his eyes rested on a baseball bat displayed in a glass case hanging on the wall. He walked to the glass display case and peered inside. The baseball bat was covered with the autographs of members of the 2016 World Series Champion Chicago Cubs.

No way!

Charlie returned to the small metal box and found a hammer and large screwdriver. He returned to the opening in the ductwork and handed the tools to Dr. Neil.

Dr. Neil took the tools and disappeared into the ductwork.

Fifteen minutes later, Charlie heard a knock on the door. A moment later, Dr. Neil opened the door.

'No problem,' she said smiling.

'Good work. Now let's get out of here. I'll check the front entrance. Wait here,' Charlie said.

Leaving the small office, Charlie quickly surveyed the damage from the explosion. The beam of his headlamp struggled to penetrate the thick dust filling the air, and Charlie covered his mouth by pulling up his tee shirt. He could see a thick layer of the dust covering everything. Otherwise the lab appeared undamaged. The inner door to the airlock was open a few inches. He peered through its window and thought the outer door looked undamaged. Charlie slipped through the airlock to the door, turned its handle and pushed hard. Nothing happened. He pushed harder, but Charlie was unable to open it. Then he noticed the top of the steel doorframe was buckled inward.

As he expected, they would have to use the emergency exit.

Departing the airlock and returning to the lab, Charlie remembered their firearms. Relieved, he saw they were still on the table. Charlie called to Jack and Brad. The three FBI agents strapped on their weapons, and with Dr. Neil leading the way, they climbed through the emergency tunnel and departed the lab.

After leaving the lab, and in a grim mood, they walked quietly toward the farmhouse. By then, the weather had changed, and a light snow was falling. Once they arrived at the farmhouse, Jack and Brad went to check on the cabins while Charlie stayed with Marion and Dr. Neil. When Jack and Brad returned, they sat at the kitchen table, discussing what to do next. The pie left on the table proved irresistible, and they all took bites as they spoke.

'All his stuff is gone,' Jack reported.

'Not surprising. He's got a head start, but Jack, we're going after the man. Brad, you're staying with Marion and Dr. Neil,' Charlie said.

'Not a good idea. Get on the radio and call for help. He can't fly in this weather. Its dark and snowing; the trail will be dangerous. He's as stuck as we are. We should wait until morning,' Jack argued.

'No, we're going. Get prepped and I'll explain on the way. We leave in five minutes. Brad get on the radio and get a plane to the Flying B as early as possible. Explain what's happened and request reinforcements. Send someone to check on the missing caretaker. And tell them we need to get Dr. Neil and Marion to Seattle ASAP,' Charlie ordered.

'We'll be ready to leave for the Flying B at first light. Be careful. This guy may be enhanced in ways we don't understand,' Brad said.

Departing in a steady snowfall, Charlie and Jack adjusted their headlamps and left the farmhouse at a brisk pace. Charlie was determined to catch up and surprise Ramsey Lewis before he reached the airstrip at the Flying B Ranch. He feared the man had arranged for a flight in the early morning hours, or he would just hike out of the area. Charlie also feared for the safety of the caretaker at the Flying B and was driven to cover ground fast.

But hiking in a heavy snowfall using headlamps was slow going, and it was approaching five a.m. before Charlie and Jack neared the river bar where the Bernard airstrip was located. Charlie and Jack were walking on a narrow stretch of trail near the river. The agents were tired and moved slowly along the waterway. Even though it was pitch dark, the white water to their right glowed with light captured from their headlamps. The sound of the rushing water drowned out the sounds of their footsteps. A steeply sloped, grass-covered hill rose into darkness just a few feet to their left. Rocks and the occasional large boulder littered the trail.

The two FBI agents slowed their pace further and moved as quietly as possible, sensing their prey might be near.

They switched off their headlamps, and Charlie insisted they stand still for several seconds while their eyes adjusted to the dark. The snow stopped momentarily, and Charlie searched the sky for the faint glow of the approaching dawn. But sunrise was still hours away.

ꝺꝺꝺ

Ramsey suddenly realized he was being followed. His enhanced hearing had warned him at about the same time other alarms starting-going off in his head. It seemed impossible the FBI agents had escaped from the lab, but there they were. The tall agent and one of his partners were slowly and cautiously moving toward him. They still had their headlamps on. He could see they were armed. Ramey chided himself for leaving their guns in the lab.

I've been overconfident.

There must have been another way out of the lab.

Ramsey called upon his training and enhancements to

quickly devise the best course of action. In a few nanoseconds, Ramsey considered a huge number of variables.

The tall agent is a very resourceful man.

He escaped from Dr. Neil's lab.

He might be the agent I shot.

In which case he is seeking revenge.

The man is supremely determined.

Ramsey quickly concluded he could use all of this against the tall agent.

He had several other advantages.

Ramsey could see and hear the two men far better than they could sense him.

He had the element of surprise.

By his estimation, Ramsey had an eighty-six percent chance of success. The only reason his chances weren't higher was the presence of two agents; he was outnumbered. He couldn't shoot and kill both men simultaneously. Not with certainty.

I need to separate the two agents.

Ramsey decided to use his pistol and wound the tall agent's partner. Ramsey hoped the tall agent would then come after him alone.

Then I will set my trap.

This will be fun.

His brain took just a few second to devise this strategy, but in that time, the two FBI agents had turned off their headlamps and now stood side by side near the river. Ramsey's night vision worked better in the absence of light, and he could clearly see the two men crouched and speaking in whispers.

Ramsey removed his gun from its holster and took aim.

Firing one round, Ramsey watched as the smaller FBI agent fell to the ground. He saw the tall agent crawl to his wounded partner. After a few seconds, the agent helped his partner to his feet and led him upstream. They hid behind a large boulder. Ramsey lost sight of the two men, but he soon saw the dim glow of a light.

After about ten minutes, and as he expected, Ramsey watched as the tall agent moved quickly across the trail and began climbing up the steep hillside.

The FBI agent is determined to succeed - too determined.

Ramsey headed down the trail to set his trap.

🧬

Unexpectedly, Jack screamed loudly in pain. His cry pierced the night for a split second, before being drowned out by the explosion of a gun. Charlie dove to the ground and scrambled on his hands and knees to his partner, who had fallen to the ground.

Charlie drew his pistol and checked to see if the gun had recognized his handprint. The green light was on, so he knew the gun was activated.

'I'm hit in the left arm; just a scratch,' Jack whispered urgently.

Charlie helped Jack walk upriver until they reached a large boulder. The two men ducked behind the rock and Charlie turned on his headlamp. He immediately began to treat the injury. The bullet had passed cleanly through the soft flesh of Jack's upper left arm.

'Did you see where the shot came from?' Charlie whispered.

'Straight up the trail. I saw a muzzle flash.'

'It must by our Mr. Lewis. Can you handle your weapon?' Charlie asked.

'Sure,' Jack said.

'We're too exposed here. I'm going to climb the hill and try to get ahead of him while it's still dark. Pop off a few shots. Keep him engaged if you can,' Charlie spoke calmly.

'We could back-off until morning,' Jack suggested.

'No. This ends now,' Charlie stated firmly.

'Charlie. Don't be a cowboy,' Jack argued.

Charlie was quiet for a few moments.

'I have the advantage. I know this country, he doesn't,' Charlie said.

'Not enough. He's enhanced. You can't go after him alone,' Jack said.

'I can and I will. I don't have time to argue,' Charlie finished.

After bandaging Jack's arm, Charlie scrambled across the flat ground and began climbing up the steep hill away from the river. He carried his gun, extra ammunition, a set of handcuffs, and binoculars. The hillside was steep, and Charlie quickly lost sight of the trail and Jack. He focused on climbing quietly in the dark.

As his eyes adjusted to the blackness, Charlie found it easier to make his way up the slope. He wondered what it was like to have enhanced night vision. He prided himself on his excellent eyesight in daylight and in the dark. As a lifelong hunter, he had worked to train his eyes to sense movement and patterns from a distance, and to function in low light environments.

Charlie knew scientists had borrowed genetic material from cats and a few other nocturnal animals to enhance the night vision of humans. But how did it work? Was it like wearing night vision goggles or better?

As he climbed, Charlie veered to his right and downstream. He thought he could make out the soft glow of the snow line far above him. Moving through sage and grass, he came upon a game trail. The trail was easier to make out in the dark and headed in the direction he wanted to go. He decided to follow it. But the well-used trail exposed loose rocks that Charlie was forced to avoid, and forward progress was slow.

Without warning, two shots rang out in the quiet night air.

Charlie flinched. It was Jack's gun.

He waited to hear a gunshot in response, but no sound came.

He kept moving.

After ninety minutes, Charlie estimated he had climbed several hundred feet above the river and moved downstream at least a mile. A faint glow in the eastern sky was barely visible when he decided to sit and search for his adversary. He found a small juniper tree and sat down silently in its deep shadow. To his right, Charlie had an excellent view of the area where he believed Ramsey Lewis was hiding when he shot Jack. Unfortunately, the area was still in dark shadow, and the little light available was not helpful.

At his feet, the grassy hillside fell steeply for a hundred feet or so before giving way to a vertical cliff dropping directly into the water. Charlie could hear the white water rushing far below him. To his left, he could barely make out the flat terrain of the river bar and thought he could see the exposed soil of the landing strip in the distance.

Using his binoculars to gather light, Charlie scoped the area for fifteen minutes, but was unable to make out any sign of the man. He carefully examined a group of trees far below him and further to his right. The trees were near where he thought the trail was located. If it was him, Charlie would hide there. He steadied the binoculars by resting his elbows on his knees.

Another gunshot pierced the night, but again no response.

DNA

Ramsey Lewis sat on the ground with his back against the base of a large boulder. The massive granite rock was imbedded into the steep hillside high above the river. He sat in its darkest shadow, and from there, Ramsey had a clear view upstream and to the south.

He chuckled to himself as the FBI agent came into view.

So predictable.

Ramsey's night vision allowed him to clearly see the FBI agent as he moved quietly up the hill. He was still a hundred feet below him and an equal distance upstream. Ramsey was impressed with how gracefully the giant man navigated the steep terrain. The man seemed to hug the steep hillside, using all four limbs to gracefully ascend the slope. Ramsey absorbed his movements, watching as the agent moved left then right in short bursts, always with short steps, following some combination of game trails that only he could see. Looking more like a rock climber than hiker, he moved like an animal.

Ramsey stopped and held his breath.

The tall man suddenly lifted his nose to the sky and cocked his head in Ramsey's direction.

Ramsey felt a deep chill passed through his body and he worked to remain perfectly still.

Then without warning, the FBI agent sat down and disappeared into the shadow of a small tree.

Ramsey worried the tall agent had somehow detected his presence. He was unsure what to do. He suddenly felt trapped. Ramsey glanced at the eastern sky and realized it wouldn't be long before the dawn's first light. He was becoming more and more exposed as the minutes went by. Yet, he couldn't move a muscle.

Did the man see me?

Ramsey again applied his training to calm down and think

about the problem. He trusted the enhancements provided by Gordon and Hawke. He was confident in his ability to make the right decision with limited and contradictory information.

Ramsey watched as the FBI agent leaned forward into what little light existed, just a few inches clear of the shadow, and lifted his binoculars to his eyes.

The man doesn't see me.

He still thinks I'm hiding by the river.

Ramsey decided it was time to act. He rose to his feet slowly and took his gun from its holster.

Time to finish what I started.

Ж

Lowering his binoculars, Charlie closed his eyes and focused his attention on the earth beneath him. He felt the tree against his back and sensed the morning wind beginning to stir. He smelled the sage deeply. Charlie knew the land was a link to his ancestors. He knew they had roamed these hills and walked where he now sat. He reached out to them, and Charlie sensed they were with him.

He recalled an old photograph hanging in his grandparent's living room. The picture was of his great-great grandfather. Charlie was named after this man. He often teased his grandparents about speaking openly and directly to the picture. But now, he desperately wanted to see them and hear their voices.

His mind drifted to memories of being lost in the back country of Idaho when he was young. He recalled watching his parents drive away, leaving him abandoned to live or die. He was proud to remember his subsequent week-long fight for survival and the journey to his grandparent's home. Smiling,

Charlie remembered the look on their faces when he arrived at their ranch with a helpless bear cub in his arms, and a new friend named Evan.

In the weeks following his arrival, living with his grandparents had been great. Charlie wanted it to last forever, and made it clear he never wanted to live with his parents again. His grandparents had been deeply disturbed by his story of abandonment and had promptly confronted Charlie's mother and father. Charlie had never learned what happened when they met, but his grandparents immediately filed for temporary guardianship with tribal authorities. Their request was granted, and Charlie felt safe for the time being.

But when it was time to decide what to do about Ursula, Charlie experienced his first serious disagreement with his grandparents. Of course, Charlie wanted to keep the cub. It was his right. But his grandparents would have nothing to do with raising a black bear. Charlie objected strongly, but in the end, he decided they were right and agreed to his grandfather wishes. Ursula would stay only until a suitable home could be found.

In the meantime, Charlie would do everything possible to increase Ursula's chances of being returned to the wild. Charlie was required to minimize Ursula's contact with people. He built a covered enclosure for Ursula and used a small door to feed and water the bear. Charlie hated the arrangement and keep working to convince his grandfather the cub needed his love and attention. But he knew it was the right thing to do.

Summer rolled toward fall, and Charlie continued his previous habit of spending long hours with his grandfather. But their lives were about to change. Evan had snapped a photograph of Charlie that he later shared with a local newspaper reporter. The reporter had shown up at his grandparent's ranch and interviewed Charlie about his adventure and taken more pictures of him with the bear. The following week a story featuring the photographs of Charlie and Ursula appeared on the front page of the local newspaper.

This was just the beginning.

Charlie's story was soon picked up by a national media outlet. Charlie became famous overnight and appeared in newspapers and other media outlets around the globe. His grandparents were forced to change their telephone number. Reporters and other interested parties found the ranch and hounded them relentlessly. Charlie, along with his grandparents, appeared on several late-night television shows. They were approached about the possibility of a movie and a book deal.

It was amazing, but as Charlie soon learned, it was not to last.

To Charlie's surprise, the media attention faded as quickly as it had arrived. Unfortunately, the damage was done, and Charlie's parents, no doubt smelling money, contacted the tribal authorities. His parents demanded Charlie's return. Charlie had never considered how his parents would respond to seeing him on television.

Charlie's grandparents were ordered to return him to his parent's home in Pocatello.

Charlie would never forget the day his grandfather had driven him to his parent's home, and the short and bittersweet reunion with his father.

'So, the famous son comes home,' his father had said after Charlie's grandfather had left.

'Not what I wanted,' Charlie responded angerly.

'Me either, but I heard you got payed for being on TV. If you got money, hand it over,' his father sneered.

'I got no money. They paid for my travel, that's all. But they were nice enough to not leave me in the woods to die,' Charlie answered smartly.

'Poor baby. We came back to get you, but you ran away. Besides, I was testing your survival skills,' he laughed.

His father was sitting at the kitchen table in the same chair Charlie sat in on his tenth birthday. Based on the number of empty cans on the table, his dad was nursing his fifth beer. Charlie could see him scratching the scar on his left arm.

The scar Charlie had put there.

His mother refused to make eye contact with Charlie, and she quickly left the room.

This was a clue to what was about to happen, and in hindsight, it still bothered Charlie that he had failed to notice it.

Charlie's father stood up and walked toward Charlie, his arms spread wide, pretending to offer a hug.

'Come here boy.'

Completely fooled, Charlie took a step toward his father.

Without warning, his father smashed his fist into Charlie's face.

'That's for shooting me you little fucker.'

Rattled to his core by the blow to the head, Charlie fell to the floor and laid still. He could feel his cheek starting to swell and warm blood flowing over his scalp and down his neck. His head spun violently, and he vomited on the floor.

Wiping his mouth with his shirt sleeve, Charlie watched as his father returned to the chair and reached for his beer.

'Welcome home, you little prick. Get to your room before I hit you again.'

Charlie crawled to his bedroom and hid under the bed.

He didn't move a muscle for hours, laying in the dark recovering from the hard blow.

Later that night, when his parents were asleep, Charlie stuffed a sleeping bag, some clothes and other belongings into his pack, got dressed, and quietly left the house through the back door. Climbing the cedar fence enclosing the backyard, he moved quickly though the shadows until he was blocks away from his house. He found an abandoned warehouse and located a room on the ground floor nearest to an exterior door. He spread his sleeping bag on the floor and, fully dressed, climbed inside. His head was still pounding, and he could feel thick blood tangled in his hair and drying on his scalp.

Feeling slightly better, Charlie woke when the sunlight made its way through a dirty window and poured onto his face. Charlie quickly packed his belongings and headed outside. He'd eaten little the day before, and his body screamed for food. It hit him hard when he realized he had no money and was unlikely to get a meal for days.

Charlie's eyes filled as he considered his situation. He was barely sixteen years old and completely on his own. Returning to his parent's house was out of the question, and if he went back to his grandparent's home, the tribe would just make him live with his parents.

Needing time to think, Charlie wandered along a downtown alleyway. Charlie came around a corner and followed a well-worn trail crossing a vacant lot. Several tall trees shaded the empty lot, and he could see the back of a brick building. As he approached the building, an overhead door rolled up and reveled a man standing near a flat-bed trailer. Four river rafts were sacked, one on top of the other, on the trailer, and as Charlie watched, the man struggled to stack a fifth boat on top of the pile.

Charlie raced to help the man lift the raft onto the trailer.

'Let me help,' Charlie said as he approached the man.

'Thanks. I'm on my own. All my guides are off to school,' the man said.

Once the raft was loaded and Charlie had helped secure the load, the two men introduced themselves and spent some time talking.

The man's name was Liam.

'So, where do you raft?' Charlie asked.

'Just finished my tenth trip this season. Mostly the middle fork and main. Did the south fork once. Got four more groups coming in. This time of year, it's all hunting and fishing parties, mostly rich folk from back east,' replied Liam.

Charlie assumed he was referring to the forks of rivers but was too timid to ask.

'How's that work with no guides?' Charlie asked.

'Just weekend trips this time of year. We take hunters in one weekend and pick them the next. Most of my kids can make it home for a weekend, but I'm still shorthanded.'

'What kind of fishing?' Charlie asked.

'Fly fisherman mostly, looking for trout, and later in the year we'll fish for steelhead.'

'I'd love to hook into a steelhead.'

'You like to fish?' the man asked.

'Love it. My grand-dad taught me to tie flies and catch fish, sure.'

'Can you handle a raft?'

'Never been on a boat.'

'Can you swim?'

'Yeah, I'm a strong swimmer. Why do you ask?'

'You looking to earn some money? I'm desperate for help. I need someone to work the sweep boat and help move gear.'

Too embarrassed to admit he didn't know what a sweep boat was, Charlie just nodded his head in agreement. He was homeless, desperately hungry, and un-employed, Charlie would agree to anything.

'Can you be here at sunrise?' Liam asked.

'Sure. What's the pay?'

'We start you at ten, but if you work hard your wages will go up. Aren't you in school?' asked Liam.

'I've been living with my grandparents and just started going to school there, in Grey's Lake. But I had to come live with my parents. Things didn't work out, so I'm living with a friend. I need a job, so thanks,' offered Charlie.

'Is that what happened to your face?'

Charlie said nothing.

'Fine. We'll talk about that later. But if you're working for me you need to be in school.'

'I'm enrolled, so I can just show up at school.'

'Great. You start classes on Monday. You can work weekends and after school. Where does your friend live?' Liam asked.

'What friend?'

'Where you live, dork.'

'Oh yeah. Not far from here. I can walk,' Charlie said.

In hindsight, Charlie knew that, for reasons he would never fully understand, Liam had spread his protective wings over him. In many ways, becoming the father he never had. And the more Liam learned about Charlie's life, the more involved he became. It didn't take long for him to discover that Charlie was homeless and not living with a friend. Liam responded by providing Charlie with a small, fully furnished room located above his warehouse. The rent was affordable, and Charlie was overjoyed to have a place of his own.

Once Liam found out about Charlie's abusive father, he

had contacted Charlie's grandparents. Together, they had petitioned the tribal court for permanent guardianship. After months of legal wrangling, Charlie's grandparents were awarded permanent guardianship. It was agreed that Charlie would live with his grandparents in the winter months and move in with Liam during the rafting season.

Liam payed all the legal fees.

Charlie became a raft guide and he loved it. He spent weekends on the sweep boat and worked after school during the week in the warehouse. Turned out, a sweep boat was an oversized raft used to haul lots of gear. This included a full kitchen, portable toilets and all the equipment needed to survive on the river. Due to the height of the boat, raft guides used a long, single paddle, a sweep oar, that hung off the stern of the vessel and was used to steer.

As the holidays approached, Charlie moved back in with his grandparents. Attending the local school required him to ride a school bus for one hour each way. Charlie used this time to do his homework, and, over time, and much to his surprise, he started succeeding at school.

The following spring, Charlie returned to Pocatello and resumed working for Liam. By then he was familiar enough with the Middle Fork of the Salmon River that Liam asked Charlie, at the tender age of seventeen, to work the season as a full-fledged guide.

This was a tremendous responsibility, but Charlie had been carefully trained by Liam during the previous fall and felt well prepared for the challenges presented by the mighty white waters of the Middle Fork.

The Middle Fork, as the locals liked to call it, was unlike any other white-water river on the planet. Just over a hundred miles long, the middle fork has fifty big rapids and three hundred stretches of white water dangerous enough to be rated. It's one of the most technically demanding rivers in the world and during high water, can easily kill the most experienced rafter.

The first month of the rafting season went well for Charlie. He led three, four-day trips down the Middle Fork without mishap. But on his first trip in June he nearly lost a family of four. He had been excited about high water and the opportunity to see some big waves. In hindsight, he realized that because of this selfish thinking he had lost his focus, and it nearly proved fatal.

The journey had started on a warm, beautiful June day. They arrived at the put-in early and immediately went to work assembling the raft. Charlie never tired of the stunning terrain of the Middle Fork river drainage. The green river flowed through a steep, rocky canyon, with an occasional flat terrace perched above the river. These areas of flat terrain, or benches, were located on both sides of the river and covered with Ponderosa Pines and a mix of smaller trees. Like watchful guardians, steep rocky bluffs spanned the tops of the canyon walls far above him. In the distance, taller snowclad mountains could be seen through the cuts in the canyon walls. The sky was clear of clouds, and the crystal-clear air allowed the sky to display its finest deep blue.

His clients were a family of four from the Washington DC area. The father and mother were named Bob and Ann respectively. Their two daughters were named Melissa and Cindy.

Once the raft was ready, Charlie gathered the family together and started giving his usual lecture about safety on the river. The speech was based almost word for word on Liam's pre-trip lecture.

'I just have a couple of things to say about safety. When on the river, quick decisions are often required and there is no time for democracy. Lives are at stake; usually one or two rafters drown each year. The captain of the raft is king and obeyed while on the river, especially in the white water. I'm not trying to be a jerk; it's just safer that way.'

'That makes sense. Is the river high?' Ann asked.

'It's high and dangerous, but the level varies every day, depending on the overnight temperatures in the high country and local weather. The best flow levels for floating the Middle Fork are between 1,500 and 5,000 cubic feet per second. The river is currently at 4,500cfs, enough to make it fun without being too crazy,' Charlie said.

'What can we expect in terms of rapids?' Ann asked, clearly the spokesperson for the group.

'Each big rapid is rated using a commonly accepted international scale. There are six levels called Grade or Class. Class VI is the hardest class of rapids and are considered very dangerous. But the scale is not fixed. There can be hard grade Class II or easy Class III, and so on. This time of year, the rapids are mostly Class II with a couple of hard Class III rapids. I don't expect to flip our boat, but if we do go over, just stay close to the raft and hold on to the ropes stretched around the outside of the vessel,' Charlie paused for questions, and hearing none, continued.

'River rafting alternates between floating through calm slow water and short, intense, stretches of white water. In the calm water, the boat moves peacefully downstream, the river as quiet as the surrounding mountains. It's a good time to swim or take a nap. Then, in the distance, you hear the roar of the white water. The boat picks up speed, and the noise gets louder and louder as you approach the rapid. The sound is amplified by the canyon walls. Your heart starts to pump faster, and you tighten the straps on your vest. The boat goes faster still, seemingly in a rush to meet its destiny. You quickly examine your existence on this planet and realize that, just like your life, the boat only goes in one direction, downstream, and there's no turning back. No matter what lies ahead, you're going to meet it head on,' Charlie had borrowed this little speech from Liam.

'You make it sound scary,' Melissa said.

'It is.'

'And a little poetic,' Ann added.

Over the course of the next few hours, they successfully navigated several stretches of white water. Everyone was having fun, and when they reached a section of the river that was calm, Cindy decided to go for a swim. She dove into the cold river and swam away from the boat, her long hair floating weightless, like black wings in the green water. Cindy stopped in mid-stream, floating on her back, letting the current pull her slowly downstream.

As Charlie watched the young girl swim, he worried about making it through the next rapid. He had almost flipped boats in the Tappan Rapids twice, once the previous fall and two weeks earlier, when the river had been lower. He was a pro and not supposed to flip boats. The event had been frightening for his paying clients, and he suspected none of them would become repeat customers.

Charlie heard the approaching white water and asked Cindy to return to the boat.

Focusing on the river, Charlie looked downstream while adjusting their course. He could see the first rocks of the Tappan Rapids fast approaching.

Charlie was suddenly filled with doubt.

Do I go left or right of the rocks?

After hesitating for a few seconds. Charlie made his

decision and moved to the left side of the river. Within seconds he knew it was the wrong choice.

'I took the wrong route. I made a mistake and you all need to dig your feet in and hold on tight to those ropes,' Charlie said calmly.

His four clients gave Charlie a worried look.

The vessel passed to the left of the upstream rocks and moved toward the center of the river, driven by the strongest part of the current. As soon as the boat cleared the rocks, Charlie saw why the alarm bells in his head had sounded so loudly. Straight ahead, fast approaching, were two house-size rocks.

The Twin Cottages.

To be avoided at all cost.

The two boulders towered stories above the surface of the river and were separated by thirty feet of raging water. A sizable portion of the river flowed between their weathered surfaces, raising a huge roiling wave that opened and closed like the jaws of an ancient dinosaur. In front of the wave, a deep trough in the river spanned the entire gap between the rocks.

There wasn't enough time to oar the craft to the right side of the river where the recommended route waited. Charlie had no choice but steered a course for the center of the two giant rocks, now only a hundred feet away.

The river was falling fast, and Charlie keep the vessel pointed to shore, preparing to turn it's bow at the last moment. This was a common practice among rafters and gave him the best chance of hitting the huge wave head on.

But the strong current forced the boat to the right. Charlie pulled hard on the oars as he fought to keep them in the middle of the river. But the river was too powerful, and the vessel continued to drift right.

The boat's bow plowed into the huge rock on their right, and its stern pivoted violently until the rafters faced upriver. Charlie pulled the oars in opposing directions in order to spin the boat, but he didn't have enough time. The boat went into the deep trough backward and slammed into the wall of water. The wave engulfed the raft and flipped it over like a child's toy. Charlie flew into the raging river and watched as the boat stood straight up and then crashed over the heads of his four clients, covering them with water and darkness.

Swimming to the raft, Charlie climbed onto the overturned boat as it passed into the calmer waters below the rapid. He reached under the far side of the boat and grabbed the flip rope. He scrambled back to the other side on the boat, and in one fluid motion, pulled the vessel up on its side until it approached the tipping point. Still standing on the edge of the raft and holding the rope in his right hand, Charlie jumped back into the river, pulling the vessel until it fell toward the water. With a loud slap, the craft slammed right side up onto the surface of the river. Charlie clambered aboard and was relieved to see his four passengers still holding onto the side of the watercraft. Charlie quickly pulled each of them aboard. The entire episode lasted about five minutes.

Three days later, after successfully navigating dozens of rapids, viewing ancient pictographs and soaking in a natural hot spring, Charlie and his four clients arrived at the take-out at Corn Creek. Charlie and the four rafters had bonded during their adventures, and the fivesome were in a jovial mood as the trip came to an end.

But Charlie's mood soured when he saw Liam and two other guides waiting on shore. Charlie was overcome by his embarrassment over flipping the boat, and he was frozen with indecision about how to handle himself.

Once ashore, and the other guides had started the long process of unloading and dismantling the raft, Charlie asked to speak with Liam alone. Bob and his family began to load their personal gear into the company's van as Charlie led Liam away from the ramp area.

'I wanted you to hear it from me. I went left at the top of Tappan Rapid and flipped the boat in the Twin Cottages,' Charlie said.

'You ran the Twins this time of year. Who you trying to impress?' Liam asked.

'Very funny.'

'How'd the clients hold up?'

'They were shook-up but seemed to get over it quick. They hardly mentioned it the rest of the trip,' Charlie said.

'That's good,' Liam spoke and stopped as Bob approached.

'I assume you talking about our little mishap?' Bob asked after he stood next to the other men.

'Charlie was just reporting what happened. I'm sorry, but as you know, the river is boss, and boats go over all the time. I hope it wasn't a problem,' Liam offered.

'On the contrary. I've come to compliment Charlie and to let you know how impressed we were with his handling of the situation. The moment Charlie realized he had made a mistake, he took full responsibility and prepared us for the danger to come. He had us all back in the boat in minutes. Well done, in my book,' Bob finished.

'Glad to hear that. I hope you'll consider coming back for another trip,' Liam added.

'Not only that, but I would recommend it as a vacation to my friends. Getting a look at the backcountry culture and its history has given me hope for this country. Charlie, if you ever need a favor just call me,' Bob said and handed Charlie his business card.

⚕

Charlie caught a familiar scent in the wind and abandoned his daydream.

Suddenly he was very certain of something.

The information flowed into him as casually as his grandfather's advice about the weather.

Ramsey Lewis had outsmarted him again.

He's smarter than I am.

He can see, smell, and hear better than I can.

He's here, right now, waiting for me.

I've walked into another trap.

Charlie heard a soft noise to his left.

It was the sound of a small rockslide. He turned his head slowly in the direction of the noise. There was a dark figure moving toward him, not twenty feet away.

Charlie froze and felt his heart starting to race. He placed the binoculars on the ground beside him and slowly removed his gun from its holster.

The dark figure raised his arms and Charlie was sure he was about to be shot.

He dove to his right and fired three rapid shots at the man. Charlie heard the man scream.

He tried to fire again, but it was too late.

The man bent low and charged at Charlie.

Gripping his pistol, Charlie attempted to meet the man at full height. But the man closed the distance between them quickly and plowed full speed into Charlie's half-erect body.

The man hit Charlie square in his chest, and with a loud grunt, the breath flew out of him. It felt like he was hit by a train, and his arms and legs flew outward.

Charlie's gun launched into darkness.

The two men crashed to the ground, and locked in a fighter's embrace, began rolling down the steep hill toward the river.

As they tumbled down the steep slope, Charlie managed to grab the man around the neck. This left his body exposed, and Charlie felt the man deliver blow after blow to his already bruised ribcage. He roared in pain but refused to release his grasp on the man's throat.

The two men continued to tumble toward the river until Charlie, using his superior size, rolled the man onto his back and managed to dig his boots into the loose soil. The two men came to a stop, face to face, fighting for their lives.

'You motherfucker. You killed my partner,' Charlie shouted.

'Thought I killed you too.'

The man punched Charlie in his midsection. He felt ribs breaking.

'You didn't kill me then, and you won't now!'

Charlie dug his thumbs deeper into the man's throat. This brought an end to the punches. Instead, Ramsey took hold of Charlie's wrists, desperately working to open his airway. But Charlie refused to loosen his grip. After what seemed like an age, Charlie felt the man weakening. His hands released their grip and the man's arms fell to his side. Charlie tightened his grip in case the man was faking. The man was unconscious. Charlie counted slowly to thirty, and then released his grip.

Charlie stood up on the steep hillside, still straddling the man. He towered above the man, panting hard, trying to recover his breath.

Charlie bent over to check the man's pulse. He quickly put his handcuffs on the man's wrists.

Suddenly, the man opened his eyes and kicked Charlie hard in the chest. Charlie slid several feet down the slope and struggled to maintain his balance.

Ramsey leaped to his feet, and holding his handcuffed arms toward Charlie, laughed, and twisted them until they snapped like threads.

Already moving. Charlie lunged at the man.

He was greeted with a fierce punch.

But Charlie was ready, and the glancing blow merely restored him to his full height, causing no harm. He quickly punched the man twice in the face. Charlie could hear bones breaking. He attempted to kick him again, but Ramsey grabbed Charlie's boot. He twisted hard and Charlie yelled in pain. He lost his footing and fell on top of the man.

Entangled again, the two fighters rolled down the hill toward the edge of the cliff.

Charlie could hear the river getting louder.

The men remained entangled as they tumbled onto a gently sloped, grassy area on top of a rock outcropping. The small outcrop of granite rock jutted out from the hillside and hung forty feet above the raging river. The grassy area was just big enough for the two men.

Charlie and Ramsey struggled to their feet and fought hand to hand, both struggling for control. They stood face to face, rocking back and forth as they exchanged blows.

But Ramsey was stronger and more skilled in the martial arts, and Charlie was hard pressed to block his punches. This realization caused him to lose focus, and Ramsey landed a hard blow to Charlie's chin. He fell to his knees, and the man pivoted and got behind Charlie. Ramsey grabbed his grandfather's necklace and began to choke the FBI agent. Immediately his airflow was completely blocked, and Charlie filled with panic. Charlie gulped for air without success. His eyes bulged out and he began to feel faint.

Remembering his underwater training. Charlie relaxed his body so the remaining air in his lungs could flow into his bloodstream. He felt his strength return and fought to loosen the leather band from around his neck. Charlie's right hand found the bear fang his grandfather had given him. The base of the long fang was pressed hard against his Adam's apple. He twisted the fang hard and felt it break away from its leather binding.

Charlie immediately reached behind him and drove the sharp fang into the man's neck.

Ramsey screamed and released his hold on Charlie.

Charlie did his own pivot and attempted to twist the man's arm behind his back. Ramsey anticipated his move and rolled hard to the ground in order to avoid the trap, holding Charlie's arm hard against his chest. This time there was nothing to stop them, and the two fighters tumbled off the grassy knoll and fell into the thin air above the river.

The men separated while falling and splashed into the cold river ten feet apart.

The strong current drove them further apart, and Charlie immediately lost sight of Ramsey.

His body in shock, Charlie gulped for air in the frigid water. The current was swift, and within seconds he was far down river. Exhausted from his battle with Ramsey, and weight down with heavy wet clothes, Charlie struggled to keep his head above water. He was too weak to swim and started choking as he floated downstream. Charlie was at the mercy of the river.

After a time, the river slowed, and Charlie gathered his strength and started to make his way toward the shore to his left. He was shivering violently and had only minutes before he would pass out from the cold.

Suddenly, out of the darkness, a long line of white ice stretched across the river a short distance downstream from where Charlie floated. It was a huge ice shelf, and there was no escaping it. Charlie would be forced under the ice by the strong current in a manner of seconds.

Using a couple of weak strokes, Charlie managed to turn his body over until he faced downstream and his legs pointed toward the ice's ragged edge. He hit the edge of the ice floe with his boots, and for a moment, Charlie thought he could hold himself steady using his strong legs. But his lower limbs were no match for the power of the river, and his feet slipped under the thick ice. He could feel the toes of his boots scraping along the bottom of the ice.

Charlie's reached across the top of the ice, and his fingers gripped hard. He managed to stop his upper body from being driven under the ice by the moving water. But it was a losing battle. Charlie felt the strong current slowly dragging his body under the ice and to a certain death. His fingernails left tracks in the ice as he lost his battle with the river, inch by painful inch. His fingers screamed, and both arms ached in pain. He struggled to find a handhold on the hard ice.

Screaming in agony, Charlie was about the go under the ice shelf when he felt a pair of strong hands grip him under his armpits and drag him out of the cold water and onto the frozen surface. His teeth chattering, Charlie turned to face his rescuer.

It was Jack.

After a few minutes, his body recovered, and Charlie rose

to his feet. Water was dripping off his clothes, and a cloud of steam rose from his now hatless head.

'That was a close call, my friend. Thanks for showing up,' Charlie managed to speak as he shivered.

'I saw you fall into the river and ran to catch up. But the river is too fast, and the shoreline was too rough. If it wasn't for the ice stopping you, I never would have caught up,' Jack said, breathing hard in the cold air.

'Well I owe you one.'

'You owe me nothing. Let's get a fire going and dry you out,' Jack suggested.

'Any sign of Ramsey Lewis?' Charlie asked.

'Too dark. I heard him yell as he hit the water, but I never saw him. I only saw you because of your coat,' Jack admitted.

'Doubtful he survived. I stuck my bear fang into the side of his neck,' Charlie said between his chattering teeth.

15

MONDAY, DECEMBER 27TH, 2050

The Devil hath power to assume a pleasing shape.
William Shakespeare

Two days later, after the FBI team, Marion, and Dr. Neil traveled to Seattle, the CDC hastily convened a press conference. By then, the story of the team's adventures in Idaho and the potential involvement of Dr. Jane Neil, a popular target of the national press, had been shared with privileged members of Seattle's press establishment. As a result, the CDC auditorium was filled with reporters, hours before the event was scheduled to begin.

This forced Dr. Peck to postpone the press conference until nine a.m. and move the event to the Seattle city hall.

At eight forty-five, Charlie and Hunter stood on the steps of city hall, waiting for Dr. Peck and the other members of the team to arrive. Charlie was surveying the dozens of reporters and their camera crews as they filed into the auditorium. The reporters were loud, and Charlie could sense high expectations among the press.

Dr. Peck and her team arrived and greeted Charlie and his boss before entering the auditorium.

Once everyone was seated, he watched as Dr. Peck calmly took charge of the reporters and confidently faced-down the dozens of bright lights and cameras staring her in the face. After introducing herself, Dr. Peck began.

'We have some significant developments to report. The CDC has been collaborating with the genetics team at the FBI since it was discovered that Quinn Conner was not murdered and may have fallen victim to the emerging outbreak. We are pleased to announce possible progress in halting the disease. But first, allow me to call to the stage and introduce the individual members of this FBI-CDC interagency team,' she said.

A quiet murmur rose from the crowd in response to this information.

She paused as Charlie and the others filed onto the stage. Dr. Peck took care in introducing Special Agent in Charge Ross Hunter, Charlie and Brad, as well as Dr. Marion Harper and Dr. Jane Neil. She also mentioned Agent Jack Lee who was recovering from his wound at home.

'The actions of these brave individuals will undoubtedly save thousands of lives. The story began ten days ago when Quinn Conner was found dead near his father's estate. His death was initially deemed suspicious, and the FBI opened a homicide investigation. During the investigation, it was discovered Mr. Conner, who worked at Genlabs, had completed a classified report on the day of his death. The report couldn't be located, but FBI agents had reason to believe it was the motive behind his murder. The team conducted its investigation based on these assumptions, until it was discovered that Mr. Conner may have been a victim of the emerging outbreak.'

Dr. Peck paused to allow this information to sink in. She took a moment to review her notes before continuing.

'At the same time, the FBI uncovered evidence related to the recent bombing at the CDC building in downtown Seattle. We believe the bombing was set in motion by Gordon Kelly, with the goal of destroying Mr. Conner's body. These events are connected and were instigated to cover-up the fact that Genlabs knew about the potential of an outbreak years ago,' Dr. Peck announced.

She paused while the crowd reacted loudly in response to these revelations. Charlie watched as several reporters filed reports. Once the crowd of reporters settled down, she continued

'So, we are waging war on an emerging epidemic, and the FBI is investigating a conspiracy to cover it up. Mr. Kelly is now in custody. However, he had an accomplice. A genetically enhanced individual by the name of Ramsey Lewis. Evidence has linked Mr. Lewis to the bombing of the CDC building. As has been reported, the FBI attempted to arrest Mr. Lewis on Christmas eve at his home near Carnation. Unfortunately, he escaped.'

Again, Dr. Peck paused while the group of reporters reacted to this news. Several minutes passed before she could start again.

'This leads me to the most significant development in this unique case. Once we recovered Mr. Conner's report, it confirmed our worst fears about the outbreak. It also pointed investigators to Dr. Neil, who lives at a remote location in Idaho. Charlie and his team, along with Dr. Harper, traveled to Idaho on Christmas day with the intention of questioning her. However, Mr. Lewis arrived in Idaho first and set a trap for the team. The FBI believes Ramsey Lewis was sent to Idaho with orders from Gordon Kelly to kill Dr. Neil. Agent Edmo and his team arrived before his plan could be carried out. To this point we still didn't have any idea what Mr. Lewis looked like. Mr. Lewis took advantage of this and pretended to be a local guide. He led Charlie and his team to Dr. Neil's ranch.'

Dr. Peck paused to catch her breath.

By this point, the group of reporters sat quietly, hanging on her every word.

'Ramsey Lewis then kidnapped and used explosives to bury them inside Dr. Neil's underground lab. Fortunately, they were able to escape. Agents Edmo and Lee then pursued Ramsey Lewis. The agents confronted Mr. Lewis near the Flying B Ranch in the Idaho wilderness. Agent Jack Lee was shot by Mr. Ramsey. Agent Edmo pursued the assailant and a struggle ensued. Mr. Lewis and Agent Edmo both fell into the Salmon River. Thankfully, Agent Edmo survived. Ramsey Lewis was injured in the fight and has not been found. He is presumed dead. FBI agents are continuing to search for his body.'

The reporters reacted loudly, and Dr. Peck could see them filing reports on their app-pads. She knew the story would be viewed by millions of people around the world in seconds. It took several minutes for the group to quiet. Dr. Peck could sense the reporters were rabid to begin the question and answer phase. She worked to quiet the crowd.

'Please, please, before questions. I have something important to say.'

The crowd of reporters grew quiet.

'For the past twenty years, and using her own personal fortune, Dr. Neil and her staff continued to conduct research at her lab in Idaho. Dr. Neil recently completed successful trials of a promising approach for halting this terrible outbreak. Dr. Neil has displayed tremendous courage in the face of unjust ridicule. Her personal life was ruined, and rather than submit to anger, she went forward with her work. We are the beneficiaries of her courage. Dr. Neil deserves our gratitude.'

Dr. Peck turned and smiled at Dr. Neil.

After turning back toward the crowd, she said.

'I'll take questions, now,' Dr. Peck said.

The reporters erupted in loud shouting as they vied to have their questions answered first. Dr. Peck selected a reporter from the Seattle Times.

'Can you tell us more about what happened in Idaho? How did the team escape?' the reported asked, as he looked over his written notes.

Ross Hunter approached the podium.

'Mr. Lewis kidnapped the entire team at gun point and locked them in Dr. Neil's lab which was built into the mountainside near her home. The suspect used a bomb to seal off the lab's main entrance. But there is an emergency exit, which the team used to escape,' Special Agent Hunter explained.

Dr. Peck returned to the microphone and called upon another reporter.

'You're press release states the outbreak is the result of an engineering flaw specific to second generation designer-babies? As it turns out a flaw that GSI and Genlabs knew about for years? How could such a huge conspiracy happen right under the noses of the FBI?' the reporter asked.

Ross Hunter again walked to the podium in order to address the reporter's question.

'Unfortunately, it took Quinn Conner's death to alert the FBI to the happenings at Genlabs. But you need to give credit to the FBI and our partners at the CDC for discovering the connection between Mr. Conner's death and the outbreak.'

Dr. Peck selected another reporter.

'Will Dr. Neil's discoveries stop the outbreak?' the reporter asked.

Marion walked to the podium and responded to the question.

'It's hard to predict before field tests. The theory of a 'selfish gene' is based on the premise that the original genetic material would over time, reject the human engineered genes introduced into the person's DNA before he or she was born. Based on our preliminary analysis, this could be what's happening. The original genetic code appears to attack the engineered genes as if it were a foreign virus. When enough cells self-destruct, the person dies. The time period between getting sick and dying appears to vary considerably. Dr. Neil has developed nanomachines capable of locating and splicing out the offending genes. The same machines can be used to splice in the original DNA sequences, or in some areas of the cell, benign genetic material. But we don't have copies of the original genetic sequences for the affected men. Only Genlabs maintains copies of the genetic sequences for their designer-babies.'

'Is there any indication that Genlabs will provide these genetic sequences to the CDC?' a reporter asked.

'Not yet. But we'll be meeting with their representatives later today,' Dr. Peck said.

'So, if I understand this correctly, the disease could affect other generations of designer-babies?' another reporter asked.

'That is possible,' Marion answered.

For the next hour, Dr. Neil, Dr. Peck and Charlie answered dozens of questions from the press.

As the questions tapered off, Dr. Peck again assumed control of the press conference.

'Our efforts to eradicate the outbreak will move forward.

The FBI anticipates a grand jury will be seated in coming weeks. Additional arrests are expected. Lastly, as was mentioned, we'll meet later today with representatives of GSI and Genlabs. We will be asking for their help. To date, nearly a hundred men have perished. There are reports from nearby states of other young men becoming sick. Given the seriousness of the situation, we are expecting their full cooperation.'

Dr. Peck thanked the reporters and concluded the press conference.

Charlie and Hunter stood in a quiet corner outside the auditorium, far from the dozens of reporters and bystanders who were exiting the building.

'So, things worked out. The Conner case will be closed, and it's likely the CDC will get what they want from Genlabs. And the best part, I get to fire you,' Hunter said.

'Why? I just showered you with glory you don't deserve. I broke this case, and got Dr. Neil to Seattle unharmed,' Charlie argued.

'You disobeyed a direct order,' Hunter responded.

'Fine, fire me. Then I'll be forced to tell folks about your little relationship with Gordon Kelly,' Charlie whispered.

Charlie's statement was met by an uncomfortably long silence.

'How the fuck did you find out about that?' Hunter whispered.

'It didn't occur to you we would be listening to Gordon Kelly's calls?' Charlie asked.

'You know nothing,' Hunter hissed.

'I know enough. And it explains a great deal about this case,' Charlie urged.

'You wouldn't dare go public. Think of what it'll do to the agency?' Hunter offered.

'Try me. The agency is better off when it cleans house occasionally.'

'You can't prove a thing,' Hunter pleaded.

'You don't know what other evidence I have,' Charlie said.

His statement was met with another long and awkward silence.

'Okay. Okay. You win. Can we call a truce?' Hunter asked.

'Not so fast. You blamed me for Hank's death. That's bullshit, and now you know it. Ramsey Lewis killed Hank and shot me, likely on orders from your friend Gordon,' Charlie argued.

'I never blamed you for Hank's death,' Hunter urged.

'You prick. That's exactly what you did.'

'Listen, you're a good agent. But I have a lot riding on the Conner case,' Hunter admitted.

'Like getting back to New York.'

'Among other reasons,' Hunter said.

'Fine, I get that. But from this moment forward, I expect you to protect me. Even if it means throwing yourself under the bus. Understand?' Charlie asked.

'Okay. I'll keep my word. But at some point, you will pay for this,' Hunter sneered.

'Not if you're in prison,' Charlie said.

'Are you threatening me?' Hunter asked.

'Yes. And don't doubt my resolve,' Charlie glared at his boss.

'Poor Indian. You were always a fucking victim,' Hunter sneered.

'Who are you to talk. You've done nothing but whine since you got here,' Charlie responded. 'And you haven't accomplished a damn thing.'

This statement was met with more silence.

Hunter's app-phone beeped.

'They're ready to question Gordon Kelly. We need to get back,' he said.

𝄞

June 18th, 2020
Journal Entry #104
Gordon Kelly, MIT Graduate Student

Today was the last class of the semester and my professor did something unexpected. She read a poem. At first, I considered it a waste of my time. I hate it when professors try to be entertainers and wondered what any poem could possibly add to a serious conversation about science. But as she read, one line from the poem by Leonard Cohen captured my attention.

"We are so large against the sky, so small between the stars."

How can twelve words convey so much meaning? For the first time in my life, I was impressed by something other than math formulas and scientific theory.

My professor followed up her reading of the poem by asking the following question.

'Given a vast and seemingly indifferent cosmos, do our lives really matter?'

The wording of the question rubbed me the wrong way, and as the class discussion heated up, I kept my mouth shut. I was convinced she wanted to deceive us into admitting the possibility that there is a higher being, instead of considering an infinite number of other possibilities.

I couldn't understand why she brought religion into the

conversation. I was convinced she had missed the point of the poem. The line from the poem, to me, compared the vast scale of the universe to the tiny planet on which we reside. It's another way of saying that on the micro and macro scales, everything is still very much a manner of perspective.

And doesn't science provide a clearer perspective and insights about the nature of the universe than religion ever could?

Yet I know of some very credible scientists who argue that the universe was built by their God to exclusively harbor life. They point to the controversy surrounding the carbon atom. The argument goes like this: Given the profound improbability that nuclei of helium and a particularly unstable isotope of beryllium would meet, and fuse to create carbon atoms, and do so only in the heart of red giant stars, strongly suggests this basic component of life should not exist in vast quantities.

Yet this is the only way that carbon atoms come to exist in vast quantities. And carbon is the basis for all life, at least on earth. We are literally made from star dust, which in all probability, shouldn't be here.

Scientists have noticed other strange coincidences: the perfect range of temperatures available for life, the suspiciously helpful properties of water and light, and other principles of physics that seem explicitly structured to support organic life. Some scientists point to these coincidences as evidence that the cosmos was created for sentient beings, subconsciously implying the hand of a higher being is at work.

Believing the universe is governed by scientific laws, I have rejected the notion that some imaginary being who lives beyond the rules reigning over matter and energy is running the whole show. Neither do I believe life is the reason for the existence of the universe. Seems more likely to me it's the other way around. However, hearing the poem made me curious about how the laws of physics allowed a species as complex as ours to exist.

There must be a lot to learn from the fact that we're even here.

I got up the nerve and raised my hand. I explained my reasoning, and asked my professor to explain why evolution, given enough time, always creates increasingly complex systems?

She claims the answer can be found in Newton's second law.

I argued the second law describes disorganization and randomness.

But she informed me that it's this randomness that creates complex structures. For instance, she said, chance mutations are central to the study of human genetics.

I was covered with goosebumps as the meaning of her words sank in.

So, is there is a higher power writing the rules? Some transcendent authority creating physical laws that ensure there is life in this vast and cold universe?

How the hell do I know? I doubt it. Honestly, I'm not that interested in the question.

In a world filled with people searching for ways to live meaningful lives, I'm happy to just live an interesting and intellectually challenging one.

Sitting on a cot in his jail cell, Gordon finished reading the last entry in his college journal. Tears poured down his face. He squeezed his eyes shut to stop the flow, but this just forced more tears to pour down his cheeks. His entire head throbbed like a drumbeat. His heart felt bruised and pulsed unevenly.

Breathing was a chore, and he closed his eyes, trying to remain calm.

It's going to be a long, pain-filled day.

He remembered the day he had written this journal entry. It was a day that ending up representing so much about his life. He was floating on air after leaving class. He had joyfully written about that day's class discussion in his journal and felt like the whole world was his for the taking.

An hour later he was being wheeled into the local hospital after suffering a major mental breakdown. He learned that day that his life was going to be a roller coaster ride. Gordon began to understand the relationship between being high on life and his subsequent decent into depression.

The doctors had struggled to diagnosis his condition. In the end, he'd been sent back to college without a clear verdict about his mental health, but in possession of an array of psychotropic drugs.

Opening his eyes, he was distracted by a cockroach climbing the wall of his cell.

Was the pest there before?

Somehow the insect had climbed most of the way up the wall without his noticing. He watched as the insect neared the ceiling. The huge bug moved cautiously, jagging left then right, following some unseen scent trail. Its huge antennae swaggered back and forth. Gordon thought he could hear a high-pitched squeaking coming from the insect.

Gordon heard footsteps outside his cell. The small opening in the middle of the cell door opened.

The guard spoke quickly.

'They're ready for you.'

It was time to be questioned by the FBI.

Gordon slid his hands through the opening in the door

and grimaced as the handcuffs were tighten around his wrists. He pulled his arms back, and the guard opened the door to the cell. Gordon followed the guard to the interview room.

When Gordon Kelly entered the room, Charlie nearly gasped at how much he had changed. He looked like someone who had already served the long prison sentence awaiting him. Charlie almost felt sorry for the man who stood awkwardly before him trying to project a sense of bravado. But Charlie recognized an unstable person. Gordon's eyes darted around the room, and it was clear he might not be comprehending what was happening to him. He looked like he had been crying. The bandage on his left cheek was wet and hung awkwardly, close to falling off. Gordon kept trying to reattach the bandage in order to cover his injury.

At his best, Gordon was an ordinary looking man. Balding, with a small belly, Gordon looked like he hadn't been outdoors in years. His pale skin looked translucent in the bright glow of the florescent lighting and the dark veins riding over the top of his exposed hands looked like they were no longer under his skin. The deep sacks under his eyes looked like teabags and Charlie struggled to reconcile the man entering the room and the one portrayed in the press.

Gordon refused to make eye contact with Charlie and sat in his chair quickly. Once seated, he stared downward at the table. Following Gordon into the interview room was Genlab's attorney, Kathleen Holden. Gordon and his attorney sat across from Charlie and his boss Ross Hunter. Brad, Lee and a team of agents sat in a nearby room, watching the interview via video. The team was recording the proceedings, and several members of the team were assigned to observe specific aspects of the interview.

As agreed upon beforehand, Charlie would do the questioning, and Hunter would observe the accused as he responded. After introductions, Charlie spent thirty-minutes working through a series of perfunctory questions. This was the first of many interviews and the questions were designed to confirm information the FBI had already collected and to establish a baseline for future interrogations.

Gordon mostly mumbled one-word responses throughout the questioning and was either unable or uninterested in cooperating. Charlie was getting frustrated, so he decided to abandon the agreed upon line of questioning and get straight to the point.

'Mr. Kelly. Are flaws in your engineering responsible for the deaths of ninety-six men?' Charlie asked.

'No comment.'

'When did you know about these problems?'

'No comment.'

'So, you admit to knowing about the fatal flaws in your engineering? I'll ask again, when did you find out about these flaws?'

'No comment.'

'Did you direct Quinn Conner to look into the problems with the second gens?'

'No comment.'

'Did Mr. Conner prepare a report for you outlining these fatal flaws?'

'No comment.'

'Did you take steps to destroy Mr. Conner's report?'

'No comment.'

'Mr. Kelly. Are you responsible for the death of Quinn Conner and ninety-six young men?' Charlie shouted.

Charlie could see the last question caught Gordon's attention. His eyebrows arched, and Charlie watched as the man's demeanor changed. Gordon sat straight up in his chair and ran both hands over his bald head. He turned to face Charlie, meeting his eyes with an intense glare. In a loud, clear voice, he began to speak.

'The death of these men is a small price to pay. A thousand men could die, and it wouldn't matter. Don't you get it? I'm trying to save our pitiful species. Don't ask me why. I want to vomit when I see how fucking ignorant you are. Don't you get it? We won't make it, unless I'm allowed to finish my work.'

'Gordon, I insist you shut up and just answer the questions,' Ms. Holden said.

'Kathleen . . . fuck off.'

Gordon jumped to his feet and shouted.

'Jane knew the truth. She knew there was a problem with the code years ago. But we needed to be the first. Don't you understand? We didn't care about the selfish gene theory. Compared to all the good we were doing, the risk was worth it. Throw me in prison; it doesn't matter, it's too late.'

Exhausted by the effort, Gordon sank onto his seat. He lowered his head to the table and began whimpering quietly.

'Quinn discovered the truth?' Charlie struggled to not scream at the little man.

'He had to die. I needed time. I can fix the problem. I just need to get back to work,' Gordon begged.

Charlie resisted an urged to throttle the man. He wanted to kill him with his bare hands. His buried emotions were triggered by Gordon's words and tone. His growing hatred of the genetic engineering industry, his own daughter's demands to change her genetic makeup, and his constant frustration with enforcing the rule of law in a society overrun by enhanced humans, were all coming to the surface.

'Get him the fuck out of here, before I . . . ' Charlie stopped.

Hunter reached behind him and knocked on the door. A guard entered the room and led Gordon and his lawyer out of the room.

DNA

Watching Gordon and his attorney, Kathleen, leave the room, Charlie remained seated, staring into space. As a result, he didn't hear Hunter's question.

' . . . if he's telling the truth,' Hunter finished.

'You mean Gordon?' Charlie confirmed.

'Right. That sounded a lot like a confession to murder. Just what exactly killed Quinn Conner? I'm confused,' Hunter pleaded.

'I think he was telling the truth,' Charlie offered.

'I agree. We need to find out what the hell is going on at Genlabs. We're shutting them down right now. I'm calling the judge. Get a team together. We leave in an hour,' Hunter declared.

DNA

Gordon returned to his cell and immediately feel asleep.

After a time, there was another loud banging on the door to his cell.

'Someone else to see you.'

'My lawyer?'

'No. Dr. Jane Neil,' the guard said.

Gordon felt shock seize his body, and he hesitated for a long time.

'You comin or not?' the guard asked.

Placing both hands through the opening in the door, Gordon felt the handcuffs tighten around his wrists. The restraints initiated an instant panic attack. He worked hard to not fight against the cuffs.

Leaving the jail cell and walking across the building gave Gordon time to calm himself, but as he entered the visitors room, panic overtook him again. His heart pounded so hard he could feel it beating against his rib cage. His body shivered from head to toe as the guard led him to a chair facing a glass partition with a small voice hole.

On the other side of the glass sat his ex-wife. Gordon tried to breathe deeply, but only managed to catch a shallow breath.

'Here to gloat?' Gordon asked in a whisper.

'Yes . . . and you look great. I wondered if this place would agree with you. You should feel lucky, this place is nice compared to where you're going,' she sneered.

'Fuck you. Why are you here?' he asked.

'I need to look you in the eye. I need to see you destroyed. I'm creating memories for my old age,' Dr. Neil said, and laughed.

'You could have been spared all this trouble if you had had the decency to kill yourself properly,' she added.

'Fuck you.'

'No can do. Sex was never your strong point. Besides, I must go enjoy my freedom. But one last thing,' Dr. Neil leaned close to the voice hole in the glass and whispered to Gordon.

'Your little company will not survive what I'm about to do.'

'What are you talking about?'

'You know what I'm talking about. I'm not as stupid as the

FBI. Just watch the news, you bastard. I hope you rot in hell, and Hawke along with you.'

Dr. Neil rose from her chair, looked at Gordon for a moment, and left the room.

Gordon maintained control of his emotions until he was back in his cell.

Then he lowered himself to the hard-cold floor, curled up into a ball, and began to sob.

ꍞꍞꍞ

The meeting was scheduled to begin immediately after the press conference in order to bring maximum pressure on GSI and Genlabs. If the two companies decided to not cooperate, Charlie knew the CDC would be forced to take legal action. A process that could takes months or even years. Dr. Neil's work would go to waste and many more men would die.

It seemed inconceivable to Charlie the two companies would not cooperate and share their data. But as he read the statements submitted by the companies' scientists, it was clear they disagreed with the findings of the CDC. They pointed to other possible causes for the outbreak. The fact the deaths had been confined to Washington State pointed to a local cause, they claimed. It was far too early to draw firm conclusions, they added.

It was clear GSI and Genlabs intended to dig in their well-financed heels.

Yet, nobody had officially heard from the leaders of either company. There were rumors Hawke Conner had visited Gordon in the hospital before he was released and arrested. The local press had also reported Hawke Conner had met with Gordon a second time in jail. But nobody knew what was discussed in either meeting. Given the high stakes, Charlie expected plenty of fireworks. He looked forward to quietly sitting in the corner and watching the show.

Charlie was worried Dr. Peck faced an impossible task. He considered possible strategies she could use to convince Genlabs and GSI to comply with the demands of the CDC. Charlie understood the real leverage was the potential for a major public relations nightmare resulting in the demise of both companies, not to mention potential legal problems for years to come. How this leverage could be wielded was beyond Charlie's experience.

With Lois in the lead, Charlie, Brad, Hunter, Dr. Neil, and the CDC team - fifteen individuals in total - entered the meeting room. Charlie watched Dr. Neil's reaction upon seeing Hawke Conner seated across the table from her. Charlie knew Dr. Neil and Hawke Conner had a serious falling out years before. Hawke had publicly insulted her and called for Gordon to divorce her. Their public feud had been fierce.

Charlie could sense the coldness as he watched the pair exchange a quick handshake.

Taking his seat against the wall, Charlie saw that, in addition to Hawke Conner, the GSI and Genlabs' team occupied the entire side of the room opposite from them. To his right, and at the end of the table, the directors of the CDC and several other representatives of governmental agencies were visible on a large video screen. In all, fourteen public and private sector entities were represented.

Dr. Peck opened the meeting and asked for all participants to introduce themselves and make brief opening remarks.

The drone of the endless introductions sent Charlie into a deep daydream. He thought about the night he had run away from his parent's home. After sleeping in a warehouse, Charlie had walked for hours until by chance, he had been lucky enough to meet Liam. Looking back, Liam had done three things that he would always be grateful for. First, he had given Charlie his first job. Charlie was proud of the time he had spent as a river guide.

Liam had also required Charlie to stay in school if he wanted to keep his job. The encouragement Liam provided during his last two years of high school led to success, and a realization that he was good at science. It was Liam who had convinced Charlie to consider a career in genetics and law enforcement.

Lastly, Liam had immediately contacted Charlie's grandparent - something Charlie had been embarrassed to do.

Frank and Joyce Edmo had driven to Pocatello the day Liam had called. Arriving late in the afternoon, his grandparents were so upset by Charlie's story, that they had immediately contacted the tribal authorities. The tribal court had again granted his grandparents temporary guardianship of Charlie, and there was a promise that tribal police would pay a visit to his parents. Among other things, they would be told to have no contact with their son.

Liam, and Charlie's grandparents, agreed that from early June until the rafting season ended for the year, Charlie would live with and work for Liam. But as soon as the raft season ended in early November, Charlie would go to live with his grandparents near Grey's Lake. He would stay with them until rafting season began again.

So, Charlie attended school and rafted on weekends until the first week of November, and then moved to his grandparent's home and transferred to a new school. In contrast to his experience attending school in Pocatello, Charlie's fame had preceded him, and for the first time in his life, he was popular with his peers. He suddenly found himself surrounded by new friends.

And for the first time, Charlie had a girlfriend. Anna George was a year behind him in school, but because of the small size of the student body, frequently attended the same classes as Charlie. It was clear to their classmates from the start that Charlie and Anna were a natural couple. Both were good students and easily the most handsome pair on campus.

Relishing his new popularity, and driven by his competition with Anna, Charlie became a good student, and by his senior year, had been offered scholarships to attend several universities. As graduation approached, Charlie decided to attend the University of Washington. Anna had enough credits to graduate a semester early and would join Charlie in Seattle during the holidays.

After graduating, Charlie worked for Liam over the summer, guiding raft trips down the Middle Fork. But as the first day of classes approached, Charlie said his goodbyes and moved into a dorm room on the UW campus in Seattle.

But the transition from the rural hinterland of Idaho to the massive urban university proved more difficult than Charlie imagined. And it wasn't just the madness of living in north Seattle. Charlie missed Anna and felt like an outsider at the university from the moment he arrived. He remembered walking into his first law enforcement class. The class convened in a huge three hundred seat auditorium, and he was the only Indian in the crowded room. Charlie was used to being stared at and was long past caring about what others thought about him.

But when his fellow students went beyond just staring, Charlie felt betrayed.

There was one episode that still made Charlie angry every time he recalled it. The professor had passed around a sign-up sheet for the lab associated with the lecture portion of the class. As the sign-up sheet was being passed around, Charlie noticed whispering and quiet laughter behind him, and it seemed like a long time before the clipboard came to him. When the sign-up sheet arrived, every slot was filled. Each lab only had ten workstations and he was the odd man out. He was forced to complete the lab alone.

After this and several other episodes, Charlie was so mad he decided to quit school and move back to his home in Idaho. But after stern lectures from Liam and Anna, Charlie agreed to stay until the end of the semester and then reevaluate his decision. But as the holidays approached, Charlie felt more like an outsider than ever, and had come to believe he would never fit in at the UW. He had not made a single new friend and struggled to hit it off with any of his professors. Charlie hated the urban environment and longed for the outdoors. As Charlie headed home for the holiday break, he was convinced he would not return to the UW.

And if it wasn't for an event that happened over the holidays, Charlie might never have returned to Seattle.

It happened a few days after Charlie had returned to Idaho. Along with Anna and his grandparents, Charlie had driven into Blackfoot for dinner. They parked and entered the restaurant, and as they were being seated, Charlie saw a good friend from high school clearing the table next to them.

'Hey dude, what's up?' Charlie asked his friend.

'Charlie. Wow! Famous boy comes home to sprinkle some star dust,' his friend said with a strong hint of sarcasm.

Charlie offered his handshake.

Instead of shaking his hand, the friend threw his arms above his head and danced as if he was being rained on by stardust.

'I can feel your magic dust,' the boy sang.

'Are you high, Jeff?' Charlie lamented.

'Fuck you. I saw you on TV. Famous and all. Going to the big city university. Bet I never see you again,' Jeff said and thumped Charlie on his chest with his index finger.

'That's hardly fair,' Charlie answered loudly.

Everyone seated in the restaurant looked in their direction.

'You want to go outside?' Jeff shouted and thumped Charlie again, this time on his forehead.

Charlie grabbed his friend with both hands and lifted him off the floor. Charlie resisted the urge to throttle his high school friend. Instead, he dropped him to the floor.

Jeff jumped to his feet and stood half erect, looking like he was about to charge Charlie. His legs were spread wide, and both feet were firmly planted in the floor. Jeff glared at Charlie.

Suddenly his friend's body language changed. Jeff stood up straight, shook his entire frame and said.

'Let me know when you're done eating so I can clean up your mess.'

Jeff picked up his dish box and walked calmly toward the kitchen.

Watching his friend walk away made Charlie realized he was outsider at home and in Seattle.

I might as well go to school. I've a better chance of changing minds in the university than here.

Charlie ended his daydream when he realized it was his turn to introduce himself.

Dr. Peck officially convened the meeting shortly after Charlie finished stumbling through his introduction.

'Thank you for coming, and I'm pleased to see a high level of representation from all the major stakeholders. This seems fitting, given the gravity of the crisis. As you all know, we are rapidly approaching one hundred fatalities. These deaths are concentrated in two areas of the state, Spokane, and Yakima. Additional cases have been reported in two other counties and three other states. Currently, there are no treatment options. We expect many more men will soon get sick and die. The potential of this outbreak to destroy human life requires an unprecedented level of cooperation between private industry and government. The bottom line is that, without this cooperation, the outbreak will spread, and many more lives will be lost,' Lois said.

She paused for a few moments, allowing her words to sink in.

Charlie noticed that Lois was looking directly at Hawke.

'You have all been briefed about how we got to this point. We don't have time to discuss what's transpired in the past. I must insist that we move forward and leave it to others to identify past mistakes and to recommend tighter regulations for governing the genetic services industry, should they be needed. Our goal today is to evaluate Dr. Neil's research as quickly as possible. If we can agree her approaches are viable, then I suggest we form a partnership and assign responsibilities as the situation merits. In this spirit, I've asked Dr. Neil to open the meeting by bringing us up-to-date on her research.'

Dr. Neil remained at her seat as she prepared to speak. The group grew very quiet as she began. Charlie watched as she took a deep breath and closed her eyes. She spoke for several seconds before opening them again.

'When I was released from prison almost twenty years ago, and after I received my divorce settlement, I moved to the backcountry of Idaho and stayed drunk for a year.'

She paused for uncomfortable laughter.

'Clearly, I was feeling sorry for myself. One day, I was soaking in my hot spring, drunk as usual, and it hit me. There was going to be an epidemic, it was just a matter of time. Men were going to start dying. I was confident in my research. But I couldn't return to my previous career. I knew the research community had rejected me and could care less about the concept of a genetic reset button. But I felt I had a responsibility to do something, and I had lots of money and time. I decided to ramp up my research. In secret, I built a lab in the wilderness, where I could work undisturbed. I hired smart, dedicated people. For the next few minutes, I want to share what we've discovered,' Dr. Neil said.

She paused, removed her glasses and rubbed the bridge of her nose again. Placing her glasses back on her head, she pointed her app-pad at the nearby screen. An image of a DNA molecule appeared.

For the next forty-five minutes, Dr. Neil summarized her research findings for the assembled group. She explained her approach to engineering the nanotechnology and demonstrated the machines' capabilities. Dr. Neil displayed the software used to control the process and presented data about its reliability.

She concluded her presentation by saying:

'The prototypes and software have proven reliable. The genetic reset button is built. I just need access to the original genetic sequences of the individuals who will potentially be affected by the outbreak.'

'That's three-hundred thousand separate sets of DNA sequences. It must be hundreds of teraflops of data. Is that manageable?' Marion asked.

'I miss-spoke. We don't need the entire sequence for every individual, just a significant sample. Much of the engineered sequences can be replaced with benign material. Once

Genlabs provides the genetic sequences for the second gens, I'll need a week to begin producing prototypes,' Dr. Neil said.

'Then what?'

'If they agree, our engineering specs for the prototypes would go to GSI. They can then begin mass production of the nanomachines,' Dr. Neil said.

This was followed by an hour-long debate related to the technical details of Dr. Neil's discoveries. Finally, Dr. Peck called for the debate to end, and specific recommendations to be made.

Everyone grew quiet as Hawke Conner asked to speak.

'My friends. First, I wish to express Abby's and my condolences to the families of the men who have perished. Even in the face of my own son's death, I hold firmly to the belief that our products are safe, and there is some undiscovered cause for these deaths. I have been deeply humbled by Quinn's death, but I remain a scientist at heart. I can't accept that his death is related to this outbreak. Until we know more, I ask that we all keep open minds. My instincts tell me it's too early for any reasonable scientist to draw firm conclusions.'

Hawke paused, taking time to review his notes.

'But regardless of my opinions, we are not here to assign blame nor discover the etiology of the outbreak. We are here to find solutions and save lives. Based on what I have just heard, I think we can all agree Dr. Neil's research appears to be valid?' Hawke asked.

Dr. Neil shot a glance at Hawke.

The rest of the group nodded their heads in agreement.

'If we agree, then I suggest we move forward. I have spoken with Gordon Kelly. We are prepared to fully cooperate. Genlabs will share the original sequences for the entire second generation of designer babies. Preparations for sending the data are already underway. GSI is also prepared to manufacture the nanotechnology using Dr. Neil's prototypes. The treatments will be offered to victims at no cost.'

Hawke paused, as murmurs passed through the group.

'Dr. Neil, our scientists are prepared to collaborate with your team. Our biggest concern is the security of the information. It's our understanding the data will be transferred to your servers in Idaho via encrypted data channels. Our technicians will need to verify the adequacy of all security protocols before the data transfer can begin,' Hawke added.

Dr. Neil nodded in agreement.

'That makes sense,' she said, and paused, 'We are concerned about protecting our secrets as well. What is the timeframe?'

'My people need two days to prepare the data transfer.'

'That will give me time to return to my lab and prepare. Once the data is transferred, we'll begin developing the manufacturing templates,' Dr. Neil said.

'Agreed,' Hawke said, and shook hands with Dr. Neil.

'I would like to accompany Dr. Neil to Idaho,' Marion said.

'I can use your help,' Dr. Neil agreed.

After the group finished discussing a variety of technical details for most of an hour, Dr. Peck ended the meeting.

🧬

Alex arrived at his parent's house unannounced. Unsure of why he had suddenly decided to drive there, he sat in his car for several minutes considering whether to enter the house. As he sat, Alex recalled waking that morning consumed with his brother's death. He felt isolated without Quinn, who often served as a bridge to his parents. He relied on Quinn's help when dealing with them. Now he had to face them alone. Alex also spent every New Year's Eve with his brother, and now faced the prospect of being without his companionship.

He felt a burning desire for the one thing his parents had historically been incapable of giving: love and comfort. But here he was, nevertheless. He felt deeply conflicted and seriously considered driving away. On one hand, he was still angry with his parents, especially his father.

There is something wrong with our relationship.

But on the other hand, Alex could also think of several reasons for maintaining a relationship with his parents. For one, he cared deeply for his mother. Second, he still worked for his father.

I may need to rethink that.

Alex still suspected his father had, in some way, contributed to the emergence of the outbreak. But Alex was also aware his brother's death had a powerful impact on his father, possibly for the better. Maybe this offered hope for the future of their relationship.

Alex also knew, for better or worse they were the only family he had.

Alex thought about Quinn again. He desperately missed his brother. The void in his life was immense. He was surprised by this, as he only remembered being angry with Quinn. He didn't want to make the same mistake with his parents. But Alex struggled with the concept of letting go. The idea always sounded so reasonable, but his powerful sense of justice always got in the way. He wanted to forgive his parents, let go of his anger, and move on. But he wasn't ready, and Alex didn't know how to talk to them about these things. He needed his brother's help.

Exiting the car, Alex entered his parent's front door. Alex

walked to the sunroom, and as he expected, found his parents being served afternoon drinks.

Predictable as Kant.

His father looked up first. He appeared startled. His mother followed Hawke's gaze until her eyes rested on Alex. She smiled at him and indicated he should sit with them.

'Please bring another drink for Alex,' his father said softly to the servant.

'Happy New Year, Alex,' his mother added.

16

WEDNESDAY, DECEMBER 28TH, 2050

Blessed are the cracked, for they let in the light.
Leonard Cohen

While the technicians at Genlabs prepared for the massive data transfer, Marion spent a long day with Dr. Neil traveling back to Idaho and the Daisy Tappan ranch. They arrived at the Bernard airstrip early Tuesday afternoon after flights from Seattle to Boise, and then from Boise to the airstrip near the Flying B Ranch. The real Pat Harren met them at the airstrip. A pistol was strapped to his waist. He planned to accompany them for the first half of the hike to the Tappan ranch.

'Thanks for helping us out. It's nice to meet the real Pat Harren. I'm glad you were unharmed, and I apologize for the unfortunate intrusion into your otherwise peaceful life,' Marion said.

'No big deal. I was pretty sure some friends locked me up as a practical joke, so I was never really scared, that is until the FBI showed up,' he admitted.

A January thaw had melted the ice along the river and lifted the snow line well beyond their view. Although no hint of spring was evident, the afternoon sun held the promise of warmer days to come. Feeling less stress, Marion was better able to appreciate the natural beauty of the river canyon. She was also pleased to have a chance to spend time with Jane and could hardly contain her excitement over working with her.

The threesome hiked along the river for several hours. As the sun descended to the canyon rim, Pat bid them farewell and headed back to the Flying B Ranch. Marion and Jane continued the hike alone.

Marion and Dr. Neil arrived at the Tappan Ranch just as darkness fell. A couple of days before their arrival, several of Dr. Neil's lab technicians had returned to Idaho and repaired the damages to the lab caused by the explosion. Several locals had arrived to help. The rocks deposited by the explosion were cleared, and the airlock's outer door was temporarily repaired. The lab was cleaned of dust, re-sanitized, and its equipment recalibrated. The crew had worked nonstop, and the lab was operational by the time Dr. Neil and Marion arrived.

The data transfer was set to begin the next morning. The technicians were still working with the lab equipment, and Marion felt like she was in the way. So, she asked Jane if she wanted to enjoy another soak in the nearby hot spring. Jane agreed, so they hiked to the pool, disrobed and got comfortable in the water.

'You've got an outstanding staff. They seem committed to you,' Marion said.

'I suppose. They're well paid, that's for sure. But I never feel well-liked. Who knows, maybe I'm just paranoid? I'm usually the last one to know anything about myself.'

'That's the foundation of all wisdom, in my opinion,' Marion paused. 'So you have children?

'A daughter, Megan. I just spoke with her, for the first time in years.'

'That must have been nice.'

'She claimed to miss me, so that's a start. Unfortunately, I hardly know her.'

'That will pass with time.'

'True enough. What about you? Kids?' Dr. Neil asked.

'Never had the time. Some of my friends struggle with being childless. But I never minded. I'm pretty selfish with my time,' Marion confessed.

'I get that. Look how I live,' Jane laughed.

'Pretty nice place. Listen, are you confident the data transfer is going to work?' Marion asked.

'I see no reason why not. I have every confidence in my IT guy,' Jane said.

'Good. I'm a bit nervous. This has got to work.'

'It will. I put a lot of preparation into this,' Jane said.

'I can't wait to start using the technology with real people. Things look good on paper, but you never know until field trials begin,' Marion said.

'Not to worry. All is going according to plan,' Jane answered confidently.

𝕯𝕹𝕬

Kaya Simon, head of cyber-security at Genlabs, stared at the three massive computer monitors on the desk and felt cold chills rolling over her skin. In a few minutes, and with the click of a button, she would initiate the data transfer. The original genetic sequences collected from over three-hundred thousand second gen babies, a data-set-worth-billions, was about to be shared with an outside lab. In addition to sending the data securely to the servers in Idaho, Kaya was charged with making sure the genetic sequences were delivered error-free.

Lives were at stake, and Kaya was justifiability nervous. Her heart was racing, and she didn't want to think about her blood pressure reading. Kaya rose from her chair and looked through the window at the group of technicians sitting in the next room. She went through the protocols in her head one more time: be sure the live connection is stable, watch for the security protocol to fully install, and be sure the data is going to the right IP address.

Kaya looked at the clock and switched on her microphone.

'Okay folks. Thirty seconds to initiations. Be on your toes, this is big.' She paused waiting for the seconds to tick by. 'Here we go . . . five, four, three, two, and one.'

She clicked the start button on her screen and watched as the connection went live and the security protocols started to initiate. In seconds, the security measures were in place and files started to transfer to Dr. Neil's servers at incomprehensively high speeds.

Everything appeared normal and Kaya started to relax. The connection was strong, and the files were being copied to Dr. Neil's servers. So far, security was holding up.

Taking hold of her coffee cup, Kaya took a deep breath.

Why was I ever worried? We're pros at this stuff.

She glanced at her monitor again. The files were still being transferred and the firewalls were holding.

Then suddenly, windows began to open on her screen. A loud chime began to sound.

Panic gripped her heart as she realized what was happening. Kaya sat her coffee cup down on the edge of the desk without looking, and the entire cup spilled in her lap.

She jumped to her feet and brushed the hot liquid off her clothes.

'Damn.'

She sat and refocused on her monitor. The moment she had opened the portal, hackers had entered the system. They had been ready and waiting. There was no other explanation. Surprise was an important part of cyber-security. Concealing when the transfer would take place and limiting the amount of time the system was exposed, was critical to success.

Someone had tipped off these hackers.

The technicians in the adjoining room started shouting. Several were running between machines in panic. Kaya could see the fear on their faces.

Kaya tried her mouse, and then the keyboard. As she expected, there was no response. She was completely locked out of the system. Based on the panic erupting in the other room, she assumed all her staff were locked out of the system as well. Her heart rate sky-rocketed and Kaya felt faint.

She grabbed her app-pad and used an overwrite function to log into the system. She typed in a command and waited for the request to be answered. There it was. Whoever had taken over the system used the appropriate authorization codes.

This is an inside job.

She watched helplessly as file after file were copied to an unidentified IP address.

In panic, Kaya grabbed the nearest app-phone and called her superior.

An hour later Kaya was forced to report the bad news to her superiors. Not only did the hackers steal every genetic sequence for the second-generation designer-babies but had managed to download the codes for all six generations of designer-babies. In fact, everything was gone. The three thousand computer servers that formed the backbone of Genlabs information system were stripped bare. Any data left in memory, including all financial and personnel records, had been erased. Even backup files in the cloud or stored on backup servers were compromised. All in a manner of minutes.

Incredibly, the FBI also confirmed the hackers had transferred more than two hundred billion dollars from the company bank accounts. This was incomprehensible, given Genlabs had hundreds of protected accounts all over the world. But once the hackers had the numbers and passwords for these accounts, it was a simple matter to steal the funds.

Once in the possession of the hackers, Genlabs' money flowed through a series of transfers that moved the funds around the world at blazing speed. During each transfer, the funds were divided into smaller and smaller amounts. Each bundle of funds passed through a minimum of forty server communities before the trail disappeared. Nobody knew where the money went.

🧬

Marion and Dr. Neil sat with the lead computer technician, waiting for data transfer to begin. Several of Dr. Neil's staff stood behind the table. Marion could feel the tension in the room. Marion didn't pretend to understand how these things worked, but for some reason, she woke that morning spooked, like waking suddenly from a bad dream. Except, she didn't remember dreaming.

The group heard a bell chime and watched as the security protocol initiated. Genlabs was right on time. The message on the screen indicated a live connection with Genlabs had been established. Another message indicated all security measures were in place and the files were being transferred.

Except, no files were being received.

The icon in the corner of the screen indicated downloads were occurring, but no files were showing up.

The technician searched the machine's hard drive, but nothing was there.

'Wait one minute and then call Genlabs,' Jane suggested to the technician.

Marion could see Dr. Neil was struggling to remain calm. Her own heart rate was ramping up and Marion's morning coffee was eating a hole in her gut.

One minute later nothing had changed so the technician called Genlabs.

Marion and Dr. Neil listened as the man communicated with his counterpart at Genlabs. Marion could see the blood draining from the man's face. He ended the call, took a deep breath and rubbed his forehead before speaking.

'My god, hackers got in and ripped off Genlabs. Everything is gone, millions of files taken or destroyed. There are no files for us to get. It's over,' he said.

Marion felt her eyes fill.

17

Saturday, December 31st, 2050

The cruelest lies are told in silence.

R.L. Stevenson

Digging deep to find some positives, Charlie thanked his ancestors for making this the last day of the year. A fresh start awaited him in the morning. The New Year's Eve party with his family was tonight.

But first, he needed to get through a meeting with Hunter.

'So, what the fuck happened?' Hunter asked harshly, as Charlie entered his office.

'It'll take months to sort out, maybe longer. The hackers wiped Genlab's servers clean. Any evidence of potential crimes is gone, at least for now. In the short term, our best bet is to go after Gordon Kelly and the scientists working with him. They must know something. But honestly, at this point, we need help, and lots of it.'

'Help will come, but might take a while, given the holiday government shutdown. Did you interview any of Gordon's co-workers?'

'Sure, the few who were at work during the holidays. They just kept citing their non-disclosure agreements,' Charlie answered.

'So, nothing. This will all land in the courts. What about the hacking?'

'Whoever hacked Genlabs used the proper authorization codes to take advantage of the open portal. We're pretty sure we know how it was done,' Charlie said.

'It had to be an inside job. Only two people knew the codes, and they both worked at Genlabs,' Hunter pointed out.

'No, Dr. Neil also had the codes. The moment the connection was made, and a couple of nanoseconds before the security protocols were blocked, the authorization codes were used to break into Genlabs' information system. Our preliminary analysis suggests the authorization codes were send from a computer in Idaho. They were routed to an IP address just before the data transfer began. The IP address no longer exists,' Charlie repeated.

'What does that mean? If the IP address was in Idaho, was Dr. Neil responsible? Why? She was about to get the data handed to her on a silver platter,' Hunter said.

'She is responsible, But, it wasn't about the genetic profiles, it was about revenge, and in my opinion, the money. The IT guys are convinced she's responsible for draining Genlab's bank accounts.'

'Damn, how is that possible? Marion was with her? Didn't she see anything?' Hunter asked.

'Marion saw nothing, because there was nothing to see. The hackers could have been in the next room or another country.'

'Our tech guys agree with this conclusion?' Hunter asked.

'Yes. There's no other explanation.'

'What else?'

'More bad news. A new web site went viral at midnight last night. It contains the genetic profiles for the entire first and second generations of designer-babies. It also leaked many of Genlabs most valuable technical trade secrets, their finances . . . everything. Whoever is operating the site promised to release the genetic profiles for the next four generations, one at a time, in the coming months. The press is going crazy,' Charlie said.

'So, it was all a hoax? Dr. Neil was a complete fraud?'

'Appears so.'

'Do we know where she is?' Hunter asked.

'Marion returned to Seattle right after the failed data transfer. She left Dr. Neil in Idaho, who was reportedly too upset to travel. As you know, we've made countless attempts to contact her, with no response. Per your emergency authorization, an FBI team flew by copter to the Tappan ranch this morning. Dr. Neil is gone. Her lab is destroyed. There's no sign of her,' Charlie summarized.

'What about the outbreak? It was real?' Hunter asked.

'Marion and her entire team are looking for answers. Nothing conclusive. But Marion does have a working theory. She thinks the nanotechnology developed by Dr. Neil was designed to create the outbreak, not stop it. Dr. Neil staged the entire thing. She killed ninety-six men to get her revenge on Gordon Kelly,' Charlie said.

'She's out of her damn mind, if you ask me.'

'Maybe. Or she's brilliant,' Charlie said.

'People can be both. Anything else?' Hunter asked.

'As you know, the outbreak was concentrated in two areas of the state, Spokane and Yakima. Brad found a link between the two places. Each hosted anniversary events for second gens around the Fourth of July. The current theory is Dr. Neil attended these events and infected victims with her nanomachines. A simple handshake would do the trick. The number of nanomachines that entered your bloodstream determined how long it took to get sick,' Charlie said.

'What about the cases from out of state?'

'It appears all of those men attended one of the events.'

'How do you know she was at the events?' Hunter asked.

'We weren't sure. But Brad located the guestbook for the Yakima event. For some reason, she signed the guestbook using her real name. Habit I guess,' Charlie said.

'The exception is Quinn Conner. He wasn't in Spokane or Yakima, right?' Hunter pointed out.

'Right. We don't know how Quinn was infected, if indeed he was. Without a body, it's hard to confirm anything. If revenge was the motive, it makes sense that Dr. Neil went after Hawke's son. She wanted revenge against Hawke Conner as well. Her plan is starting to become clear,' Charlie responded.

'She got her revenge. That's for sure. Gordon Kelly is in jail, and Genlabs is shut down. Jane Neil is probably sitting on some tropical island enjoying a cold drink. Any leads on the stolen funds?' Hunter asked.

'The electronic trail goes cold after forty transfer points. But there is one very interesting development. We received an alert from Interpol. It appears small amounts of funds are being deposited in thousands of accounts in banks across the U.S., Europe and Asia.'

'Are you implying these are the missing funds?'

'No way to know for sure, at least not yet. But the total amount taken from Genlabs is close to the amounts being deposited in banks. We'll figure it out. Recovering any funds is another story.'

'Dr. Neil fancies herself a modern-day Robin Hood.'

'And a mass murderer. Speaking of, has the director approved expanding the investigation?' Charlie asked.

'Not yet but could be as soon as tomorrow.'

'And I'll lead the investigation?' Charlie asked.

'That's the plan.'

'Good. I intend to find Dr. Neil and get to the bottom of this whole mess,' Charlie promised.

'She'll already be out of the country.'

'No doubt. But that won't stop us. So, what happens next? What's being shared with the public?' Charlie asked.

'Communications is working on a detailed press release. Basically, the story line will be it was much to do about nothing, that Dr. Neil was brilliant, but turned out to be crazy. How else could she have fooled so many experts? Over time, memories will fade, and the outbreak, hopefully, will be forgotten,' Hunter said.

'So that's it?' Charlie asked.

'Life goes on. I expect to get fired or transferred. I'm sure you're safe. There'll be Congressional hearings, and no doubt some type of internal review,' Hunter said sadly.

Charlie didn't respond.

18

JANUARY 1ST, 2051

Write injuries in dust, benefits in marble.
Ben Franklin

Charlie was exhausted, but not too tired to do some drumming and singing to bring in the New Year. He sat next to his grandfather and two cousins in the living room of his home. The four men used wooden beaters to play three small powwow drums. Charlie and his grandfather shared a drum. He could think of no better antidote to his frustrations with the Conner case.

His grandfather suddenly switched to a new rhythm and began to chant an ancient vocable. Charlie and his cousins joined in.

Leaping to her feet, Anna started doing a dance of her people. Several guests clapped, and the drummers responded by playing louder. Charlie watched as droplets of his sweat fell on the buffalo skin of the drum and danced in time with his rhythm.

His house was full of party goers filling the living room, spilling into the kitchen, and populating the porch. Smiling, Charlie was pleased to see some unexpected guests. Agent

Seaman had arrived with a date. They sat near the drummers and seemed genuinely interested in the music. Marion and Lois were watching the drummers along with the other members of Charlie's extended family. (Brad and his wife had finally made their trip to California.) His daughter, Esther, chatted with Jack Lee and his wife.

At the stroke of midnight, Charlie exchanged a long kiss with Anna as the crowd welcomed in the Year 2051. As they hugged, she spoke quietly in his ear.

'I have a secret,' Anna said.

'Do tell, fair lady.'

'Your daughter has changed her mind. Don't make a big deal, but she decided to not have the genetic treatments. You won,' Anna said.

'I didn't win. Esther won. And you and Frank showed great wisdom, and a decent knowledge of human psychology,' Charlie laughed, and kissed his wife again.

'Yes. I am wise, and you would do well to remember that. Let's get to bed soon,' Anna whispered, smiling.

As the party wound down, Charlie sat with Marion, Lois, and Jack. Anna stood near the front door thanking the departing guests.

'This will be a holiday to remember,' Marion observed.

'Crazy two weeks, that's for sure. And if the boss gets his way, we're just getting started,' Charlie said.

'Good. I like working with you guys,' Marion added.

'Same here. But before we celebrate, there is some news. Hunter may be done,' Charlie reported.

'You mean he'll resign.'

'That, or get fired,' Charlie said.

'There'll still be an investigation into Genlabs?' Marion asked.

'Sure. A grand jury will be seated. We'll have our work cut out for us. We can also expect congressional hearings and an internal investigation to be hanging over us. Heads will roll. I suspect Hunter will be the first to go,' Charlie said.

'He's an ass, but he doesn't deserve that,' Marion said.

'I guess,' Charlie answered.

'I can't help but wonder about a few things,' Marion said.

'What's on your mind?' Charlie asked.

'Gordon Kelly. If he had done nothing, the man wouldn't be sitting in jail,' Marion said.

'Oh, the ironies of life. Jane did her best to nudge him along, but he made his own bad choices. Gordon staged a cover up, but there was nothing to hide. He was brilliant, no doubt, but emotionally unstable, and she took advantage of that. In the end that was his undoing. How many times do you see a genius fail because he or she is an emotional idiot? Most folks think it's about having a high IQ. At the university, I see plenty of smart people, but most of them act like children. It's about managing emotions, not having a high IQ,' Charlie said.

'I don't disagree. We don't know our own mind well enough to mistrust it, ' Marion said.

Charlie, Lois, and Jack laughed.

'Yeah. I'm not sure evolution has adequately prepared us for this crazy world,' Charlie added.

'I thought genetic enhancements were going to fix that?' Jack asked.

'Not so far,' Charlie laughed.

'What about Dr. Neil?' Marion asked.

'She'll be the focus of our investigation,' Charlie said.

'The CDC will open its own investigation,' Marion submitted.

'The FBI will look forward to collaborating with you,' Charlie said.

'What will happen to the Conners?' Jack asked.

'That depends . . . they already lost a son. GSI will be investigated. They're being punished plenty. But remember, the outbreak was not real, so they committed no crimes in that respect. It's still not clear to what extend Hawke Conner participated with the crimes committed by Gordon Kelly. And the charges against Alex are being dropped. For the moment, the Conner family is in the clear,' Charlie said.

'What about having a genetically-enhanced son and a natural-born son in the same family?' Jack asked.

'The Conners will be crucified by the press, but no charges will be filed,' Charlie reported.

'What I keep wondering is how Quinn Conner got hold of Dr. Neil's research. None of our guys could find anything in the research base. I wonder if Dr. Neil was feeding him info. There were a number of emails containing data that later turned up in his report,' he added.

'Who sent them?' Marion asked.

'Agent Seaman could never locate the point of origin,' Jack said.

'Had to be Dr. Neil. She thought of everything else. Not sure I've ever been played so badly,' Charlie observed.

'How was she able to infect so many men in the first place?' Marion asked.

'She shook a lot of hands, I guess,' Charlie said.

'And how did she infect Quinn Conner?'

'The airline confirmed she was in Seattle and we think Dr. Neil attended one of the public events where Quinn made an appearance, on or around the Fourth of July,' Charlie said.

'Has she been formally charged?' Marion asked.

'Yes. Ninety-six counts of murder. There's a long list of other charges. She's a mass murderer and we'll catch her,' Charlie said.

'Will she be charged with the death of Quinn Conner?' Marion asked.

'She is not yet charged with his death, but that may change. Another scenario is Ramsey Lewis murdered Quinn Conner on orders from Gordon Kelly. I think he killed my partner and shot me as well.'

'Why would Gordon have Quinn murdered? He's Hawke's son.'

'He wanted to cover-up the existence of the report.'

''So, Quinn Conner didn't die from the infection?' Marion asked.

'I think Ramsey killed Quinn before the infection could. If Gordon had waited a few days, there would have been no need to murder him,' Charlie reported.

'Gordon panicked when he saw the report,' Marion said.

'Makes sense doesn't it. Gordon stood to lose everything, and in the end, he did,' Charlie added.

'Certain symmetry to your theory. But lots of gaps too,' Marion said.

'Agreed. No doubt, there is more to the story. If we could just question Ramsey Lewis,' Charlie lamented.

'And no sign of him?' she asked.

'No body, has been found, which is not surprising. It may never be found. It's possible he survived,' Charlie admitted.

'He could come after you,' she said.

'Unlikely. Nothing to cover-up anymore.'

'True, but he might be pissed,' Marion concluded.

'I'll take my chances. He killed my good friend. I would love to get my hands on the guy,' Charlie said.

'Listen, I want a chance to make things right. I feel responsible for not spotting the ruse. Jane fooled me first and foremost, and I'm pissed,' Marion admitted.

'We were all fooled. You'll get your chance,' Charlie stopped and turned to Lois. 'If you will allow Marion to stay on our team.'

'Marion will be assigned to your team for three months. If needed, I can extend the assignment. Depending on progress, of course,' Lois offered.

'Excellent, she's a real asset to the team.' Charlie stopped, 'For now, let's all get some rest, because on Monday morning, we start looking for Dr. Jane Neil,' Charlie said.

Marion, Lois and Jack smiled.

If you enjoyed the story, please consider writing a review on Amazon, Goodreads, or Barnes and Noble. This would make me happy, and also help make it possible to write my next novel. Thank you.

Made in the USA
Las Vegas, NV
13 March 2021